LIES AND HYPOCRISY

Mel Vil

ISBN: 979-10-94007-16-7
ISBN-13: 9791094007167

"On the chess board lies and
hypocrisy do not survive long."

Emanuel Lasker

BOOK ONE

Book One

The whole time I spent trying to sleep I was plagued by the 'if only'. I was lucky to have gotten away as lightly as I did, escaping their set-up, and there I was wishing I had hurt one of them or come away with some kind of souvenir. The cop's handcuffs perhaps—I fixated on them—perhaps some money or the drugs they were trying to plant on me: something to say I got out of it on top. Just getting away evens wasn't enough. Besides, I wasn't even.

I slept eventually, but then my dreams were hounded by reoccurrences of the same events that had been keeping me awake. Some were related to what actually happened, or how I remembered it at least. Others continued where the story had left off. And despite my dreams, I woke up every twenty minutes or so struggling to distinguish memory of reality from memory of dream.

The next morning was the same. I woke eventually, but convincing my brain of the truth had become a harder task. I still needed a souvenir, some kind of proof that would unconfound my doubt. In the end, a new sense of fear provided the evidence. I feared that after breakfast, after my morning rituals, I wouldn't be able to get out of the front door; I wouldn't be able to walk in my streets.

Leaving the house wasn't necessarily the objective of the day. I am known, and not by many, to stay in the house on many a day. But not to have the capacity, after summoning the will, wasn't a comforting sensation. Besides I did need to leave the house, I had things to do.

I sat and watched t.v., but I couldn't concentrate. The twenty-four news cycle was too repetitive, besides I couldn't focus on what was going on in the room around me let alone inside some insignificant box that invents what is and isn't important in the world. I switched it off, as I needed to formulate a plan. I needed several plans, in fact: one specific, implementable plan that would get me out of the house, then a more global plan that would change the course of my life. I had to do something. I needed some kind of positive action.

I couldn't just sit there thinking about this guy wandering around doing the same thing as the day before. It's the kind of thing that happens to tourists, not to me. I don't really care too much if it happens to tourists, perhaps in my neighbourhood, but generally not at all. Nevertheless, I still felt I needed to get out and get revenge.

Let's have some definitions: 'my streets' and 'revenge'. I guess they both easily conjure up mafia hit men and bloody Italian coffee shops. Well, in my humble case it's not like that, although there is a bloody Italian coffee shop, but it's bloody for different reasons. So, my streets: I live here. I didn't grow up here, but here grew up in my head. So, when I had arrived, I had felt at home, and had continued to do so—without interruption—until the events of the previous night. And, because I no longer felt at home, I felt also the need for some revenge. Somewhere out there was a kid—he was a kid, barely out of his teens—who got his kicks from ripping people off. So, I needed to get back at him. Although I'd never had any opinion, knowledge or experience, I considered myself to be in favour of a reasonably just punishment.

The strangest part wasn't being scared: it was the shattering of my inner peace. I'd never pretended to own this neighbourhood, in fact most of its inhabitants ignore me or look down their long noses at me. But they left me alone and I they. So why was it interrupted? What shift in the stars caused such an upset? Harmony had been kidnapped, my thoughts too, taken off in a wild direction. My mind settled on fixing this apparent injustice with a bit of revengeful justice. Today would be Big Wednesday.

It was time for the little boy inside me to get revenge tribal style. I would step justly on the feet of those who had stepped so unjustly on mine. Whatever revenge meant to other, to me it meant restoring my confidence: getting up and getting to, and out of, the front door. It wasn't for 'the don' or for 'the family' or any other moral cliché. It was purely to reset the balance.

I'd never had fear of going out the front door. I can't suppose many people have. It's not nice. It wasn't then, being the first time. But I knew I had to do it, for myself. My paranoid mind, I suppose they all are, was already conjuring the mania houseboundness would cause. It blew things out of proportion as usual. But my imagination held all the cards that morning. Thoughts of revenge made me salivate. And as the fear soared out of control, the little means I had for fulfilling my imagination's careless spending also said goodbye, taking my creativity captive too.

It's broad and detailed picture, but not unlike the majority of people's backgrounds. Here, however, it doesn't start years ago with my childhood, with being a victim of abuse or anything like it. It started that morning, or at least the night before. It was a trust thing.

You know when you buy something and then get it home only to find out it's not what it said on the packaging? Say for example you picked up a book and read the back cover, which was written in a language you understand, but you overlook flicking through the pages. Perhaps the cinema is a better example. You pay to go in to see a recent release only to find out the movie was dubbed into a language you don't understand.

Well, that's the way I feel about people too. When you talk to someone, in your own neighbourhood, on a warm evening in the square. When they tell you their name, you expect it to be their name. No, am I wrong? Did I fuck up that bad? It wasn't as if he'd said, "Hi! My name is P... B...

W… L… Fred… I mean Bob… Err Dick, yes Richard that's my name, Larry." I had no reason to not trust him.

So this is the picture I give you: there's me—stretched out on a bench to the fullest possible extent without actually lying down—in the square of the balmy suburbs of the nice part of the city, where all the doctors, lawyers and other big noses live. It's a nice area, as I said already, where we all leave each other alone. Not this guy though. I mean people do sit on benches and talk to each other. It's what I do too. Any stranger can be my best friend. In that sense, I have a new best friend everyday and could even be described as a hobby, like I collect the sum of all their lives. Generally it's good company.

That is to say the big noses don't come and sit down that much, at least not next to me. Generally they'd say they have too little time, or too much business, but I think it's more about too much shame, to sit in the square, to talk to the unoccupied guy. They could call me a vagrant, but they don't. I can't quite explain why; it's some phenomenon I guess.

So that was it. I bought the guy's story, not all of it, we all bullshit after all, but the framework at least: who he was, what he was up to, and so on. It wasn't the most interesting life story I had ever listened to but he kept me interested. Now I see that it was his plan.

The next morning, I stood inside my front door. My finger hovered by the key holder. The other hand rested on my forehead, I held my elbow against the door trying to remember the kid's name. It had completely escaped overnight. It would come eventually but not at that point. So, me, the door, the fear and revenge. It occurred to me then that even his name might have been bullshit too. In fact, it made good sense that it was. You don't give your name to the victim of your crime, right?

So, while leaving the house was the plan, the terrain was unnavigable. I stood there trying to do it, trying to summon the courage. It was the time for doing things not the time for dwelling. Wednesday, what would Wednesday hold? Streets, cars, people. Same as Mondays right? You would think. First step was the front door. And I went.

Tropical Bill gave a long hard cold stare across his playing field. Scanning was how he described it. Accurate enough. He was looking for someone, a target, a sucker, a dupe, or a mark. Call it what you will, he looked for it. He took a small, glass cocaine sniffer from his jacket pocket. It resembled an anti-allergy inhaler, and with the same motion of a patient who would use one he took it to his nose. In broad view, he sucked the white dust towards the rewarding membrane. He had spotted someone. He lifted his head, sniffed several times, the rush took him and then he began his approach.

Taking a packet of cigarettes from the same jacket, but a different pocket, he flicked out a cigarette and replaced it. The jacket was light creamy beige; perhaps naturally coloured light summer style. Underneath he had a blue shirt, chequered with alternating light and dark blues, made of a fine material. He jeans were black denim, his walk, his dress and his mojo were all working to the same rhythm. It was all going well, the sucker was still there, didn't look like he was going to move, all going to plan. Tropical Bill screwed the white cigarette into his lips seconds before entering the visual world of the dupe.

The dupe was enjoying the evening, warm and balmy. Mentally engaged; he didn't let out the complexity or the engagement of his thoughts. To the outside world, he could be in a world of pain but quite oblivious to it or seriously digging mentally into something whimsical. He spotted Bill.

Bill took the white cigarette from his lips. "Hey, uh, you don't have a light do you?"

The sucker looked at him, disentangling his brain and nodding with a polite smile. He reached into his trouser pocket and passed a metal lighter. Bill took it with a nod of thanks, pushing the cigarette back into his dark lips and pulling the lighter to his face.

To the casual observer he lit the cigarette, but the casual observer wouldn't have notice the cold search Bill performed under the guise of habitually hand shielding the flame. The air was perfectly still and only that small detail would have given him away. But Bill's act of smoking was just that, an act, not just to deceive but some sort of flamboyance or bravado. It was still hiding something, he was searching the field again. This time he was looking for an accomplice.

Bill flicked back his head with the first heat of the blank cigarette, sucking its white essence in to his lungs and receiving yet another boost of confidence. The act continued, as if he were some method actor. He rolled the lighter through his fingers as he passed it back to the dupe.

"Thanks man."

"Don't mention it." The stranger was back in the world now, he looked the friendly type.

"Ya don't got tha time too?"

"Yes, it's nine-thirty."

"Aiight, cool." Bill checked his mental agenda, still lurking ominously over his dupe. He sat down. "You don't mind do ya?"

The sucker looked to him as if to say, free world, be my guest, your welcome, why would I and every other possible answer without saying one.

Bill cast his arms over the back of the bench broadening his width, surveying the scene in front of them. "Got tha evenin' free."

"Yes, me too."

"You live round here?"

"Yes, just a few blocks away." The stranger turned his head to face Bill for the first time fully, he jolted his chin up. "You?"

"Who, me?" Bill looked genuine, that was the plan, he took a cigarette's pause for composure, as if waiting for the affirmation. He sucked the smoke in loudly. The sucker nodded yes impatiently.

"Nah man. Arm from outa town. Ma brova lives up in here, just visitin' nim an all dat. He at work tho now. So, you from round here then?"

"Yes. The answer carried a hint of impatience, but just a hint."

"Yeah? Whereabouts? Ah mean like in this hood or what?"

The sap gave Bill a raised eyebrow to offer him warning of the intrusion. "Just a few blocks away."

"Thas cool, I kinda likes it here ya know. Relaxed an all that. So what you be doin' here?" Bill took at his cigarette again, unfazed by the sucker's offence.

"Here? where? Right now?"

"Yeah."

"Nothing. Nothing much at least. Watching the world go by, you know, taking a minute out." His confidence was of a different source to Bill's hardness, it was smooth and relaxed. It belonged inside that same body. Nevertheless, Bill pursued him as the target.

"You see this old guy here," the sap pointed across the street in front of them, "This one here, with the blue jacket, looks really old. The jacket I mean."

"Which one… oh, yeah! Yeah, I sees him."

"This guy has been to every restaurant on this block at least four times. He stops at each to read the menu as if he was going to eat there. Watch him."

Together they watched the man hop from lectern to display board outside each restaurant as he ran his fingers over menus and lips in some lost decisiveness. Never deciding on anything except to check the last menu again. He massaged his moustache and nodded his head agreeingly as Bill and the suckers heads and eyes followed him harmoniously.

The warm suburban evening provided a warm relief to the days heat. The traffic had become sparse around this square, human traffic had increased. Tropical Bill and the sucker sat ensconced from across a broad sided paving of the square and the three lanes of one-way traffic as it thinned in the wanderings of a senile old man. The eateries and restaurants and street side cafes that surrounded him filled and the humid air breezing in and out of their open fronted facades carried their welcome chatter freely into the night.

Bill made a grunt like smirk and made a joke about the old man's habits, breaking the ice between the two. The white boy looked at him inquisitively, but still with a playful look on his face. As he turned back to the cafés Bill looked towards him and made a similar assessment. Similar to the casual observer that is. The keen observer would have seen the evil glint in his eye.

"What you say ya name was?"

"I didn't…"

"Aiight. So what is it?"

"Sammy." He raised a hand expectantly.

"Bill. They call me Tropical Bill." He smiled showing the full contrast between his black skin, pink gums and shiny teeth.

They shook hands, gripping fingertips before Sammy asked, facially, for an explanation. "I live up in a black neighbourhood, but ma paren's moved here from the Caribbean an' most o dem who live up in der lived der all dey lives, they used to the cold winters an' shit. But I ain't, I got tropical blood in me. Iss aiight now, with the summer an all that but you know, dis why dey call me tropical."

"So when did you move here?" Sammy had taken an interest and unknowingly the bait.

"Nah man, when I was like six. It's a school ting an' dat, the name. You know, ma homeboys be callin' me since den.

You know how it is right? Not too many get up outa der. Cept ma brova, but we all got the same nicknames since we was kids."

"I see."

"You? You grow up here in da city?"

"No, I grew up in the country side, my parents had a huge house in the middle of nowhere."

"Like a mansion or somfin?"

"No, no, nothing like that." Sammy laughed at the thought. "It was old all right, but old and falling apart. We used to call it the barn. We were quite poor but we had a good life, simple, but good. But I never liked the countryside much. I always wanted to live in the city." He looked introspectively turning after a few seconds to Bill who was sucking the end of the cigarette, nodding.

"That's cool man, I can hear dat. I ain't one for da countryside neiver, all them cows and dirt don't do nofin for me."

Sammy looked at Bill, examining his clothes. They clearly matched the self-description of a city dweller. Everything was well-coordinated, spotlessly clean; he was dressed rather than clothed.

"So when you move here den?"

"When I was twenty. About eight years ago."

"Damn, you don't look twenty-eight."

"That's what you get growing up in the countryside, clean air, good food, no stress or pollution. Besides I have some sort of medical condition, my immune system, it's really strong so I never get sick."

"So, you like superman or sumfin?"

"No," Sammy laughed, but not sure about the seriousness of the question. "No, not quite. More like this. If I cut myself it bleeds, leaves a scar like everyone, just doesn't take as long to heal. And I never get sick, I catch the flu but it never gets me, no fever or anything, just goes away over a day or two."

Bill knotted his eyebrows sucking his eyeballs deep into his face. He looked suspiciously through them, analysing what he had been told, deciding whether or not to infer significance. He drew the last of the cigarette and flicked straight from his lips into the street in a shower of monotone sparks. He relaxed and decided it had none. He relaxed a little. "So wha you do? Whas your job I mean."

"I don't have one."

"So, what, you, you like a student or sumfin. You a bit old to be studyin."

"Study? No, I am not one for, for mental application. Let's say." He turned to Bill with a cheeky smile. Bill held a closed fist out in recognition.

"I hear dat." He nodded for Sammy to put his fist out to and tapped it gently as he did initiating Sammy to do the same back. This pleased Bill. "Der you go, so, I mean, what you doin, you know to make ens meet an' dat?" He smiled realisingly, "You sellin' weed right?"

"No, not me, not my style either."

"But chu smoke it doe right?"

Sammy looked back, looked around him in some kind of practised surveillance then looked back bashfully. "Who doesn't?" His answer carried enough weight to make up for the lost face.

"Der you go man, I hear dat too. But how yo pay fo dat? And, you know, bills an' dat?"

Sammy continued studying Bill as he was distracted a moment by a passing girl, scrutinising for the smallest detail telling him not to trust him. He looked deeply, as if he could see more than just the skin or the clothes or the social stigmas, he looked as if he could see further inside him. But there was nothing there, nothing Sammy could see. He could continue to trust him as a random passer-by. But Sammy was smart enough to proceed with caution and suspicion.

"I get uh… It's not that straight forward. I go to the

university hospital here, you know it? No, anyway it's—well—it's not embarrassing, but they pay me. They do tests and things every six months. I'm kind of like a lab rat."

"You serious?" Bill looked half in disbelief at Sammy and half on the brink of laughing. "You a fucking guinea pig or somfin? Tha's fucked up yo!" They laughed, Bill with a pinch of amused disgust and Sammy with the same sense of slightly embarrassed shame. Bill stopped, sobered by a thought previously delayed. "So they pay you!? Fo real? Like enough to live on?" Sammy nodded, sobered too by Bill's shocked question.

"Do you think I would do it otherwise?" Sammy struggled to gain back some face. You have got to be kidding me. Sure there is some bigger picture, they're trying to solve the worlds diseases and problems using me but...

"I feel you man, I feel you; see, I knew you was a player."

They sat in silence, watching the world as it carried on, Bill commented on the girl that had passed but it didn't make any conversation. Eventually Sammy turned to Bill and asked about him.

"Young, black and unemployed. Imma fuckin' statistic." He smirked as he said it but watched carefully fro the response from the corner of his eye. He was trying to win his confidence not scare him with social stereotypes. He watched, Sammy didn't let it phase him, he appeared to Bill to be stronger than that. Cooler. "Nah man, I just finished college this year, studio engineering, you know music and dat. Me and ma brova we tryin' to set up some shit up but it ain't happnin right now, so I be workin' for ma dad still. He a carpenter, he don't pay me much but um still up at home so it payin' the rent on top."

"Wait! Your dad's a carpenter? So you know how to, how to, you know."

"Build shit from wood? Yeah." They laughed.

"Not the phrase I was looking for but I'll keep it in mind next time." Sammy shook his head in acknowledgement.

Bill looked at him in slight surprise, genuinely amused.

"Fuck this, I am going for a beer!" Sammy nearly leapt from the bench. Bill looked at him surprised, the situation had just left his hands. He struggled for a lie or line to get it back.

"Uh what time is it?"

"Beer time." Sammy had become very matter of fact and entirely in control of his providence. He looked at his watch too. "Ten p.m."

"Where you goin' fo a beer?" Bill was definitely below full energy levels. His face looked like a pet dog saying goodbye to its owner. Sammy looked somewhat bewildered by the upset his randomness had caused. He tipped his head to one side briefly then pointed across the street.

"To the kiosk. Sure enough, there was a little kiosk wedged between to eateries. You want to come?!"

"Uh no, um mean nah, you go ahead man." He looked more upset now, less sad and more ashamed. Sammy smiled and let a small laugh out.

"I wasn't serious!" He looked at Bill's face, and felt bad for a split second. "You want a beer?"

"Yeah, aiight." Bill wasn't sure what to say, he was not used to this, usually he would buy the beer or they would leave a place without paying after he had said he had. He was not used to saying please or thank you. He watched Sammy randomly wander though the night to the store meanwhile fishing the little coke sniffer from his pocket. He put it alternately to each flared black nostril and replaced it. He rummaged the rest of his pockets for small coins, watching Sammy all the time, as he absentmindedly and innocently bought two bottles and gum. He put the gum in the left shirt pocket of his white short-sleeved shirt as he waited to cross back. Bill was stopped again by his thought processes and cast an anxious and surprising look around him. He had become so entranced by this kid that he had begun to forget what he was doing there.

He hadn't found who he was looking for when Sammy arrived back at the bench and handed him a beer. "Here! Did you lose something?"

"Nah man, I was just, uh lookin' fur. The old man, yeah the old man." Sammy added emphasis to a face already showing doubt, spun around again and pointed him out. And sure enough, the vagabond was still deciding which restaurant he was not going to eat in. Sammy sat down pulled the lighter from his pocket. The old man pressed his face against one of the windows, hands either side either trying to look in or impress someone to feed him.

"Look at this guy. You need this?" He waved the lighter at Bill. Bill pulled a metal opener from his pocket.

"You need dis?" Waving it loosely at Sammy, who in response popped the metal top off with his lighter. "No." Bill experienced further surprise. "So you carry a beer opener but not a lighter?"

"Thas sum funny shit man, funny. Openin' bottles with fire."

"Hmm, I don't know, I like the idea of carrying a bottle opener."

"Why when you can do dat?"

"I don't know, just seems pretty cool."

"For me maybe, you couldn't pull it off. Nah man. I'm tellin' you, white boys carryin' bottle openers everyone will fink you's a wino man."

"And what makes you think I'm not?" Bill took a sip from his beer.

Sammy took the cap from his and looked back. "Aiight player, I ain't fuckin with you no more."

Bill examined Sammy more closely, he was white, but he was too good looking to be a wino, slightly olive skin, nice clothes, shame about that medical thing, makes him a bit strange. There was something that didn't fit. Something that was not quite right. Maybe the short hair.

"I don know man," he said reflectively and calmly as he could, "But I do know you ain't or no nazi KKK sonamabitch either."

"But why would you think that, because I am white and have a skin head?"

"Nah man, but thas wha um sayin', doe. You don carry a bottle opener wivout a reason, same as you don't cut ya hair so short wivout a reason. You ain't bin in no army right? And you good lookin an' dat so why don't you let it grow like da rest o dem?"

"Hey fuck you! That's like me saying you are going to rape my little sister because you are black and you 'ain't iced up'."

Sammy's minute knowledge of the opposite side of cultural divide cut deep. Bill didn't want it to get out of hand and took the less threatening root. But on another day, he would have reacted differently.

"You gots a lil' sister?"

"What? Fuck you." Sammy saw Bill was smiling and wasn't sure what to do.

"Is she cute?"

"No, I haven't, and besides..."

The tension came back.

"Besides what?"

"It isn't about whether I have a sister or if I am a wino, or if I want to see 'yo black ass' hanging from a lamp–post. It's not even about whether you are allowed to come to those decisions, morally, socially or literally. The thing that really pisses me off, is that sometimes you can tell these things in someone. Sometimes it's so fucking blatantly obvious you can't deny it, it's only because at some other times it isn't so obvious that we cant generalise like we want to. If I want to make it obvious, I can; if I want to disguise it, I can. I can even make it obvious when it's not true to set you up. And if I am, and I don't want you to find out, I can still do it just to tease you. So, when it's not obvious it could mean I am not, or I just don't want you to find out. You are fucked these days anyway, a guy can have as many black crosses and swastikas tattooed on his head, even a nine-inch nail he wants to stick through his flesh, he can tear his denim and you still can't judge him. You still can't assume anything; even if that's the most likely reason why he put them there."

"That's what um sayin do, why go to all dat effort if you ain't like that?"

"If you wanted the entire world to think you aren't a nazi what's the easiest way to do it? Dress up as something else."

"So you are a nazi then?"

"Fuck you." They burst out laughing.

"I see your point dough."

"You know, it's not about whether you think you can tell or whether you are allowed to decide. It's about whether you actually know. You can sit here next to me for four fucking days, talking, and I still wouldn't know if you wanted to rape my sister."

Sammy slowed himself and began to breath again. He had stopped at some point during his rant, but it appeared to have been settling. He took a sip from his beer. Bill checked his brain for something to change the subject. He was glad Sammy had got that off his chest but it was a little intense. He remembered he had been looking for change. He hooked a coin from his pocket.

"Can you break me this?"

Sammy reached the coins in his pockets. "What do you need?"

"I got to call ma brova?" He waved the coin again.

"I meant what coins?"

"Oh yeah, umm, tens or twenties."

"Here, keep them." He handed a few coins, which added up to less than would have broken the bigger coin.

Bill took them with little acknowledgement or thanks and got up looking determined. He walked towards a payphone, running and rerunning things through his head.

How was he going to tackle? This one was quite volatile. He reached the phone, picked up the receiver and looked back to check on Sammy. Still sitting, enjoying life's idiosyncrasies. Bill turned happily; this wasn't a problem. He revised the phone, put in the coins and marked the number. He turned and watched Sammy as he waited for an answer. His head jerked up when it came.

"Where you at? Wha ya doin all da way over der? Aiight man, but you see this white boy? Yeah! Fuck? Whatever! So? You comin' or not? Huh? Fuck you man, you gonna or not? Aiight, I call you in a minute."

Tropical Bill slammed the receiver down looking distressed. He started to walk, looking focussed at the sucker. He remembered the sniffer, took it out and took a hit. He reached his neck to either side until it clicked, pulled the jacket higher onto his shoulders and swayed to the bench, where Sammy remained completely unaware of everything except the wanderings of the old man, which still had him fixated.

A hard night had enslaved Gil. The cell phone was the major weapon of its duress. Between Bill and Gil's wife he'd had enough and wanted to throw it away. The bank had called earlier as well, like the national anthem, their familiar reminders and nagging had opened this Friday's derby between partner and partner. His wife was leading though. Why do banks call you with bad news on Friday evening when they know you can't do anything until Monday? Only leave you to stress about it. Monday morning isn't a great deal better but at least you can apply yourself straight away. Al had called too, about some money Gil had borrowed two months before to pay what the bank had been complaining about then. That was going to turn sour soon. He had borrowed that to pay the mortgage and should have paid it back already. Now Al was behind on his rent.

Money was the general problem, not this Friday's specific

problem, but the theme at least, the flavour. He rarely made enough. Enough, more so than most people's standard he just had more outgoing than John Normal. He blamed his wife. It was the small holes at the bottom of the pocket where he was losing out. And the kids too. He felt bad blaming his wife, he loved her. The kids too. But who has heard of kids taking it in turns to be ill. They span all twelve months, never a full set of clear noses or eyes in the house. If it wasn't doctors then it was antibiotics. He didn't even really agree with antibiotics, but his wife was in charge and a peaceful life was more highly prized than an ideal one.

It was antibiotics that had him dragged away from where he should have been when Bill called him. It pissed him off. His wife had just called for the millionth update, and he had already told her he was on his way with the medicine. He shouldn't be so far away from Bill when they were in the middle of a set-up. But he thought the same thing when he was in a set-up and his wife called. He had thought it when he left the square to by the medicine.

The routine should work like that, he should be watching all the time, it's not the most precise science in the world but like all good art, it requires good timing. Bill was already pissed off at him, and that pissed Gil off, as if anyone had the right or privilege of being pissed off it was him. He was the senior, but Bill was too fast and cocky for him, the truth, should it be known, was that he didn't like him and even less working with him. Bill gave Gil more stress, but Gil wasn't aware on that level and so was unaware as too why. He just assumed it was because he was too loud, too cliquey and too black.

They lived in neighbouring neighbourhoods. Gil's was nice, but poor, mixed but generally friendly. Bill lived further across, in a black neighbourhood, it was poor, black and possibly friendly, depending on who you are and what moods the other people are in.

Gil and Bill had been doing this scam for only a few

months. It had been going OK, but not as it should have been. This gave Gil stress. He was more aware on this level, he had been hustling for thirty years, he might not be able to recognise stress but he knew how to recognise a sucker. This was the problem Bill was having, he was picking the wrong type. The scam used to be easy, you used to just pick a tourist. But the tourists had become too smart, that was why Jose, the Spanish kid, had given it up. Too hard and too close to home. It wasn't Bill's fault that they got too smart, but Gil knew it didn't rely on foreigners, anyone is a sucker, but Bill wasn't so good at learning from Gil. He didn't respect the chain of authority. He saw Bill like the rest of them, couldn't give a shit. Bill would go to jail, he didn't care, it didn't make any sense but Gil knew it was true.

The last few weeks had seen too many get away. If too many get away everything changes. If you hustle a person well, they keep their mouth shout for years, but if they get away they don't stop talking about it. And if it was going to carry on, everyone would know the scam and worse, they would get picked up for it too.

Gil couldn't face the thought of being arrested. Sure enough, he worked on that other side of the law, but he wasn't a criminal, he couldn't go to jail. Gil was like a piranha, swimming the current until a weak fish comes along and then crushing it. Besides going to jail would leave his wife and two kids with nothing, her mother surely couldn't or wasn't going to help and his parents didn't even like her. That gave Gil stress too.

Gil stressed about Bill a lot. Even over things such as: how could the son of a priest be so reckless? As bad as the rest of the homeboys. He was too reckless and was going to end up shut up. If Gil was one of the boys he would be OK, surely Bill stick up for his boys, but not for Gil. He had paid his dues and that was why he got the easy part of the job. Now, it was all stress, the fun had gone from the job.

Gil had ulcers from the stress. Excess acids, he had been

ordered to the doctor, by his wife. But the ulcers didn't bother Gil, sure, they hurt, but it's not the ulcer that matters, it's having reason to have them. Every time an ulcer calls it doesn't just hurt it reminds you how fucked up your life is. Gil's life was going really badly.

IN response to his wife's call Gil had rushed from the square, thinking foolishly that if he rushed, he would get back in time. He had been watching Bill and the skinhead sucker from the corner of a street that led into the same square. He picked up some antibiotics from a pharmacy as his youngest son had vomited the last three pills into the toilet. He looked at the packet, why did he have to buy twenty-four when he only needed one. The thought didn't last long; his kids never stayed healthy for very long.

Gil worried about his kids, they had been on more courses of drugs than he had, he worried they would have completely useless immune systems by the time they grew up. David, the youngest, had the worst luck, it was bad luck; other children got clothes handed down, David got respiratory infections. Then he would get mixtures, so Gil's wife would get him to buy mixtures of medications. She panicked too much, Gil argued.

Bill interrupted Gil's mental preoccupations. He was on the bus. Gil had predicted it and had planned to an extent how the conversation would follow. Bill didn't take well to the fact that Gil's family seemed to be dying slowly. He had even once commented that they didn't seem to be carrying the right genes. That led obviously to an argument. They argued more than Gil did with his wife. Somehow, this time Bill didn't mention anything, only stressing Gil more as he couldn't understand why not.

He got off the bus and walked quickly, turning into his street. The corner was familiar and it always came with the familiar thought of having a car. He would love to pull one day into his street with his own car. Or even just driving one. He had never driven himself around that corner, his last car was lost in the price of the deposit on the house. Only in taxi or by foot had he passed this corner. He would love to do that.

He reached the big stone steps that led up from the street. The house was a big old stone house, it had presence despite being the width of one room, it had three floors plus the half submerged cellar. It was big enough and it was the one happy solid thing in Gil's life.

He took a breath to cast out the thoughts and rang the bell. There was always someone in the house. He didn't even know where his keys were, it could have been six months since he held them last. He did everything outside the house his wife would do if she wasn't so tied to the kids. He paid the bills, he did most of the shopping, took the kids to school—when they were well enough to go—and to the doctors when they weren't. If the house ever was empty it was a mystery to Gil and it obviously happened at the time of day he was never around. Fortunately he thought as his eldest son opened the door.

It was like a royal or presidential house, always someone there to open for you, always someone expecting you. The important things these people have on their minds, Gil could never imagine them on a mad search for their keys. He didn't share this view with anyone, his peers did not talk often about politics or the like. They were all like Gil, political thoughts came and went but political words did not.

The house was a damp steam pot as usual. He could smell the illness in the air as if he lived in the eighteenth century. He wondered at other times which was damper, in the house or outside. It was one-hundred per cent humidity outside, but it was worse inside. He patted various children on the head as he squeezed past on to the kitchen at the rear of the house. Having safely navigated the darkened minefield of toys and children in the lobby he found his wife in front of her orchestra of modern cauldrons. Each one full of his step mothers best kept secrets. Most people don't appreciate cooking for six people. Perhaps for a dinner party occasionally or when family visits. But to cook three meals a day for six people was a logistical exercise. There was always something on the stove. He didn't know what it looked like without pots on it, or without the blue glow of gas underneath them. Anyway they ate well, and the kids always had cooked food, even to take to school, better than the sandwich and other cultural things to which his wife's family tried so hard not to adopt.

He kissed her and leaving the medicine and the promise he would be back provided the skinhead paid out. She knew what went on, she wasn't proud of it, but she knew. He wasn't the criminal he had been when they met and he still dressed it up to her. She didn't even have time for socialising anymore so she didn't have anyone to look down on her, she saw Gil's point of view and did her best to accept it. Her best on the surface was quite convincing.

Gil had a more vigorous dream. He dreamt of being on the black side of the lines. Where everything was more tranquil. His wife would give a quite smile when he mentioned it as if to say it was her dream too but its nice to have something to dream about. He asked briefly after the child but he had bought the medicine more for his wife's peace of mind than for the child. She smiled a disapproving smile, knowing that whatever it was it was out of her control. She loved him and she shared the same dream, she just had more time to dream about it.

He thought briefly of the dream on this way out of the house after kissing his children on their foreheads as they looked up to him. He had much less time to think about it and that was why no movement towards it ever happened. But the dream was there and it lived and breathed inside Gil. "One day," he said, one day.

He felt better to be back outside, on the street. The air

was breathable and he felt assured for having visited home. His stressful life still circled ominously above his head like air traffic running out of fuel and threatening to fall at any moment. It would have been nice to drive out of the street to he thought, but not today, another bus.

He got off the bus a few blocks before the square, Bill still hadn't called back. Gil stood on a street corner in thought. He didn't want to appear again in the background and fuck it up, he didn't know what was going on in Bill's 'playground' as he called it. They were a team he told himself. They worked for each other, if one fucked up neither of them got paid. He told him that when it went wrong and when they argued. He told himself that a lot. He didn't bother putting up a fight in the arguments, he knew Bill didn't see his reasoning and that his big bold attitude wasn't good for this job. This contemplation restored his usual stressful mental ambience.

He didn't like being under the thumb of a kid but completely lacked the subconscious rage necessary to stand up to him. Bill had a mirror reaction to anger, his spitting and swearing increased as his opponent's did. It wasn't just him, Gil wasn't good at standing up in general. And it wasn't just Bill, he was calm compared with some of the other kids from that area. Gil contemplated Bill's neighbourhood for a while and wondered if it was OK to think that he was happy he wasn't born black. He wondered if it was some divine intervention, a sign to tell him to move on.

Bill sat back down quietly, picked up his beer bottle and looked into the neck. He raised it slowly close to his mouth but couldn't drink it and returned to looking into the neck. Sammy had barely noticed his partners return, after several minutes of silence he looked at him. "Everything OK?"

"Yeah, man."

"You look like you want to jump into the bottle."

"Nah, nothin man, just me brova got held up an' dat so I gots to wait around longer." Sammy looked at him as if to say is my company not good enough and as he did Bill realised looked to him in an attempt to add more sincerity to his act.

"Thas all." Sammy nodded in acknowledgement, drained the rest of his beer and stood up.

"So, you want another?" He held the beer bottle up a bit for reference.

"Uh yeah, aiight." Bill drank down the beer and put the bottle under the bench, Sammy stood watching him expectantly his facing showing the kind of disbelieving surprise you might give a child when it immediately does something you just asked it not to. He shook his head, Bill seemed to be distracted.

"You gonna give me the bottle? I need to return it!"

"Ah shit! Sorry man." Sammy turned to leave. "Hey, uh we gonna go back to his place, ma brova's, you know hang out an' dat. If you wanna come an, you know…"

Sammy continued to look impatiently at him, he took the bottle. "Um, maybe, I uh, I don't know. I am going to get the beers, OK?" He walked off his expression unchanged, a little confused and a little suspicious.

On his return he didn't seem to have thought about it much more. Or anything for that matter. He said nothing and passed Bill his beer. Bill opened it and again passed Sammy the bottle opener not having noticed Sammy had opened his already with the lighter. Sammy's expression moved slowly from suspicious to confused and frustrated.

"Yeah, you know, we gonna chill an all dat. Smoke a lil' somfin."

Sammy responded with little more than a grunt, sitting quietly contemplating his beer.

"He live close and dat."

"Maybe," Sammy finally responded, but I am a little tired. If I do I would like to go home and take a shower first.

But thanks anyway.

"Watch some movies maybe, play playstation, drink some, whatever man." Bill spoke as if her were mentally checking off a list of activities designed to provoke interest. He was. "Anyway, I told you he ain't gonna pass by for a half hour an' dat so, you know." He relaxed back to the chair, consciously taking a time out, he looked at the beer, decided a cigarette was more what he wanted.

"Know wha I'd like righ' now?"

"What's that?"

"Fine ass bitch."

Sammy half spat half coughed into his beer at the change of subject. "Yes?"

"Yeah man you know?" Sammy didn't know, and looked at him trying to demonstrate it. He was losing interest.

"Get ma dick sucked an all dat." Sammy looked back at him, not surprised or shocked but with the face of something else, a little wry smile not really giving it away.

"Like I told you I am a little tired." They laughed, Bill perked up having realised a successful subject.

"Der a place round here with girls."

"Are you asking me or telling me? What do you mean anyway, like a bar or club or a whorehouse?" Sammy shook off the question not knowing why he had taken so much interest. Bill was regretting both the subject and having picked this topic. But he hated being wrong, especially in front of Gil. Besides he had wasted how much time? Forty-five minutes. No, he would fold, push on, just pick another subject.

"Nah, nothin man, just what I'd like righ now."

"Yeah, me too," Sammy sarcastically added without the slightest hint of conviction. But like I said, I am a little bit tired right now.

A moment of silence was followed by, "So you wanna see if we can find one, I fink der's one over dis way," he held out his lanky black arm pointing a lazy finger.

"Really?" Sammy looked confused, not only buy Bills random behaviour, but because he lived in this area for eight years and still didn't know that there were brothels let alone where they were.

"Yeah come on man, le's see if we can find it. Anyway, if not we can call ma brova, he'll know, he likes to get down like dat." Sammy laughed shortly at Bills description of his brother and shook his head slowly.

"No, seriously. Besides, then I would really need to take a shower."

"For a ho?" Bill looked confused, clearly Sammy didn't know too many hookers, but neither of them wanted to get onto personal hygiene as a Friday night conversation topic. "Aiight man." Bill relaxed into the no–go–ness of the idea.

"In fact, I think I am going to go home now." Sammy made a small movement, but was interrupted.

"No, uh, um mean stick around man, you know we go to ma brova's, and still I got to buy you a beer man, you already bought me two."

Sammy didn't really want to go home, but he was becoming a little suspicious of what exactly Bill was after. He decided to stay. "Ok, but I don't really fancy waling around looking for hookers at this time of night. Or at any time of the day for that matter." His tone was stern.

"Aiight man," Bill wasn't really in the mood either, besides the cocaine wasn't on his side either. But nevertheless he was stuck for angles, the topic of fellatio was a last choice, a fail safe.

"But still man, I could do with gettin' ma dick sucked righ now. Mmm. You know? Ma brova, he hat dis girl, she always bring friends when she come. Anyway, last night she brought dis one bitch, sucked ma dick straight for a half hour. Shit! I was nearly cryin' when she was done."

Sammy sat, now looking slightly interested in Bills bragging, he was enjoying listening at least. The subject matter wasn't choice, but to him it was they way they were told.

"Yeah man, somfin else. But you know, if we go back der later, maybe he call her an' day come over." Bill gave the black equivalent of nudge–nudge, wink–wink. Sammy remained unmoved and unconvinced, he nodded and hummed his yes's. He distracted himself whenever he could with what ever he could, but Bill caught his attention back leaning close to Sammy, resting his elbow on the back of the bench. He prodded Sammy. "You know what?" Sammy was intrigued by this sudden increase in confidence between the two. He leaned a little towards Bill.

"One time I had a guy suck ma dick…"

Sammy struggled to keep his composure but changed his smile a little to be sure he felt acknowledged. "Really?" He gave nothing away, he could have even had the same experience for all he gave away.

"Yeah man," his voice was lowered, "it was good an' dat, nice. But I had to close ma eyes an' shit dough, you know? But it was a good one." Bill looked with a smile half of embarrassment and half of pride. He had exposed himself, at least his character.

"I don't know if you have noticed, but the level of this conversation has really gone down hill."

Bill couldn't understand what was meant and examined Sammy's face, which was still staring straight forward, for clues.

"Wha ya mean?"

"Nothing," Sammy turned now, just that we were having a civilised conversation a few minutes ago and now you are talking about going to brothels and this. Sammy waved a snobbish arm at the subject and then regretted doing so.

"Hmph, we different, thas all. Black people don't got shame like white people, we more open an' dat." He nodded intelligently at Sammy. "White people more conservative, right?"

"Maybe, but do you let all you homeboys know you let

men suck you off?"

"Aiight player, so maybe we ain't so open about everyting."

"I don't think its about black and white, it's like I told you before, its about different people, people are different, like you and I for example, we find different things interesting to talk about. Don't take it the wrong way, I am interested in what you say and how you say it, you just picked a topic I wouldn't have done. Two, in fact."

Sammy relaxed, feeling his rant again, but he was sure he had suit him up this time. Perhaps even got him to think about something else. But it only took a few seconds for it to change.

"Yeah, but you act like you interested, but can't bring yourself off your throne to talk with a black man about it. Like iss ok fort me to entertain you wiv it but…"

"Don't go there," Sammy cut him off, "Don't go there. Anyone can sit down and start talking to me. And talk about disgusting things and I would listen, be they black white or orange, and just because I was listening or because I was interested doesn't mean I am going to share similar experiences. I am interested not in what they are saying but why they are saying it. But what I would prefer above all that is to have a normal conversation. You know, life and bullshit, not about who has had the best sexual experience."

"Aiight man, le's talk about dat shit then."

Sammy let out his steam in a long controlled sigh rolling his eyeballs ion the process. He started to speak but hesitated.

"It doesn't work like that," he said eventually.

"Wha you mean?"

"You cant just say, 'let's talk about something interesting' and it happens. A good conversation evolves out of a basic one and sometimes out of a bad one. But you," Sammy paused feeling an accusation or prejudice coming. "You, I mean to say, I don't know if it is you or black people of just some kind of people but its just impossible. For example you can't even see the conversation was bad, let alone explain why. You understand." Bill shook his head. "Ok, for example: tell me why you started talking about finding a brothel."

"Wha? You mean why I said it?" Bill became defensive as he became paranoid. "I do' know, makin' talk an' dat."

"Ok, but there must have been a reason, talking about blowjobs isn't the most usual conversation topic thirty minutes into a relationship." Bill cringed at the word relationship. He had become addicted to every word from Sammy's mouth, expecting every next one to accuse him. He was on his guard. "Something must have made you talk about prostitutes."

"Uh, I do' Know. Perhaps, yeah, that bitch form last night. The one I told you, suck me for half an hour and dat."

"Ok, but why were you thinking about her?"

"Because I had invited you to ma brova's place." Bill was sure he had fucked up somewhere, he could easily employ his righteousness to get himself out but he was in a corner and people act differently when they are in a corner. Especially when they are confused as to why they are there and who has them there.

Sammy was all but aware of Bills fear, and so carried on his interrogation playfully. "So why did you invite me there?"

"Wha' you sayin man?" Bill sounded more aggressive than he would have liked.

"Nothing, I am just trying to get under you skin, to understand, to get you to tell me your motives. You don't need to get defensive." Sammy notice then that Bill was a little shaken. "Look forget it, I wasn't trying to upset you or piss you off."

"Aiight man." Bill returned to his beer and his secrets.

"I didn't literally mean forget it." There was still silence, Bill was recalculating, his eyebrows twitch when he recalculates, but Sammy didn't know nor did he notice. He turned to his beer instead, shaking it off. He pulled a cigarette from the packet he had taken from his trouser packet and lit it with the least movement possible.

Sammy's smoking drew Bill's attention as it was the first time Sammy had smoked. He shook it off. He went back to planning, he needed a new angle, quickly, he was determined not to give up on this, he know too that Gil would be back soon, he had to make progress. He wouldn't be able to find someone else now anyway, maybe later, but much later.

"What time you got now?"

"Ten twenty."

"Cool man, imma call ma bredrin den see if he finished." Sammy looked at him and as if he could see past Bills green eyes he saw a red flame in Bill's soul, he already knew something was wrong but this sealed it. He didn't feel worried, a little nervous or anxious but not worried about the final outcome, it always worked out OK.

Bill limped off, he took his beer this time, throwing the bottle high above his face as he drained the last few drops almost walking into a guy coming the other way as he did. He threw the bottle into a bush casually as he approached the phone. Sammy watched this attributed it, and for some reason everything else, to the 'bad attitude' not unique to this particular kid. He sat back and laughed to himself.

At the phone Bill dropped in the coins and dialled the same number. "Where you at? Bill, who'd you fink? Aiight, whatever, listen jus tell me where you at? For real? Cool, You see me den? Cool and the gang." He hung up, checked himself once more and sauntered back to the bench. Not sitting this time.

"So, uh listen, ma brova all finished, he on his way back, you wanna pass by or not?" He tried to remain causal, Sammy had already started shaking his head, but Bill was determined. He had done this before, so he kept cool, just a formula, he told himself. He wondered how much Sammy knew, had he clocked him or was it just blind coincidence. They didn't normally act this way, usually they just walk away, no formalities or politeness. Didn't matter then anyway Bill reassured himself, just a script, they always did this at this point.

"Come on man, come chill fo a minute. Smoke a little, chill out." The first bait was taken.

"No really, thank you but I am going to hit the sack soon."

"Aiight but I'd like to pay you back for the beers you know." Second bait.

"Really, thanks."

"Aiight man, but you don't have to smoke, we can get some powder or whatever." Second Bait. "Call some girls." Third bait. Play some playstation or watch some James Cagney–Edward G. Robinson shit." Fourth and Fifth. It was working but slowly.

"Really, thanks, but no."

Bill looked at him, he had never been played so well, he knew he was being watched by Gil, but it felt like he was on trial at some kind of audition. He felt the pressure.

"Come on, maaan! Look, we'll buy the beers on the way." Sammy started to budge.

"There you go! Come on, he only live a few blocks this way." Sammy acquiesced with the reluctance of someone heading to be executed. They stood side by side for the first time. Sammy strode above Bill as they set off, he wasn't that tall but his strong build and good looks made him look god–like next to Bill. Bill carried on in his disjointed and random fashion.

"Der you go man, now you doin it, lef leg, righ leg an all dat." He smiled, he was on top at last. They walked away from the bench were it had al taken place. Bill occasionally pointed his finger in their direction. The vibrant aromas of good food and cigar smoke, the happy warm vibration of the square passed them on the air. They came to the street and waited to cross, then left behind their island patrolled by dwindling traffic moving onto other things.

"You gonna like ma brova man, he like you, dat intellectual type." He looked to Sammy for confirmation. "Not that I ain't, but I think you a bit above my head an' shit."

"I don't know, I think there is more to you than meets the eye."

"Wha you mean," Bill inquired innocently deaf to the irony by this point.

"Nothing, I just think you are smarter than you think."

"Yeah I hear dat a lot man." He did, and had, he was the kind who teachers really wanted to believe in, always telling him to apply himself and how far he could go if he just did. "All that shit about applyin' maself. Tha's wha you was about to say righ?" He looked again for conformation, smiling smugly as he received it.

"You are right I was, but I don't need to know, you have just proven my point."

They walked a few steps without words. Then Bill, who although being smart and having the script well by heart, took a step to far. He knew the script but was useless at improvisation. "You know if you wanna buy some weed or somfin, you can do it from ma brova." Bill noticed Sammy did not react, so searched through his pockets, it was habit, he generally knew where things were in his pockets, but he liked the randomness of searching for a few seconds for dramatic effect.

Just one block away from the square everything had changed. Bill had noted the direction Sammy had pointed when he asked where he lived and had purposely taken him the opposite way. Here the lights were sparse, the air was still and with an odour of rubbish and engine oil, there was no traffic, no life and the outlook was less than promising. The walls of the buildings seemed to lean in on the middle of the street, casting themselves into their own shadows. The half moon hanging above could have been covered by cloud moving at irregular speed and it wouldn't have seemed out of place.

Bill kept rummaging, he had been 'taught' this, and this is why he over did it and over used it. He pulled a pinch of green from a pocket. "Here look, 's good shit man, one-hundred per cent natural. He held it to Sammy's nose." Sammy reluctantly smelled it.

"Mmm."

"I got some coke too," he frisked himself briefly again with more hurry this time. "Here! Look."

"Hey, put it away man," Sammy looked around him warily. He looked at Bill offended by his tactlessness.

"Aiight man chill, *no pasa nada*"

"You speak Spanish?!"

"Nah man, just a little, a few words, from school." It was true, he only knew a few words, those few. But he had learnt them just for that reason, 'to act to distract'. Funnily enough, this was his own idea, he had needed to ask a few people to learn a good phrase. He didn't tell anyone that, he liked people to think he was smart and he loved it more when they told him to apply his brain to life. But he knew that by not doing so he benefited more as he felt more powerful by being the only one in control of his life. If he became smart and applied himself he would think up a follow-up line in Spanish, but he wasn't going to so he didn't have one. And so they turned the corner in silence, they turned right and walked along the plain wall, at the end of the wall the front of the houses were set further pack from the street. Bill stepped up to a doorway and pressed a buzzer. Sammy watch anxiously from the street. Bill stepped away from the door as if to hide himself and beckoned Sammy to do the same. It made Sammy very nervous and in that moment of seeing Bill pressed against the wall away from the door he knew it was bad. He looked around with a moments bodyguard paranoia and shook his head at Bill. He didn't want to go into that recess. Bill looked at him hurriedly motioning, he didn't want the person in the apartment he had just buzzed to see either of them. He looked up, calling Sammy again.

"Why the fuck do I want to go there?" He shook his head and turned back the way he had come. "Fuck you! I am out of here." But no sooner had he turned on the spot he spotted a police officer making his way along the wall. Hugging it tightly with the look of a lion approaching its next meal.

With lack of anything to do except wait for Bill's phone call and the oppressive heat having returned to its confusing level Gil was stressed again. He looked at his watch, ten-fifteen, great, but what did that mean when he couldn't remember when Bill had called. He couldn't remember how long ago either, he calculated from his activities, perhaps thirty minutes. He walked towards the square, keeping a blocks distance he turned left and took a parallel street, then back right and ended up on the far end of the square to where Bill was. He looked to his watch again but not to check the time but to look across the square. Then walked over to a paper stand to wait. He read the headlines of the scandal filled tabloids, his interest in scandals stretch a little way past his in politics but was kept just as well guarded. He was distracted by Bill standing up and so stepped back to the street he had come from. As he did the cell phone began to buzz in his pocket.

"I'm back, right on the corner of the plaza, Bill?" He hesitated for a second, not sure if it was Bill. "Nothing, I told you I am on the plaza." He stopped again realising he wasn't and turned back around and walk towards the paper stand again. "At the corner by the paper stand, you see me now? Yeah I can see you, you're ready then?" The phone cut off and Gil looked at it half in surprise and half in sadness.

He went back to watching Bill. The guy at the paper stand watch Gil curiously. Gil often forgot he was wearing a police officers uniform. Especially when he was stressed, like this moment. People came up to him sometimes to ask directions, he was always with it enough to just direct them rather than panic. But he dreaded the day someone came up to him with a real problem. Jose had always reassured him, –not in this neighbourhood, man, nothing bad ever happens here. But Gil was just another one changing that.

He ignored the looks of the paper seller and walked off trying to look as purposeful as possible. He skirted around the square stopping at a corner to talk with a taxi driver. He was counting the entire time. Forty seconds and he walked down the street he had seen Bill and the sucker take. He doubted how well he had counted, he kidded himself, in fact. He sped his pace, even if it was forty seconds it was too long, it was supposed to look like an honest drug bust, that meant he should look like he was following them closely. He went through his lines trying to expel his doubts and stresses.

He had been doing it for years, he didn't have a problem with the act, but it would be nice to forget about life while doing it. He thought of how Bill was going to critique everything when they finished. The stress wasn't going to go away. He stopped at the corner to expel all these thoughts. He had been doing it for years, it didn't matter what Bill said, it would be wrong and he didn't know any better. He clenched his fists, threw them to the very bottom of his arms, sighed through puffed cheeks and stepped around the corner into the 'playground'.

What was the white-boy doing standing in the street like that? The peace of mind went as soon as Gil had taken the corner. What was he doing? He kept his face straight and walked with his walk of purpose. It fucked up again, his conscience told him. He tried to banish it, just go ahead as planned, he cursed inside. The boy looked petrified, that was a good sign. They caught each others eyes.

The white-boy looked like a trapped animal, he looked both ways and in a panic walked towards Gil. Crazy kid Gil thought. He carried on, trap him at the end of the wall. Sammy looked at Bill with a face that spelled 'you bastard' that was good too. He reached them.

"Ok boys, let's see some identification." His voice in character was firm and authoritative.

Bill pulled out his ID quickly. Too quickly in Sammy's eyes, but he didn't see the small wrap of cocaine he passed at the same time. It didn't matter, Sammy clammed up. The game was gone.

"Don't have any."

Gil made straight to grab him as he tried to pass, pinning him against the wall; he reached to try and plant the coke but Sammy wriggled out of his reach. Gil grabbed his shirt pocket. The kid was quick and smart. Gil tried several more times to plant it but couldn't and it was just making Sammy more agitated. Gil's heart raced. There was no time for thinking now; he grabbed the handcuffs from his belt and waved them at Sammy. Bill stood in quiet support.

On seeing the handcuffs Sammy got even more restless, he started screaming "I'm not with him, I don't know him!" Louder and louder. Sammy and Gil turned to face Bill together both showing their disgust at him. The taxi Gil had spoken with scooted around the corner, Gil waved it down with the cuffs, getting Sammy's attention back. The driver pulled over, it was already fucked. A brief moment of calm in the storm set sadness in Gil's heart, what kind of cop needs a taxi anyway. Sammy let his voice to full wail, the driver of the taxi decided he didn't want to be a part of it after all and left. Another risk of the useless idea. The screaming was now drawing the attention of the neighbourhood, lights came on, faces appeared from behind curtains and shutters. Sammy felt a wave of support, despite the neighbours not actually doing anything. He started to drag Gil by the arm he was held by, still tightly creasing Sammy's shirt. Bill was lost, he tried the occasional line to try and calm Sammy but it didn't work, he followed like the coward he was in these situations. He was thinking too that it was fucked, and if he stayed shut up he could blame Gil.

Sammy became exasperated by the lack of community spirit and dragged Gil further, turning his vocal efforts to him also. "You're not a real cop! Let's go and find a real cop! Come on!" It seemed a little over the top to both Gil and Bill, they weren't going to hurt him at any point after all. But that didn't matter, Sammy was dragging them all back to the square. Then it could get out of hand.

Time slipped away, as they reached the square the grip on Sammy's shirt loosened. Gil and Bill looked at each other in disguised desperation, Sammy saw them gripped Gil's thumb and twisted against the grain. Gil had to let go and did. Sammy stood for those split seconds, free but ignorant of what to do. Bill and Gil had the same moment of panic, what would he do. Ninety-nine out of one hundred times they ran, no one ever knew for sure Gil wasn't a real cop. That was the fail safe. You cant go to another cop just in case.

So they stood suspended momentarily, all three heads spinning inside, three hearts racing. Sammy moved first, scanning the environment in his first moments clarity. No one, neither cop nor obstacle. And that was it. He left, sprinting around the corner, not looking back and not stopping for about twenty blocks, only for a busy street. He looked back then, but finding nothing he still ran. He didn't go straight home, just in case someone was following.

The argument that ensued was just as Gil had seen it. Bill, having lost sight of the dupe, took his cue to be angry. He didn't see the future in such a pessimistic way and therefore never concerned himself too much with what he was going to say. Gil on the other hand did, and he had everything planned already. He gave Bill a sour glare.

"Shit!"

Bill shook his head like a critical father would before launching into a detailed analysis. "Fuckin' righ, shit!" But in the moment of having to think of something to say to support his anger his brain failed him. It didn't matter, Gil knew the lines.

"Why do you pick them like this?"

"Wha ya mean, like dis?"

"You've got to pick stupid looking ones!" It had sounded right in Gil's plan, but the soft words lost their credibility in the harsh night air. Bill smirked.

"Truss me! It ain't about stupid. This guy was as likely as any, it ain't a fuckin exact science you Know. Anyway, wha we gonna do now?"

Bill was ready, he had said his piece, despite all his downsides, he was quick to forgive and move on. He didn't hold a grudge. Gil, however, hadn't finished. 'Exact science' was a phrase Bill used all the time, and now Gil had remembered the answer he'd thought of a few nights ago when he couldn't sleep. He saw Bill like the thick kid at school who needed to be burned fifty-nine times before he decided it was time to stop touching the heaters. "You don't give a shit do you?"

"Wha?"

"About this." Gil waved his hand towards the recently deserted space in the street. They both realised in that moment the majority of the crowd that had gathered had stayed to watch the developments. Gil grabbed Bill by the shoulder and dragged him away, lowering his voice, he still looked like a cop to the crowd.

"What happened? Why was he standing in the street like that? Why did he start screaming? How did you manage to fuck it up again?"

Bill tore his arm away from its grip. "Wha the fuck you mean wha happened, you was der. I din fuck it up was ya fuckin problem man, you win some you lose some, le's just get on with it." He looked to the square, he saw another hundred suckers. "Always fucking complain at me like iss always ma fault," he said to him self. He gestured to the playing field. "Look!"

Gil looked, only seeing a blur of people. He turned back to Bill, his tone was quieter. "Look, you have to learnt from you mistakes or this will keep happening."

"Shit, you stress too much Gil, man. Der's plenty mo fish out der, le's go get some. Relax for four fuckin seconds."

"You don't understand, we cant try every person out there. It supposed to be low key. If everyone goes through it or knows about it, it doesn't leave any fucking fish." His tone started to rise again. He remembered the exact science. "You're fishing with a shotgun like your homeboys in paper store hold ups. It might not be an exact science but your accuracy is lacking." Again Gil felt his words lacked a certain something in their reality.

It didn't matter how the words came out, Bill and Gil thought differently. Nothing would change either of them, least of all themselves. Their age, their race, their upbringing, cultures, moral values; everything worked against them. But the main factor in this situation had been Gil's expectation of failure. Bill on the other hand kept his hopes high, perhaps it failed perhaps it didn't, he knew he could try again. It had failed, he was ready to carry on. Gil though knowing it was going to fail wanted to argue it out all night.

They did argue, and in the end they didn't find any knew suckers and so they got on the same bus together, still arguing in quiet voices. Bill remained calm throughout, some internal beat keeping his blood pressure in check. Gil felt his ulcers and was happy when he left the bus, they didn't say any nice goodbyes, he just got off and left Bill staring intently into the gutter.

The bus carried Bill into his neighbourhood, he sat waiting on the bus watching the eyes of those people on the blocks the bus passed by. They became more like him, but they were all waiting. Some for buses, some for friends, taxis or food. Some were waiting of morning and some just waited. They all shared the same look in their eyes, tired, hot and glazed, tired of waiting for something to change.

He watched traffic lights run their routines as he waited by them. Her cleared his mind, he didn't know stress, he had the same problems as Gil he considered. Without the kids. He had to pay those amounts for his life to carry on. So he couldn't figure out why Gil was so stressed.

He though of the conversation with Sammy, but he couldn't figure out why it was on his mind, nothing stood out to him. He nodded his head to the beat inside. He thought about girls and sleep. He wasn't going to go to sleep though, he was hungry and he wanted to find something to do. Once he was back in his neighbourhood he would find something comforting. He felt at home there, something would be waiting for him.

So that was pretty much how it happened, can't say I felt exactly the way it was described, but I am not going to be picky over something none of us can prove. But the next morning, at the door, I had other things to worry about. They were obviously related.

Those first steps out of the front door that morning after were like the first ones I took when I moved to the city. Nervous, somewhat paranoid. This time I had more reason to suspect someone was hiding around every corner. I looked both ways across one way traffic less streets. The streets were always deserted, as much on Wednesday as any other days. But I wasn't looking for cars. The blocks close to my house were always deserted.

With every old block my heart rate dropped and every

new one it went up. My fear of finding someone exchanged frequently with my want to find the one. I walked to the main street in my area, but turned the opposite direction to the square. Every policeman or uniformed person sent me into near hysterics. I felt like a wreck, but I need to do it.

I walked and procrastinated long enough to be hungry. I took this opportunity to take a break from my task or re-adaptation that was half a search. I sat outside a restaurant, I have two types, nice because they are cheap and nice because the food is nice. This one was the former type. I eat out a lot and so I am used to eating in this type.

I sat outside, as usual, but picked a different table, one that offered me a better view of the intersection I was sat at. If he passed by from here I could see him easily. I ordered my usual as compensation for moving seats. It works well if you are being followed, and if you are paranoid. AS I waited for my food I tried to establish if I was hunter or prey. Surely this guy wasn't looking for me, and surely I wanted to find him.

I wanted nothing more than finding him. I wanted to grab him and assault him. I sat staring blankly into space planning my revenge. In doing so I didn't achieve much observing. Everything was a little glazed over, I felt punch drunk. The soups arrival snapped me out of it.

I considered then that my chances of finding this character were pretty slim. It put me off to a certain extent, but it wasn't just revenge, I had to restore my confidence. Further, considering my options, what other methods did I have of locating him other than chance?

I had no idea who he was, I couldn't remember his name, and on the basis of assuming everything he told me in that conversation was a lie to win my confidence I cant assume that if I did remember it that it would be the truth. It would be worth remembering, even as the most frail of foundations. Even still I feared chance was my best ally.

I watched the street for a while, but my mind soon

returned back inside itself. I played the events over, many still blurred or uncertain. The what if plagued me still, but they were slowing becoming future what if as opposed to the regret filled ones. I considered this a step in the right direction, but it made me wonder, exactly how can I revenge this, what is appropriate. I had a lot to consider, I didn't want to be disproportionate, as a result of my personality. But it occurred to me also I didn't know what was proportionate. What are the emotional and physical costs I have had to pay? I had run, I had screamed, so there is both energy expended and social consequences. Adrenalin too, there was plenty of that. I felt like a stranger, scared in my own neighbourhood.

My pasta arrived, before I had touched the soup. I told the waiter to leave them both and I began with the soup. This mental process was ridiculous, besides, did I want revenge on the cop too. If not why not? I imagined briefly how far the chain goes, how many more people were involved. That taxi driver. Probably not, but they could all be protected by someone. Paranoid and conspiratorial, but still I dint want to get into something I wouldn't get back out of. The thought of mafia lightened my mood briefly, I doubted the existence of organised crime, except with parking tickets.

The consequences worried me, I was too busy thinking about his consequences to think about mine. My line of thought is that people below the law are generally not very well covered by it. But that was a risk too, they could play dumb and besides it's not a moral justification. Going to the police was a waste of time, no witnesses anyway. They wouldn't help me when I needed it why would they waste any more of their precious time.

The quick thinking told me not to worry about mob reprisals or that kind of trouble, police included. Quick thinking is the type I usually refer to, long thinking doesn't figure much ion my life, or at least hadn't. Quick thinking had got me out of the set-up and helped me chose the seat in the restaurant and pick the food I wanted to eat. I would do it here too. Do what you want to him and quick think afterwards.

I thought about asking someone else's opinion on the subject. That was long thinking, that would involve lots of consequences. Besides which I had very few people I consider confidantes, back in the country perhaps there was one old friend I would have told, but his ideas of revenge wouldn't be easily followed, given the restrictions of law, time and space. I didn't really need to talk to anyone, I had got on ok so far, why do some people always need to have someone else to talk to, to help them with their ideas. I read a proverb someone once that said when you look for advice you look for an accomplice. And that wasn't what I needed, I needed to handle it myself. I knew it was going to end up sounding like some bad American movie, stinking of standing up and being a man and so on, but like it or not it had to be done.

A truck woke me out of the trance, the soup was truly cold, I pushed it away and began on the not so cold pasta. I managed to eat that without further drifting, but also without keeping an eye out from this character, like he was going to walk past the restaurant. When I had finished, I walked to the square. I felt it was ridiculous him just sauntering by, best to return to the scene of the crime.

One-thirty on a Wednesday, quiet. I picked a bench, different bench, sat and watched. I soon drifted in to a dream like state. I watched the familiar elderly faces taking advantage of the peaceful timetable lapping the square slowly. I watched the dog walkers struggling with their valences of dogs, pondered how they manage to keep them all quiet at once, and how did such an obvious profession exist. Why have a dog if you haven't the time to walk it? It's half the reason of having it at all.

So it was fated to become the most left to fate manhunt in

history, my personal history at least. Not since I moved to the city and a passer-by asked me if I wanted to by some marijuana had it been so relaxed. I watched, but the storm in my brain overran the process. Its different now anyway, drug dealers don't walk by any more. It's too fashionable. No one I wanted to see was about to walk by, but I sat anyway, thinking about the night before and the revenge I was probably never going to get a chance to enact.

The crowd of unwanted faces passed me by, unaware of what had happened to me the night before, unaware of the extreme mental activity of my brain, and by the looks of them unaware to a lot of other things too. Time moved on, step by step, as if the world had become time–lapsed. Usually when I sit around I set a time limit, a period of inactivity or activity. Sit, watch, walk, eat, smoke. Doesn't matter what it is, it's a process. Today I forgot, today routine had been ruined. Why would I sit down and not say to myself, fifteen minutes if you do not see him move. That is how I work, today I wasn't working.

The populous drove by, step by step, I watched, my head nodding from side to side in irregular jerks. The torment of mental activity disturbed the normality of my vision. I needed to find this Bill. That was when I remember his name. Bill, if I could find him I could get on with my life. If I could settle this lack of normality I am suffering, it would be OK.

His face sprawled across my brain, how could I ever revenge such a face. Some things in life are impossible to imagine purely based on the likelihood of their occurrence. A guy so helpless looking. No matter what his mouth issued, he wasn't the type you would ever plan to physically abuse. How could I hurt a face like that? It would be like torturing a kitten or a baby child. It made me cringe. He was helpless.

Uniformed people circulated as I sat, scaring me each time. Those utility belts were extremely close from my reclined eye-level. The confidence was coming back, just slowly. As it did I could focus more. The first thoughts were simply violent. Violently simple. Grabbing him and pounding him. Perhaps I could find a way of putting this fear into him. Was I that menacing? Perhaps, but most likely not. What else, anonymous, smashing him from behind with a bottle or a pipe. Has its advantages, but down points too. No, I needed some more questions to be answered. I could play his game, approach him as if I believed the whole set-up was real, would he believe me? Too complex, but It would give me time and resources to enact my revenge.

As I ran though this melody of revenge I freed myself from the fear, the hypothesised future looked good. All I had to do was make a plan, a decision. Not always the easiest thing. Especially for me. Perhaps I was better to keep all options open. Pick one on the spot. Or perhaps just blag it. Play it by ear, that's what he must do. I am as good as he is. I have to be. Besides, look at how random and impractical this method of finding him is. Blagging has always worked for me, so where is the harm in trying again.

So if blagging was to be the way forward I would have to be in the right frame of mind. Alert. Quick. It had its down sides. I would have to get off the bench and do something. A guy approached me for the time. "Two-thirty p.m.," I told him, "you're welcome." Damn the whole lunchtime wasted. Nothing.

With this though fresh in mind I looked up, sure enough the melee had reduced, people scurried from the corners of the plaza and filed back to their jobs. The time guy hurried off, probably late too. I hadn't even seen his face. Perhaps it was him! A surge filled me and I leapt off the bench, turned away from him but keeping an eye, circled around the grassy patch quickly to catch a glimpse of his face. No, not him. What were the chances anyway, slim to none, right?

The adrenalin had however reinvigorated me, the desire to catch up with this Bill guy was back. And more importantly the energy too. I headed for a kiosk for a drink, new thoughts rummaged through my processing centres. I needed a plan to find him first. Nothing was going to be straight forward. Plans. Detective work. Private eye. Guesses. Coincidence. Should have done it the night before was the only conclusion I had. Not much use without a time machine. Still shouldn't have run. Shut it, no use to me now.

You thought they were better than you, two people is too much for you to handle. Rage came back with the 'what if'.

I bought cigarettes too, I don't smoke much, except when I am stressed. Even still I usually have a packet anyway, useful. I took one straight from the packet. Using the lighter at the kiosk I sucked in the smoke and told myself its all better.

Walking along the street I came across Raffael's coffee shop. I had used to go there all the time, until Raffael had retired and let his son run the business. Then it had turned into a pile of shit, not to mention that we didn't get along. So I'd stopped going. He'd also stopped my tab, although that had been a while back, six months or more. I'd since heard Raffael was back and had been meaning to go and say 'hi'.

Raffael was one for playing it cool, so even after six months his greeting was as relaxed and Italian as ever. "How are you my friend? Such a long time." I played back the standard greeting, wishing I hadn't for the sake of having to find some way of covering up my abnormality or having to explain to him. And even if I did want to explain it I would have to find a branch from which to tell him. I hate social conventions.

The other thing I feared was Raffael giving me the entire history of how badly it had gone wrong. But I didn't have any reason to not start going back, so if I had to have picked a good day this one was it. I sat and listened waiting for the only bonus, a complimentary coffee. My brain was really elsewhere, but I caught the important points. Built the place with bare hands, really fucked it up, how could you do it to your father. It was worse than I had imagined or thought. He had stolen money and practically run the place in to the ground.

"How can a child do that to his father's business? Huh? I ask you?"

There was no reply from me. The waiter brought over a cappuccino and a sympathetic look. I smiled and raised my eyebrows. Turning back to Raffael I realised I had lost the plot.

"Sorry, Raffael, but what were you saying, I have got a lot of things on my mind." I ventured the branch not knowing if he would even recognise it let alone accept it. I didn't know if I was ready to tell anyone, whether I ever would be or not is different. But it occurred to me if I could ask anyone in confidence here was my man. Besides, his brother was a cop and he was always with his ear to the ground. I recognised my priorities had changed. First I needed to find the guy and Raffael could be useful.

The train of thought was interrupted by snapping fingers.

"What's the matter? You're sitting there like a loony. You haven't said anything for three minutes." He tapped his watch under raised eyebrows a little too close to my face.

I took it as a sign. I told him the story. Five minutes later he sat a little confused looking and with his mouth open a little, he looked lost for words. He sat back and slicked back his grey hair. It worried me a little. Eventually he said, "what kind of scum would do that to a nice kid like you?"

I told him I felt exactly the same about the subject. So then I told him I was thinking about finding the guy. It was a mistake, I knew from the point it became concrete in Raffael's head. They didn't even come out right, I had over rehearsed them. What had happened to blagging?

However it came out I regretted it, why would I want to

look for the guy. It was admitting, albeit to a good counsel, that I wanted to revenge somebody. It made me think about the finding accomplices in counsel, but it had become, look for counsel and find a witness.

My brain scrambled to explain itself in a non threatening way to Raffael. It come up with this. "I want to expose him, you know, to let people be aware of this scam." It wasn't far from the truth but it covered, I thought, how deep and dark my feelings went. Raffael sat with deep doubt in his eyes, shit. No good, didn't play with him. But I kept my mouth shut just to be sure. Time to play it cool.

It seemed like an hour, but it was more likely thirty seconds before he said anything. It was thirty fear filled seconds. Doubt pounded and pounded inside my head until I thought I was deaf and would be able to hear him. Every paranoid thought combined to form a worse case scenario.

What if I had made a mistake in telling him? I fumbled for the cigarettes again. I looked over to the waiter, "Steve, you have some matches?" He followed this with a small book of matches. I took a cigarette from the paper packet and was about to light it when Raffael interrupted his silence.

He sat up, pulled his chair closer to the table and leant his elbows gently on the surface. He leaned his head over the table giving a quick look for prying ears. I felt as if he was about to tell me his deepest secret and if not give me some sleeping with the fishes routine. He did neither, instead breaking into a fatherly routine.

"You gotta be careful. You go to think first, I know you are all wound up and hot right now but you got to wait. The fact you nothing about this guy, I don't care if he is a weakling or not, should tell you to not do anything." He was right, it was obvious, I hadn't thought about it like that. Just that I knew nothing about him and wanted to find something out. He told me he would 'see what he could do' he got up and busied himself with something completely unrelated.

I enjoyed my drink in peaceful thought. The atmosphere was peaceful, the thoughts weren't. I lit another cigarette and soon drifted in to the fog that was my brain. I woke up as it burned my fingers only to find Raffael shaking his head at me from behind his counter. I wondered if he had offered to help out of sympathy more than anything else. Who would mess with a guy like me.

I drained down the rest of the coffee and left a few coins on the table more out of habit than anything else. I passed by him on my way out and shot him a quick look as if to say sorry, or something. I wasn't sure why, perhaps for my sorry state, I said don't worry about it or about me. He shook his head again and told me to come back when my head was straight, good advice I thought. But I think that he meant stop thinking about it then come back, not find the guy, sort him out then come back.

The fresh air hit me straight away. I became alert again and returned to eagle like movement, scanning and cross referencing every face that passed. I decided at length that I should go home and rest my brain. It was beginning to dawn on me that it was all having a deeper effect than I had thought. I thought of Raffael and having gotten at least some of it off my chest. He had treated me well too, perhaps because he was in the process of disowning his own son and was in the market for a surrogate.

Home was a paradise away from the streets. I never thought before now how lonely and unrewarding they could be, so unfamiliar but they had become that way. I put on the kettle and searched the cupboards for something to eat. Cooking would help. I wasn't greatly hungry but I fancied the idea of doing something. I went out to buy some vegetables coming back to find the kettle boiled dry and the kitchen steamed out.

I sat down, after sorting the mess out, and stared at the

wall, my head spinning into some space again. I asked myself over and over if I really knew what was going on. How could one small event have left my head so drained? My confidence so dented. The harmony of my life had been upset. So much and so quickly.

The previous day had been such a normal day, I had gotten up early, about ten, which is early for me. I'd had breakfast and walked in the park, say under a tree and slept a while. Enjoyed the peace and returned home via a video store with a black and white and spent the afternoon on the sofa. Where was the premise in those innocent actions?

Tension grew over the next days, little success and great more arguments. Gil's problems weren't going away and neither was Bill's attitude. They fought every time it went wrong. Bill didn't have much of a problem with it going wrong, he wasn't keen on arguing but he lived at home and was supported more or less by his father, so for him not making money didn't have a great downside.

This kind of scam had little other downsides, he was less likely to get caught doing this and that was the price you pay for little return. But as time moved on they began to drift. Not the greatest partnership in the history of semi–organised crime, probably not the shortest either, but definitely in the list of most doomed.

Bill was the type to drift between jobs, friends, lives and fashions and so drifted. He began to spend more time helping his father, who was the priest in the community church, and less time.

Gil, having made more partners over his history than he usually cared to remember, found it was less stressful and equally as unprofitable to reconcile a few broken ties. The money arrived in dribs and went out in the usual fashion.

Life passed them both by leaving them with only one common thought, that their chapter together had passed them by.

* * *

Raffael had been having a relatively easy life until a few months after leaving his café in his son Frankie's incapable hands. Frankie was his second child. The other, the first, Paolo, continued to be a success. But he doesn't figure much in this story. Only to serve the distinction between successful and useless.

Frankie's first job took twenty-three years to surface, in the meantime Federico had already achieved his undergraduate degree, with honours, in business administration. He had won several scholarships and reorganised organisations in his spare time. He had gone off to study for his PhD while turning down seven figure salary offers.

Frankie was fired from his first job after just seventeen days. In fact every job he started in his career had ended in redundancy (if he was lucky), expulsions, police charges and court costs, explosions and fire and in some cases bankruptcy. He had managed to quit a few companies before destroying them, but that was generally under some brokered deal.

Frankie bummed between family members, renting or borrowing spare rooms and enjoying the strong family welcome at the dinner table. He doesn't figure much in the story except for the scar he left on his father. Raffael had been thinking about retiring since he laid the last brick in the coffee shop walls thirty-five years earlier. He wasn't desperate but it was his dream to retire with a clean sheet. One job, one goal and one success. He didn't count sons in his tally.

So there it had been, Raffael four months before his fifty-fifth birthday took Frankie under his wing. More of a gesture of hope than sympathy. For three months Raffael came religiously everyday to check on Frankie. He hadn't been the quickest but he picked it up and after three months Raffael took a step back and came every other day. And when fifty-five came, he spent just one day a month, not for Frankie or for his paranoia but for his nostalgia.

Six months later it was a burning wreck of china and red letters. Money was leaking through every hole in the wall that had appeared since he took over. Holes easily described as engineered from stupidity and greed. And there were a lot of holes.

Raffael obviously blew his top at first. At himself. He had preoccupied about how his lazy son would act around the customers than check how thorough and disciplined he would be in the office. The stupidity had let the backbone break, the laziness the shop floor and the greed the bank managers friendliness.

Frankie had let relations with all the suppliers slip, hadn't made orders for the new fiscal year, he hadn't been doing repairs, except to his pocket from the till. He hadn't treated the customers how he had been taught. In general he did as he always did.

Raffael fired him when he found out, then shortly afterwards disowned him. One month later he was in the process of getting the business back on its feet. He was in the brink of recovery, the only problem then was for his blood pressure, as on the other side of the brink was bankruptcy.

Plans for early retirement went on hold. He was still on course for getting the business recovered in time, but still trying to get his head around the sums of money and stupidity when Sammy walked in the door. Raffael hadn't seen him for a long while, he knew Frankie and he didn't get on so well and hadn't been so attached to him as to do anything about it. But he had a soft spot for the kid they used to spend lazy afternoons chatting after the lunchtime rush. Raffael was depressed that morning and Sammy looked so too, he told Steven the only waiter he could afford to keep on to make some coffee for them and made Sammy sit down.

He had given him the most enthusiastic welcome he could. "I heard you were back," Sammy said.

"Here I am, in the flesh." Raffael cheered a bit.

"No reason to stay away any longer, then?"

"Don't even go there."

Raffael had always had a soft spot for the kid, quiet and simple, things that appealed to him. So, seeing him a little bit down reminded him that he was too. And that meant of he was going to get better, the kid would too. They sat and chatted.

"So what's the matter with you? Frankie fuck this place up too?" Raffael looked briefly at Sammy before smiling, the swearing was unusual, but the sharp wit familiar.

"Don't you start on me too, thirty-five years in the black and six months he ruins it all. He's got to have some kind of curse."

Sammy didn't say much on the subject.

"He never fell well with you though right."

"No," Sammy said matter of factly.

"Tell me something."

"Uh, I don't know, you shouldn't have let him have full control of the place. Sorry for being blunt."

"No, you're right, absolutely right. But it's my kid. And he's never had much luck. You got to assume its luck when it's your kid, you cant just label him a loser. Anyway, it was his chance, and it's the last I am going to give him, with this place at lease."

"So much for early retirement!"

The waiter brought over the coffees.

"Can you believe the little runt was taking money from the till, like he wasn't taking home a salary," Raffael turned under his voice. His face went red and he felt his blood surging.

"How can a boy do that to his father," Sammy forced out the last sarcasm-laden words on the subject.

"You got good instincts."

"Yeah? You think?" Raffael watched Sammy blowing spirals into his cappuccino. Raffael took account that he had been going on about his situation after not having seen the kid for four months. But it was the first steaming letting off of the day so he pardoned himself. Something seemed to be bothering the kid.

"What's that face for, by the look of it you would think your problems are worse than mine."

"I have things on my mind." Sammy looked up briefly as if only to ensure it was a response to a question rather than distracted drivel. Raffael wasn't so sure, he looked at the kid, then his watch then out of the window. When he looked back the kid was still blowing into his cup with the same look of contemplation. He watched him impatiently waiting for him to do or say something. He began to time him, after exactly two minutes and forty-five seconds, he reached his Italian genetic impatience limit. He knew how to do impatient, but it wasn't working. He snapped his fingers in Sammy's face.

"Are you ok, three minutes you sit there and don't say a word."

Sammy looked knowingly at Raffael and began to tell the story of his encounter the previous night with tropical Bill and Gil.

How Bill had come up and sat, started talking, how they drank beers, how Sammy had always had a funny feeling, all the details and some commentary on how he felt at various points. How he would have preferred to have gone through with it than at any other time be rude. Raffael didn't say a word instead sat ensconced in the story, which although not a worse problem was infinitely more exciting than the things that go on in his life. Not shocked that things like that happen but that it had happened to such a nice kid.

"Call that good instincts?"

Raffael's brother, Paolo, was a cop and Raffael was

already thinking in asking him to pick this guy up and give him a lesson or two. He thought it a bit much and so didn't say anything about it to Sammy, just in case he changed his mind or something else happened. Besides, the kid got away ok and didn't lose anything except Face. But he had a soft spot for the kid, and he looked a bit shaken up by it all.

Sammy broke into talking about finding the guy, Bill. This concerned Raffael more. Sammy wasn't stupid, but he wasn't tough either. He was good looking and that did even less favours with crooks. Raffael felt some fatherly urge to do something and decided he would at least talk to his brother about it. Even if it meant just keeping Sammy out of trouble it would be worth the while. He told Sammy not to do anything and that he would see what he could do. The kid fumbled with a slim cigarette in his thinner lips.

Raffael got up after that leaving the kid in his thoughts and did some work things. He would help him out, but he wouldn't get involved. Too much on this plate. Maybe for the next course. So much for early retirement.

He called Paolo as casually as he could later in the afternoon. He asked him to find the characters real name and if he could shake him down a little. They weren't the closest of brothers, but in true Italian style they would be able to not talk for a month or two and immediately get on to the same wavelength. Paolo was very quiet on the phone, but not without his complaints. "I'll see what I can do, but I got to be careful at the moment, they're being a real pain in the ass right now, we've been fucking around too much lately. Besides I'm a homicide detective now, I can't always get away with finding someone to come with me to pick up these little niggers. Beside they're too fucking mouthy, they know it's crooked and never shut up. Stand on their little fucking toe and that's it, two weeks without pay. I'd like to do you the favour Raffael but…"

Paolo was as crooked as they come. Raffael knew it, didn't like it, but had to accept it. He had always been the same, the younger brother, by a good few years, the bullshitter of the family. Something went wrong he was the first to look for someone to blame, be it Raffael or a passing stranger.

This time it didn't matter, Raffael didn't want to get any further into any of it, Sammy or his brother. He had done his part, his brother would do it anyway. He always did things for Raffael the only thing that had changed was that he didn't have to say things over. Unless he wanted them done quickly, and that was something he had given up on a long while before.

He looked around the coffee shop actively building his sense of achievement as he looked back on the favour he had done. That was his good Samaritan-ship for the week. Enough of helping others, back to helping myself. Things are looking up he told himself. It washed well. Things are on the move, and the following few weeks were exactly that, the neighbourhood, he overheard from the returning low fat drinkers was back on the fashionable scene, new people coming and old people returning. To live, to work, to go out, to shop, to eat and most importantly to drink coffee. The fashionable centre was unfashionable and they were coming back. Only to leave in six months Raffael added mentally. They don't need fashion magazines they need a climate chart.

Raffael often laughed or poked fun at his customers in his head. His personal and business centres were in direct opposite areas of his brain and he kept them as equally well separated. He felt bad about the way he felt, but they were built from different fibres. They weren't shy about showing how they dressed either. He had good customers too, ones he truly liked. Besides the pinstripe-suit, cell-phone rush-hour customers, who only manifested between seven-to-nine a.m. and twelve-to-two p.m., the rest of his clientele were good, quiet friendly people. Like Sammy. It was peaceful. That was his secret he would admit only to himself. Daily.

His public secret was good customer relations, not far from the truth, but much more thickly spread. He would tell people daily of his public secret. His customers supposedly knew it, his friends definitely did, relatives, pretty much everyone he knew and some he didn't but were ok with listening. They all loved him though, they loved him for it instead of in spite it.

It took Raffael's brother two months to call him back about the favour for Sammy. "Some of the boys who run patrols cars heard of him. Little punk, no real friends, drifter, you know from one set of losers to another." He didn't add much more except answering his name and address for Raffael. The son of a catholic priest in some shitty poor black neighbourhood. There wasn't a great deal more to add, the boys biography was somewhat repetitive and didn't have much insight into life… Raffael tried to determine whether this was just information or whether Paolo had seen him and spoken with him or what. Paolo wouldn't answer, which told Raffael no he hadn't done anything. But he guessed, more hoped, tha Sammy would have given up on it by now.

Raffael hadn't seen Sammy more than a few times since that day, less talked to him about it. It didn't occur that he hadn't come more often because he wasn't looking too good. But then out of sight out of mind. Raffael made a mental note of the details anyway, just in case Sammy ever asked him.

He spent the rest of his Saturday evening doing the kinds of things coffee shop owners do on their weekends, watching made of TV movies, ignoring account books and thinking unprovoked about kids who needed given a direction in life but by the people least likely to do so. He wanted to protect Sammy from it. He wasn't tough enough to do this kind of things. The two thoughts wouldn't cross.

Sammy and direction pointing? No.

Raffael become more philosophical as the night drew on. He didn't suppose the kid Bill, for that was his real name, was any danger to Sammy, besides he sounded a bit harmless. Like a cat in a china shop he thought. Even still there wasn't any reason to tempt fate. Raffael tried to decipher what life wanted him to do with the information privileged to him. He couldn't decide in the end and instead decided to sleep on it.

Sundays, Saturday evenings, they are all the same for coffee shop owners. He used to open the shop occasionally on Sunday afternoons to catch drifters, but always in the hope of collecting some group of some kind, crossword or chess players, something along those lines. His Saturday morning plan had worked, part time staff in the clothing and record stores came before work and in the lunch breaks as well as eager shoppers eager to rest from their shopping. So in the end, or what was the beginning of a new chapter, hopefully near the end, Sundays were free. He got up late and had lunch. He sat looking at his wife, wanting to ask here advice, knowing that if he even ventured near such a subject she would fly of the table and plant various saucepans in various anatomical weak points. She wasn't a safe choice, she wouldn't support anything so below his level, anything near the level of his brother. It frustrated him and they sat instead in silence.

It sat on his mind in the afternoon too. He decided that he needed to get it off his mind. This was his criteria for calling Sammy, if the only other option was to not tell him and he couldn't keep it contained somewhere it had to be done. If he told him it would go away. Too many more silent meals and his wife would spring the trap anyway. He could deny 'something was wrong'. Then he would get accused of something much less, like having an affair. 'At my age he would laugh' then she would carry on until he admitted it. He would break in the end. He always did, we always do, he wondered who we were. But even when it was in the open she would screw up her eyes sceptically and purse here lips and call him a liar and return to the affair charge. That was the worst. Not bad by any means but it would be over several weeks. One phone call versus weeks of mind games, old, repeated mind games.

He picked his well thumbed address book from the coffee table and sat back into his armchair with the telephone. He played with the thoughts of the mental games, they became more fun as the problem began to go away. Decision made he thought. Not getting into it again, no matter how fun it is. She never enjoyed it and she would be mad for weeks afterwards. Not again, not over this anyway. No, they were happy in that moment, no point in changing it. Besides, things were on the up.

While Raffael and his brother spoke, Bill and his father spoke. Alone in the church, Sunday evenings preferable for a service than the tradition of ten am, not to say that the people didn't come. And it meant that they couldn't put off cleaning until Monday morning. They walked slowly, side-by-side down the rows of seating checking for handbags, hats, children and the other items that churchgoers tend to leave behind in their enlightened state of mind. Bill checked the left hand side, his father the right, so they didn't look as they spoke.

"What are you going to do this afternoon, son?"

The church was modern, although its interior somehow created the classic ambience of a church, not of most modern churches which feel more like empty cinemas or deserted inner-city school gymnasiums. The air had the damp and religious feel to it, cool like it held dew before the crowds arrived and damp like a morning bedroom when they left. A lot of people came and went through the church in the morning, more than you would expect, Bills father took it as his biggest achievement. He would start his sermons by thanking the congregation, either straight forwardly or not. "There are two things we should be proud of, two things that are ours, two things we have created, and have created to the highest level of indestructibility, he would start with empirical conviction, our race and our religion. And not always in that order. Black people keep this religion alive."

Priests from other dioceses had no choice but awe when they met and were told of the numbers of attendance at Bill's fathers church. It was his momentous achievement, his next step was to use religion to help keep black people alive.

"Not much, I don't have a lot to do, maybe I will go to the park."

Bill was a different person around his father, quiet, humble almost like a disciple more than a son. His father was the only man he held respect for, real genuine respect that is. And so, while they were in the same room at least, he was always respectful. His father knew of his misdemeanours but being the man of faith he was he didn't let small things interfere with such an important relationship. He had to have faith in an entire neighbourhood, to hope they would improve, and forget their misdemeanours, then eventually stop committing them. He was the same with them too, a font of advice, not a flood of criticism. And so he was with his son, he pained him to have to do it. More than anything. He knew his relationship with his son reflected not on him but on his perception by the community. Bill had gone to school, and then to a community college, he had made his mistakes but he was smart and he would get his break, soon. To be seen interfering in his son's life would suggest that there was something wrong.

"Ok, son. Will you go on your own or are you thinking of going with someone."

"If I go, I'll probably go on my own."

They reached the end of the pews and stopped to look at

each other. Bill looked up and faced his father, "But don't worry about me, pop, I have friends." It struck his father's heart, partly because he felt very transparent in front of his sons amazing perception, but mainly because that was his major worry. Bill didn't have any good friends, the ones he did have were transient and generally up to no good. It was a hopeless struggle, all the kids in the area were bad influences, there was little way around that. And if anything he would prefer his son to be mixing with his own people.

They turned and walked back towards the altar. Bills father stopped after a few rows, Bill turned to him, a fresh polygon of sunshine appeared on his chest. It descended from the skylight in a cone of settling dust. It was like some divine sign to ask the question everyone in a fathers position should really ask.

"Did you ever think about following in your fathers footsteps?"

Bill stepped back to face the direction they had been walking in, the ray of light fell back to its dividing line between the two. It was out of the blue, "How come you have never asked me that before?"

"I don't force religion on anyone, when I can help it," he smirked, less on to you. A pause. You have never needed religion, guidance perhaps, but you carry the guardian angel you mother had around with you.

They smiled at each other. "So why are you asking me now?"

"I don't know, I don't know. I guess I had to ask you one day, I never thought I would, but soon you'll be too old anyway and I would only regret not having asked you. Besides now you are old enough to tell me the truth!"

"I couldn't do it, dad. I don't have the faith you have. Not in myself let alone these people." He gestured a hand to the empty chairs.

"I know how you feel, remember we have had this conversation many times, but you have a vacancy, and you do have faith, you just don't know where to aim it. You waste it on foolishness. Hanging around with the wrong types." Bill's father bit his tongue.

"Don't worry about me, I am going to do something with my life, I am, I promise you."

"I know, I am not worried about your future, I am worried about your now. It makes me feel bad you know."

"Why?" Bill's voice was the first to break the silence threshold. He felt his fathers suggestion of pain.

"It reflects on me. I have always tried to keep you in the neighbourhood. Selfishly, so you grew up around your own people, and so you didn't mix. But you should. You should be getting out, get out and … mix."

"Pa, don't worry. Please, I do get out. I do mix. Maybe not enough or with the right people. But don't worry, I get myself into these things I'll get myself out too. Besides its better that its always transient than the other way, right? Anyway, I never needed you encouragement or support to hang out with the neighbourhood kids. That would be the worst if you told me you didn't want that."

"I don't," his father tried to put in, but Bill carried on preaching to his father.

"That's what it is to be black and poor after all. You taught me that, you cant get out with selling out and the last thing you ever do it sell out. The catch-twenty-two of being young black and poor. Trapped."

Bills father smiled at the irony. He wasn't worried, after all. "Don't worry, he put his hand on Bill's shoulder and led him along the aisle. You'll find the answer one day."

Bill kicked himself for falling into another of his father's lessons. Somewhat hurt that he was still being so mischievous at his age.

While his father went to the little 'office', Bill took a broom, making kung-fu movements with it as his father wasn't looking and began to sweep the dust as it settled, only stirring it into little eddies in the prisms of light falling from the midday Sun. He played with the conversation in his head, reflecting on how things had changed since he had stopped hustling with Gil. It occurred to him that he had been clean since, well OK, he hadn't spent any time with anyone. But that was the same thing. Maybe he could keep out of trouble. The hustler lifestyle didn't appeal to him, it never had. He had just found it exciting, a challenge. A puzzle, a brain teaser against the most intelligent opponent. But then he was easily influenced, he knew that. He didn't see Sammy come in but he was still thinking of the last few times he worked with Gil. He liked the black braggadocio style, it made him feel powerful and, not important, but in charge, in command. That kind of thing was the opposite to being a priest, but being humble had a deeper calling in Bill. That was were Bill was when Sammy came in, stuck between power and humility, not being able to make a choice he floated between them as life demanded or dictated. Or at least as he calculated life's intentions for him.

Fate doesn't knock anymore; he rings your cell phone with an unrecognised number. It was Raffael, I found out after seconds of hesitation. I don't remember my number too well, I have it written down in my wallet for filling out application forms and so on, but banks don't call on Sundays right? The phone was for emergencies and banks. I don't remember when the last of either was, but it was why I had it.

It was Raffael, and no he wasn't going to tell me how he had gotten my number. He did tell me about this guy Bill and where he was from and that he didn't know why he was telling me.

The mist returned after I put the phone down. It had become a legitimate point in my life for making decisions. It wasn't that a decision had to be made, but at least I had to decide to make a decision or not.

I knew of the area Raffael had told me about, but never

had been there. It was, after all the lies, a black neighbourhood. The reason I had never been there. The kept themselves to themselves, or at least that's how the deal was supposed to work, now it had changed. He had come to my neighbourhood. Not that it is exclusively white people here or anything. In fact being the crime free, clean street type place it is its more a money thing than anything. Bill's justification became clear for a few flitting seconds. Then it came back that I had no problem with Bill doing what he wanted to do, just as long as he didn't do it to me, and he had unfortunately crossed that line.

I got up and left the comfort of my sofa, of my apartment, of my neighbour hood. I traded it all for the back seat of a cab. The driver asked me if that was really where I wanted to go. I didn't bother to answer him but that didn't seem to bother him either. It was a bit blurry, perhaps I was focussed, or perhaps in shock, whichever it was I was a little out of the zone of optimal control. The driver carried on regardless. Recounting stories of newspaper headline and cabbies stories all advertising 'don't go to this neighbourhood'.

My head skipped back to the day after, my plans of revenge, now they had a playing field, now they could be realised. What was I going to do? Reality was lagging, perhaps he was somewhere shouting taxi follow that zombie before he hurts himself. Reality didn't exist. I just sat in the car allowing my actions and decisions to be automated by my revenge. My subconscious had been planning this moment for weeks now. It surely had everything fine-tuned and executable. I didn't need conscious decisions. In fact I would probably, having crossed the threshold, be better off without them.

Fate was written, had I not taken the taxi life would have carried on. Because I took it, it wasn't going to just carry on. It needed a new adverb. Perhaps scrape on, or tear along or life would just be on.

I didn't know exactly where I was goin in this foreign land, so when the driver asked me exactly where I was going I opened my mouth silently. In the end I told him to leave me somewhere were they would be people on a Sunday afternoon. He told me the park was the place I wanted. I told him really. He told me there was always people, during the summer sun at least, some kind of Caribbean thing. Volleyball, barbecues and beer. What did we know?

As we approached my brain paid some Attention. A new town. My thoughts concentrated their limited capacity on what was happening outside the windows just for a Change. A shitty neighbourhood. The streets dirty, the house boarded up if not scaffolded. People hurried along the streets even though it was Sunday. Newsagents and kiosks served through grills, unusual, I have seen it in my area, but only at three a.m.

The park, the park was a little different. The air was relaxed. People we relaxed. We skirted one edge and I peered through the buzzing railings. The population was younger. Drinking and listening to music they sat in groups, there was an underlying tension. Almost as if they were gangs. Hostility Sunday style.

The driver unlocked my door. Had I noticed him lock it, had I got in the other side? I paid him. He only unlocked my door. He reiterated to me that I should be careful. Mm whatever I told him. The adrenalin was at full pace. I stepped out, the thought of my appearance was the last thing on my mind but you need to imagine a young white male with a shiny shaven head entering an entirely black area. If you have ever stepped onto the streets of another culture you will know that a six sense exists, you will know that you can feel the stares. But I didn't feel scared or apprehended, but I felt that perhaps I should have been.

The entrance to the park was littered with the usual signs

about littering and opening and closing times and how they should all be respected. The details were hard to make out under the graffiti. I walked in, it surprised me that the park was actually really nice, looked after and well laid out. Green and surprisingly clean and fresh aired. There was little traffic today and a little breeze my negative side told me. The sun shone through the trees and in one area of grass a group of youths had sat them selves, shirts off watching a volleyball game enjoying the sunshine. It reminded me of what tropical Bill had said about the black man and the tropical sun.

I fixed my eyes on them, walked over, my confidence was strong, despite the stares. I could hear the comments as I walked past other groups and even from individuals. I stopped by a tree , the sun breaking gently through on to my face. I watched the scene and took a few deep breaths. My heart was pounding. What was I doing here?

My moments were, expectedly, interrupted by one of the youths from the sunbathing group, barely five minutes into his teens his confidence had outgrown mine a long time Ago. That racing pulse of mine skipped a beat.

"What you doin up in here?" Nothing else, no swear words, no threats or motions of threats. No more words. His eyes said a lot. His mouth too, but not verbally.

I paused to think, fortunately he respected my right to do so. I had come for a reason, no point in fucking around. "I am looking for someone."

"Aint no one here want speak with yo."

"It's a private matter," I swallowed after that mistake flashed across my screen.

The questioner stepped back and threw his arms up as if to say you've just offended me. It alerted the group he had been sitting with. Their response, probably practised, was quicker than anyone who would have come to back me up.

"There definitely ain't no one who going talk to you on a private level, brother."

I was slightly paralysed. Slightly in the sense nothing moved. Time carried on, but I had lost the ability to interact with it. The trees actually began to spin before he swung his fist. When it hit me everything else began to spin. But it woke me up. That was the positive side.

"The fuck's wrong with you white boy?" Bad timing on my part I guess.

"Look," I bargain, "I don't have anything with you guys. I am looking for a guy I need to… settle a score with." I almost made the face to go with my uncoolness.

"I am going knock this white boy the fuck out," was the response I received. He reeled up again ready to strike me a second time. I managed to react this time, I threw my guard up. The entire crowd burst out laughing, except the guy directly in front of me.

"What you think this is some kind of fight? You don't fight back around here bitch. I tried to walk away."

"I told you I dot have anything with you. One of the crowd pulled Mr. Punchy away form me. As I stepped off another called out to me."

"Who you looking for anyway. Word travels fast."

"Tropical Bill."

Punchy had calmed down by now and was still the most inquisitive. "What the fuck you want with that little punk" was the emergent answer after a few minutes of consultation.

"I have some err, I tried to be more cool this time, unfinished business with him." It didn't work.

"What you think you some kind of gang-star bitch," the joker of the crowd let out.

"You be lucky if you leave this park alive motherfucker. You asking us for help you better step the fuck down, whitey."

"Look, punchy told me in confidence, no one round here like that little bitch, but you cant just go round fucking with him neither. Don't mess around with what you don't know."

Funny I thought, those words rung a familiar peel. So what was this anyway, Bill was untouchable or what? They weren't going to help, they were just playing with their pet white boy, I turned to walk away. The crowd dulled their enthusiasm, some walked away. Punchy stepped up to me. "So are you going to tell me or not?"

"You fucking hardcore ain't ya?" He almost smiled at me shaking his head. He told me I could find Bill at the church. He cracked a smile full of diamonds and gold and bright white teeth. Then he told me to be careful in this neighbourhood, funny, I thought the other guy was the joker. I walked away and felt my jaw, pushing it to one side it let out a loud crack. I cringed. It was going to hurt later on.

A church? I found my self asking myself as I left the park. What would he be doing in a church, such a moral place for such a, perhaps that was it, an immoral person. I decided to stop with the premature judgements. I had made enough this lifetime. My mind went through the calculations, what would he be doing there.

The kids in the park had told me not to mess with him, no directly him, but it was obvious enough. Then they seemed to show about as much respect for him as I had. As usual I didn't even think about it for more than a moment, and definitely took no notice of their advice. Subconscious was still in charge. In fact, I hadn't made any of the decisions that had led me to walking down this street, in this neighbourhood, in this particular moment in time except for buying a guy a beer one evening.

Nonetheless, I was there, I supposed that I was supposed to be there. Whatever that meant. And on top of that I had to deal with it.

The streets were deadly on this other side of the park. It reminded me of the urban myth that quiet streets are more dangerous. How people watch you and so on. I dismissed it, again, as myth. It made me chuckle. I was glad, I still am, that although I wasn't in control that I could see what was going on. Experience it.

Even the growing swelling on my cheek couldn't bring me down.

I saw the church from a few blocks away. It wasn't old, but certainly newer than the crumbling buildings around it. My pace increased, my sense of intrigue had given it new vigour. It became my primary objective. Out of control of the rest, my passive audience took to armchair betting.

He appeared then in my mind as someone who belonged in a church. But his lies and deceit warped that vision. I saw him picking notes from the collection tray. Looking over his shoulder to see up women's skirts and taking advantage of blind pious gentlemen. Social prejudice struck my mind. What did I know? Nothing. Do criminals go to church. Do they confess? Was this even a catholic church? Why do the rest of the pious get away without confession?

By the time I finished another useless train of thought I looked down to see my feet skipping up the stairs at the front of the church. So I was really going through with this then. No questions, debates or cost-benefit analyses, just pure confidence, unintelligent, unsupported bravado.

I looked briefly around to check for, well, witnesses I suppose, before entering. I don't know why I assumed he was in the church, regardless he wasn't around the church. What had they told me?

I pushed the large door slowly open, looking behind a quick, last time.

The church was empty. I looked around quickly and slid quietly behind a pillar. It wasn't, I saw a figure sweep his way from behind another pillar further into the church. It swept its way closer. It was Bill. My heart obviously raced. How simple.

I stepped out. He froze on the spot. I smiled in response

to his obviously being trapped, even though I didn't think about why he felt trapped. He even looked around without alerting my intelligence from its slumber. He was looking for help, obviously, but why should I have assumed there was some so close by.

I walked a few steps to wars him and smiled, whispering to him, "I have a bone to pick with you. I don't know why I whispered, not even from being slightly religious. Perhaps it was a secret respect thing."

"OK, OK just not here," he whispered back. I was obviously setting the trends. "Lets go out side."

I was a little hesitant. But the streets were empty, I couldn't imagine it was some kind of set-up. Besides, the secret respect said something about houses of worship.

So I took him outside, he let me pull him by one arm, showing me he was going to be submissive. I pushed him into the alley way between the church and the next building. A few metres down there was a sub-alley, a dead end of a few metres that backed onto a wooden gate. I pushed him into it and blocked his exit. Perfect. I swung my fist at him, square on the cheek bone.

My fist reeled back. I wasn't used to punching people. But it opened a gash on his cheek which made me fell particularly proud of my efforts. I couldn't punch him again so I kicked Bill in the stomach, sending him flying against the gate.

As he fell a black object fell also from the back of his trousers. I had to look twice. It was a pistol. I had no time to think, as I looked at it the second time my sixth sense told me he had stopped looking at me and was also looking at it. What do you do? I realise that was the trap. The back up.

We both lunged for the pistol. He was closer and so reached it first. But I was coming from further away and so had more momentum. I landed on top of him and sent his head rebounding to the tarmac, it must have knock him cold, giving me a few seconds to grab the gun and gather myself.

When he came around the gravity must have hit him pretty quickly. Bleeding, having trouble breathing and his head ringing.

I looked around to see if the crashing and banging had alerted anyone to what was taking place. Realising that even if they did know what was going on they surely didn't want to be involved, but could nonetheless be watching.

Bill looked at me, with a sheepish look, I raised my head as if to say what do you have to say for yourself. The gun, rather limp in my hand was pointed generally at him.

He remained silent. It unnerved me as I couldn't tell if he was scared or not. I wondered if it wasn't the first time he'd had a gun pointed at him.

"This isn't the first time I have had a gun pointed at me."

Too funny. The clichés were mounting. I told him to be honest or it might be the last. He didn't seem phased.

But just as I was about to unleash the reel of questions I have crated over the last few months we were disturbed.

My head spun around to see what the disturbance was; the gun just went off. I looked back to Bill before I had recognised our disturber; Bill was dead. I turned again, automatically pointing the gun at whoever was there. My nerves needless to say, were reaching their ends. The priest stared at me and raised an arm up in calm protest. Bill grabbed my legs from behind; another accidental discharge. This time the victim was surely dead. I turned back to Bill, he was in a bad way and for some subconscious unknown reason I put him out of his complaining.

My stomach reeled. I looked around as if I would execute any other witnesses who happened to be nosey enough to let me know they were watching. I saw no one.

Reality began to dawn. Everything all of a sudden became very bright and obvious. Me, a gun still in my hand. Two dead bodies, shot at no distance. I had just executed, what looked, even at the time, like a priest. It all, needless to say, got a bit too much.

I ran.

And ran.

My muscles began to exceed their capacity of using lactic acid around the time I reached the expressway. It was a good milestone, it separated this area from a much nicer one. I cut straight across the first carriage way. Three lanes of speeding Sunday traffic. On arriving at the central reservation I decided two things. First, stop waving the gun around quite as much and second, to look where I was going on the next three lanes of traffic.

I made it across alive. I began to walk. There was a huge shopping complex in this neighbourhood. Perfect I thought. Air conditioning and bathrooms.

I crashed into a stall, much to the surprise of the bathroom attendant. Slammed the door behind me and threw up into the toilet. I sat with my back to the door on the cold floor. My breathing still wild form the running and vomiting hadn't made it any calmer. My wild thoughts couldn't help but appreciate my luck in finding such clean toilets. Reality sound-bit back, Bill hadn't said father to the priest but dad or pa or something that designated he wasn't trust his spiritual leader.

I threw up again. Now my stomach was definitely completely empty. I stepped out of the cubicle and slowly went to wash. I found I couldn't look at my reflection. I concentrated on my hands. The attendant asked me several times if I was ok before I looked at him. He told me I had some vomit on my face. This made me look at the mirror, just in case. And it was, it was blood. I washed it off and thanked somebody's lucky stars. I looked at my clothes. True to form I was wearing black combat trousers and a dark grey hoody so blood wouldn't have shown, but it was the thought the worried me. It was done now, I had killed two people and all that was left alive was me, the evidence and the consequences.

I began to look at my options. Policeman began to invade my cerebral space. Real policemen. Then forensic scientists giving testimony. The long years in jail. I stopped there. Jail didn't sound like a very good option.

I made my escape from the shopping centre toilets, back into the free world. The free world of shopping centres on Sundays. It scared me to think that these might be the last few hours of freedom. What a place to spend them. I escaped in to the real free world and into a taxi. The first cab home.

It was approaching the end of the afternoon and the traffic that had ventured out in the face of mad boys in fast cars was gaining confidence. I sent myself to the splendid comfort of the land of thoughts. My mindless gaze merely glazed over the weekend rush hour.

What had I done? The events of the last few hours represented something major. Something from which I couldn't really turn back. Before all the thoughts had been in my control and indeed the actions which I had planned too. This time nothing was in my control. I could already see the police knocking on my door. It couldn't take them that long to find out who did it.

Two dead people. I didn't execute people. This wasn't me. How could I have done such a thing? Sure I had planned revenge but nothing of this magnitude.

All the thoughts came at once. The driver tried to strike conversation. The words eventually reached my ears "Are you ok, you look very pale." I grunted a response, but decided I should keep my consciousness in check for the rest of the journey.

The traffic seethed by the window. So much for Sundays being slow. Eventually, and predictably, my brain went back into its shell long before I got home.

Home was a relative tranquillity. I tried to arrange my thoughts. It occurred to me that of all the people involved in this charade, none of them were likely to go out of their ways to incriminate me. Raffael, so what if his brother was a cop, he would want his name tarred with knowing a murderer, even if it was just between he and his brother. Well, perhaps. The kids in the park? What did they give a shit? Well, they didn't look like the most law abiding citizens, and besides I am sure punchy wasn't going to go out of his way to get charge with assault, regardless of what I had done. Perhaps there would be a bad feeling in the area because someone had killed a religious figure. But what did I really know, I was making assumptions about people I didn't know.

I had killed a priest, shit, what the fuck was I going to do. This was going to be big. The maths didn't fit properly. There would be no leads for the police to go on. Provided they didn't speak to Raffael of the boys in the park. Why would they? Of course they would the whole neighbourhood had seen this white boy walk through the park on Sunday afternoon. There was a reason there was no one around in the six or seven blocks between there and the church, they were all in the park. But why would they assume it was me. That one small band of kids wouldn't say anything about who I had asked about. Unless they wanted to give me up.

What about Bills partner? How did he fit into the difficult equation?

What about the gun, that was still in my pocket. That was both in and out of my favour. It wasn't there at the crime scene, covered in my sticky fingerprints. But it was in my pocket and being the murder weapon it was an obvious lead for the police.

My mind was far from clear. My breathing and cardiac rhythms were up and down with each new or old thought. I tried to lay out the facts without writing them down. Get rid of the gun and cross your fingers.

I put the kettle on, coffee. Like I needed stimulants. I left it on anyway. I meditated as it heated. I needed to move past the panic. It came to me. What if I was easily linked. What if they knew it was me. That was the other side of the coin. The side that had eluded me. I would have to run. Hide. Escape and avoid capture. Jail was not an alternative. My life was quickly turning into a movie. I expected pinstripe gangster to come past my flat with their Tommy guns blazing any minute.

Have you ever thought about leaving your life. Just dropping anything and everything knowing you would never have it back. Your house or apartment, you life, your neighbours and neighbourhood. It's not an easy one to say yes to. My life as fine, it didn't need changing. Besides I had no idea how to go about it how do you go about it? Can you just buy a one-way ticket and leave your country? Never looking back. Did they keep a list of priest killers with the immigration police? They must.

The kettle whistled me out of that awful meditation. I think it had been whistling for a quite a while. I made some coffee and was all of a sudden hungry. I looked around the kitchen for inspiration. I reached into my pocket looking for matches and found the pistol. Shit, too much to think about. I put the gun down on the work surface. And looked at it.

I looked at my hand, it looked clean. I raised it to my nose. I could smell the gas discharge. How do you get rid of that?

Bill saw Sammy now. He had appeared seemingly from nowhere into the middle of the church. And from even more nowhere into the church. Bills heart sank, his balls shrank and his sphincter tightened. All simultaneously. He instinctively stopped sweeping, but he couldn't move to find where his father was. He always dreaded the payback. You never know who or where it's going to come from, but you can pretty much guarantee it's going to come and that it's going to be uncomfortable. It was part of life in a neighbourhood like Bill's. It was accepted. If you fuck around you lay around. Bill strangely thought for a split second that he didn't know what the white-boy equivalent was. What ever it was it was likely to be unpredictable. And to Bill, Sammy looked scared. And there was nothing more unpredictable than a trapped scared white bunny.

Bill took Sammy outside, not wanting his father to get involved. It was a childish instinct and he regretted it as Sammy pushed him into the alley way and he remembered he had a pistol in his trousers. His heart stopped for a second time.

Bills head was pounding, the world was closing in around him. It all seemed much worse than it should do in that situation. And he couldn't tell why.

Bill was now six years old, stepping out of a friends house with a toy gun, forgotten, in his jacket pocket. Walking from the house but not wanting to say anything for fear they would think he had stolen it. He could put it back, he had told himself, the next visit. Hopefully no one would notice, or they would think it was lost and he could find it. It hadn't worked out like that. The plastic gun had fallen from his pocket as he got into this parents' car, clacking as it hit the street. Alerting the entire world to the fact it had been in Bill's possession when it would have been much better off anywhere else.

Bill was nineteen again. He wished that the real gun was in a toy box somewhere; it would be much safer there. Bill wasn't strong enough to resist Sammy, and he even doubted if he was fast enough. Sammy was much bigger and clearly much stronger and Bill had lost the boldness he might have summoned on any other day.

Bill had lost control of this situation before it had started. All he could think of was the gun, he could feel its every lump and corner. By the time Sammy punched him, it was destined to fall with a familiar clack onto the concrete. Being beaten up seemed tame in comparison for those few seconds between it being a worry and a reality.

Bill didn't want to have to use the pistol. But street karma wasn't going to make him bullet proof. So he decided to grab for it anyway. Time froze.

Bill's father had actually seen the interaction in the church. But he hadn't overheard. He left Bill to it as he seemed to recognise they guy. But it was strange a white skin head in the church. And it was his church.

So when he heard the clattering outside the open side door of the church, which he had opened to let some of the lovely day into his life, he stepped out without hesitation.

Sammy had got the gun by the time he could see what was going on. He stopped taking steps forward. Sammy had his back to him. He looked over his shoulder in to his sons eyes. It all began to unwind. Bill looking at his father alerted Sammy to the presence of a third. Bills eyes filled with pain and horror, he didn't want his father involved nor to see him in such a bad predicament.

Sammy reacted in the worse fashion. His body tensed in every muscle, including his right hand. The had holding the pistol, a slim, long, white finger already curled through the trigger guard. His broad palms tightly pressed against the brown parcel tape that was holding the handle on. His bare wrist, white, sinewy, athletic. His entire arm up to his bicep was bulging with strength and blood pressure.

Bill must have know the end was close. Time had slowed infinitesimally. He monitored every detail of the scene although prohibited in interacting in some way to change what hadn't quite been written. He saw his fathers face morph from inquisitiveness, to shocked puzzle, to horror and finally to pain. To Bills inner ear his voice sounded like the air horn of a rig or the fog horn of a ship. He called his father, without anything to say.

Sammy managed to pull a few muscles loose to look behind him, but the chain reaction of muscles and tendons flashed before Bills eyes. The flash never went away, it became everything Bill could see.

The gun followed Sammy around, now pointing, although involuntarily, everywhere he looked. He raised it to Bills father, the man who had interrupted them. He swallowed, causing the second bizarre chain of events, the gun, however, wasn't going to point out that it shouldn't have fired and just did its willing.

Bill, had survived, and was groping his way towards were Sammy had been standing when he could see. Then, on hearing the second shot and what it had t have entailed reached a blind bloody hand out in front of him. He grabbed a leg which quickly removed itself from his grip. Sammy shot Bill once again in his blind face.

How do you get rid of a gun? Throw it in the river? Do you need to tie a brick to it? My brain wasn't working as efficiently as it should have been. Especially given the need I had at that point in time. I sipped at the coffee and continued with the food preparations.

I had picked a culinary walkover for the fear it would all go wrong. That meant pasta. Again the meditative nature of cooking helped to sooth my mental process. My thought pattern came, for a short period, back under my control.

But at the same time I was thinking that the investigation must already be under way. Two dead bodies can't have to lie around for this long to be found or at least reported.

Perhaps they already knew who they we looking for, perhaps they were on there ay over here right now.

The paranoia was driving me to the early stages of insanity.

I took my pasta and a fresh cup of coffee to the living room, sat down and stared hard at my home.

I realised soon, before the first mouthfuls of the food I had made but didn't really want, need or know was there, that I didn't want to leave what I was looking at. My TV, for example, it was almost as old as I was, I had brought it from my parents house when I moved. With its brown plastic imitation wood case, goldfish bowl shaped screen and eight channels. Where would I find another like it? The books on the bookshelves? Well, they could be replaced I guess. But I would have to write a list of them.

Then I wondered what would happen to all these things if I went to jail. Do they keep things like that? What if I did a runner to the exterior? Would they keep the stuff then? Probably not. What about my sofa? It had taken me years to mould this arse groove (dixit H. J. Simpson)

I ate to calm my anxiety. My head span a little at the reality I was facing. Everything was so comfortable, down to the sofa.

I went to my bedroom and instinctively packed a bag of clothes. Should I stay or not? Could I face the consequences? After several minutes I realised I couldn't face the decision. Leaving would be suspicious, staying would be, well, the easy way to get caught.

My stomach wrenched again at the thought of leaving my life. Where would I go, I knew nobody in the city let alone in another city or another part of the world. I lay on the bed. The ceiling began to spin, by the time it stopped I was seeing strange irregular patterns in the plaster. Then I fell asleep.

What a relief sleep was for my brain. I woke from it about three hours later. At least Sunday afternoon had been spent in the normal fashion. And at least I didn't wake up arrested. The world was however, still spinning.

As I sat up I did so half expecting someone to be there. I looked around the room. Who would be in my bedroom apart from the police? From there I wandered around my apartment several times. On the first circuit I kind of looked in cupboards and behind doors looking for people. Then I began to examine smaller objects, ornaments, books, kitchen utensils, as if they held the answer. I wondered if this would be the last time I would look at them closely, the last time I would see them.

My apartment isn't huge, one bedroom, kitchen, a little hallway, and two bathrooms (one en-suite, go figure). And I don't own a great deal of items (last ornament count: three), so the few circuits I did didn't last long.

I stopped in my bedroom, shut the door and looked at it. I lived the unintentional minimalist life the entire fengshui generation struggle so hard to imitate. My bedroom: it was just that a room with a bed. White sheets, two pillows (one for my neck the other for my legs), two bedside tables (natural wood, polished) and one alarm-clock (albeit dysfunctional, it had been a while since I'd needed to get up for anything). Incidental items: an empty glass (short, straight edges, slightly conical), a few coins and some dirty clothes on the floor.

The bed linen was a mess. I looked at the clothes on the floor. I opened the closet. The laundry basket was spilling over. Since this whole charade had begun my personal hygiene levels had plummeted. I always made the bed. A half-full laundry basket was a three-quarters full basket. A three-quarters basket, a full one. Now all clothes were dirty, even the ones I had packed.

In a moment of distracted despair I went to the fountain of introspection, inside the temple that used to be my bathroom. It was still my bathroom, the only thing that had changed was that a slob was using it and not cleaning up after himself. I checked my pupils between flecks of soap and toothpaste on the mirror. There were more dirty clothes in here too. The little black dots encrusted in soap around the basin momentarily filled my with the positive news that I had been shaving, but its alien appearance in my temple of cleanliness was overall upsetting.

With my self-esteem back down to where it should be after weeks of slacking and hours after a double killing I went back to the bedroom. I would decide if I was going to stay before cleaning. Life had to continue, obviously, I just wasn't sure how.

I thought briefly over the advantages of tossing a coin. My head was spinning but not landing.

Despite the obvious incongruities this was not an unusual situation for me, that of indecision, so I opted for my time proven technique of, if you cant make a decision don't, carry on life until its too late or someone else makes it for you.

Leaving the country was defiantly a mistake. Perhaps if they come looking for me then I will, but let's at least give them a chance.

The exterior. Why would I want to leave to there? Unfamiliar culture, language and customs. What I needed now, outside my status as a murder/fugitive etc, was stability. For my own mental and physical health. Perhaps that is the punishment dealt out when none is dealt out?

I looked at the bag, everything stopped. For a second even the world stopped spinning. Peace. I knew I would stay. I dropped the clothes bag back on the floor, I looked at my watch, then to the window; the sun had set and it was beginning to get dark. Perfect. The day was ending, there I can hide, in darkness, in sleep. Perhaps in the morning it would have all gone away.

I smiled at the thought. Sarcastically. Like all this could go away. But my vision couldn't show me 'all this', the severe abstractness didn't betray its seriousness. It was so unrealistic it couldn't be real.

Life has normal days and abnormal ones. Then there was this particular Sunday, which didn't really fit in to the bigger scheme of things. It was like those imaginary situations you create, telling a teacher a dirty secret. Two friends from different walks of life meeting, just to prove it will never happen. The brain has a somewhat predictive nature. If you cant imagine your wife's face when you tell her that you sleep with transvestite prostitutes when she is away then you can keep the secret. If you imagine her response, and it fits with her character, then she is going to find out.

I roamed around the flat, turned out the lights and drew some curtains. In the living room I stopped with my hand on the dial of my TV. Was a I really that big a sucker for punishment? I had a deep desire to know if the story was on the news but the options were uneven. If I turned on the TV and there was the story it would (a) confirm my suspicions that all this was real, (b) give me a weighting of the seriousness of what I had done (given it was real!) and that was the positive points. The negative points were, (a) it would confirm my suspicions that all this was real, (b) it would give me some idea of the trouble I was in, and (c) it would plague me for the rest of the day, until I managed to get to sleep. Then it would plague my dreams. No TV was the answer.

I watched one of my neighbours cooking through a gap I opened in the curtain with my hand. His window was beginning to steam up, I watched him until it steamed completely thinking about regret. I had been dealing well with regret so far. In so far as I hadn't begun to regret it.

That was a lie. Of course I regretted it. I regretted it in the natural gut response. The vomiting, the running, the racing heart and sweaty palpitations. It was all there, the common reactions to doing something wrong. But it was completed. In a holistic point of view, it was whole. Complete. Nothing earthly would change the situation.

Remorse was a different concept was the arrival I had come to by the time my neighbour had disappeared. I knew the media portrayal would fuck with my conscience. Father and Son Killed, I could already see the headlines. The pun was too obvious. I would be made the scourge of society. The only man doing anything positive dead. Son witnessed father's death shortly before his own or vice versa. They would get facts wrong and I would want to scream out the truth. Expose their stupidity and my situation. I would be made the bad guy, they would give no account of what had driven me to do what I had done. If they did it would be quickly forgotten.

I went back to the TV, turned the switch and began a 'I am in control' mantra. I fell on to the sofa, literally, tiredness was getting the better of me. The adrenalin faded. I flicked the channels. Nothing, for fifteen minutes my heart and soul calmed. Too much time was passing without real or predicting consequences.

I had thought at one point I would have been apprehended immediately. It made me feel a little sad, melancholy even. A little depressed. The thought of dealing with this until the day I would die or get lobotomised was unpromising.

Retribution and rehabilitation began to appeal. It amazed me how bright the bright side was. Maybe it wouldn't be so hard after all, optimism wasn't far behind. Yeah, right. They left quicker than the setting sun. Only to come back tomorrow, and daily until madness came. Then I considered perhaps it already had.

Those fifteen minutes flew under self analysis. I came back as the hour approached, nipped to the bathroom and came back just in time to catch the headlines. The main news started, I felt I couldn't be that important, that famous. Yet, I waited in anticipation as political failures flashed across the screen. I blocked them out, not because of their unimportance but their quantity. Digression struck again as I justified myself once again, how did my actions have any effect compared to this kind of scandal and corruption. What did I know?

The shining teeth and glossed lips reached the real world, filled with more scandal and corruption. I could feel the sports section rapidly approaching. Had there been enough time? Had the press been told? I began doubting the people involved forgetting my suspicions.

A million new questions crash-landed my head, occupying it. Do people in this neighbourhood actually call the police? Do they 'hear' gunshots? Do they go off all the time? The alley was kind of out of the way. Do the police go to the neighbourhood? What kind of person doesn't report double murder? What kind of people don't report it? Besides priests have wives and families and other children and so on. They must be missing, they cant still be lying there in the alleyway?

The train of thought was sickening. And had made me lose my attention of the box. Sports. Damn. Was it there, had it passed and I had missed it? It would have caught my attention.

It was a sign I was sure. I convinced myself. I turned the set off and went to begin the going to bed rituals. Tomorrow, I told myself, the world would be aware or what you had done, you can be sure of it. I would know what I had done.

The next day in my new life, I should be well rested. It would be a hard day, I could already sense a lot of anxiety.

Inevitably it was the menial task of undressing that reminded my of what I had done. The gun returned. It had, believe me, escaped my mind.

I sat on the edge of my bed and examined it carefully. Two thoughts came to mind. Firstly, I understood why criminals get caught on such obvious details. It just happens.

Secondly, and more importantly, I recalled the many discovery channel type shows I wasted my daytimes watching. The forensic scientist certainly have no flies on them when it came to linking guns to bodies, dead and alive. If the police found the gun it wouldn't be more than an open and closed case. As far as they were concerned that is.

It was in my possession, despite being Bill's I had it. Why did he even have a gun? Was it his? Was it registered? Did the police have the serial number? What about a record of the gun's unique footprint? Had it been used in other crimes? What would happen? I have less alibis than Arabia. Why did he have a gun with him then? What was going on or does everyone carry guns around on Sunday afternoons? Was someone else trying to kill him? Perhaps it was that fake cop. Perhaps that's why those boys warned me to be careful? What if Bill was going to be knocked off that very same day? Coincidence? Perhaps. If that's the case I was almost glad I had gotten in while the window was open.

If all that was the case why would the police ever suspect me? How would they ever connect me? No one carries a gun around like that with no reason. How many people have a reason to kill any one person at anyone time?

Bill's father entered my equation maker again. He was the unknown quantity, how would he balance the chain of event? I pondered over it. If there had been a witness they might be more likely to speak up to help a priest. The words 'white' and 'skinned' lead the police out of the area. Complex.

I stopped, it is impossible to try and solve a case you know the answer to. I had the clues they didn't, and they, the ones I lacked.

The ridiculous number of known and controllable variable were too much, before I considered the unknown and uncontrollable. My problem solving centres were not serving their function, they needed to rest. At least, I told myself, nothing was going to happen tonight. I put the gun, in this security, causally on the bedside table. I took off my clothes and thought twice before throwing them on the floor. It was unconscious but the gun was going to serve as a good reality fetcher in the morning.

As I lay down I appreciated the means of self defence so out of focus next to my head. Like some kind of virtual reality glove I could slide my hand into and dissolve my real reality problems.

The lack of consciousness we all refer to as sleep crept quickly over me. The bed side light stayed on.

Gil's life had been quiet since he stopped acting up with Bill. He'd had less to complain about and ultimately less stress on his mind and more time on his hands. Nothing had been said, nothing verbal at the time that is. They both knew how they felt about each other and that feeling had slowly initiated their disassociation.

Gil had ventured successfully into some other scams of equal moral and criminal ranking and had come out shiny. He had paid his friends and less reputable financial institutions back their money and was now arguing with the only lender who would fold, the bank. He would pay them back, but not if they were going to let him get away with such low interest rates.

The kids had their noses dry and were looking at breaking their ill streak. It was good in one sense, but as Gil lazed his Sunday afternoon away in his arm chair their antics made him reconsider, albeit quiet and remorsefully. Gil's head flopped from side to side trying to watch the hopping channels as the children took it in turns to molest him. He was smiling, ever so slightly, somewhere in the background he was contemplating the future. He was in the somewhat unusual but simply comfortable side of the line that is thinking positively.

A little dream of his was beginning to flicker when his front door was charged with a heavy knocking. It rattled in its frame. It shocked Gil, simply because no one ever knocks at the door. Not that he ever remembered, but then he couldn't even remember if there was a door bell. It seemed likely there was, so Gil's next thought was: who would be so disturbing on a Sunday?

He told one of the kids to check. Jumping on to the old

brown sofa in the bay window the child carefully pulled back the lace curtain. "It's a man."

Gil looked over to the innocent face, "What kind of man is he?"

"I don't know, but he must be important," the kid double checked quickly, he has his own policeman!

Gil was the type to startle easily. It was his motivator for working so far from the criminal line as he could. He knew it, accepted it and even preached it. He would tell his friends, that, if in the parallel dimension, he existed and was a police man he would be an investigator of some kind. A forensic scientist perhaps, the guys who turn up after the action was through, the guy who drew chalk lines for example. He knew the bad guys were dead by that time.

Gil, in character, startled. It was getting a bit active. He shifted forward onto the front of his arm chair and looked towards the kitchen doorway bellowing steam. Sunday was no exception in the kitchen. He didn't want The Wife to see the police, even if they were looking for a lost cat.

Gil told the kids to go and play somewhere else. Away from the front door. "But stay out of the kitchen and don't bother your mother."

The kids scattered and Gil braced himself. Gil wasn't the kind of person with a lot to worry about, but he had a certain affinity for worrying. He pushed that feeling as far down as he could and yanked the door open, making the well dressed gentleman and his police officer pull surprised faces.

Gil never opened the door, no one ever came, so what did he know about safety chains, let alone asking who was there before opening. However, it had handed Gil a slight advantage to the situation.

"Err… Gil, err." The well dressed man fumbled embarrassedly with a note book.

"Yes," Gil replied before the gentleman had a chance to get his own composure, how can I help you. Two points to

Gil.

"My name is Paolo," the gentleman stopped to stare at Gil's smiling innocence. He forgot his surname for just a second, and already being two-nothing down he skipped on to his profession. "I am…"

"Nice to meet you Paolo," Gil cut in again.

"Err," his authority pinched him. "That's err, Inspector Paolo."

"Oh sorry, that's your surname?" Gil tilted his head.

"No, my name is Paolo, I'm an," Paolo was interrupted by the uniformed man's sniggering. It stopped on the command of a sharp look from Paolo.

Gil smiled, chuckling to himself at the antics of the two policemen on his door step, almost forgetting the remote possibility they could be there to arrest him for some kind of crime.

Paolo looked concerned baffled. He was sure Gil was the guy he was looking for, but how could a guy who had murdered two people, including a priest, but a few hours ago, be so relaxed and nonchalant. He decided to forget the introductions.

"Uh, Gil, we need to speak to you concerning your associate…" he paused again, the notebook came to hand again. Gil watched the seriousness notch up a gear and stopped entertaining the idea of inviting them in and switched to watching the man in front of this, this Inspector Paolo. He wasn't a bumbling fool. He looked crooked. Gil had a better knack than most for spotting either crooks or bumbling fools. This guy was clearly one and not the other.

"William, I mean Bill."

"That little prick isn't an associate of mine anymore." Gil let out before thinking.

"Yes," Paolo felt the situation come crawling back to him, "We know. Somebody killed him a few hours ago."

Gil closed the door. After having stepped outside.

"And, so, you need what exactly from me?" He asked as

if it were rhetoric.

"Well, unfortunately, Gil," Paolo went for the note book again.

"What? What is it that you have in there that I don't know? That we knew each other and I don't know him now because he is dead or something else?"

The inspector stopped, the note book's contents would come to memory if the case lasted longer than that day. And if not, it didn't matter.

"But you knew him? Before his death, that is. You aren't trying to tell me something else?"

"Yes, I knew him, and no that's not what I'm saying. Anyway, if you're on the hunt for information I cant tell you much. I haven't seen his for a week and we haven't seen each other much before then for about a month and I don't plan to see him again. Not that that's going to happen of course."

"Unfortunately Gil we haven't come for information, we have come for you. You are the only suspect at the moment and I am going to have to arrest you."

"Arrest me?" He spluttered. At least Paolo was straight forward, either that or he was disguising his crookedness cunningly, Gil thought. "On what basis? His voice lowered. You can't seriously think I killed him, I've been at home all afternoon," he lowered his voice some more. "And I guess he was murdered, don't give me that, 'no one said anything about murder' shit."

"This is where I come unstuck Gil, because I know that if you didn't do it you know who did, but at the moment I have nothing on you. What I do have however is a large list of misdemeanour, long enough to hold you long enough, if you know what I mean."

Gil let out a little laugh, disbelieving and high pitched. This guy has to be kidding, he thought, stunned at the obstruction his life was facing on the whims of some bent copper. Innocence comes so much more easily when it's honest, but, Gil, sighed to himself, these days doesn't count for much.

Anyway, he hadn't done it, not that afternoon, at least. He would have remembered.

But Gil did begin to worry about it. It was clearly a mistake, but he still didn't want to get arrested for anything. Seeing the bluff he decided to call it. What harm could it do, other than to his marriage and his Sunday afternoon. Besides, if dirty coppers were going to put him in jail what did either of those matter.

"So, I take it if I come along with you quietly for free you wont book me for anything?"

"You're a quick one, that's absolutely the way I'd like to do it." Paolo smiled crookedly.

"Wanker," Gil thought to himself not for the first time.

"Let me go and grab some things," he waved a thumb over his shoulder. The uniformed man shuffled a bit.

"Go ahead," Paolo replied.

"Don't worry I am not going anywhere."

"Doesn't matter," Paolo thought to himself, "you don't have anywhere to go out the back, there are more uniforms there."

Gil walked into his lobby and was greeted by several pairs of eyes. "It's ok kids you can come out now." The eyes became growing bodies. "But daddy has to go out with these gentlemen now. So come and say good bye."

Gil rummaged through his things on the counter in the lobby, keys, identification and so on. He sorted through a list of things to tell his wife. He could lie, he assumed he would be out in an hour or two and she would be none the wiser. But then he could get caught up in a lot of bureaucracy. He sped off quickly to the kitchen.

"Friend's been in a car accident, going to visit him in the hospital, back soon." Dialogue with his wife often read and sounded like a note he might have left here had she been out. But she never went out, that was the beauty of it. She never left and his friends never came round. They would never meet, until retirement perhaps. Gil hoped that by then everyone's sense of humour will have flourished. He then wondered if he was in for the prospect of retirement.

Her face dropped, "Oh, is it bad? I hope he's OK. Which friend?" She was just being polite, he could have told her any name and gotten the same reply.

He said goodbye, telling her he didn't know when he would be back, but hopefully the same evening before she went to bed.

Gil grabbed a brown suede bomber jacket that was hanging from the banisters on his way to the front door. Keys, he thought to himself, better take some keys. He wasn't sure why it just seemed that he would need keys at the police station. But that was is, he didn't know what else you needed to be questioned about murder.

He patted the children on their various heads and stepped out to the front of his house, leaning his back against the door as he shut it as if to make sure he closed it quietly.

The two policemen were waiting at the bottom of the stairs that led to his house, Gil stepped down.

"Ok Gil, come with us, we have a car at the end of the street."

He followed them nervously, looking around at the sets of eyes as they disappeared from windows. Disguising their inquisitiveness behind their lacy curtains of their own secrecy, not that they had secrets of their own to keep, but they stored up those of their neighbours. They watched through the lace when they knew people were looking, but not now. This was too much, not one of the old hags will be able to resist the vivid colour of this scene, Gil cursed them as they watched him being paraded down his own street.

How can they live lives purely vicariously? Let them watch, Gil told himself. They don't know what's going on. Even more suspense then, let them guess. They don't even know how you earn a living. I am sure they are suspicious. I am sure they have their wild guesses not too far from the truth. But they wont work this one out, even if Gil's wife happens to entertain them one afternoon while she hangs out her laundry in the back yard.

Get out and do something! Gil laughed at them. The thought took him to his wife, she had things to do, perhaps it wasn't the most perfect family but she enjoyed the kids and the cooking. And he had traded off a lot of chores, such as shopping and occasionally ironing. But were these women equally housebound or was it their choice. Could they leave the house one morning and go to work, or to the park or to a museum, fair enough they are retired or house wives with nothing to clean? But did they really have nothing better to do.

He shook the thought from his head and paid attention to his situation. The officers chatted coolly in front of him as they approached the end of the road. Out of the three of them it would be difficult to select one being more preoccupied than the other. Paolo was convinced he had his man, and he was walking into the police station. The officer had his own life, he had a twenty minute drive to the station and he knew Paolo would probably do that anyway. Then he would get assigned to something else. And Gil, complete in his innocence, trying to calculate how long it had been since he had last spoken to a real police officer.

He was painfully free in the security that not having done it was his best defence. A waste of time he told himself, these coppers don't know the right end of a gun to point let alone who was pointing it. But he didn't fancy getting charged for stupid little crimes and so with his arm, so to speak, behind his back he went along.

If he had thought a bit more about it he would have realised that the police were wild cannons, all dirty cops were loose cannons. Free radicals or fireworks, once they are lit that's it. You cant go back to check on them and you aren't really safe anywhere in the vicinity. It didn't occur to Gil, ironically, given that he often dressed as a crooked cop for his own employment.

He wondered instead of the many things he had done wrong, and which of those they could pin him on, on pin on him. They must have known of the scam he ran with Bill. Te thought sobered him a little. If that was the case, then they knew he dressed as a cop. That had to be against him. Sure to piss them off. He made a mental note to steer as clear of it as possible.

What ever else he had done carried little punishment, and as far as murder he was innocent. He repeated the thought over and over for the rest of the silent journey.

After being made to wait twenty minutes, Gil began to sweat a little. No doubt that was why they were making him wait.

Paolo came along with another well dressed man and the two led him into an interviewing room.

The second suit sat down on a chair against the wall near the door they came in without saying a word. Paolo sat at the desk and went through his interview rituals, loading cassettes and laying his notes and pens out in front of him. He explained the formalities to Gil as he did it.

Gil wasn't paying attention, he was far more interested in the second suit. He had seen him somewhere before. But he couldn't remember when or where. The suit examined some paperwork he had bought with him, while Gil cross examined his brain as to where he had seen him before.

The next thing Gil knew Paolo was telling him they were ready. He started the tapes and began taping the introduction. He read the spiel from a sheet and even got the names right. Gil say patiently, waiting for the questions to begin. His heart sped a little, like the first day at school of the first hours in the city.

"Ok Gil," Paolo began, this is the good cop, he pointed

back to his colleague, Gil had taken mental note of his name and recorded his face while Paolo had been introducing the interview. It would come to him. The suit was an old man, probably a little older than Gil, not too long from retirement. He sat happily ensconced in his papers, barely acknowledging what was going on until his introduction as the 'good cop'. He was close to last base, there was no more struggle for promotion, he had it easy, interview sit-ins and paper work. His hair was growing clearly greyer, receding too. His stomach was on an opposite march, just beginning to break the lines of his jacket.

"And you, I take it, are the bad cop."

Gil smiled and smirked. It was too rehearsed for one thing. It was a little unexpected and also the topic he most wanted to avoid. He began to wonder just how crooked Paolo was, the formalities and formal appearances so far had lulled him into a sense of bureaucracy and justice. The tapes, the furniture, the old greying detective. He felt duped.

"Do you think this is funny?" Paolo's voice had no clear intention, it was serious and stern, but was he just setting the mood or was he really mad.

"I think it's rehearsed." Gil's rebellious streak shone through and grabbed the suit's attention. He was interested now, he gave Gil a quick eyeing but didn't seem to recognise him.

"Ok, Gil, you know this is more than about your friend Bill, who was murdered this afternoon. Because he wasn't the only one."

Gil pricked up from his gaze at the other policeman. This was news, who else had been killed. Who else did they think he had killed. He measured is reactions and language.

"Not that it is OK that Bill was murdered, as low-life as he may have been I still have a job to do. But then I guess that's why he was hanging around with you." Paolo's slander campaign deepened, forcing Gil to really wonder if the tape recordings wouldn't just be thrown away at the end of the interview. Questioning, he reconsidered.

"So, who else was killed?"

Paolo was dying to start the hard nose. To use Gil's scams against him. He could feel the pressure from his boss behind him. He had priorities. Some of which fell outside the sphere of his job.

Some things he would get away with, like arresting him on pathetic hustling charges, to buy time. His techniques however might not go down so fluidly. There was a reason behind it, both Paolo and his boss were worried about their jobs.

On top of that for Paolo there was a random personal connection to this case, one he couldn't talk to anyone about and get let off the case because it would immediately be used as the strongest lead. And he didn't want his brother being involved in a murder charge.

Although the connection was random and probably unrelated, or at least related via Gil, Paolo couldn't get it from his head. His brother asks about a little crook one day and the next he and his father turn up executed. Raffael hadn't done it, but it was a little too close to call. He would have to find out the old fashioned way.

Fortunately for Paolo it wasn't the first time he had to keep a distinction, once a liar always a liar. Furthermore it wouldn't be the last time either. He could always talk to his brother later.

"Ok, lets get through the basics. Where were you this afternoon?"

Gil answered all of the questions, honestly, to his surprise. He even began to relax as the mood lightened a little. Paolo forgot about the good-bad cop thing and went through all the routine things. The two cops left at one point allowing Gil to take a breather, he stood by the window over looking the police car park considering what was happening.

He began to feel uncomfortable being so comfortable. He remembered the anecdote of five suspects. The guilty one is the first to relax, knowing he has been caught. Was there anyone else? Should he be more or less tense? Was there any point playing the game? The games they see everyday? What are the chances of the next guy being better at playing than they are? The real smart guy perhaps, or the guy who had studied up on it. But Gil? No, not little old staying well out of trouble Gil. There was no point in lying when you hadn't done anything wrong.

Technically he had done lots of things wrong, but those, would they stick? In any case, at that point in time it was irrelevant. They didn't care about them, they wanted him for killing Bill and whoever else had been killed. If they wanted to accuse him of the other things he would reconsider then whether or not he was going to lie. Until then, not having done it was working in his favour.

The movement had made him feel a bit queasy. He stared at the uniformity of the cop cars lined up. The absurdity of it all made him chuckle briefly. Tropical Bill. The fact he was dead began to sink in, but not in the usual way death sinks in, he chuckled instead. Life had its ironies for Gil, like the situation he was in for example, but this was mint. He had always seen Bill as a good kids a heart, but it had never gone as far as to persuade him to like him. Let alone tell him so and persuade him to leave the life alone. Bill was smart and quick; he had just lacked good society. Gil wouldn't miss him, although he felt a little depressed by the injustice.

Gil wondered how he had died and who else died with him. His creations were far from the truth. He looked at two street kids, mixed up in something, a hustle gone wrong, toes stepped on or some longer vendetta he knew nothing about. Two shirtless kids, shot each other, stabbed or kicked to death. Gil hadn't known many people die, some old associates he had heard had gone out violently, but Gil always saw it coming years ahead and had always stepped out. Old faces drifted through his mind, Gil had never considered himself lucky, or questioned these deaths. He just told himself he made the right decisions. Stay out of trouble.

Seconds before Paolo and his boss came back in it began to dawn on Gil that Bill was to smart for getting on the wrong side of some homeboy. He had enough mouth to talk his way out. He also thought it strange that anyone would step up on the priest's son. It gave him a tinge of disgust. The thought was interrupted.

Paolo was ready to give some more ground in return for information. Perhaps Gil would react and give up clues.

They sat back down. "So you hadn't seen him for a few weeks?"

Gil examined Paolo's face, he didn't trust the new confidence and honesty that had just re-entered the room.

"Last week, Tuesday."

"Are you sure it was Tuesday?"

"Of course not, I don't keep track of the days, but it's that or nothing."

"I know the feeling," Paolo's approach had definitely changed.

"And you had seen him much before then."

"Less, we were together quite a lot, about a month ago. But things changed."

"What things?"

Gil want to explain what a little prick Bill was, the words filled his mouth but he held them down. Meticulous control would keep him afloat.

"Nothing changed really, he was always the same way I just got tired of him."

"And why was that?"

His throat filled again. "He was too young and arrogant, know-it-all but don't-know-shit type."

"Disrespectful?"

"Perhaps. He was just a little to fresh for me." Gil felt he was going to far. But it was just a personality difference. And people don't kill each other just because they don't get along. "I know it wasn't a marriage or social arrangement, but you got to get along with a partner in this type of scam. You have to trust his next move, and I couldn't."

"So it was just a personal thing. He didn't rip you off, set you up or try to, you know, cross you."

"No, he was smart enough to do it, but he didn't have a problem with me. To be honest it was me who had the problem. He didn't need the money, I have no idea why he was doing it. I guess he enjoyed it, but then we argued a lot and I guess he stopped enjoying it. He wasn't the talkative type, you know, sharing his emotions, so I can't tell you what his motivation was. I guess it was a phase or perhaps it was fashionable. Perhaps some rebellion, he told me his dad was a preacher of some kind."

Paolo nodded, pondering whether to take the next step.

"So you never met his father?"

"No, I got about as much reason to go anywhere near that shit hole as you."

"It's not your job fishing out the dead bodies."

Gil sat back in his chair, a little defeated by the inhumanity for the second time.

"So you never met or saw his father, spoke with him on the phone. Any contact what so ever?"

"No, why?"

"Because his father's dead."

Gil looked at him as if to say, "So what, he lied to me. Wouldn't have been the first lie anyone ever told me." But said nothing and stared blankly.

"Recently."

Still no reaction. Gil portrayed nothing, because that was what he knew. Paolo began to get the message, it left him with a sickening feeling that this was going to be a long drawn out case. He didn't fancy the idea of it. Locking Gil up that afternoon would have been much more rewarding, not to mention easier. Morals aside. Perhaps Paolo would pick up his moral attention if that was the case.

"How recently?" Gil finally said, also picking up the picture.

"This afternoon."

Gil's eyebrows went up. "So, they were..." Paolo nodded.

"And you don't know anything about this?"

Gil shook his head. Paolo shook his. He didn't have any evidence that the two bodies had been made cold at the same time, it had looked that way. There had been signs of a scuffle, he assumed Bill was into something and the old man came out to see what was going on. It occurred they may have shot each other. He noted it down.

Gil looked under Paolo's puzzled brow for an explanation. "We found the bodies together. Both dead, both in the same alley way." He said it in the most matter-of-factly way he could. Not entirely dissociated from the reality and sickness of the crime, but knowing he should be.

Gil swallowed, both the detectives noticed him do so. But they kept their interpretations to themselves. He looked as genuinely horrified about it as they had when they heard. Father and son. Literally. Paolo got up and went out. He took a few steps away from the room before putting his hands on his hips and looking deeply at the floor. He sighed heavily and ran things through his mind. He told himself he was a real detective and that he could handle it and he could find out who did it. He had solved difficult cases before. They weren't all easy, they weren't all like this, he hadn't had one in a while. Not one was going to be quite so public. The media love mysterious and unusual case, and he was going from an immediate solution to not having any leads what so ever. The outlook wasn't pretty without Gil somewhere in the equation. But Paolo knew he could do it.

He went back in with an approach that actually

considered Gil as a witness, perhaps he did actually hold the clue. He could keep him as the number one suspect, but he didn't have to treat him like it.

Gil and Paolo's boss were casually chatting when he went back in. Gil was trying, still to work out where and when he knew him from, but in an indirect manner. He was also trying to distract himself from his train of thoughts. He was a little dazed by it all. He could conceive they might hold him suspect for killing Bill, them being associates and having fallen out recently. However, the thought of killing his father too was a little painful. It wasn't his style, it wasn't even within his capability. And to have someone think that about you was craziness.

Paolo sat down opposite Gil, "So lets try a new angle. Who do you think might have done this?"

"Me? You two are the detectives."

"Ok," Paolo said frustratedly, "Who do you think had reason to do this?"

Paolo had very little to go on. Gil, his only lead and witness, a dead boy with no friends, a dead priest with no other family and little public private life. Gossip was very rarely true and good for nothing in the long run. All he had was that the priest was likely the unfortunate one and Bill was the one who got what he'd had coming. No witnesses in a neighbourhood where there never are. He wanted to scream it out. He had one lead, his own brother. He couldn't tell Gil that.

"I have no idea. I didn't meet a single one of his homeboys, family nothing. He went round on the bus, called me from pay-phones. Nothing, I don't know anything about him."

"So how did you meet him?"

"Fucking kid knocked on my front door." Gil was still as surprised by the fact as he was when it happened. The two detectives eyed him doubtingly. "I swear, told me he had heard about me from some friends of friends. You know how it is. I told him where to go, obviously, but he kept hanging around me, like some Buddhist monk."

"And who were you working with before?"

"Little Spanish kid from my own neighbourhood. But he retired along time before, several months."

"So they never met in front of you?"

"No, he was long gone."

"And what were you doing in between."

The second man was interested in the verbal tennis, but remained being silent.

"Other things."

It went on, Gil became more interested by the case as it went along. Paolo's analytical questioning was throwing up questions he didn't know the answers to, and ones he wanted to. He remembered how he had thought Bill was a cop in the first instance, trying to set him up. He reconsidered it, but the detectives denied it. But then they denied all of the questions Gil asked in the three hours they questioned him.

When Gil left he took over the role of detective, he began walking but eventually decided to take a bus. As he sat down, his brain hooked on to the right path. It could have been any one of the people they had set up together. And for that matter any of the ones Bill had done with other people or on his own. Risks you take, Gil surmised, why you have to fish carefully. It seemed likely that it was someone who they had been successful with, perhaps they had gone back for the money and so on. He couldn't picture anyone directly who seemed violent enough. And then if they were they would probably have been one of the ones who got away. So he discarded the thread.

All the suspects were just random faces. He didn't know anyone form Bill's life, and surely it contained more random faces than their common life. It didn't matter, but Gil's brain was hungry and so he spent the rest of the day sorting through the faces he did know, as nameless and uninvolved as they all were.

He spent the night thinking about it, he took it all the way to bed, even there it stopped him sleeping directly. It wasn't him , but they wanted it to be. He didn't know who it was, but it might be in his favour to find out. It was going to be a long week.

Paolo spent the rest of the afternoon filling out the associated paperwork with the case and the interview. He talked things over with his boss and didn't answer the phone. The press had heard about the story and the few journalists at it were doing their best to break his concentration. Tomorrow would be worse, once reaction to the story was felt they would be hounding him. Besides Sundays are not the days for press conferences.

That was tomorrow mornings task, writing a press statement. It was really Sunday night's task, but by the time he wanted to leave he still hadn't written anything. That was partly why he wanted to leave. There was nothing. He toyed with the connection to his brother. He imagined that statement. The ironic thing was that my brother asked me not long before the youth's death to look him up and rough him over. I, personally at the time, was on bad terms with my boss over similar incidents of brutality and similar coercion methods and decided against it for my own personal reasons, instead passing out the youth's details freely, what now appears to be within the twenty-four hour period leading to his death. Along with the other members of his family. Fortunately there were only two. Although even I find it difficult to believe, there is no connection between the member of my own family, who shall for personal reasons remain unnamed and the events of yesterday afternoon.

It was a dire situation for Paolo. He shook his head and ran his hands through his hair. Resting his elbows on the desk he looked around the office, the offices joined by glass dividers around him were all empty. His desk light was the only one on.

He cursed his brother. The strongest bond in the family was one of protection. He couldn't get him involved. Even talking to him about it was a chance. Besides his brother was having trouble with his own son, Paolo's nephew, so he had enough trouble as it was. Even if he did bring it up he would have to do it initially in passing such were the family ties.

Hopefully his brother would pick it up from the newspapers or TV. It would make it more awkward, Paolo would then get the 'why didn't you come to me about it' treatment. But at least it would be open ground. If he could get help from his brother great, burying them would be a different matter, but one to deal with when it crops up.

The bad consequences would be bad. With both Paolo and his brother tied to the murders it would look very suspicious. No matter who they were trying to protect. It was too early to start the negative thoughts Paolo told himself, but he already felt it was too far in. He put his mind back to Gil and decided to call it a day. Gil could take the fall, not the most obvious subject but he would go down with little resistance.

It would have to be Gil or some new third party unrelated. He would wait to see what forensics would dig up. His heart skipped a beat as the possibility of his brother being the actual culprit. It was a wild thought but it was there. The crazy pictures followed him away from his desk and out of his office. Paolo did have the luxury of driving home, but like Gil he couldn't shake the detective work from his head. He played the crime scene video in his head trying to create the events, placing the characters in their places, fixing in assailants in the place of the killer. He went through various stereotypical situations. The gang fight, the robbery, the revenge, the family feud, he put the gun in different hands, he put more than one gun. He went through endless examples, but the only common factor he could find, except the bodies was Gil's face. His cheeky attitude when he had answered the door and his surprise when he had told him the facts. All the while, he played real detective still imagining Gil going down.

Paolo had only ever planned to send someone away for murder knowing their innocence. And it had made him feel really guilty even though it never came to reality. So bad he had been reasonably straight since. He had done it for a friend who had killed his wife in the middle of an intense argument, it wasn't the first intense argument but he sympathised somehow as he couldn't imagine this friend would have wanted to kill her. He would have gone down for it so Paolo had gone out and picked up some chain-snatcher, walked him around his buddy's house under the cover of an insurance set-up, which he would get nicely cut into. He had sat him down in the kitchen, talked him through the plan, made him coffee, went through a list of things they planned to steal all the while the body was cooling off. They went around the house, unplugged all the electrical equipment, Paolo told the kid to go upstairs for the jewellery while he did the kitchen. So the kid went up to the room only to find the dead body just inside the door of the bedroom from there it went wrong for Paolo and his chain-snatcher, Paolo's buddy sneaked out from the spare bedroom and let the kids head explode all over his dead wife.

Needless to say it worked, although Paolo and his buddy fell out soon after. Paolo had felt bad at the time, he pitied the poor kid and he pitied his friend. His stomach turned at the thought of going through it again. He didn't want to have to do it again, but he would be protecting family this time. He decided he would follow Gil the next day, he would be on his own, so would Gil. All three of them were on their own, Gil, Paolo and Bill.

Paolo stared hard at his hallway telephone when he returned home. He re-convinced himself that if his brother was dragged into it he would protect him, but he wasn't going to be the one responsible for pulling him in. Besides, there was no reason to involve him unless necessary, if he could let Gil go down or get directly to the real killer, were it not Gil, there was no need.

He examined the case of setting Gil up. It would have to be more in his control than last time, a lot more slick too. Paolo's emotions rose as he considered it. He considered it all night, waking up the next morning with a nasty recollection of it. His first weary thoughts were that he had already done it. He must have dreamt it during the night. Slowly he came round, clawing back reality and removing the build-up from his eyes. It annoyed him, that being the first thought of the day. Worse, the first thought of the week.

BOOK TWO

Book Two

Gil had spent his Sunday nights' sleep in turmoil too. His list of suspects was now challenging the city phone book for wordiness. Most of the names on it ran very low scores on his likely-o-meter. He was lacking a lot. For example first hand access to the crime scene, years of training and practice, the sequence of events. He had to keep in mind that Bill was dead, every time a new face cropped up he planned to call Bill and ask him whether he thought that could be the one. Killing, he thought, it was too much for a Sunday.

Mondays, however, were more like the weekend for Gil, the end of his working week. He shook off his dreams. He had also had reconsiderations when he awoke. Had he really killed Bill? Had he been arrested for it? Had he found out the real killers identity? Why couldn't he recall it now? He felt as if he had lost a Sunday, consumed by another's murder.

Gil was worried. He was a worrying person. But dirty cops made him nervous and in this instance he felt justified. His innocence was not his guarantee. It set the mood for the week. Definitely, Gil told himself, he would have to go the distance on this one. If the police weren't going to protect him from false accusation he would have to.

Paolo was going to make it his week's objective too. He had several other cases assigned to him, but nothing had changed in any of them during the last week, besides he prioritised this one given the sudden media attention. Most murders go unnoticed by the surface. Only the high profiles and bizarre circumstances are deemed worthy of unnerving the comfort of the masses. It was a paper cut for Paolo. On the one hand, the media bore upon him added pressure and vigilance, but on the other hand, it justified him cutting corners.

Gil could go down. All that was needed was a small stitch. A wife who stays in the kitchen for hours at a time. Kids? Kids don't make good alibis. One small stitch and he could make it seamless.

But the pressure on Monday was to work, not to cheat. To deduce and not produce. Better to find the real person on all accounts, provided that was possible. Give it a week, and then review, if there is nothing, then go back to square one.

Upon awakening my brain took full account of just how scary my dreams had been. I had only had a few short ones, I guessed on account of the fatigue. It was still early, but it seemed like I had a lot to do that Monday. I searched for some form of functional timepiece while comparing the similarities of the morning after my first encounter with Bill and his budding policeman partner.

It was uncanny, the hand gun, sitting so calmly on my bedside table. Dictating the truth to unbelieving senses. The brain ever slower on the uptake.

It was seven-thirty. I considered the myth of dawn raid and whether they were myths or not. So far so good was the only conclusion reached.

I went for the shower, I dragged the clothes I had worn the day before with me. It occurred to me, in one of my dreams, that I had been covered in blood. Further that Bill had been clawing my leg, leaving all sorts of evidence under his finger nails and so on. Needless to say I felt dirty. My brain reeled at the reality, did I step in blood. Did I leave footprints, would it all have left my shoes before I reached home, was there blood on the carpet right now? Would they follow the bloody footsteps?

The answer could easily have been yes judging by the amounts of blood that left my clothes. I eventually gave up and threw them to the sink. They would have to go. I proceeded to scrub myself, hard, my whole body ached. Adrenalin and running.

As I washed my face memories of my altercation in the park flooded back. It ached when I touched it. Inspecting it in the mirror revealed a thin blue-yellow line from the left corner of my mouth, along my cheek bone to my eye. I could barely touch it, let alone shave. Best disguised by stubble in any case.

I stayed in the shower a long time, even to the point of getting out and back in again to use the toilet. The air outside wasn't too cold, but the glass walls, steamy air and warm film of water offered higher levels of comfort and protection. The bathroom resembled a Turkish bath by the time I dragged myself from it. However it had been it had worked. I stumbled around the house in a towel hypnotised into my usual routine. Coffee was the key, a preparation so meticulous in its method. Refined over many years, an impeccably obeyed ritual. It shook out the events of Sunday's actions, the rich aroma of freshly ground beans blocking the malodour of the previous day.

The consumption stage of breakfast was a more sombre affair, the nonchalance ended with a small laugh of self pity concerning the ordeal in general. How could I have ever thought even for one second that it could have all been a figment of my imagination. Anymore than life itself is. Hallucination of this magnitude existed only in ones of greater proportion. Hallucinations of this magnitude cannot be real. I mused it while I ate.

The event's outrageousness, its outlandishness, astounded me, these memories couldn't possibly begin to convince me that they were anything but real. But my acceptance of these realities was not going to be something I could easily decide upon. In the haze, the mist soon took my attention so fully that I the cups and bowls in front of me on the table were empty a long time before I had noticed. The repetitive clanging of my spoon against an empty bowl, actions that may have continued unnoticed for several minutes, eventually broke through the misty reality barrier.

I stopped. I thought. I needed a plan of action. From the small details to how to get through the week. If I was, as I planned, going to stay and stick it out I had to cover my tracks. The decision was still firm in the day's new light. Regardless I had to eradicate anything that tied me to the two black corpses I left lying in an alleyway the previous day.

The clothes, the gun, a word with Raffael. I thought about writing the list down, smiling at the stupid duality of my brain. It amazed me how inefficient our brains can be more than the fact it didn't happen all the time. I needed to destroy the evidence, not leave around pieces of paper with the title, Sammy's to-do-list in regard to The cover up of Tropical Bill and Tropical Bill, Sr. But still, my recognition of this stupidity heartened me. Perhaps I would get through it after all. As long as I could see where I was going to screw it up it would get by ok. Stepping in the right direction.

My brain stopped to argue the opposite argument. Developing a criminal mind was not really stepping forwards. Did I really want to become a criminal? No. Should this type of thinking, then, become my new personality, my logic? My new approach to life. The 'how am I going to get my way out of this one' method would surely soon become the 'how am I going to get my way out of the next one' shortly followed by the 'how am I going to get my way into the third one'.

The trance ended and I decided it was actually time to do something, instead of musing the benefits to my id. I had no problem with burning my clothes, or at least any other method of destroying. Not throwing away or tearing up, but destroying them. The gun would be different, to destroy it would take a lot of force. It would surely be better to clean it and put it somewhere where no one would find it. The simplicity of leaving it in the trash to be buried in some landfill toyed lazily with the lazy side of my psyche.

The evidence engrained on my own body bothered me. The smell of the gun's discharge for example. I smelt my hand again. Something bothered me, not that I could smell it, I couldn't, but it bothered me that I didn't know more about it. I wasn't sure whether the predicament of my ignorance bothered me more.

It struck me around this time that there was a possibility, that other than Bill's finger nails, I had left some evidence behind at the scene. Something really obvious that would not leave me here logically debating the finer details. Hair fibres, blood, saliva or clothing fibres, what I knew did haunt me, what I didn't did so too but also pointed a big finger at me too.

But despite these things pointing a finger at me that was all. I had left the house particularly empty-pocketed on purpose. Perhaps Bill had left some account of our first meeting. A diary or such, it seemed unlikely, but I wasn't trying to remove possibilities at this stage. It bothered me that I had been almost entirely honest with him. Anything he would have written would have been true, down to my name, down to my neighbourhood and the fact that I have a very easily identifiable physiology.

Then there was the accomplice. What did he know? I didn't share much with him except my sudden disliking of his profession. It was still a blurry memory, but I wondered what they might have spoken about afterwards, why it had gone wrong and so on. And all this was still under the huge assumption that he wasn't a real cop. Maybe they had followed my up, wanting their own revenge.

It was a big ocean, what I knew less than an island. All I could count on was that I had a small sphere of control. This accomplice would, undoubtedly come into the equation on one side or the other. He looked like a regular guy, honest, a little too old to fit your average street crook profile but in all cases a person that was destined to haunt me a little bit longer.

I left the kitchen in defiance of the tasks I had set myself, although determined to carry them out. Perhaps Raffael could help me again in finding this unknown assailant of mine. My freedom balanced in his hands was all I could think. I needed a judgement risk on his likely interference to my peace.

Physical evidence was my first priority. The things lying around in my own apartment. They should be removed before the police arrived was the immediately obvious thought. The bloody clothes were still wet in the basin in my bathroom. I decided immediately to dispose of all the items I was wearing, down to my underwear and shoes. Nothing holds that much sentimental attachment after all.

The fact the clothes were wet bore little consideration in the end. I lived in the middle of a city, in an apartment without a garden. Lighting a fire was not really an easy option. I didn't fancy a long bus or train ride to the countryside to light a fire in the middle of I-don't-know-where. Where do they burn things in the city? No ideas, I could wait months for the next riotous protestation and their tyre burning.

Distractedly I picked up the gun. It still felt good having a gun in the house, but I shook the idea of keeping it off. If I felt that unsafe with it gone I could find a new one, somewhere. I attempted to disassemble the weapon.

The ammunition case came out easily. After that it was very trial and error. Eventually everything sprang apart sending springs and bits everywhere. This would be easy I decided. I would just clean each part and dump each one in a different place. Then it would just be gun parts. It belonged to Bill, well it had belonged to him. So without my finger-prints it wouldn't be traceable to me. The criminality of the underlying mind bewildered me. The next thought was that I was lucky to not have a job to go to. Definitely not the average Monday morning.

I searched my bathroom, finding some surgical alcohol, which I used to clean all the parts of the gun, carefully not leaving more prints. As I was doing it I thought about dissolving my clothes in acid. It seemed extravagant, but I could work. I decided I had no idea where you would get hold of such a product, and surely it would be traceable. It was getting out of hand. But it was working towards it all being over, to my brain returning to normal.

Perhaps it would never start, I bagged each gun part into supermarket carrier bags and tided each entire bag in a series of knots. Only the clothes and the conscience to go. My confidence was seemingly very high, the thing that had preoccupied me was now dead. Providing other things didn't change I could get some serenity back, it was such a lovely thought.

I found I had more reason to live my old life. Being pushed by small amounts to live a slightly more discreet life. To tell people less of me, not to do or say anything that would even link me, let alone incriminate me. To live the rest of my life as a harmless and unrelated butterfly. And given laissez faire environs it wasn't too far from being the truth.

I analogised myself to an animal, I forget which, but one who when cornered will never surrender until the last piece of flesh is torn from his bones, and if coming out on top will walk away serenely as if nothing had happened, least of all to him. I was that animal. I finished the gun preparations and stepped into the real world.

I hadn't prepared myself in the slightest for the outside world. It was luck, my high confidence had pushed me unknowingly over a threshold I wouldn't have otherwise crossed. The sun was warm, the air only slightly disturbed by a breeze. The calm passing of cars and birds chirping very slow songs was too realistic, too unedited. My street was full of hard working, honest and definitely very normal people. It was, therefore, very empty at eleven a.m. All at their respective tasks the street was once again mine. A surge filled my torso.

I had taken the gun completely to pieces. I even disfigured a few smaller parts. I had put each of the bags in bags with other things to disguise them to the bored rubbish collector. I even dismantled the ammunition, I didn't want to hear about a round having gone off and hitting poor Otto the garbage man in the leg one day in the newspaper.

I walked with my head quite high, my deviousness had shown its true colours in the light of a difficult situation. It would save me from the confinement of prison, the humiliation of the press and the inevitable ostracism of the public.

I wondered as I walked what I really knew about hour of need. This was by far the most intense situation I had ever found myself in, that may not be surprising, but if looking at the previous two years of my life and calling them eventful would be a gross mis-description.

Inevitably I began to question the value of my life. Hoping as I did that fellow beings of my species do the same calculations, and as regularly. It sickens me to have to question my existence. And to be forced to do so by none other than myself. Having killed two people changed me? Am I more or less valuable? Can I consider using these events to change my life, to make it better or worse? What if I were to go to jail? Would that make me a better person? I doubted it. Rehabilitation needs inner strength and motivation, not bars and confinement. Did I even want to change my life? Was this entire situation initiated for the very purpose of initiating my own change? Some divine signal saying, "Hey you! Get off your ass and do something."

It made me consider again leaving for the exterior. Perhaps I could do something worthwhile. There were starving people out there, I could help people. I could set up a new life, a new start.

The though collapsed. I wasn't trained in any of this. I couldn't get a job, I didn't know how to have a job. What kind of employee would I make? No, it wasn't an option. If it was a signal it was one telling me to stay still. Whatever happens.

I continued my mission. I dropped bags in every third bin along the high street, then cut off and left random bags in random bins of random houses until I had got rig of them all. Heading for home I began to think about what to do with the clothes. I did some high street research. How do you get rid of clothes, without having to burn them? I passed a charity shop. It seemed like a god idea. Perhaps they would send them to the exterior for me. They would even clean the clothes for me. A bit risky. An electrical appliance store showed me a huge protest in the capital zone, so much for having to wait months. I could take the clothes down there and throw them on one of the tyre fires, burn the evidence in front of fifty police officers.

I cursed my society for making it so hard to hide evidence, then considered if I could really call it my society. I wasn't a regular donator. To be honest the last thing I contributed to it was two dead bodies. And there I was having to answer a million questions no one else will even have occur to them.

The acid idea came back as I passed a chemist. It was becoming quickly my least favourite idea. The conversation in the store would be bad. "I need some acid." "Ok, what kind?" "I don't know." "Ok, well, what is it for?" No, it would be a bad idea. It would rouse suspicion where it wasn't needed. Burning was much more simple and at least I knew how to do that. Two millennia of civilisation and I could just about manage something we master several millennia before.

I was fighting what I saw as a losing battle, but I had no choice. Freedom is worth fighting for as they say. I am sure they don't mean it to be applied to this particular situation. How many smaller, less significant or less consequential had I given up on? Too many surely, like everyone I suppose. But not this one, perhaps that was the sign.

I wanted more than nothing to get back on with the nothingness that was my life. I enjoyed having no job, no responsibilities no friends or preoccupations. Time to do nothing but think. I had many theories on thinking and on things in general. Life. The way I saw it was that most people fill their minds with this list of things. These priorities, pushing the vast gap of knowledge so far down the list they never stop to think about it. As if they are scared of the truth or of a void in the knowledge. I could see it then, with the mess I was. I was no longer the observer I had been made a clown in the circus of life.

My head spun as if it weren't attached to my neck. Reality check, what was next? Before getting back to normal. The gun. Gone. Even if by slight chance they found it, it was unconnected to me. It hadn't occurred to me that the police might have been following me. They would have to have been pretty smart to have caught up with me in less than twenty-four hours. Even if someone had casually seen me dumping the parts it was pure circumstance. The gun. Gone.

The clothes were next then. I began to worry less about them. If they really wanted to get forensic on me I am sure they would find some fibres from the clothes in my apartment, even after the clothes themselves were long gone. It didn't mean I was going to leave the items, still stained with blood in the bathroom too much longer. What it did tell me was that it was self-defeating to go to measures that might arouse suspicion over the clothes. I would do it low profile and low stress.

I threw them in the washing machine when I got home, I threw in a few items of old clothing, things I hadn't been wearing recently and two hours later I bagged them up and dragged them to the charity store. Call it confidence or call it laziness but I took them to the store in my neighbourhood. It was more obvious to take a bus or taxi to go to another area, but at the time it just didn't seem worth it. The clothes were very well received and I even walked out with a few extra pennies in my pocket.

And that was, as they say, the end of it. I got home, had a spring clean to allow the energy to flow more freely once more and washed the clothes that had piled up. Generally I cleansed. Taking away the evidence, not of the murder, but of what had preceded it. Everything that had lead up to it. I decided life would be back to normal from that point. If I concentrated on it, I could will the police to never find me.

I could return to watching movies like they weren't making them anymore and watching the world like they were about to take it away. Life would be once more the way I like it. It wasn't just about the murder, life hadn't been the same for over a month, since I first met Bill that night, I had tried to get on as normal but it had never left me, never gone away. I would think about it everyday at least thirty times. I had returned to the point where I could smile at the world, fell it smile back at me and put the kettle on.

I did just that, put the kettle on, sensing the end of one chapter and the beginning of the next. The coffee came out just how I liked like, weak and full of sugary substances. I even made it as far as the television news. Confident that whatever was there would pass by my confident shield. Looking back it was one of those win or trip situations. With the cocky front I had put up a fall wouldn't have looked out of place. Fortunately, it didn't work out like that. The story had made the news, and it was a big story, someone out there in TV land had obviously been shocked by it enough to want the whole world to think it was important. But despite all the power that one person had he or she could do nothing to change the smile inducing facts. The police knew nothing. They complained about the community and its lack of spirit and how this kind of outrage should be bringing people together not extending the barriers. They did blab on though, talking about how there were no family members, who might, in such a case, be suspects. The fact a community leader was shot in a neighbourhood which people don't go into unless they live there. No witnesses, one suspect and no signs of clear motive. The story was given a how can we have confidence in the police spin and finished attacking them more than the murderer.

It surprised me as I switched the channel how that only twenty-four hours before I had been considering leaving the country. My conscience couldn't have been cleaner at that point. I boiled it down to the fact that I wouldn't survive in jail, I didn't belong there and I was never going to go there. My lack of humanity surprised me also. I guess humanity comes second place after the survival instinct.

If I hadn't been the murderer I would look down on such behaviour, it was the kind of unnecessariness that the world was too full of. But yet when it's the choice between being an observer and being the one behind the wheel perspective is easily shifted.

I wouldn't have known what Bill had been done. Bill would have been the other person who was killed. Not being a particular subscriber to any faith didn't lend much to my opinion, but you can imagine those lesser blessed in the imagination and faith department would see it in an even darker light.

The ironic thing, perusing the religion one a little longer is that while neither atheist nor agnostic if I had to pick a religion, my own philosophy would make me tend towards Buddhism, which doesn't have religious leaders. No gods, no rules, each and every man for himself within the sphere of his peers.

The hard fact in this case was that someone I didn't know, who pushed religion on the people, the kind of behaviour easily analogised with a drug dealer, had been lost. It wasn't going to end the world. I have my own answer as to why god allows these kind of things happen. If he was strong enough he would sort it out. These weren't answers to answer. What I had done was done. Nothing could change it. I could look back no more. So I didn't.

Gil's week was yet another of preoccupation. For everything that had gone on it had changed Gil's life. Sure he would have been stressing over something else, but the fact he was stressing over something he had no involvement in stressed him more. The cop had called him at least twice a day everyday. He had even seen him a few times. He wondered if the cop was following him, it was a possibility.

It seemed a bit extravagant that he would follow him, Gil thought. How could he be that serious? Nonetheless Gil stayed out of his normal situations that week. Giving it a rest was not giving the cop any unnecessary ammunition. But by the time Monday came around again everyone found themselves status quo. The cop had clearly got nothing new, and Gil had noticed also that he'd been silent on whether the media knew that Gil was a witness.

The persecution began to be normal; the lack of work, however, was becoming a more pressing issue. Whatever the consequences were, the ones that came with doing some work was preferable to those of not doing it. He contemplated his options for the week alternately with his longer term plans. The remedy for his short term situation was not in the long term plans, but a change of lifestyle was not only attractive but difficult for Gil to de-consider.

It was enlightenment for Gil. He had passed the point of knowledge a long time before. He had for many years wanted to 'go straight,' the idea of working an honest living was not new. What was new this week was that Gil now had direction and motivation. The point at which the path is not only clear but approachable.

Gil wasn't sure how easily it could be done. Could you do it in one day? It is a process at all, or is merely deciding the entire transition. But as he made his way on Monday morning he considered he could do it in one day. In his criminal life, he had no boss, he worked for no one, he had no ties. There was no family; he wasn't going to be dragged back in by anyone except himself. He bought a newspaper. After briefly scanning the headlines he threw it away, all except the classified sections.

He carried on walking, tucking the section under his arm. He hadn't planned any of this. He had a large variety of scams up his sleeve and had reached the point in his line of work were he could just 'freestyle'. Walking around until he spotted a sucker. But as he walked he could feel the print under his arm burning. And being the opportunist he was he felt this was his opportunity to make money this Monday morning.

Gil sat down in a coffee shop and let his eyes wander over the sections while he stirred some coffee and waited for a glazed donut. It wasn't the first time he had bought a classified section to a coffee shop. A favourite scam of his was calling numbers to go round to see furniture or antiques and pulling some sort of scam. But he pushed the urge to read those sections and moved to the employment. The reality of the real world was implanted and was now beginning to germinate. He would have to answer a lot of questions. Where have you been? What have you been doing? Why haven't you been paying taxes? The beginnings of frustrations crept into his jaw muscles. He sat back letting the paper relax onto the table. Using his glazed eyes instead to stare into nothing ness. Once the coffee was cool enough to drink and the donut arrived he would be able to look at the paper again. Sugar and caffeine. He sat back and invented some slogans for his new campaign, running them through various sections of his brain to see how they sounded.

The cop had become such a common sight on the back horizon Gil was barely surprised enough to snap out of his thought pattern when he sat down in front of him.

Paolo was trying to take things easily too, he had already ordered his coffee before sitting down and brought it with him himself. He sat it down and looked across at Gil. He was blowing into his coffee with a lost look in his eyes, their emptiness was reflected in the shiny surface of the coffee cup. The white china and black coffee the contrasting opposites of Gil's pupils and the whites of his eyes.

Paolo looked down at the paper, noticing it was a bit thin he rummaged it and realised it was just the classifieds. "What are you after eh?"

Gil wasn't impressed by being socially cornered. He didn't like Paolo's cheeky grin either. He was in the middle of trying to change his life for the better and here was the worst thing in his life laughing at him about it. As if a lifetimes worth of not being arrested was being paid off somehow. If only he had kept the rest of the paper.

"I was about to ask you the same thing." Gil replied coolly but already feeling the heat building up inside. As if it was already getting beyond a joke or misunderstanding. "I don't know why you're following me around. I didn't do it and if, after a week, you still don't know that we should switch jobs."

"Didn't do what Gil?" The cop was almost openly sarcastic.

"Eh?" Gil hoped that is was an honest misunderstanding. He soon realised it wasn't and sank back down. "You have got to be kidding me?"

"About what, what would I joke about with you?"

"No, you're right, you wouldn't, we don't know each other that well. But I'll tell you what, why don't you come around one day, we'll have something to eat and get to know each other better. Meet the wife and all that. You know where I live don't you?"

"Now you're joking with me, right?" Both of them were getting angry, Paolo was just doing a better job of keeping it under covers. Gil's anger was more short term, he was pissed off since Paolo had sat down. Paolo on the other hand looked as if he was on a slow build up since his adolescence.

"So what are you looking for?" Paolo reiterated lifting the corner of the paper.

"Renta-cop-killer. What's it got to do with you?"

"Nothing, just making conversation. You don't have to tell me if you don't want to."

Gil sat and examined the cops dirty eyes, was there any advantage to telling him of his life changing plans. His playful mood was about as genuine as when Gil put on his cop uniform.

"When you come to dinner, was the final answer Gil could come up with."

Paolo smirked almost genuinely. "Ok, Gil," Gil was already getting tired of the constant repetition of his name. It was either patronising or paternalistic, he couldn't decided, it could be both. He cut into Paolo's speech.

"Where have you go to go?"

"Well," Paolo said recovering from both the look Gil had given him and the interruption, I was actually going to ask you that.

Gil eyed the cop again. What was this crook up to now? "Really? He ventured, and in what? ... why?" Gil gave up talking and gave in to the misunderstanding with a facial expression.

"Being honest with you, I haven't gotten very far with

finding whoever it was who killed your friend Bill. In fact you are still my main suspect, we both know you didn't do it. Well, I am pretty certain of it, unless you want to tell me something I don't know." Gil shook his head sorrowfully. "And, well the point is, that you know sometimes the wrong people get blamed for the wrong thing and go to you know… the wrong prison."

"Really?" Gil wished he'd had something better to say but then realised it was better to not say anything.

"No, not that often, but I really was hoping you were going to tell me something new. Something that might help me. Perhaps you have some ideas or notions of who it was? I know you lot aren't that famous for being talkative, but…"

"What are you getting at?" Gil asked, suspecting he was up to something.

"I guess that being under suspicion for something you didn't do, assumedly of course, might have initiated you into doing some research. Or if not, perhaps it will."

"And why would I do that?"

"I don't know, perhaps to save your ass."

"It doesn't need saving, I didn't do it and this would never even make it to a court room." Gil was finding his enlightened mood being slowly shattered piece be piece. His strange reference were like some cry for help.

"So you have been thinking about it then?" Paolo said with a smug grin. It reminded Gil of why he hated cops so much. The greasy, slimy fucker in front of him was the pure example of what he didn't like about cops. He couldn't be too blunt with him, nor could he be subtle.

"If you think I know, you're wrong. If you think I would tell you, you're wrong and if you think I am gong to listen to much more of this, guess what?"

Gil watched Paolo transform in front of him. His eye's grew in their beadiness. His cheeks swelled and fattened, his nose flattened. His ears began to point up, then flopped to their sides. His words became garbled nonsense.

Gil was repulsed, he wanted to get up but only made the motion to do so, eventually sitting back down again. He would hear it out. What ever he told Paolo, he did want to find out who did it, he wasn't wrong, just out of place and out of order.

"Let me get this straight then," Gil started, finding his good humour again, "You're making a threat or you're having trouble figuring out who did this?" Gil wondered if Paolo actually had the balls to set him up. He looked like he was contemplating the thought and like he had threaten people like this before. Paolo was analysing Gil's answer and his demeanour, looking for flaws in his logic and points of weakness to attack.

Gil found the strength he needed to get up but before he had a chance Paolo had something that would make him stay. "So what are you going to be doing this week? Are you going to work?" It seemed as if he was making threats, don't do any crime this week because someone will be watching you. Gil felt himself shrink, Paolo's expression changed. "Or is that what you were looking for in the classified section? Don't flatter yourself too much Gil." Paolo had a wry smile on his face. "But then we don't want you being picked up on some small misdemeanour do we."

"And if I am not working what might I be doing?"

"Oh I don't know, finding out who killed Bill and his dad for me."

"I already told you I have no idea and that I wouldn't tell you if I did."

"Look!" Paolo's vicious and impatient side leapt out at Gil. "I already told you that you are the only suspect, there is nothing else, no weapon, no forensic evidence, nothing, absolutely bloody nothing." He calmed down and wiped a some spit from the side of his mouth before calmly saying, "Nothing that will say it wasn't you, that is."

Gil shrunk back more visibly by the sudden attack. It was a little too much, he didn't like being backed into a corner either. "So? I really don't know what you are getting at. If you are trying to say it was me who did it because there is no evidence it only says you are either bad at the detecting business or you are trying to threaten me. In the first case, well I guess the first case is the truth, and secondly, no motive, no weapon, no nothing, I may not be a lawyer but I have a rough idea of what and wont stand up in court." Gil was shaken and clearly beyond the range of his usual daily mood swings, he stood up proudly and definitely, adding before he left, "And if you are trying to set me up then, well, I don't really know what to say. But it sure as hell makes me feel better about myself." He swept the remnants of the paper of the table and walked away.

Paolo fought it as Gil walked off, "No motive?" But it was too late, Gil was upset and a little offended, not because of Paolo, but because life was treating him so. He had been sitting contemplating a better life, a more morally correct life and look what he had thrown in his face in return. Reminded of how low people sink. And now this guy is shouting that I don't have a motive. What motive does he have for doing this to me?

Paolo stayed after Gil left with his coffee and some moments of thought. A few faces had noticed Gil's loud exits, but Paolo's snarl quickly made them forget. He decided to give Gil a day off, not follow him, let him cool down. If he was going to carry through with framing him he would need Gil to be as docile as possible.

He analysed the conversation, ensuring Gil was a long way a way before he left. Just to rid the temptation. He found it strange that Gil had been angry and upset over angry and frightened. Why was that? He didn't bother checking his own moral standards at that point in time, instead he concentrated on some other angles. Perhaps even do some work on some other cases. Last weeks sneaking round after Gil and the crime scene stuff was enough real police work to get away with doing some bureaucratic things for a while. Gil wasn't going anywhere, he needed some time to cool off, breath, get back into the swing of things. If he cant work he will get frustrated and he wont go near anyone either. By the weekend he would want to get this off his mind, he could find out in that time.

Gil was more determined than ever to find out who killed Bill. He had very little else on his mind. The conversation with Paolo would not go away, anyone who deals out that kind of bad attitude and grief on a Monday morning was not going to leave him alone. And wouldn't until he had what he wanted. He hated cops. He wondered briefly what it was that Paolo wanted so badly. What was it about this case that got him so hot under the collar? He couldn't be like it for every case, he wouldn't have made it to that age without having had a heart attack.

The story had been in the news, people had been talking about it. He hadn't pursued the story himself, but Gil was not considering that there might be a certain level of gravity at the police station. Paolo could have been having his ear chewed by someone about the case. What else could it be. What drives a dirty pig cop to set up a person he knows to be innocent—of the crime at hand, at least—and to whom he has no other connection. There could have been many reasons, Gil considered, but none of them seemed believable over the next. The only plausible solution was that he had a personal link to the crime.

As he walked he concentrated his efforts towards sorting the problem rather than explaining it. The rest of his troubles took back seats in the bus that was his mind. It wasn't a conscious thing, he was just stressing more on hi new primary goal. The cop was not playing the game nor was he playing fair.

Gil went back through the list of suspects he had compiled the week before, adding more names for the sake of getting a good base. Some names of people Bill had spoken to on the phone and all so some of his own friends who might at least know who to get hold of some of the people on his list.

That would be the job for the week. He went home to get started. The sooner he knew who it was the sooner he could take the next step.

From his armchair he made some calls. With his slippers and greying moustache the way he flicked reminiscently through his phone book he looked like someone twenty years older enjoying retirement. He wasn't, he was finding an excuse not to carry out the life change he had wanted so much an hour before.

He was forty, he thought his hair was greying from premature ageing. It was doing so from stress. He thought his job wasn't as bad as anyone thinking about it for the first time might think it was, but it was. He thought his family was healthy and functional, but his kids were malnourished and he hadn't had what anyone else would term a conversation with his wife in what was probably months.

When he did consider these problems he made up excuses, ignored them or found something else to stress over. He was bad at dealing with his life, he wasn't built to deal with his life, yes he had to everyday. And everyday he looked at life he did so through the eyes of his own dirty cop. As if he had some filter between him and reality. He didn't see himself as real, he knew people could see him, but he was fake and he couldn't see how his decisions would actually affect anyone.

When he was in his cop uniform it was the same. A dupe would walk away after a successful hustle feeling lucky, lucky he hadn't been arrested or if they were smarter, hurt or even worse. What ever it was there was always something keeping him from reality, something preventing him from dealing with the issues that he should have been concerned about. It wasn't as if he was short of them.

As he spoke to old friends and reminisced it dawned on Gil that his could be the last one. It could be the last unnecessary preoccupation. By the time he had exhausted the phone numbers he realised it didn't matter, as long as there was one left another could come along. But he made an effort to try.

The phone calls had come up with little. Gil had dissociated himself from the underworld some years before through motives of fear and in attempt to elevate his own self image. But it didn't mean he couldn't call people from time to time. He had been looked down upon for leaving but it was his choice and he had never been high enough up the rankings to have been important enough to not want to lose.

But he was empty handed from this time around. He left the house thinking he could go and have a walk around Bill's old neighbourhood, detective style. He laughed at the thought of being a detective, he imagined himself with the pigs head he had seen on Paolo that morning. He could solve this quicker than Paolo, he told himself. He was more sensible and had the necessary motivation to find out who did it instead of just blaming the first criminal who came into sight. Paolo couldn't just be lazy, there was some other motivation with him. Perhaps Gil would find that out what it was too.

Gil's mind freed up, he thought of his breakthrough into the free world as a police officer. It had its appeal, car chases and snooping into private lives. It wasn't a serious thought, but for Gil, it was good in the sense that he was free for a while.

Gil ended up walking all the way to Bill's old neighbourhood. He didn't actually know many people there. It was more of a chance thing. See who he ran into. There was one old guy, an old neighbour, not a crook, he had an electronics store, Gil headed for it.

The old guy had always had the store, but back when it was a really dangerous area he used to live in Gil's street, a few doors away. The old guy used to come and go with all his repairs daily, in the end he got fed up with carting things back and forth and so he bought the three floors above the shop and moved in. It would be a good starting point, even if it wasn't helpful.

Gil's face appearing in the store made the old man react immediately, "Heeeey!" His voice creaked out. Long time no see! Gil was used to him saying that, it was always a long time between them meeting. The word 'friend' in Gil's vocabulary meant 'casual acquaintance' in anybody else's. But the old guy was the friendly type, always greeted people with a smile and always treated people like one of his own brothers.

Gil noticed the smile he made himself, and felt his mood climb even higher.

"So what ever brings you into this dark neighbourhood?" There was a good question, Gil thought, wishing he had prepared an answer.

"Actually just looking for an acquaintance. But I passed by and thought I would drop in."

"Well, that sure is a nice thought Gil. How the hell are you? Boy it's been along time. Who you after anyhow? Anyone I know? What you up to at the moment? Same old dirty tricks I suppose." The old man was harmless, his questions would go on and on with no direction or purpose. Gil told himself to relax. The old man carried on asking questions as he put some project to one side. "Well, look at me would you? Demanding all this information from a man who hasn't been offered anything in trade. What can I get you? Something to drink? Tea? Coffee? Or something?"

Gil instinctively accepted, justifying it with the long walk he had just taken. It would give him time to rest his feet and get a fresh perspective.

Gil pulled up a stool and lent on the glass counter while

the old man unplugged a tangle of wires replacing it with the end of a kettle half buried in some electrical carcasses. "So how are things with you?"

"Good, you know me, cant complain, don't know how to. Food on the table, game on Sunday, kid's about to go to a good college." Gil nodded approvingly.

"Glad you moved?" Gil couldn't actually remember if he had seen the old guy since he had moved out.

"You know something? I actually miss that old street. The peace and quiet isn't as bad as them old papers would have you believe. Round here isn't no fairy tale neither." The old guy furrowed his brow the infinite black fold looked like rubber, stopping into an impossibly smooth skin where the old man's mixture of grey and black hair used to reach. Busying himself again with the task of coffee, Gil took time to examine what he might look like in a few years time. The old man interrupted his activities occasionally turning his attention to tell Gil something that just had to be true. "I mean, did you hear about this kid and his father? The priest? I mean who would go round shooting a holy man like that?" Gil tried to swallow his surprise, the old man went back to pulling items from the least expected places. "It just isn't right. And you know what, they say they came looking for the kid first. The priest just got it for looking out for his own child." Gil feigned a different kind of surprise. "So you didn't hear, huh? Well, that doesn't surprise me either, cant see no one caring about what goes on around this neck of the woods. Just so long as it doesn't leave that is."

For Gil it was too obvious to go into it, and the old guy seemed a bit worked up over the whole subject. "But as far as work? You're finding it easier, living closer I mean."

"Oh yes, of course. The only thing I would tell you Gil is that I am getting lazier and lazier in my old age. You know I used to complain about dragging all this stuff home, loading it all in the car, driving home and, well, you remember, and now," he lowered his voice and gave a quick conspiring look around, "Now, I cant even be bothered to take it up the stairs. It's a shame though, his voice picked back up to normal pitch, because I used to like sitting with the family, chatting, fixing things and watching the television. Now I end up down here all on my own hollering things up and down the stairs all night." He smiled and shook his head. Half buried, "Funny isn't it."

Gil looked at the old man with a hint of awe, he would have given anything to spend his Monday in the old guy's shoes.

"So how is the old place? I bet it hasn't changed a bit. I should go by one day just for old time's sake." Gil nodded reminiscently.

"And you, Gil? What are you up to? Same old tricks I can tell. I can see it in your eyes."

"Yes, still looking for a way out too." Gil replied reluctantly.

The old man finished the coffee and handed Gil a cup.

"Thanks." They stirred silently for a few moments. "So what was this thing with the priest?"

"Why would you be interested in a thing like that?" The old man began to stare him out but stopped short and added, "Never knew you one as one for a gossiper. Quite the contrary if I remember."

"Me? No, gossip no. Not me, besides who would I tell?" They both laughed, somewhat sadly at the loneliness they both felt.

"Well, it's a strange thing Gil. I'll tell you the story just for that. There's this young lad, bit of a drifter, went to school with my boy. Never met him mind, but you know how you find out about other kids and that. Say he was a quite type, unless you pushed him of course, but still, never had many friends. Always into something different, like he couldn't find his place. Anyway that's all she had the chance to write. Some white boy came stalking through one day like a nazi on a mission, blew that poor kid away. Meantime, his father is the local preacher, he comes out springs the white boy with his boy in a corner, I mean this is so they say, but that was it, the boy shoots his way out leaves them both cold on the street. Leaves without a trace."

"Really?" Gil sipped his coffee, still too hot. "And? He said putting it carefully down on the glass."

"And?" The old man laughed "And shit!" His cheek and neck rolled. "Not one of these fools around here talks to the police. Like some kind of conspiracy of silence. But then you would know that." He gave Gil a knowing look.

"I could have told them, but what do I know, just some white boy. There are plenty of them around. He went on, in fact they came round here, because they went to school together, he and my boy, some boys zipped up tight in their flack jackets, asking me if I had heard anything, I told them it was some white boy, but then they went on asking how I knew it and so on, and all of a sudden I remembered why we don't talk around here much."

"But how did you know he was white?"

"Hehehe… you sound just like they do Gil, why if I didn't know you better!" He stopped laughing, pulled himself serious again and carried on. "It's all politics with these young kids. My son told me he heard it was some white boy when it came on the TV one day, in passing because, you know the demographics of this place. There isn't that many white boys running around with shooter that aren't dressed in blue lights. Apparently some boys from the school had seen a white boy looking for this same kid the same afternoon with the devil in his eyes and the rest of it. And that was me, just trying to help out these lost policemen a little but you tell them something and they don't know how to get off asking you were you found out. As if every police case ends up with the big bang! Anyway, I didn't want to get the kids into trouble so I sealed up, like most parents would I guessed."

"So they haven't arrested anyone?"

"They haven't got anyone to arrest! I seen them dumb cops on the TV, looking all serious saying things like, 'we have several leads to follow up' and 'we are waiting for word from out forensic labs'," the old guy's impressions made Gil laugh, almost forgetting his own charade. He picked up his coffee again and began to sip it.

"They are never going to find out who did it anyway, damn shame if you ask me. I mean, who goes around shooting religious people anyway."

"It's a crazy world."

"You said it." The old guy sipped at his coffee too. "So who was it you were looking for?" He said after a short pause. "But I feel like I keep asking you that. Didn't you tell me or is it that I shouldn't be asking. Don't mind an old man, I don't mean to be nosy or anything."

Gil wasn't minding the intrusion, he was wishing he could think of something to say. The old man didn't mean any harm but that did mean he wouldn't cause any.

"Just an old business associate."

"Ok, Gil, you don't have to say anything else. It's your own business, don't say another word about it. Tell me something else, how's that little basketball team of yours? They all ok?"

"I'll bring champagne the day they are all ok," Gil joked glad of the subject change.

"Still sick huh?"

"You said it. But it's improving slowly, we're down to one at a time now."

"I don't need to tell you not to worry, it's what happens when you have that many."

Gil nodded his head in agreement. They drank in silence again for a few moments, Gil transfixed by the instant darkness of his coffee, the old man by Gil's transfixation.

"Gee, it sure is good to see you Gil," he let out as if he had stopped being able to hold it in. "Thanks for dropping by to see me, I sure do appreciate it. I don't get many visitors nowadays. Hardly ever leave the old place. Not like before when I used to walk in the street at least twice a day. I guess I am getting on."

Gil didn't know what to say so he stuck to the clichés, "Cant be stopped, we all have to face slowing down one day. That's the way I see it."

"It isn't so close for you, the end, I mean, when you are as close as I am and you've already slowed down a little you start to regret it. Start to try and pick things back up, or at least wish you could. Such a shame getting old, don't you think?" Another pause finished. Gil finished his coffee and remembered what he had come to do.

"At least we're getting the chance," he said slightly from the side of his mouth. "I should be going."

The old man laughed a short laugh. Gil got up and gave a look around the workshop, almost every spare piece of space filled with a pile of TVs, stereos, and every manner of electrical item, dusty and piled mainly as high as the ceiling allowed. He comparing the 'to be fixed' with the 'to be sold' piles.

"So how is the business going?"

"Just like you see it. They bring in one to be fixed one week and come back a week later with money to buy a brand new one. Crazy really but I cant complain. All I need is something to do with all this. I just can't bear the thought of throwing it all away."

"Well, maybe I'll drop by when I have some free time see if we cant get them sold."

"Alright then, I'll see you then."

Gil left feeling refreshed, he turned purposefully to the right, continuing his journey, determined to finish what he had come for. He had come away from what was another procrastination with a brand new perspective. As he walked, he wondered exactly how the word Nazi was going to fit into all this. He crossed off over half of his suspect list; Nazi meant he had to be white-white. But it didn't stick to well with Gil. How could it have been a white person?

He considered the school kids; he couldn't go around asking kids in a schoolyard and especially not street kids. It would be too suspicious, not to mention other problems it might bring up. The police wouldn't be the only group of people willing to deal out punishment for this kind of crime. It was, at least, Gil bargained, a last resort.

Gil stopped outside a cab office to finish off the thought then popped his head in the door. "Is Steve around?"

"Nah," the operator replied, "you need a cab?"

"No, I just need a few words with Steve, is he on today?"

"Yeah, he's on his way back, five minutes. I'll tell him you're here. What's your name?"

"Gil." Gil went outside, dug his hands deep into his pockets and watched the sky and the tops of the buildings. The sparse clouds moved gently behind the buildings. He listened to two cab drivers sitting in the front of a cab parked nearby as they read and laughed at things in the newspaper. A cab pulled up behind and the driver leaned to the window "Gil!"

"Steve!" Gil snapped out of his trance with a jolt.

"Come on," the driver signalled Gil to get in. Gil quickstepped around the parked cars and climbed into the passenger seat.

"So what brings you around here old fellow!"

"Don't ask! I actually came to ask a few favours." Gil looked across at Steve, the guy got bigger every time he saw him. He had to crane his neck to see under the window frame, didn't need a seat belt he was pressed against the steering wheel so hard.

"Yeah? His voice matched the depth of his torso, something bothering you?"

"This kid and his priest daddy who got shot somewhere

around here is bothering me."

"Steve didn't say anything in return." Gil felt his heart skip, he had told Steve openly because he was one of the few people he could tell openly. He looked at him now to see why he wasn't saying anything. Steve's face was serious, but the subject was getting the vehicle safely around a corner. They pulled down a narrow residential street packed with parked cars and kids playing in between them.

"So how'd you get mixed in with that?" He finally replied, still not giving much away.

"Mixed isn't the fucking word, I got a cop following me around every other day determined I did it."

"And did you?"

"You know I didn't do it."

"How am I supposed to know that?"

"Because you know it was some white boy." Gil gambled.

"Who you calling a white boy?" Steve laughed and shot Gil a quick glance, still concentrating in a specific route but having moved onto a more freely moving road. "So this cop seriously thinks you did it? Why's that? Stupid is he?"

"I have no idea what's going on in his head, he knows I didn't do it but for some reason he's willing to out his own neck on the block saying I did it. And he's a cop; of course he's stupid."

"Hey! He's not following us around now is he?"

"No, it's his day off."

"Alright then Gil, so what is it you have come looking for?"

"For you to tell me what to start looking for."

"I don't get it, you didn't do it. What are you after exactly?"

"I didn't do it, but I don't know who did."

"And why do you need to know who did it, you're better off not knowing that kind of stuff, you doing the cops job for him?"

"You could say that," Gil said reluctantly.

"Yeah? You mean if I was a cynical bastard." Gil looked at him and they both laughed, although it took Gil a little while longer to crack a smile than Steve. Steve pulled the car to a halt and motioned to the outside of the car. "So, you had lunch yet?"

"No," Gil said feeling the coffee drain form his stomach.

"Good, what do you say to me buying you a slice of pizza? Come one."

Steve levered himself from the car against its frame and strode over to the window, ordering two slices and taking a large bottle of soda from the refrigerator perched in the door way to the house turned pizzeria. He went and sat down at a plastic table where Gil had positioned himself.

"So you're in a bit of a pickle then?"

"To be honest, I don't know, I really don't know what's going to come out of this. But right now I feel like I can't get on with anything until I get on with this. Besides I can't hustle with him following me around, and now I have him threatening me every time he speaks to me."

"Got you by the balls then?"

"Pretty much."

"So why does he want you so badly."

"I wish I knew, I wish I knew," Gil said wistfully.

"Fucking pigs." They sat for a moment contemplating that.

Gil stared Steve out for a moment, it had been a while since they had seen each other, but that happened between them, months without any contact then they could get together as if it had been half an hour.

"So what can you tell me?" Gil asked.

"What else do I know, you're the one playing detective. It was some white boy that's all anyone knows. Anyway how they going to arrest you Gil, you aren't no white boy."

"I was hanging round with the kid, tropical, a few weeks before, running a scam together. He looked me up and bothered me until I let him work with me, it didn't work out too well, kid was a loser if you know what I mean, and that was it."

"I heard he was a loser."

"So you didn't know him then?"

"I knew who he was, everyone knew he was the reverends kid, but I am where I am, and I can't let the squirts hang around me. No offence?"

"No, none taken." Gil let slip even if it wasn't necessarily true.

"It's a damn shame though," Steve offered.

A scrawny young kid came over from the window dragging his thonged feet and bringing pizza. They started eating.

"So, what you need is to find out exactly who did it to get your ass off the red line?"

"Something like that," Gil said between mouthfuls.

"And you need what from me? I don't know who did it. Some white boy is all I heard."

"So you really don't know anything else?" Gil's pizza drooped in anticipation of the answer.

"Gil," Steve's mouth was full of pizza. He swallowed eventually in response to Gil's look of impatience. "Gil, you know how it works, what ever goes on around here its better not knowing things." He paused and looked at Gil, feeling slightly sorry for him he finally broke. "Alright, let me see this afternoon. I know the kids who saw this white boy."

"I heard they saw someone looking for Bill that same afternoon." Gil felt like talking but wished he hadn't.

"That's what they say. Give me this afternoon to find out what I can."

"Thanks, really I mean it."

They ate in silence. When they finished Steve offered Gil a lift home. Gil had to accept, not knowing where they were.

Steve eventually drove him home while listening to Gil's plans to go straight. They talked about getting him a job with the cab firm and maybe even letting Gil drive his cab. They said goodbye and Gil went in to his house, out on his slippers and spent the afternoon sleeping in front of daytime TV.

Paolo spent the rest of the week thinking about Gil, but giving him the space he would need. He could lean on him whenever, but if he did it too much it could go wrong. There was a limit where he would settle for the lesser charges and make a complaint. That would make it very difficult.

He was being pressured by his boss and by his mind. The press barely figured, that was just a small teacup rain shower. But he began to worry about his brother; the bigger picture began to evolve. Once a story has been covered by the media it is on twenty-four-second standby, they can resurrect it when they like. And is brother figured in the bigger picture. Paolo began to wonder how his brother was involved. If it fell apart, if Gil was set up and it fell apart they would all fall, and Paolo and his brother would fall the hardest.

He found it hard to believe there was no connection but still didn't want to bring it up. If he did and the next day Gil either tells him who did it or confesses it would be involving him for no reason. But what if Gil came across the truth and that involved Paolo's brother.

What if Gil already knew? The thickness amongst thieves was the hardest barrier a cop had to face and Gil was the thickest. It didn't appear like it, but he wasn't the kind who played dumb, he was smart enough to soak up the questions and feed the wrong information.

Paolo saw it slipping from his fingers. And worse, he saw it falling into Gil's lap.

Steve called Gil back the same evening to tell him he had

spoken with the kids who had seen the white kid, they had spoken with him in the park the same afternoon, he had been looking for Bill, there had been some kind of fight, Steve didn't know what about, but it didn't seem important. The kids had told the white boy Bill was in the church, the kid looked surprised that Bill would be in a church and that was it he left. They didn't know much else; the white boy had appeared from nowhere then disappeared. They didn't say much about what he looked like, white, skinhead, tall but not huge.

Gil thanked him and told him he owed Steve a new favour, but was told to forget it. He sat back in the armchair he had just woken up from and thought about what new information he had. There wasn't a great deal of information concerning the killer but he did have a better reconstruction in his mind. The white boy comes stealing into the neighbourhood, gets roughed up in the park, putting him in a foul mood and then heads off to find Bill for some reason. That was the key, Gil concluded, the motive. What had he wanted with Bill, old debt or grudge? Was he after money? That was the most obvious thought. The killer must have been some kind of crook, Gil couldn't think outside of that thought. He didn't have the catalogue of criminal faces Paolo might have but still no one came to mind.

He didn't think of any white skinhead, who packed a gun and wandered around executing people. Even if he was some Nazi it seemed unlikely that he would so freely kill a priest. And on top of that he would be hiding behind his group. They love to admit they killed even if they never give up the killer.

Gil wasn't any the wiser when he decided to go to bed, but he would go being somewhat happier than when he had started the day. Things were beginning to swing his way. He thanked Steve for confirming some things and setting him on the right path. Sleeping on it will make it seem clearer Gil reasserted as he switched off the TV; it would do Gil some good too. He walked dreamily into the hallway, switched out the lights and dragged himself up the stairs to where his wife was waiting for him. Albeit it two hours into her night's sleep.

In the bathroom he wondered if his hair had turned a shade greyer, his moustache made a caterpillar motion on top of his teeth brushing, tickling his nose every time it went past the middle. Almost enough aggravation to shave it off he thought, but not quite. His motive? It was the perfecting touch to the cop uniform; it made it so much more official, so much more believable. It was only when he brushed his teeth that it tickled, that was four minutes out of each day, nothing. Perhaps, he wondered, when the new life come into effect it wont be necessary. His toes crunched up inside his slippers as he marvelled at the thought of a new life.

Tuesday was a slow day for Gil. In a change from Monday he was beginning to have two preoccupations. Not making any progress on his mental crime scene video he began thinking about money. The money he had made less than a week and a half ago wasn't going to go much further, he hadn't made a single cent since this policeman had turned up on his doorstep. Not bad, he thought, that it had lasted so long, but not the point. He would have to get out this week somehow.

He mused the offer of becoming a cab driver. He thought also of calling some other favours in, but with the heat on him he didn't need anyone getting in trouble because of him. Nose had to be clean all week.

The one thought that kept coming back was taking up driving a cab, but the reality was a hell of a lot of bureaucracy, which Gil might not get out of the way until he was fit to retire. And gypsy-cab? Well, he didn't have a car for that, so he was a little out of luck.

He ended up in the bus station. It was a deal of shame to deal with, but he could work alone and effectively. Well, within his capability and not somewhere he was new to.

It was many years, though, since he had last been there, even to take a bus. The bus station was the place you honed your hustling skills on tourists and out-of-towners. More like a finishing school than a place to make money. It didn't matter. It was the easiest place and Gil was feeling lazy.

He bought a newspaper and looked around until he found a quiet corridor. Sitting down on a row of chairs made without their end purpose in mind he took out a pocket-knife and some notes from his pocket. He put the Bills on the newspaper and cut around them. When he had cut out several hundred money sized slips of newspaper he rolled them up and put the real money on the outside and stuck a rubber band around it, making it look like a big bundle of cash.

Standing up he threw away the rest of the newspaper and checked through his pockets. He was wearing a long light brown trench coat over a white shirt but no tie. He went to the toilets to check his appearance in the mirror. Good, he thought, too fucking old for the bus station, but its easy money. His professionalism returned. He told himself how good he was, how very few people can do this alone, on a whim in pretty much any place. Doesn't matter where you are, if you walk away and in pocket there is no problem. The thoughts of Paolo, the unknown white boy and all the drama washed away with the tide of the chase. He was a lion, he chose his prey from the heard, spot a weak one and show your teeth to the rest.

He made several circuits of the bus station on a semi-reconnaissance. It was a huge building, with several floors, built into the side of the hill with escalators, lifts and stairs going in all directions. A nightmare for the first time traveller. Locals buzzed around, up and down from arrival platforms to departure gates and taxi ranks, in and out of little stores and eateries. There were a few security on patrol, but no police. Gil was too old and dressed to respectably to be kicked out for loitering.

It was busy for a Tuesday, making the security staff thinly spread on the ground. Gil buzzed around, picking good spots and cut off points rushing from the nostalgia and the adrenalin.

He thought of the dirty cop, where was he at that moment? In the station? Unlikely he hadn't seen him on the way. Perhaps outside Gil's house waiting for him to come home. Perhaps sense has finally penetrated the thickness of his skull and he has given up the goose chase. He shook the nice thoughts and concentrated.

He picked a young kid, looking completely out of place. Could even be from the exterior, Gil thought. Easy prey. A good place to start. Gil watched him from the level above the ticket offices, the kid got passed along from one window to another, eventually buying a ticket and lugging his huge backpack towards the escalators. Gil made a circuit, going down to the same level on the escalators, walked past the top of the next escalator passing the kid's back and made the next descent on the stairs. He almost slid down the stairs and came out perfectly facing the kid with a gap of about ten metres. He was close now, he could see his acne and braces, a teenager now doubt. Gil hesitated for a second but decided he would do it anyway. He knocked into the teenager.

"Hey," Gil looked at the teenager, who had spun around to apologise, "You dropped something." Gil pointed down to the bundle of cash and newspaper he had just dropped on the floor. The teenager just stared at him, it was generally quite on this level, but it must have been nearing the hour as the flow of people was picking up.

"You dropped something." Gil reiterated to snap the teenager out of his trance.

The teenager looked down, his eyes brightened.

"Well, is it yours?" Gil turned on the pressured voice.

The teenager started to shake his head, but couldn't speak. Gil lent down and picked it up.

"Come with me," Gil grabbed the teenager by his shirt sleeve and pulled him out of the flow of people, down a little corridor towards a janitors cupboard. Once it was quiet and they were out of sight Gil fingered through the bundle.

"So, it's not yours?"

The teenager shook his head.

"You want to split it?"

The teenager nodded his head.

"Well, if that is the case son, I have some bad news for you." Gil reached into his trench coat pocket and pulled out a black wallet. The teenager swallowed hard.

"I am a police officer, Gil flashed a fake police ID, and by agreeing to take some of this money, you have committed a crime."

The teenager's eyelids nearly came through the back of his head. He swallowed again, completely bemused by the quick turn of events; he felt his asshole go tight. He looked down at the ID, but that could have been cut-up newspaper as far as he would have known.

"You got some ID, kid?"

The teenager pulled out his wallet from his jeans pocket, it was attached by a chain to his belt loops.

"What's the chain for, son, so you don't get it stolen or is it a fashion thing nowadays," Gil joked with him, sliding deeply into his character. The kid slowly began to open the wallet, his hands shaking. Gil nodded his head and put his hand out. "Give it here."

Taking the wallet he flicked it open and help some various different photo ID's against the teenager's face. He took a sizeable stack of cash out of the wallet at the same time as saying, "Danny, I am going to let you go this time."

Waving the cash as a warning, folding it and then tucking it into the back pocket of his trousers allowing the teenager to swallow again at the sight of the wooden handle of the pistol holstered on Gil's belt.

"Think your self lucky this time! Now go on, you'll miss your bus. The kid put his wallet back in his jeans and scurried off. Gil followed him closely, making sure he knew he was being followed. Once the kid was on the bus and the bus had left, Gil turned around and walked back into the heart of the station. Easy money," he said to himself, stupid kids.

He stood on the next level against a glass window watching the bus mounting the highway. He took the cash from his pocket, expecting it to be a lot, he licked a thumb on his bottom lip and counted it, but not that much. Leaving the bottom lip out he nodded his head in approval. Time to go home, then. He smiled and decided he would take a taxi.

Gil whittled his Tuesday away; he thought of the bus station scam of the previous day, he considered his character, his 'Gil the Police Officer', as some kind of oasis. As if there he could get away from the tediousness, the aridity and the inefficient struggle of life and as if it were an added bonus, he could drink the modern water of life, money. There were no problems when he was acting, it was a play, scripted, directed and even prompted. All that mattered was the size of the applause.

But as Gil wasted the day away in his living room, he came to another conclusion, that he preferred the desert. He couldn't understand why, but he did.

Paolo was spending his Wednesday 'on the case.' He was unaware of the shared nature of his first thought that morning. The next ironic similarity was that for both of them it meant sitting down. Paolo sat in his car outside Gil's house. If Gil had left the house Paolo could have molested him, but he wouldn't leave. It worked for Paolo. Molesting Gil was like scratching a rash: it felt good but wasn't going to heal things. For a few hours in the morning Paolo watched Gil through a small gap in the curtains of the house. He went to lunch and came back to find the scene unchanged. He wondered to himself briefly whether it was some kind of cardboard cut out and Gil had escaped through the back door. But it wasn't; unfortunately it wasn't. Paolo set as his afternoon target not knocking on the door. Leaving him alone and just watching. Thursday was the day for bothering him.

So this was Wednesday for both of them. The midpoint of the week, the peak and the trough. Sat in deadlock each protected from the real world by thin sheets of glass and minds full of thought. Gil in his home, in the company of his kids. Paolo in his car with the company of peanuts and coffee.

Paolo sat with a pile of files on his lap and on top of that his notebook. He flicked through the pad reviewing scribblings and 'to-dos'. He came across an underlined note that read '<u>white Nazi</u>'. It had a name next to it. It was the name of a police officer he had spoken to at some point in the last week, they had handed him a report at his desk and mentioned something about someone having witnessed a white male in the area the same day as the murder. The officer had been on a detail to interview all known friends and associates of the kid and the priest. He dug out the file and read through the reports. There was nothing there, but the cover page of the report mentioned 'a large quantity of unsubstantiated and unreliable' evidence and witness reports.

Paolo looked up, leaving the files in his lap, and took a good look at the quarter portion of Gil's head. It moved in and out of sight as he lent back and forward. Was Gil white? Given he wasn't a Nazi, but you don't have to kill a lot of black people to get that label. Paolo picked up a small pair of binoculars and shot a quick look towards the house. It didn't make it any clearer.

He questioned himself objectively, what would you say when some asked you? Perhaps white, he looked up Gil's surname, but that gave even less clues.

He looked up again and found Gil laughing; he guessed so by the movement of his head and shoulders. What an injustice, Paolo chastised himself.

Going back to thinking about Gil's race, Paolo examined his own face in the rear view mirror. Pulling to face him and closing in on it himself too. Paolo knew his racial roots, his skin was a light olive colour, and he was that as he examined it, but he never recalled having been called anything in reference to his skin colour. He concluded that he would call himself white. If someone saw him from a distance they would call him white. He looked back to Gil and asked himself again, objectively, would they call him white. The answer he kept giving himself was no. And what about in a black neighbourhood? Would they call Gil white? Perhaps. He made a note to speak with the other officer. To clarify things.

He began to consider how he could use this description. Did it work for him or against him, could he manipulate it? Was there a witness somewhere? All the notes went in to the pad pushed against the steering wheel. Paolo sat afterwards staring blankly into the rear of the red car parked in front of him, chewing the plastic cap of his disposable pen.

His thought train was heading along neutral tracks. He had begun to review this case with a more mature and detective like approach. A careful and objective review of the facts and semi-facts. Thoughts of crookedness had momentarily climbed into the back seat.

In control of an objective mind, Paolo questioned himself over his thirst for Gil. Why did he resent him so much? What did Gil have that was so beautiful he had made it a life mission to destroy? It was clear to Paolo in that moment that destruction was the exact description of what he wanted to do to Gil. He wanted to destroy his life.

Leaving this brief moment of clarity Paolo could feel two things, firstly that his inner rage had been stirred from its slumber and secondly, and very close to overwhelmingly, a sense of self-pity.

The answer was not there, he knew he wanted to destroy Gil, but he couldn't establish why. Instead, he became entangled in the larger question. The part of his personality that allows him to destroy people's lives and had allowed him to do the things he had done in the past.

He looked over to check on Gil, he sat motionless, watching TV Paolo supposed.

Paolo made a list of his motives. Sometimes he did the wrong thing to make the job easier, that was applicable here, he kidded himself. Sometimes for favours, to make life easier, or to make the job easier in the long run, that was the converse here; this would make everything in the future difficult, even dealing with the never-ending consciousness. Sometimes he did the wrong thing in the spare of the moment, instinctually.

Was it laziness, perhaps, but if it was why pick that job, why pick a job where you cant be lazy. Perhaps he wasn't lazy when he took the job; perhaps the job had made him lazy. The thought spiralled out of control sucking into far too many character flaws for Paolo's ego to handle. Picking out one thought he concentrated on a girl he was seeing. She was one of the so-called moral infractions. He thought about her because he would go and see her that evening. He thought about having sexual intercourse with her and lying with her afterwards. He thought about her because, despite being part of what he didn't want to think about, it was better than thinking directly about it. He had worked very hard on dissociating the circumstances through which the relationship was initiated with its continuance.

Wednesday's head was never going to have been a quiet place, and Paolo's mind soon moved on from its pleasurable hopes. He thought of his brother. Randomly as it seemed there was a deeper reason for having made the connection. Mainly relating to shame. He hadn't spoken to his bother since the case had started, so he wouldn't end up questioning him over his involvement. Paolo, being a little brother, was good at keeping secrets, the girl he had just been thinking about was a perfect example. If his brother had found out Paolo was most likely have been pressured out of the relationship by the family and not just because of the circumstances but also on general principle.

Paolo had his confrontation speeches planned, various episodes of confrontation, and confession down to deathbed. There was no way the secrets would get out, Paolo was too professional in covering his tracks for that to happen.

Gil was having his own thought patterns. He had been laughing as Paolo had suspected, laughing at his children's antics. The older two were dressing up the youngest. The third being in bed, ill and missing the fun. They had found Gil's old costumes from the time when he was a kid and used to dress up and act for his own entertainment. Gil had been an only child and had therefore taken to this kind of performing. He used to dress up, first, in his father's suit, pretending to be a businessman, bank manager or someone important, feeding his lifetime aspirations of the time. And the hobby developed from there.

It put Gil into a trance. What had happened over the last thirty years? A lot had happened, that was accepted, but was he going to let it keep happening. What was going to happen to his kids? They thought he was a police officer. They were too young then to realise the truth, but one day they would. What would he tell them then? A stroke of panic inflated his chest, as if it was the first time the consequences had occurred to him.

Of course it wasn't the first time the consequences had arisen, but it was just another sign, that Thursday afternoon, telling him to change. The same goal as Monday with a different motivation. He should be shielding his kids from lies, protecting them from ending up in a similar state of affairs one day. He would be shielding them from the problems he was facing in that moment; it brought the reality back to Gil.

He needed to change. The impulse was so strong his body moved. I can change, he told himself, I will change. He could go straight, get a regular job and make honest money. The only problem that he was left with was would he make enough money to keep the family afloat? How much does it take to keep a family of six above water, he had never done that maths, it was generally you go out and work when there is no money. He didn't keep track of it, different days different pays, was his slogan.

Would his wife be able to get a job too? Perhaps she could get a part time job to start. Together surely there would be enough. Thoughts of doing something together, setting up a business together filtered through Gil's brain. But the process was stopped again by Bill. Why had Bill been killed? Sure, he was a pain in the ass, but who gets killed for being a pain in the ass. What made it worse that even after his death he continued being a pain in the ass.

Gil took a mental step back and realised nothing could be done until he had sorted out Bill's murder. It pained him to think it, because two weeks ago, had he thought about it, he was the master of his own destiny. A man who could have picked up the pen and signed the paper to change his life. Selling his soul to the anti-devil. Buying it back perhaps.

He balanced his thoughts out by convincing himself it was a process, one bit at a time, he had been in possession of the goal for a long time and he had acquired the motivation, all that remained was the timing.

Then he could start fresh. A youthful rejuvenation free of crooked cops fake or real. No more scourging it, no more side-lines of the underworld. No more Bill's or bus stations. No more scams in city squares.

Gil's mind clicked into place, and from nowhere a face clicked into his mind.

With every day that passed I said to myself, Sammy, with everyday that passes, you're helped a step closer to freedom. I guess that one day I would walk so far I wouldn't be able to remember what I was walking away from. That line was a good goal, but it remained for the two weeks directly after my little, let's call it a, mistake, a distant goal.

I did however rediscover my passions which were more like two months lost. I got back to watching people from park benches and Raffael's windows. My telephone, once again, went quiet and I even indulged myself in some marijuana, to take the edge off things. The next item on my life's agenda at this point was a hospital visit, but it was almost more distant than the next item on my 'to-do' list!

So my life had returned to being obstacle free. The slight possibility of anything cropping up diminished with each day.

I took to seeing Raffael as my liberator, not a mentor or role model by any means, but a man who had done something good for another person. Without him I would still be suffering under the fear and loathing aftermath of my incident with Tropical Bill and his cop friend.

The first day I walked into his coffee shop he greeted me with a knowing smile. Not giving a single thing away, but he did little to deny the knowledge. Or at least that was how it seemed. It was how I had wanted it, a topic of non-discussion. It reassured me that if he wouldn't talk to me about it, he was unlikely to with anyone else. One more loose end tied and sealed and Raffael wasn't the kind of rope to fray.

On top of his character, Raffael was still deep in his own circumstance, or so he told me, he was past the point of losing the business and onto the point of just having to make concessions. He added we all have to do that and because of that, he wasn't so upset any longer. The thought of having to start fresh I assumed would have made upset him.

So, I tried very hard, but in vain, to repay my liberator somehow. From the way he reacted to my efforts I began to wonder that if I explained it to him slowly in words of less than three syllables he still would have not accepted my thanks. Regardless I made the efforts and he understood whatever it was that he understood. We could rely on each other in that frame of mind.

I did consider at some point whether he was trying to offer me a job, not being the most direct person ever to speak it was never clear. I thought about whether I would except it until I realised that he was about to employ an ex-murderer like I was about to confess. Especially when he was implicated in the murder, somehow, I was sure, at least it made me feel better to think I wasn't in it alone.

So, as it was I dropped by for a coffee at least once a day, had a chat with Raffael ask after business and current luck and make idle chat when it was quiet. I sat and analogised the last few months of our lives, he had found out about how his business had been run into the ground around the same time I'd had my incident with Bill. We both suffered during the initial period after that, then we had somehow managed to get along. To live with our grief for those months that had passed in between. Then the same week I, let's say disposed, of my problems, Raffael is back on two feet and taking the punches with a wink and a smile. I had no idea how he had hoisted himself out of Frankie's hole, but he had and he wasn't about to tell anyone, not directly at least. But it gave me another thing to speculate.

I postulated the philosophy of lives inextricably linked and that of lives following their own pre-planned destinies. Raffael had stepped in, in the middle of probably the most hectic period of his life, to help me out and do me a favour. I am sure it didn't take him a lot of man-hours or money, but he took time away from his life to make the decision to do it. That I guessed came from empathy. I hadn't owed him anything, nor him me, and it even continued that way.

I watched him, never enquiring to whether I owed him anything, but the image that always prevailed was one of pure balance, almost of forget. I waited with unknown patience for an opportunity to do something, but it never came up.

Autumn blossomed, people in the street smiled catching all of the last hot rays. Life was not only buoyant but in abundance. To say that my life was free of worry, nerves or anxiety would be a slight fabrication. From time to time remorse came, either in the shape of a bad dream or a flashback. At other times paranoia visited, generally if I had been smoking, but sometimes also in the faces of the world. I would see in a complete stranger in the street, a facial feature of either Bill, his dad or the unidentified cop. My fear of police officers didn't see any downward turns. I resigned to thinking it never would and quickly filed it alongside breathing, taxes and teeth brushing.

The feeling that someone else was in control had always been with me, the first week after the 'mistake' reinforced that. The flashbacks and dreams were like little reminders. Like remembering a something you learnt at school out of the blue, still not having any application for it but feeling spirited for having remembered it. I wasn't going to do it again, so I started telling myself the reminders were harmless.

It was a very euphoric state to reach in such a short space, but I guessed that I had been storing up a lot of philosophy and not contemplating it. I was no longer in control, I could make the decisions, but it didn't matter which one it took, the choice had already been made for me. That seemed quite strange at first appearance, but once I had mulled it over for a few days, I realised how much easier it makes life. Everything became clear, no decision was ever going to cause worry or stress. Only when you see the no wrong decision can be made, that the consequence is not important or not your responsibility, can you make decisions about important things. Similarly afterwards you could relax in the heavy mist that wasn't regret. Occasionally picking the odd lesson here or there from hindsight. Consigning it to memory and then moving on.

It was something like the Buddhist teaching of the way. To me I called it freedom, mental freedom. And it was a necessary element to peace of mind and to enjoying life.

With this kind of freedom I had regained the ability to walk in the city (other's may prefer a walk in the country, but I did that when I was a kid), walk and enjoy the river, the bridges that spanned it, the buildings, the little quirks in life that no one pays attention to when the rent is due. Like traffic lights changing when there is no traffic and the ant like movement of our species on the larger scale. The people, the faces, the twenty-four neon lights. The entire world would see all these things if only they stopped worrying about their lives.

My life also slowed, instead of waiting for the season to change, I felt like I was just waiting for the month or the week to end. Like a train passing through a station but not stopping, so too my life decided that even though no planned stop was scheduled it was better to take things easy and not rip anyone off the platform and suck them under my carriage. It gave me time to react and others time to get out of the way, I guess that was what Raffael was doing in not talking about what had happened.

So I watched a milestone in my life flutter by the windows of the coffee shop carriage, what the milestone was I couldn't see from my position on the planet, but I was strong in the faith that the heavenly signal controllers had a pretty good idea.

The smaller scale of life was affected to. The smaller decisions were no longer decisions. There was no further: which fork is the right fork for this meal? Which brand and odour of soap or deodorant? The choice of movie or book. Fate became my guide. Life became, in the most simple form, simpler.

If the current decision had no consequence, of serious consequence, then there was no need to thing about the decision. Conversely, if the decision did have serious consequence, a step back had to be taken, and a judgement made on whether the decision had to be made at all.

In trying to list these changes it was clear that there is a lack in the quantity. It was as if nothing real had changed, just the way I would see it. My routine remained, give or take a little, the same, yet every choice was no longer a cause for stress. Nothing reflected on me any longer. The factors of life remained, unaffected; my actions and behaviours, my tastes, my turn-ons and turn offs.

Although this would make a good ending, my inner peace not only restored but enlightened, it makes bad on the moral side of things. The murder the problems out of your life maybe good when you have a conscience as wipe-clean as I do. Whether that is reality or semi-reality is not the issue, I would argue that yes, finding this kind of freedom is a possibility for anyone. What it doesn't do is solve the problems of the social matrix we have woven ourselves into. The abundance of wrongs and rights, so much black and so little white. We can no longer see the door of the room from where we are: stuck in the corner we'd painted ourselves into and no longer open to debate the issue of murder.

The value of the story I feel is here already, but the events that took place so soon after this epiphany of mine doing nothing if they don't underline the important issues. And if they do then they also serve as worth reading, because two weeks later life span back out of control. The train left the station and the driver forgot to warm his passengers to strap themselves back in.

I had been too busy enjoying the simplicity of life to notice the complexity. My philosophising over life's inextricably linked lives was not thought through to the end but probably interrupted by some near miss involving angry car drivers or the passage of a blonde showing off her long legs with forceful strides. I had thought about the detectives finding me, because I knew who did it, I had no idea they would try and find someone else, I hadn't really thought it through. And when it dawned on me, it stung. Fortunately, I had been smoking that afternoon and it helped to take the away the sharpness of the sting. Nevertheless, the blunt side of the knife is far from safe.

Raffael's week was quite quiet in relation to some that had recently passed him by at a high speed. And particularly so compared to that of his brother and then man Raffael had no idea he was chasing. Moreover, Raffael was ignorant to all of it. His coffee shop was on the road to recover now, it was not longer in intensive care but well on its way to being a day patient. Nothing out of the ordinary happened, if you discount broken cups and one customer covered in hot coffee. He had been somewhat disturbed by the news item concerning and priest and his son being executed in an alleyway, but the name William meant nothing and the coincidence passed without anything clicking. Raffael didn't think that he knew anyone who executed people, especially priests, not even his brother. The kind of thing Frankie would do, he was easily capable of getting Holy

Communion wrong, but Raffael's wife would have heard and that meant he would have known.

It bothered Raffael more thinking that about his brother than his son. It even put him into thinking that he hadn't heard from him in a while, the thought he might be working on the same case came one evening while Raffael was cleaning down the tables, but there was still nothing there.

Of course Raffael had no circumstance that would have made him recognise the stranger who walked into the coffee shop late Friday evening; late but still busy. Raffael greeted him politely but welcomingly and served him coffee and paid no further notice. As far as he was concerned it was just another customer. Another passer-by come in to rest his feet and examine the world as it rushed by the window.

Raffael stood cleaning and shining cutlery, staring over the strangers head also towards the multitude, not seeing individual people just a train of evacuation. He consoled himself with his love of his coffee shop. To want to leave, even by Friday afternoon defeats the point of coming on a Monday. The sad irony of it was that by the time Wednesday came around they are soaked up their gratefulness of being granted time off that they forget they imprison themselves voluntarily. It was time off to Raffael, doing this, he looked at the five spoons he had in his hand, stopping before he polished the last one. What he was doing at that exact moment was time off. He didn't need a weekend, being in the shop was relaxing, it was happiness.

Raffael had opened at weekends, generally on a whim, but weekends were for sin, and Raffael's weekend sin was sitting down. Not being in his feet was pure weekend pleasure. That Friday evening he was thinking about enjoying weekend of sin.

His train of thought went to his son, Frankie, what would he be doing at the weekend? Not visiting daddy that's for sure. Raffael felt the first pluck of the Frankie heart string this episode. Maybe the wounds were beginning to heal, he cheered himself with the prospect. He couldn't be mad at him forever, it didn't work like that in his family. He pushed the thought a little further in surmising perhaps it had been the long awaited licking Frankie needed.

Raffael laughed at the thought, coming out of his trance, he looked at the reality passing the window and let out a second laugh and shook his head, smiling.

Gil knew who the murderer was. He didn't know how he knew, he would have to see him for that. He wasn't entirely one-hundred per cent sure either, he would have to confront the murderer for that.

The thought scared him a little, the face he had in his mind was one that didn't like to be trapped. He remembered his face so close to that Friday evening. He had seen an animal backed into a corner and the incredible strength they can summon when their freedom is threatened.

Gil had been scared that night too, so he couldn't work out why he was apprehensive. Gil found it strange that this young lad had set out to kill Bill and not even bother to find himself. He worried that was next, the white nazi would come stalking though his neighbourhood like a black ninja and leave him bloody on the side walk. Perhaps the reason he found himself in the coffee shop in this kids neighbourhood was because he was being drawn into a trap. The kid was clever enough to work out they were both part of the set up after all.

Gil didn't understand much but his mind was set on locating him, he reassured himself he was in control and set himself firm on finding out who this kid was, where he lived, why he had felt so trapped and why he killed Bill. How had he even found Bill and where did he get the balls to kill him?

That Friday afternoon, in the unsuspecting coffee shop none of the answers came to Gil, just more questions and more doubts. Would he recognise the kid, was his mental image of him warped by other peoples descriptions of him? What would Gil do when he found him, wouldn't the kid just run away again? It was like the school crush, knowing the person you fancied the most, but then getting so physically close to them just to speak changed the entire perspective. You can see them close too, you forget the best thing you had planned to say, it was a situation that required composure.

The irony of the situation was that Sammy didn't walk into Raffael's coffee shop that Friday evening while Gil was using it as an observation post. Life for everybody would likely have been much easier.

During this time, as if some unknown force was penetrating Gil's mind, he discovered the idea that linked the two unwritten chapters in his mind. The one titled what do I do when I find the murderer and the one what do I do with him. The cop deserved to go down, even if Gil was dragged with him. He knew he wouldn't, he could work around that, but the fact this was going to symbolise the end of his badly drawn career meant to Gil that he should gout with fireworks. The thought flashed repeatedly through his mind, "Let's use this opportunity to teach the fucking pig cop a lesson." And every time it went through it gave Gil the satisfying feeling that it would keep him smiling for the rest of the straight life he had been planning all week.

The feeling would satisfy him all weekend, all Friday night with its endless pursuit, Saturday and its lazy but fruitful search and all the way to Sunday afternoon when he would knock on the murderers door.

It disguised the stress; it disguised the worry that was eating away at his insides. He was so accustomed to controlling his nerves he didn't see the endless questions knotting themselves in his brain. The thoughts of a new life, of finding and approaching a murderer, setting up a cop and generally having his life changed either for good or for worse.

It wasn't invisible, it was the grey in his face, the acid in his stomach, the pain in his neck and shoulders. He just didn't relate the two. The dim light at the end of the road too bright to challenge the stamina needed to get there.

The light outside, however, was getting dimmer, the stronger lights of the coffee shop beating the dull hum of the street lights, turning Gil's window into a mirror. He got up and paid realising that he was the last customer and that they were waiting for him to leave. The owner didn't look impatient and gave him the change with a broad smile. Gil wandered around in vain for twenty minutes or so before going home. Friday night was a working weekday for Gil, but he decided instead to take some unused holiday time.

Friday evening had been beckoning Paolo with a bony finger. He had achieved nothing all week and without knowing why had a feeling the case was slipping. The invisible quantities of information, frustration and direction seemed to have exclusive ownership rights. Leaking out of Paolo's unguarded head leaving him without his sense of control. He had spent the last few hours of his week snapping at people and slamming telephones down. He had little concept of how far ahead Gil was advancing on the information battlefield nor that they were at loggerheads on the stress battlefield. Perhaps if he had known the latter he could make some gains. Paolo was, however, fully aware of his stress levels.

His boss walked in, "Paolo," he began before sitting down, "I guess you aren't going to like or even agree with what I am going to say to you, but you don't seem to be getting anywhere with this priest case. And you know its not an everyday case."

The bad effects of the week coiled up inside Paolo, he

could feel a period of shouting deep in his chest. He liked his boss less that usual when he was being patronising.

"Come on! Leave me alone," it wasn't quite shouting but it released some pressure. "It's not like it's me, there is nothing on this case, one suspect, no weapon, I got," Paolo moved towards some papers on his desk but fell back into his chair and sighed.

"Look, you know what I have and don't have, and why it's not leading me anywhere, so why are you coming in and busting my balls about it?"

"I told you. It's because it's an important case." Paolo's boss relaxed a little into the chair disguising a smile.

Paolo sat up, checking himself, "So what is it that you would like me to do?"

"Have you thought about handing the case over?"

Paolo shuffled uneasily, knowing he was getting at something else. "No, I hadn't, but I err..." He hadn't thought about it, didn't want to and as he did briefly he realised he didn't want to, not because he hadn't done it before but because he was after all protecting someone. The thought of his brother being in a bad mood with him was the worst outcome, by a long way.

"Well, I want you to at least consider it. I don't want you off the case, it wouldn't look good, and I am not going to force you off it either. It's more for your own good, you know. Why don't you give it a thought over the weekend?"

Paolo checked himself again. His boss looked like a huge Mickey Mouse doll blocking his way down a dark alley in the middle of a chase scene from a nightmare predator. "So, you aren't going to set me one of your famous deadlines then?" Paolo laughed as genuinely as he could, but a little too loudly. Paolo kicked himself in anticipation.

"Well, I wasn't, but if you think it will help?" His grey eyebrows raised making his eyes bulged. He raised his arms behind his head smiling, revealing half dry salt lakes in his pale blue shirt, disguising for the first time the grey rug his chest sported.

Paolo fought against the physical urge to be sick. "No, I need some new perspective, not more fucking pressure."

His boss's arms came down and his smile disappeared. "I didn't mean it like that," he defended himself somewhat with the palms of his hands. "Tell me what it is that you need and let's see where we are by this time next week. Sound good?"

"What do you mean we can see where we are? What's that if it's not a fucking deadline?"

"You're right, Paolo, I'm sorry. But at least tell me if I can pool some resources on this."

"What I really need you can't get me." He needed another analytical mind, but at the same time didn't need what one might uncover.

"And what is it?"

Paolo's turn to patronise. "Let's see. Some evidence, some witnesses. Someone who can torture everyone in this godforsaken neighbourhood into talking. The only new lead I have was fucked up by some uniform asking too many questions. But that's the bigger problem. That's your problem to pass on."

"I know, I know. It's not your job but it's your problem. Don't forget I have been in your shoes. You know the first job I had in that neighbourhood was a shooting in a nightclub? I ever tell you that one?"

Paolo humbly shook his head not remembering him having told him any stories.

"Crazy!" He laughed a little. "Three kids come barging into a club, long gone now, probably turned into some TV church, anyway, one shooter and two big fellows to push the crowd for him. And it was a crowd, it was five hundred capacity and probably overfilled. Some famous jazz singer or blues musician, not the details you look for really. Anyway, these three came barging through to take out, so it seemed, one guy, who was part of the band. No one knows what for, what he had done, just seemed random. So by the time I arrived, the uniforms had managed to get about three-hundred names and there was at least one-hundred who weren't walking anywhere. I guess we missed about two-hundred people, but what difference would it make. We interviewed every last name on the list. Four hundred and thirty something people. And you know what they all said? And I mean four hundred and twenty something people."

He waited for Paolo to give some kind of answer.

"'You see, officer, I didn't see what happened because I was in the toilet at the time'. And we checked the toilets and there sure as hell wasn't room for two-hundred people in either of them."

Paolo shook his head, nothing had changed and nothing would.

"You see Paolo, it's a layer of bullshit, it's not the truth. It took me several tries to get through it and I hate preaching to you about it but you have to break through. Especially with this one."

Paolo nodded accedingly.

"It may have died out of the media, but the church and the head shed haven't finished having their puppies over it yet."

"Don't worry, I'll get it done." There was a personal tone in Paolo's voice. He looked at his boss through lying eyes, they should have been I fucking hate you eyes. You're the most straight cop in the world and you know I am bent so why don't you fucking hate me eyes. You should have me fired, with your bald head, your fake fucking smile and your sweaty fucking shirt. Why did I end up with you, why couldn't I have landed a boss slightly sly?

He imagined the outcome of using his crookedness to get back at his boss. He would feel better for it; more in control and above his boos fro doing so. It soothed him, a brief thought with no reality, adding a glaze to the world. Once the boss left he could think of a good way to do it.

"Good, that's what I like to hear. Listen. Why don't you take some time out this weekend? Don't think too hard about it. Play some golf or something to get your mind off it. Perhaps that'll bring you the fresh perspective you need." Paolo's boss wished him a good weekend and went out leaving Paolo to contemplate whether the last remark was patronising or not. Fresh perspective was the detectives second wind. What they used to tell each other as a means of support and good hope. Sometimes it showed up, and even fewer times it helped.

"So what if he was being honest or patronising," Paolo said once his boss was out of range. He went back to the euphoric thought long enough for him to connect it to his overbearing reality. It was so obvious, getting clean away with sending the wrong man to court would seal the euphoria.

He had the means and the lack of morality. He had also written off the fresh perspective with his perseverance of Gil. There was no way he could believe it was anyone else even if they came in and confessed. So what if he wasn't white, that little detail wasn't going to make as far as the courts. And by that time, the lawyers would have their hands all over the shitty end of the Gil stick.

He looked around the office. Another week wasted. Lost somewhere between obsession and laziness. He questioned himself along the lines of why does the dirtiest cop work the latest. He didn't wait around for someone to phone with the answer. He picked up his jacket, his keys, sorted the file into a folder and picked it up, a pen. He paused and threw the folder back down. He then picket it up again and leafed through it, eventually pulling out a note which he added to his wallet. He switched off the lamp over his desk, put his jacket on and blindly searched his way out of the dark set of offices.

He mulled over the prospect of talking with his brother,

the fresh perspective would do him good. Besides there was no guarantee that it would go away if Gil did. There was the grand possibility that Paolo would still want to know who did it. And the case may even come back to him. He had an armoury of reasons not to talk to his brother, his avoidance was at the top of the list. You could find a million ways to tell him something and all he would do is find a million related or unrelated other things to tell you. Paolo decided his brother lacked directness. And worse, if he had to label it, honesty. The reason he got away with it? Probably years of practice. Paolo would leave conversations not feeling angry because he wasn't given the information he had wanted, but frustrated he couldn't think of the angle that would have released it or purely in awe of what must be one of the planets greatest bull-shitter.

Raffael's wife knew he was a bull-shitter. And he liked it that way. So when he arrived home that Friday evening he did so safe in the knowledge that by the time he hung his coat up he wouldn't have been pressed for information, and by the time he washed his hands he wouldn't have been pressed for information and by the time he went to bed he wouldn't have been pressed for information.

Raffael's wife only greeted him on Fridays, in some kind of blind revenge. This Friday he challenged it. "Why don't you greet me everyday, why only Fridays?"

"I don't know, why have you never asked me before?" Raffael sighed the sigh of a successful teacher.

"I made you raviolis," she said raising her eyebrows suggestively.

"You're amazing," Raffael said trying hard to hide his happiness, I've never had a wife so easy to keep happy. Raffael emptied the contents of his pockets on to a table in the hallway and answered the phone.

"Pronto!" His wife went happily back to the kitchen.

"Paolo! Where are you? Yes, I can hear you are in the car,

little brother, but where exactly? Well, why don't you come over? Homemade raviolis going to persuade you? We can talk about that when you get here, come on, I know I am in a good mood tonight, so? I don't care, just come on over." The conversation went on like this until Raffael finally hung up on the words "I am not going to talk to you on the phone anymore, if you need to talk to me do it man to man."

He wandered into the kitchen. "There's enough for my brother to eat, right?"

"There is always enough for your brother, besides," she turned around and pinched his stomach, "you don't need to eat it all."

"You're a funny woman, I don't think I have ever had a wife so funny."

They were still at it when they heard a car pull up outside. "There's my brother, let me go let him in." He kissed his wife quickly and made for the front door. He stood proudly over his green lawn, miniature hedges and concrete path, waiting, the calmness of the neighbourhood destroyed only by the roar of insects.

"How come you never call me," Raffael announced to the street as his brother mounted the kerb.

"What do you mean? I just did," was the reply, as he got closer he lowered his voice. "And besides, what kind of way is that to greet your brother?"

"Ok, but you haven't called me for two weeks."

"You have a telephone too, it makes outgoing calls?"

"It takes incoming ones, that's for sure."

"Anyway I have been busy with this priest case."

"Yeah I heard about it? How did you end up with it?"

"What' that supposed to mean?"

"What I don't understand, Raffael changed the subject only very slightly, is why it's the priest case. I can't imagine they set out to kill his holiness first. And are you ignoring the kid?"

"What do you mean?"

"Like there is more kudos behind the priest's death and no one cares about his son."

"You watch too much TV at work. Besides the kid was a shit bag, he did deserve to die."

"You watch too much death."

"Don't joke about it. It's not that funny. Seeing dead people isn't something you ever get over."

"So what do you know about it?" Raffael said changing the subject for what already seemed like the millionth time.

"What do I know about what? Dead bodies?"

"No, the priest."

"And his son?"

"Yeah!" Raffael was playing upset.

"Nothing, not a god damn thing? What do you know about it?"

"Nothing?"

"So why are you breaking my balls?"

"Because you're my kid brother. So I take it that it's going badly?"

"Yeah, but why you so interested all of a sudden? Not the first black kid to be killed this year."

"Did you forget your religion, leave it in the car perhaps?"

"I've got littler fish to fry, you worry about yours and I'll worry about mine. Talking of which you up to defending that little squit's actions yet?"

"When are you getting a new car? This one's starting to look a little old," Raffael pointed out to the street hiding yet another smile.

"When I crash this one… I don't have too many high-speed chases at the moment."

"Let's go inside."

In the kitchen Raffael's wife smiled openly, "Hi Paolo, how are you?" She gave him a big hug while Raffael went off to change, then took him to one side and gave him a few minutes normal conversation before they sat down to eat.

* * *

On the street, Gil racked his brain as to where he had seen the guy in the house before. He couldn't see clearly enough but he recognised him. He thought perhaps it was the cop from the interview, the one he couldn't place back then. He gave up in the mind that he could come back any day and find out who it was. It was coincidence enough for Gil that he saw Paolo sail by as he waited for a bus. And that Paolo hadn't noticed him.

Gil's proposed time at home was also being eating away. He could be waiting for hours while Paolo was inside and he didn't have enough cash in his pockets to fund many more manic taxi chases.

Inside, Paolo and Raffael heckled each other over the dinner table. Raffael was not giving in on the subject of the murder case, Paolo couldn't even decide whether he knew something and wasn't letting on because of the present company or whether he knew nothing.

They gave up and relaxed into the family and food atmosphere instead.

But even by the time he left two hours later it was still niggling Paolo from the back of his mind, only once or twice had he got carried away by conversation enough to let go. He climbed into his car and placed the objects from is jacket on the dash wondering whether he did the right thing not asking Raffael directly. He put on his seatbelt and weighed the options. It really wasn't worth getting Raffael involved. If he was as innocent as he seemed he can't know anything or doesn't know that he knows anything.

He decided to put the dilemma to sleep. Raffael was out of the equation. He had been through too much and was now as happy as he had been before Frankie messed everything up. There was no point being another thorn in the family's side. Gil was available and had no prior commitments. Paolo started his car and decided to go and see what Gil had found out. It had reached Friday after all.

Paolo parked in the street housing Gil and his family immediately opposite the usual window. Gil was there as usual, his head amplified grossly against the lace curtain by a lamp on the other side of his head. Paolo sighed as the engine's sound stopped and peace returned, his long drawn out breath ended with a twinge in his jaw and the return of ringing to his ears.

The street outside was less populated by eleven p.m. on Friday evening. Gil sat drinking what looked like beer and was laughing and even appear to be having a conversation.

Paolo stared with his beady eyes, straining them and his body towards Gil. How could criminals have such peace of mind? Then as soon as a cop breaks the rules they have to deal with morality? He clenched the steering wheel and dragged his eyes away from the window. Staring out straight ahead of him he struggled to conjure up some moments of internal peace of his own. It wasn't the way he saw it in that moment really, it was just that seeing Gil enjoying it was a great injustice.

Gil felt someone watching him. He lifted the corner of the lace curtain in his living room and peered out into the dark street. He saw Paolo's car. Paolo sank down into the driver's seat. Gil just smiled more and raised his glass in a toast to the dark car parked outside.

He couldn't actually see Paolo, as the streetlights were reflecting off the windows. So, he definitely couldn't see the knot in Paolo's stomach either, but he knew about the vexation. He glanced up and down the empty street before closing the curtains on another day's survival.

Paolo woke on Saturday morning with the feeling of shaggy rocks in his stomach. He had fallen asleep in his car in front of Gil's house the night before, woken at around one-forty a.m. and driven home and crawled straight to bed. Still in his work clothes.

He had planned other activities for his Friday night, but they had all fallen victim to his anger. He had decided he wouldn't confront Gil at his house but couldn't understand at what point sleepiness had overcome him.

He walked straight out of the house, without performing a single morning ritual, climbed into his car, drove to Gil's house and parked up in what was becoming his usual spot.

There was slightly more cover with Saturday morning, but Paolo considered Gil must know the car by know. Especially after the previous night. It didn't make any difference, Paolo would stop him as soon as he left his street. But as he cooled down and woke up a cold fact drew over him. Gil wasn't in his chair. He saw no sign of him. Nor much movement in the house.

Paolo struggled for his wrist, but he hadn't put a watch on. He strained to cover the dash clock but realised he had the time on his cell phone. It read ten-thirty a.m.

Paolo sat back in deep thought. Gil could be anywhere, in bed, in the kitchen or shower, gone for the day, gone forever. He sat for five more minutes with nothing except a dull calling from his mid-section. He folded, started his engine and roared out of the street to find something to shut his stomach up. With every intention of coming straight back.

Gil was at home. He watched Paolo's movements from the upper level of the house, through a pin hole tear in a black curtain that shielded the junk in the attic from the sunlight. He had known Paolo would turn up that Saturday morning. It was another gut feeling, and being so close to the truth he was willing to go out of his way to shake Paolo. That last thing he wanted was Paolo finding out who the real killer was.

Gil knew he had to react quickly; the increased vigilance was a sign that time was running out. But Paolo's unexpected departure left him a little puzzled. Gil decided it was a bluff and decided best to stay at home. It wasn't like a cop like this to work the weekend, surely when he left next it would be for good.

Sure enough he saw Paolo's car back outside twenty minutes later. Gil pottered around the house in his slippers doing some odd things he had been putting off, questioning Paolo every time he came near a window facing the street.

When Paolo left, Gil did too, feeling glad of having had the time at home. He rounded the corner only to find Paolo's car tucked against the curb. He leaned over and opened the door, it bounced silently on its hinges as it swung open.

"Get in," Paolo was less than polite.

"So, what's a cop like you doing on a Saturday? Boss on your back?" Paolo told him to shut the door, Gil did so and they drove off.

Paolo didn't say anything in reply, he shot a quick look at Gil, seeing he had several layers of emotional protection and anything he said would bounce right off.

"I didn't wait around all morning to bull-shit with you. It's quite simple for here on in. Find me who did it on Monday or I'll knick you for it."

"Ok," Gil nodded his head but he didn't follow up his intonation.

Paolo still not looking at Gil seemed fixated on the empty road in front of them.

"It's quite straightforward," Gil said finally, but you didn't answer my question.

"What question?"

"What's a cop like you doing hard at it on a Sunday?"

"It's Saturday." Paolo replied spinning another glance at Gil.

"Same applies."

Paolo slowed the car a little and looked at Gil.

"Do you normally work on a Saturday?" He reiterated.

"I'm a cop. We are always at work."

"Don't give me that shit."

"What's your problem?"

"I don't like dirty stinking cops."

Paolo slowed the car almost to a stop, took a disguised deep breath, "And that is supposed to what? Hurt my feelings."

"Ooooo, Gil faked a shiver, still in his good mood, you've got a real pathetic sense of humour this morning."

"It's nearly two-thirty," Paolo snapped back, proud of his increased chronological awareness. He snapped out of it seeing Gil's look of nonchalance. "So do you know who it is or not. You can tell me now if you like get it out of the way. Then I can enjoy the rest of my weekend."

Gil studied Paolo gently. "How do you make your decisions, cop?"

"What?"

"How do you set your moral standards? Daily? You clearly don't read your horoscopes. Or did the I Ching tell you to break all the rules and arrest innocent people all day?"

Paolo dragged the car to the side of the road, "Get out, get out of my car."

Gil sat still, his emotional armour still fully intact. "I am asking you? Really. You don't have an answer?" Gil's good humour left the car as he opened the door, "Who do you do you consider when you make your decisions? Who wins in your little fucking predictions?"

Paolo's retort held no weight but he told Gil he seemed very bitter anyway.

"It's a problem I have with fake cops and their lazy and immoral attitudes towards other human beings." Gil's specific rage for this individual pinched him as he got out of the car. He leant back in the window. "Ok, I'll find you your white boy. I'll give him to you on Monday. But if I find you following me the deal's off and you wont find me alone on Monday morning. Or for quite a while afterwards. So, unless you want to explain this conversation to a lot of people you better get lost until Monday afternoon."

"How am I supposed to trust you?" Paolo stuttered.

"You don't know the meaning of the word. It's too late for you. Just leave me alone. I'll find him alone; all you will do is scare him off."

Paolo sped off from that meeting with only one thing in mind, to get things off his mind. He got drunk. During his binge he contemplated whether Gil would go through with it. He decided it didn't matter. He didn't care. Not caring is second nature when you are drunk. And Paolo was very drunk.

Gil set off to his old hunting grounds. He wondered up and down the high street, in and out of shops as casually as he could. He scared some kid who had been shoplifting by staring out to the street from behind the shelves of a stationer's store. Gil laughed at the irony, or the lack of it.

The afternoon dragged, Gil wasn't happy about giving up but his feet were tired. He decided to go and sit down, out side this time.

He entered the square with the dawning remembrance that it was the same square he had seen who he was looking for the first time. It brought reality; there was nothing to say he was even from this neighbourhood. It's fashionable enough to visit for shopping and so on.

Nonetheless Gil spotted the back of a promising head. He skirted behind the bench, the head was with someone else, but it wasn't obvious if they were together or not.

Gil had seen so many dupes fall on this square their faces had all merged into one. Even getting close to this head revealed nothing except Gil was unprepared verbally.

Gil sat down despondently, far enough away to talk to himself but not be overheard by the head. But still in visual range. He began talking to himself. "It's the wrong time."

He explained to himself that he had to do it and that anytime was the wrong time, but also the right time too. He would follow the head, see where it went, try and get a view of its front. He could even follow it to its house. "Perfect," Gil snapped, at home.

He ran some icebreakers through his head. Some good punch lines, things that would keep the kid quiet.

The head said something to its neighbour.

To Gil it was all too familiar. He knew how to sit and wait, how to judge the mood and character of a person from observing them. He rehearsed the lines in his head with the head. He began to grow confident.

The head got up after several minutes and walked away from the plaza, although to Gil's surprise away from the high street and towards a residential side of the square. Causing Gil to panic a little. He followed anyway. Like he done so many times before. Counting his distance against lamp posts and doorways.

The kid was clearly going straight home. Gil stepped up a little. They walked three blocks then the head turned left. The next street was even quieter, still wide but the buildings somewhat too high to make it a nice street for a walk. Apartment blocks but of three or four floors each. Gil stepped up more and waited on the corner watching the head's movements over his shoulder in the window of a convenient van. The head crossed the street half way down its length.

Gil's heart raced, he spun around and walked sternly across the street in a long diagonal. He arrived outside the head's block just in time to see him enter a ground floor apartment. Gil swept past with his hand to the side of his face, doing a lap of the block in mind.

Before he had made it around the second corner of his circuit the doubts had entered Gil's mind. It didn't take a lot of convincing. Sunday would be a better day was the only justification Gil could or did come up with. He carried on walking until he reached home.

Sunday was another morning of empty stomachs all around. Gil's was accompanied by an extreme lack of motivation. Even to get out of the bed. When he did he spent a good deal of time looking in the mirror examined various grooves in his face. He thought of it, but didn't even try to smile.

He did manage to persuade himself to leave the house. Without any morning rituals other than getting dressed and taking a gun. He also managed to walk himself to the kid's front door. And ring the buzzer.

And that was the next step taken. Without breakfast and without contemplation. Like a clockwork mouse he followed his destiny without much general consideration or thought. The cop, the kid, god or even Gil could have been in charge as far as Gil was concerned, he was just following orders. His balls had been tied, and whoever was pulling the fishing line they had used, had tied it just tight enough to stop him arguing.

He had a nervous look around. The cop was good to stick to his word if he thought he was getting a free lunch. Provided he didn't think Gil was going to fuck him good and properly. It had escaped Gil that it was exactly what he wanted to do. But now the moment was here, the idea of Paolo and Gil both walking away reasonably unscathed and the real murderer getting what he deserved, had an easy ring to it. Gil wasn't one-hundred per cent sure of any outcome. He was sure he didn't want to miss out on the chance to screw a bent cop in a royal fashion.

Added to this Gil was becoming nervous, a feeling that only made him more nervous. All ex-suckers were difficult given their unpredictability. Especially the fighters. He gave another look around. A thud behind the door forced Gil to put his hand on his revolver.

* * *

Fate's cell phone was obviously low on battery that Sunday afternoon as it rang my doorbell instead. It shocked me, as the doorbell very rarely rings, and that I had only recently found out why and had it fixed.

It has a little video phone, but I was so intrigued as to see who could be at the door I went straight to the door, straining to the peep hole I banged my head against the wood sending me into a giggling fit.

Outside there was a stranger, of about forty or so years, with a stern face residing below a worried brow. He seemed to have a big nose and definitely knew I was watching him. Although I think the peephole was to blame.

He looked around nervously and then strained his head to the peephole, the exponential growth of his head sending me into further giggles.

I flipped the locks with unusual ease. Decided I should act a little less stoned and opened the door.

Our eyes met undistorted for the first time. A bolt of biological lightening completed a dot-the-dot figure, starting in my adrenal gland and going via eyeball, brain, heart and asshole at great speed. My blood became very heavy as I looked at what could have been a real cop in plain clothes or a fake cop on his day off.

My split second of paralysis was a split second too long to get the door shut before his shiny black shoe found its way in. I looked down at it, he pulled out a gun, I looked up at it, then at his face and then let the door free.

He snaked his way into the apartment. My first visitor, not just for a long time, but forever. I sobered reasonably quickly.

In the living room he strangely put the pistol back in his pocket and offered me a seat. He seemed calm, but worried, as if he was having one of his worst bad days, but not the first.

He began talking and I seemed to have been removed of the ability to listen, dumbstruck by the silent banging of this new nemesis's lips. I had no idea what was going on or what was about to happen. The story that had just arrived, armed, on my doorstep was unfamiliar and definitely unplanned. I tried to read the expression on his face.

My face must have betrayed my lack of confusion as he lifted his head towards me to get my acknowledgement.

I couldn't speak either. His face dropped and he shook his head. I stood sullen with a familiar feeling creeping over. I looked down at this strange man in my living room. No matter how dangerous or unpredictable he may have been he had been transformed into who needed help. Whether I could trust any of the words I couldn't hear was another decision, but he was definitely on the back foot.

He sat looking at me for several minutes, the colours and background noises came back. The fear and shock disappeared and I came to the conclusion he needed my help. He started to stand up and I snapped back to life.

"Excuse me, but what are you doing here? I'm sorry but I didn't catch much of what you just said."

"Look, kid, you know exactly why I am here, and if you don't then I have made a huge mistake. But I haven't, and I intend to exploit your weak position to get at least me out of mine."

I shook my head. To which he replied something about it being a last resort. There was clearly some logic in there, it just wasn't very clear. I nodded, but the situation was still confused, he should have been much more in control of the situation. His face contradicted that thought.

"I am beginning to get the gist but there are a few elements I think I am obviously lacking."

He explained that the murder I had committed was abut to be stamped on him. I restrained the will to laugh at the irony and my own oversight. It turned out that the cops even knew it wasn't him but had no idea who did it and were trying to set him up for it. If only he hadn't turned up on my doorstep to tell me this.

"I can't get back to my normal life until this thing's out of my mind."

"I know the feeling, but what do you want from me? You expect me to just walk in and hand myself in? Or do you have some evidence against me?"

"Let me be honest with you, I wondered what the word meant to him, it's not about making someone go to jail, its about making the case disappear. You're a smart kid and I'm not going to try and force you to do anything. But I am asking you to help me. The way I see it, it's a midway meeting, I began to recognise this as the same speech I missed, if you don't help me I can hand you over to the cop tomorrow, if you do we can both walk away quietly."

I didn't understand the 'how' but the result sounded ok. Despite having been in that ending twenty minutes before. The room span a little bit. I considered it could be a trap, I put my finger up to say I needed some silent time to think. I went over what he had said. Why should I trust him given his short but one-sided track record? I went through my options, the 'I don't know what you're talking about' dialogue was above my head. Besides if he was recording the conversation it would be good for nothing unless the police were doing it themselves. I reached instead for my cell phone.

Instead of producing a hostile reaction he began to beg me not to do it. Like he knew!

I walked towards the hall and looked out of the peephole, then opened the door and looked back. Still no reaction, just a look like a lost rabbit. I looked to the street, nothing seemed out of place. No strange cars or shadowy figures in the building opposite. I hesitated briefly but took off and did a lap of the block, returning only to find him still there sat on my sofa, the front door wide open.

When the kid left the apartment unexpectedly, Gil reiterated his correctness to himself. People are unpredictable. He was still stunned by the kid's weird behaviour, but he could smell the stench of the drug. He cogitated, his brain had switched drivers since leaving the bed two hours before.

He decided not to tell the kid the plan he had thought of, it would be too much for him. No reason to scare him off.

The kid had been very careful about what he had said; he must have been thinking Gil was wearing a wire. But he had given enough away to tell Gil he had killed Bill.

He would call Paolo's bluff. If he was right he had all the time in the world, if he was wrong he had the kid.

"How do I know you aren't working for the police?"

"Did you see anything outside?"

"Do you think they would be sitting in a car with blue lights on top?" My newfound caution was definitely on my side.

"I can't... prove anything to you. But you cant pick up the phone and call them to find out. He had good reasoning, it may not have been improvised but it was good." I went to a cupboard and pulled out a bottle of whiskey, not that I had been waiting all my life to do it, and put two glasses on the table. Helping myself to one.

"Firstly," I said with my newfound courage and the knowledge I could live up to it. "Firstly, I don't believe you; and secondly, you need it like I need it." He sat contemplating it while I weighed the options. The police call was out, once I was in the frame I was in the jail, simple. If they already knew it was going over the top to get a confession in this manner. I stepped back onto the board.

"I can play this game as long as it takes you to prove you're being straight forward. If they know, they already know. If they don't..."

"You," he pointed his finger above the empty glass, "can think what you like. I need to tell this cop something tomorrow, perhaps if I am lucky that would be the end of it. I just thought you and I could come up with another alternative." He sounded angry and almost upset.

"Bullshit." I chanced. "You just don't want to end up like your friend."

"I didn't start this," he replied. I told him I disagreed and why. He didn't have an answer to that. He looked into the glass of answer, but I told him it wasn't there either.

"Ok, let's just pretend for a moment you are being honest, what exactly are you proposing?" I said on some gaming instinct. And assuming he had come prepared with a plan. He stumbled around his lack of plan and how intelligent he assumed I was and how I was going to help him with a plan. If he had a plan he certainly lacked the confidence to tell me what it was.

"You are joking then?" I said with a certain control and honesty. The fact he was armed had long fallen from my mind. "You cant blackmail me like this, besides your cards are shitty. I can see how easily I got away from you last time."

He sat still motionless and despondent. I he must have had the confidence at some point to come here. Or he was being backed into a real tight corner. Failing that he had some real evidence against me, or a witness. There were too many possibilities and I didn't feel in a position to examine any of them.

In the worst case scenario he could even have been setting me up for someone else, or himself. Some kind of crooks revenge.

This guy had made a fool of me before, I wasn't about to let it happen again. Besides, my freedom and health, even my life, could be back on the line. And they were all worth fighting for.

My senses were deceiving my logic again. Like they had with Bill I looked at this guy on my sofa wondering why he looked so sympathetic and honest. What was it? Was it me? Was there something about my face? They say you can't judge a book by its cover and it's turning more and more into an anti-prejudice slogan that the original metaphor is being lost. There are a million books where the book defines the cover perfectly and a million the other way. Teaching kids not to prejudge is good but only if you tell them the logic behind it. That it is fallible. It's a fucked up situation. It would be easier to teach people to be prejudice but that sometimes it goes wrong and that in that case they should just hold their tongue. You cant complain about racists when there are some bad black people.

It is too one directional. You can pick out a good guy, who looks like a good guy; a bad guy who looks bad, but when you start to cross them up logic fails you. It happened to me the first time and looking at this character on my sofa gave me the impression it was about to happen again. Perhaps if I had turned him upside down there would be a label with instructions and warnings on it. Caution: this model may cause serious problems to your life if it judges you to possess more money or greater status.

"If I'm going to help you—and I haven't decided on that yet—it has to work out for both of us, ok?" This was my opening bid, through which I hoped to buy time enough to consider the higher question that had arisen that afternoon. He nodded.

"So, the first thing I need is for you to leave, so I can have some time to think this over."

He said nothing, just sat for a minute or two staring blankly into space. "Ok, give me an address or phone number where I can reach you."

"You know where I live, I told him, give me your number and I'll call you, and if I don't, you still know where I live."

I offered him the door with my head. He got up quietly but reluctantly as if to say what I had said made sense but was the last thing he had ever expected.

He said to me in a very rejected voice before leaving that it was a little more urgent for him than it was for me. I nodded in agreement and showed him the door.

I don't think he had planned on leaving so early or with the little progress he had made. But then it could have been another bluff, my brain told me. Thoughts like this were going to be the end of me, my brain was contradicting every idea that came to it. It was making me sick of being awake. Besides, I figured he had made progress, I had started thinking about helping him.

I slept a few hours after the fake cop left, he hadn't told me his name, or anything about him, at all. I awoke, then, with that familiar 'it was all a dream feeling'. It hadn't been; the whiskey glasses gave account.

I sat back on the sofa and went through the details. If I was going to help him, he would have to follow me, not the other way around. If I walk myself into a trap then I deserve it. But I didn't feel like being suckered by the same guy twice.

That was the very beginning. Whatever followed had to be based on that. But what followed wasn't going to be easy, how could I help him? Character witness? They surely wouldn't fall for that. Alibi? The same. Handing myself in? Not going to happen. Provide anther suspect? Another murderer? I didn't like the idea but it sounded like a plausible last resort.

I didn't have many ideas, they were all very straight forward and generally too obvious. It didn't fit in, this guy was clearly a professional bullshitter. Why didn't he have a better idea? Why didn't he tell me what it was? A bigger plan of his?

Paranoia was making me sick. It made me sick thinking I would never get the upper hand. The thought of having to call him made me sick.

I moved onto different directions. The police had been in touch with him. They thought he had killed Bill. They would probably be following him or something. They would probably knock on my door eventually then, with this guy in the back of the patrol car. Surely he was smarter than that.

These types of thoughts were becoming more and more common. Thoughts which arrive, hard, impacting the brain into panic, fear and pain.

I stepped out. If I was going to find a solution I was going to first have to stop worrying about the consequences. To have the free mind again. With clarity and objectivity. My brain felt its task and demanded chocolate, I grabbed a jacket and walked out into the Sunday dusk.

I still felt the pinch of life as I unlocked my front door. Something was telling me it was dangerous outside and warm and comfortable inside. I checked myself in the hall mirror and left.

Life can be clear; it just needs work. I needed to meditate, focus and get to grips with the problem at hand. There had to be a problem-solving corner to my brain. It had been a long time since I had willingly applied it to reality, if ever at all.

My short-term instinct was my water; if it had been incorrect I would have dehydrated and died by now. But now, with the long path ahead, with the only facts being the ones already behind me and with nothing tangible to hand, I was suffering. My long-term instinct was my food, but the feeling in my stomach told me I wasn't hungry, marrying well with the feeling in my head that told me the source of my next meal was still unknown. Why couldn't I just know the way out of this latest situation? It vexed my walk not having an essential resource.

I needed that inner peace, mental distance or perhaps mental approach. Perhaps it meant waiting. Waiting until the decision was upon me and relying once more on the one-way instinct. Wait to get put on the spot. I didn't like the idea, despite its track record. It was paradoxical. To get ahead in the planning I need to relax. And to relax I need to have a plan.

While all this processing was going on, the search for something to fuel it was becoming increasingly frustrating and my patience similarly thin. About to swear and head back home I found a corner shop open and dived in. At least one thing went in my favour that Sunday.

The chocolate clearly wasn't the reason I left the house. There was a higher motive. A higher hunger. The mission was the species-old task of finding food, but a chocolate bar clearly wasn't going to cut it. I headed for a restaurant.

The first thought came before the soup. We could get this guy to leave the country. It had its problems, its farfetchedness causing most of them.

I needed the guy on tap. I had no information, nothing to work with. What had he told the police? What did they know about him? Could he just get up and leave the country, didn't he have family and a house or was he a forty year old single crook who rented?

Nothing I had thought of had involved me so far. He could have done any of the workable solution on his own. What would I get out of this? It wasn't as important as putting this into the past, but I want more out of my new relationship than just being implicated.

I pressed on, processing every option I could. Coming to no conclusions other than I had ordered too much food.

I decided to walk it off. It was a cool evening with a slight breeze, it was beginning to blow some of the browner leaves from the trees. The air was fresh and made me feel sleepy, but I had eaten a lot and needed to keep moving for fear I would sit down and never be able to get back up.

I headed for the park, with no intention of making that far. But before I knew it, I was there. The street lights had been on a while but it was only at that late hour that they'd relieved the natural light. That was far enough. I turned, went home and slept.

Sleep was all knew. No dreams or nightmares, no

midnight-toilet runs, no thinking, arguing couples or cats screaming. Best of all no reality.

Gil had left the kid's apartment feeling confident. Things could continue from that basis in the right direction. They could, however, easily go the other way. Gil tried not to focus on it, but there was a pervading air of uncertainty in his mind. Would Paolo show up? What would he do or say?

There was a twinge of nervousness. Like meeting someone you've already gotten know face-to-face for the first time. But he knew the cop's face. It was the one that looked like a caricature of a pig.

Nevertheless Gil went to bed that Sunday feeling confident, upbeat having all the angles covered. And because of that he slept soundly. So soundly in fact, his Monday morning didn't start until eleven a.m.

He woke with the feeling of having slept through a storm. In the kitchen he was told no one had called or stopped by. Gil had expected the cop to be dirty enough to come at nine a.m. instead of at four p.m. On top of that, he needed something to have happened without him. He felt it had, but if it really had, it would have given him a jumping block for the day. Without that he was just at home on a Monday.

He kept his guard up all day. Once outside of the law most people are out of moral standards as well. After his morning rituals, he put his slippers on and sat in his armchair and went through the Sunday paper with a more careful eye than the day before.

The cop would come or he wouldn't. Either way it was best to be in the house. As for the kid, the murderer, he could wait for him to call provided Paolo didn't show up. And even if he did he wouldn't be able to arrest the kid straight away.

Paolo was having a bad start to Monday. His hangover had

kept him in bed until late. He was planning to see Gil early then let him a few hours to come up with someone. He went straight to the office instead. He found his boss at his desk tidying up the file he had left scattered on Friday.

The sight caused his motivation and mood to capsize. He slumped into the chair on the wrong side of his desk. Waiting for whatever his boss had to tell him. Like so many people, his boss was more of a Friday-evening man than a Monday-morning man, so he was obviously going to put across what ever he hadn't on Friday. Was he going to work with him this week? Friday was a deadline whether he admitted it or not. The thought of deadlines made Paolo feel sick again. He had been sick several times over the weekend. His lethargy grew. He would sooner be thrown off the case than have to spend half the week being patronised and not actually learning anything.

He stood up and walked out before a word had been said, the boss still reading and sorting files. Paolo came back with two cups of coffees, but feeling it might be interpreted as sucking up, he left the second one on the side of the desk at which he was sitting. He sat down and watched his boss. Did he even seen me when I came in before? He asked himself. Probably, was the conclusion. He was a sneaky old bastard and always up to tricks. Paolo began to feel quite playful. He blew the steam off his coffee and worked on clearing his mind.

"Not much here, is there?" the boss began.

Paolo stopped blowing his coffee as his mood plunged back to the depths from which he had just dragged it. Was it honest or was he trying to imply laziness?

"What ever happened to the days when murderers left clues?"

"And had motives, you mean?"

Paolo thought of Gil at home, not being bothered by anyone. "They don't make them as stupid as they used to. This one's a bitch anyway. If it was just the kid, I'd say gangbangers. Just the old man, an angry parishioner, and had no one spotted a white male asking after the kid, I'd say it was probably a black guy."

"So you're convinced it was a white male, not a bluff or misdirection?"

"It didn't make much difference to me, 'white-male' isn't going to get us anywhere."

"And this ex-partner? Where does he figure?"

"Nowhere, look for yourself. Small time, dresses up as a cop would you believe it?"

"Yes, I would. It's becoming too common and no one seems to care. Anyway, what's the story. Does he have and alibi or not?"

"Yes, but it wouldn't stand up in thick mud."

"So why haven't you nicked him then? You've got motive haven't you?"

Paolo paused. It could easily have been a trick question. If he affirms, it's going to trip him up later down the line. If he denies, then Gil steps out of the frame. It was a sticky dilemma for a Monday morning.

What's more is that Paolo wasn't in a logical mind set. And the obsession he had for Gil was causing more damage than good. The bottom line is that it was causing damage. He was ready to ditch the case and take a chance on his brother. Paolo's face was covered in sleep still. He looked lazy and tired of life. His insides looked exactly the same.

"I was so sure it was him I brought him in for questioning the same day."

"But do you think he did it or not?"

"If he didn't, he's definitely got a finger deep in it," was the best compromise Paolo could find.

The boss hummed a little and looked through the paper in front of him. He looked back at Paolo with a critical look. "You didn't get much sleep this weekend, right? Well, at least you got this off your mind I hope."

"Yeah, but I'm fine."

"So what do you want to do? You have anything fresh? More games."

Paolo gave a long sigh and held in a yawn. "Well, if you don't mind I'd like to keep hold of it. I know it's not going anywhere, but its got some kudos to it."

"I think it's going to be open for a while, which is a damn shame, I'd liked to have gotten this one tucked away."

"Yeah, I know. So what do you think is the best way forward?"

"Let me take it off your hands for a week or two. I think you have enough other things to occupy yourself. But I won't give this away, I'll just hold on to it myself. See if I can't come up with some fresh perspective. If I get the time that is." He laughed and stood up. "What do you think?"

"Sure, sounds like a welcome break."

"That's what I thought. Now why don't you head off out, get some breakfast and some decent coffee and try starting again in an hour or two."

Paolo realised he had reached the bottom of the dejection slide and consoled himself with the thought things could only get better. Besides, he could not think about the case for a while. Forget Gil, forget his own brother, the old man wasn't going to do anything that involved leaving his office. He wouldn't find anything leading to Raffael without the murderer nor to the murderer without Raffael. At least he hoped.

Paolo left the office, feeling sick still, but also still too lazy to care about anything. He felt a little slack for having let Gil get off the hook like that, even if it was just to be temporarily, but he had probably been too far out on a limb to make anything stick this time around. And Raffael was safely tucked away.

Gil was worrying. He was happy Paolo hadn't shown up, but nervous. If he was bluffing, he would still have shown up... unless he had something else up his sleeve.

After a few hours of the afternoon he began to think a bit further forward. Perhaps it would be ok. No, was the conclusion. He got up and went in search of the cop. Something fishy was going on.

He sat in a coffee shop opposite the police station. After forty-five minutes Paolo left. Gil was surprised at his relaxed demeanour and smile. He decided to follow him, only to be further surprised to see Paolo make a house call to a young girl and then go drinking in a bar. He then went home, surprisingly early and assumedly still sober enough to drive.

Gil followed him on Tuesday as well. The same thing. Work, with a smile. Leaving early, visiting a young girl, then the familiar guy again and then back to the bar. Gil left him in the bar and went to see the familiar man. He still couldn't figure where he recognised him from. Even from closer up.

He was on his way back to the bar where he had left Paolo when he realised he would never know if he was still inside, without going in. So he went home instead. Trying to figure out what was going on. He got home just in time, the kid rang. Gil explained briefly that he had an idea but didn't want to go into it in too much detail.

Things weren't balanced, and that in Gil's sphere was not a good sign for moving forward. The kid would be up for getting the crooked cop. He seemed like the overly moral type. But the cop was up to something. Gil had no idea what or whether it was even related to him, but it was too late to step back.

Blind to the circumstance Gil set his mind to planning something. He decided to meet the kid and talk it over with him. Gil wasn't too sure the kid would be up to it. He wanted to do it, but perhaps he wasn't cut out. It would be a nice payback for Gil though, for all the shit he had been through in the name of being the killer. And it meant he could give the kid the hard work.

The kid did take to the idea. Even enjoyed the idea of it. It wasn't clear to Gil why the kid wasn't interested in screwing the cop, but it hardly seemed the point. He was interested in getting on with his life. Equally was Gil.

I left Monday to the dogs. I woke up late, ate, had a nap all afternoon and watched t.v. all evening.

On Tuesday I started thinking. Monday was lost at the thought of having to spend my whole day playing 'people chess'. Tuesday I had to do it. I was in a mess again. I wasn't alone this time, but I realised it was actually better in the bigger scheme even if it felt worse.

I called him in the evening. As the phone rang I remembered I still didn't know his name. I hoped he would answer, so I wouldn't have to say something like "Is the master of the house there?" It made me smile at least. It answered. It was him. I could instantly recognise that voice now. So deep but smooth, normal but so controlling. I put it to the fact we had a less than normal relationship, but that he would make a good actor. I soon realised that technically, but not legitimately, he was. We decided to meet in the city centre, away from everyone. Amongst no one we knew and in a place no one would find us.

It was the third time we had met. It already felt strangely like I was meeting an old friend. Being in a situation such as I was and having only one person to talk to it about binds you. He had something I needed. The same way a job has something you need to survive. Everyone nowadays needs money to survive and as much as we hate to be caught into the system, the system has what we need. The necessary evil.

I sat down with my necessary evil and we had some coffee. I was proud of how well my anxiety was under control, it returned every now and then, but as I examined my partner I realised he was looking more worried than ever. Not physically, he was a mess before and still was, but he seemed very strained. I thought of how I felt the morning after our first encounter. It can happen I concluded.

I wondered what was eating him so badly. But it wasn't my business and at the end of the day I didn't care. More curiosity at this creature in front of me.

I called his bluff and told him I would help him if he could come up with an easy way of doing it. A good, quick and easily executable plan. A plan that would leave us to continue our lives in the manners we wished to.

Leaving it to the last minute had pulled through again. When there was no script, no words, when what came out of my mouth was all that would ever be said in that moment, there was no problem. When you can't go back, you can move easily forward. Only then are the words actually effective, not in terms of relative effectiveness, but in terms of affecting the real world.

Coincidence had it that they were also effective words. He swallowed slowly and a bead of sweat even appeared on one of his temples. I was used to life being full of clichés so I ignored it and listened to his plan.

His plan was simple, effective and probably the most risky thing I had ever considered doing. Bearing in mind I hadn't considered killing Bill, it had just happened. It was so far from anything I had been thinking of and completely in the opposite direction I had wished to be going.

BOOK THREE

Book Three

The coffee shop was a good place, as I felt sick and there was no one I knew to judge me. Deciding to sit on a high stool was a bad idea, however, as I want to fall off them. I stared to my side where this horrible character sat, then back through the window and its coated people. It was an obvious plan, the man next to me was as innocent as the cop trying to arrest him was crooked. And what better way to deal with crooked people than to feed them their own poison.

Yet another confidence scam. Just what the world needed. I could feel my personality toughening. I felt that Monday morning internal dialogue. I didn't want to be doing this kind of thing. When would the nightmare end, when would my brain wake up and go to work and let me be awake in peace?

Why did he want me involved? Well, I had kind of spoilt his chances of using his old partner. But he could have found someone else. "You just want me as implicated in this as possible."

"Kid, I have been trying to put it to you easily. But at the end of it all, you killed someone and you shouldn't expect to get off scot-free."

There was an entire meta-physical and socio-moral argument my stomach wouldn't let me get into. Put me in front of the man who wants me the most? It had its charm and its bite. And acid bite. It bit my stomach. I ordered up another coffee, believing I could dilute my problems with espresso.

When it arrived I waited for it to cool before standing up. I drained it down including the grains. "OK, it looks like a good plan, well, for the least, a plan, maybe not even very good. Where it highlights itself is that it is a million times better than anything that I would have come up with. Its functional, that's where I will draw the line. Functional but not incriminating."

The man next to me looked with horrified intrigue at my sudden punch drunken state. He nodded in agreement once he realised that I was actually thinking straight.

I stumbled out into the metropolitan street, getting bundled and shoved in various directions. I turned past the coffeeshop and looked back briefly only to find my recently departed coffee neighbour staring at me with callous eyes. I moved on like the village drunk, half cramped over from the pain in my abdomen. I don't know how long or where I wandered to, realising I was 'lost' in the city, I fell into the back of a cab and told the guy to take me to my neighbourhood. Slipping into a semi-meditative, semi-sedated trance. I was like and empty shell, a zombie aware of his horrible actions but unable to control them.

The cabbie had to lean over and shake me when he realised he didn't know exactly where I wanted to go. I told him I was fine where we were, paid him and got out in front of a neighbourhood restaurant. I sat straight down for lack of any other possible movements and was soon ordering food with what surprised me to be relative straightforwardness.

My restaurant dialogue showed a clearing in the fog. The sooner it cleared the sooner I admitted I would have to do it. What did I know? Nothing, I had no choice, no argument to justify saying, 'no'. Why would one guy go to jail for murder when he knew who did it and didn't know him well enough to care about him? He wouldn't? But then if he didn't actually do it how would he go to jail? Were they going to make evidence up? Surely that wasn't allowed.

Nevertheless, unless I could back out of it, I would need to be prepared, mentally and physically. I slipped a cigarette from the crumpled pack in my pocket, slipped it into my dry lips and slipped a match. The seductive dancing flame showed me my soul's reflection with a perfect meticulousness.

If I did this, how could I be sure it would last? Once you step out side the rules, the rules walk away, shunned. They don't love you anymore; they are no longer your friends. They wont back you up. There was a clear line. Perhaps I had already stepped over it. Freedom is perhaps a socially constructed necessity; it made sense.

So, the over-the-line me had little choice. Go with the flow. If it becomes too rough you can still jump, or carry on killing people until nobody knows.

I still lacked the positive edge to this spoon. What would I get out of naming and shaming a stinking cop? Fame? Unlikely and less wanted. Moral high ground? That's like saying I would be able to absolve myself. I was fucking absolved.

Some smoke slipped stingingly in to my eye. I winced and a tear fell down my cheek. I could feel it as it slipped over the light fluffy hairs on my cheek and then got caught up in the thick but transparent stubble.

I wondered if it had a significance. None probably, just that sometimes smoke reaches your eye and other times it doesn't. It made me alert anyway. Perhaps life was trying to tell me something. I looked around. Quiet lonely diners. Working their way up from greasy waiters. Everyone deeply involved in their own introspection. Worrying about their problems. Involved in their meals and their little lives. Everyone was the same. The people passing in the street, waiting for busses. Busy with where they were going, the mistakes they had made and how they would fix it all tomorrow. Down to the cockroaches, although I was hard pressed to imagine what they were worried about, losing their heads perhaps.

If yesterday is history and tomorrow a mystery, I sure as hell couldn't figure out what today was supposed to be. It was no gift. I had witnesses to that.

Life was definitely trying to tell me something. My analysis was clearly flawed. Was it that I should be concentrating on my own problems? Strange. Because that is what I had been doing when it stole my attention. Should I be paying less attention to my problems, and worrying more about that guy's? Or the guy I left in the coffee shop? I would remember to find out his name, although not knowing it had advantages too.

The universe's continuity began to slip out of life's control. But then what did I know about him? Nothing? He was a crook who dressed up as a cop. At least I had that one thing settled. But criminals have scruples and problems too. Whether they let them show is different. But he must have a life on the other side of the line. A family and family problems, a house and house problems and health and health problems. Just as the same as everyone, just the same as the cockroaches.

A waiter bearing soup interrupted me, telling me indirectly that I had reached my conclusion. Whether it solved anything was not supposed to be a question answered.

I was still left on the empty side of the deal. I wasn't sure what that signified. To me. I wasn't the criminal type, but at the same time I wasn't the law-abiding type. If laws were morals, it would be different, and to me paying back a dirty cop wasn't going to change the world despite it having an element of balance.

It wasn't high on the one-hundred things to do before you get married list: run a confidence scam. And although I had already been through the dirty end, I was still asking myself where was the appeal of being in control. Was this another adrenalin sport? Not likely.

The relative period of mental peace and the rapidity with which I attacked the soup told me whatever the stomach muscles were saying they weren't sticking to the truth.

It came to me more as a post-soup revelation than a product of good process. I was thinking greedily. Whatever I wanted out of this, I wanted nothing more than nothing more. Why would I need some more evidence, something else to link me. I wanted my peace back. I had it myself, I could reward myself with that. When it was all over, I would never see, hear from or speak to this guy or any of the players ever again. That was prize enough. Just because I hadn't started the whole mess didn't mean I should expect it to cough out a sympathy prize.

Perhaps this time around I would find a souvenir, a little trinket to clean up and put on the sill of my living room window? Evidence wasn't really going to be a relevant worry factor given the 'in our face attitude' to which my new partner in crime had brought to the table.

I guess I would be playing Bill's role, the innocent liar. What if Bill had been like me, innocently dragged under the world. I doubted it, I hoped so at least. Nonetheless I would need to start lying and acting, or acting and lying.

Acting was always a pipe dream, not being famous, but being able to do the things they do. To assume a role and become a different person, even if just for a season. Then be able to drift from one character to the next. Then never be the same person two days in a row. It had reheated the oldest of embers. It gave me the positive angle I would need. It even went as far as giving me the buzz of anticipation. Perhaps I had been wrong over the adrenalin sport idea.

It would be the most criminal thing I would do in my life. Bearing in mind it was premeditated. The fact that we would probably get away with it made it all the more scandalous.

I wasn't one-hundred per cent sure it would be that easy. There were little facts to support it. Perhaps it was stupidity or confidence or both. How to stop a police officer doing his job wouldn't be the easiest task.

What did my new partner know that I didn't? My imagination took over and displayed to me all sorts of crazy wildness. It made me smile. I had always been accused of being slow in school, but I knew it was more the fault of my overactive imagination and paranoia rather than any dark lethargy or lack of intelligence. I ate the rest of my dinner before the slight joviality withered. It was a nice break,

I spent the rest of the evening reading, then laying on the sofa with the remote control and the TV guide.

The outlook wasn't comfortable, but I made myself comfortable that Monday night, just in case. Life had its chances of returning to normal, but it also had its chances of not.

By the middle of the week, I would usually get the days mixed up. I can get to grips with the weekends because everything changes. TV, traffic, shops. Opening and closing times. But week days merge. Sometimes I sleep the afternoon away, or stay up over night. But now the week that was just starting had the promise of being more regimented, but even that would take some getting used to.

I waited everyday for my partner to show up, never wanting to leave the house in case he did and still not wanting to call him. After a two days of this I freed myself. What was the big deal, he could come looking for me, provided he didn't go asking for me. But I was sure he was quicker than that.

Regardless I needed to get out of my prison, into the fresh air before it became cool air. I needed to get out more, home is after all supposed to be a refuge from the world not the other way around.

I visited Raffael. Coffee and other people's problems would take my mind off it. He had become accustomed to sitting down with me and having a coffee when I came in. I made it my business to drop in during a quiet period. This day was no exception. The clock behind Raffael's counter read ten fifty-six a.m. as I sat down.

I looked across as Raffael, I wanted to tell him what was going on. Could I break the silent seal we had put across this? The answer lay in, would he have the advice that I wanted from him. I decided he wouldn't and left it alone.

We beat around the bush instead, talking about mundane neighbourhood bullshit, things we had heard and films he had watched.

Since the Sunday he had called me and told me Bill's name I had put him under the suspicion category. I never knew how he had managed what he did. Had he talked to his brother, who I knew was a cop of some sort, or whether it was some more obscure connection to either the police or the underworld?

I had figured a long time ago, regardless of whether it was clichéd or paranoid, that a city of this size has to have its own organised underworld. There is so much crime there is no way it can all be the workings of unrelated underground loners.

The fact that I was looking at framing and blackmailing a city detective began to nail the coffin firmly shut. I couldn't imagine that there wasn't some kind of hierarchy regulating this kind of thing, a system that provided for starting and stopping the appropriate flows of information. I would have wondered where I would have been placed, but Raffael began talking to me.

I tried to push some hints in at him, but he didn't answer straight questions so this was futile. He was very causal about it too, I reckoned the secret to it is a combination of playing it cool and always making sure there was enough going on in your life to keep you talking longer than the next guy.

Things had stopped getting worse since Frankie left. He started feeling less cold towards him. He spoke to his brother for the first time in two weeks and the second time in months.

"Sammy", it gave me a warm buzz when he used my name, "if you ever have kids, make sure you teach them the kind of morals that you have."

"Hmm?"

"I wish we had been brought up like that, I became the way I am, and I'm not confessing to being the straightest of cats, but you look at my brother or worse at Frankie." I had never liked Frankie and couldn't remember having said more than two conjoined words to him. "Frankie fucked me. He literally tore the trousers from my ass and fucked me. I still can't understand it. I don't feel as bad as I did a few months back but it still hasn't lodged yet. You know? What I did wrong. He looked at me as if I was there specifically to tell him the answer."

"What makes a son fuck his own father, eh? I built this place with my own fucking hands. Not literally of course. But the business, this. Entirely one-hundred per cent mine, and do you know good that feels to have something to pass down, something that is yours? And look how they pay you back."

Raffael's soliloquy went on for some time, but still it felt better to have someone else's problems pounding entrance to my skull, than mine own pounding their way out.

I wondered if I would ever have anything to pass down to my next generation. Who ever they would be. Perhaps my malformed endocrine system would turn hereditary. Not a great gift and it probably wouldn't always be such an easy source of income. Before that there was the mating problem; it had been what seemed like several generations since I last looked at a female, longer since one looked at me.

It was hardly a subject to be worrying about, but it was good to have something new and different. Like sweeping dust under cupboards.

I also felt for Raffael. He was a nice guy and he had me under his wing now. He had always been good to his kids, especially Frankie. In fact, he must have known Frankie would fuck it all up but probably still let him have a go at it anyway. Besides it was more than my father ever gave me, but from what Raffael had told me I think my gift was probably that I had a greater moral value than commercial. Besides, as far as I could see the fast-track to a skewed moral education isn't any more streamlined anywhere than in the city, the super express highway to bad manners.

I drank coffee and listened to Raffael's stories, as enraptured by them as I was by the way he told them. We moved onto life and how to solve the world's problems in a few easy strokes. I left and had lunch at home for once and came straight back as soon as the lunch time rush had finished. We chatted some more, sat outside on the side of the empty pavement. The afternoon sun warming us, but only thanks to the still air.

That day, whether it was Tuesday, Wednesday or Thursday, was the beautiful, peaceful and serene eye of the storm. We drank beer and chatted nonsense. What I would hand down to my kids, the crazy movement of fashionable people in and out of the neighbourhood.

It raised a lot of issues about my life that I hadn't discussed openly with myself let alone a third party. They weren't things connected to this story. And at the time this story was all that should have been on my mind. At this time I wanted to not be in that period, so I could address these issues. Issues that concerned my life, issues that are so easily covered up with the mess of everyday life.

I returned to my apartment in a day dream and found no signs of my partner. I stepped back to the street briefly and had a quick look around. Peaceful tranquillity was king. And remained so for the rest of the night, as far as I knew over the entire street, but definitely in my life. Undisturbed reflection.

At one point I felt anxiety, it didn't last long. It did make me question the length of this period of calm. When would things go back to normal? It wasn't like a school holiday, there was no calendar to dictate my anxiety, nothing to make my metabolism go up.

But like school I wanted it to start, I wanted to get on with it. Anxiety isn't all bad. I wanted it to start, not only not to be left where I was, but also to get to where it would take me. Its time would come, it was inevitable and the anxiety did nothing, if it didn't remind me of that.

I woke the next day with that feeling of excitement that you get on the first day of school, apprehension mixed with adrenalin and an empty stomach. My mind and body told me they were ready for something they didn't want to do but to which they were already committed.

As it turned out the morning went slowly. I contemplated speeding it up by calling they guy. But instead I made the breakfast rituals carefully and slowly, so I could enjoy them.

I breakfasted. I washed. I cleared away the weekend from my life. Around midday I decided to stop lazing around and made for the outside world. Wondering if the mystery man would come looking for me again, I was a little torn. My gut feeling was still reading off the chart. The school child inside had set me free.

The sun was out again, keeping summer alive. My spirit was free and the weather reminded me I hadn't spoken to anyone for a long time. Other than Raffael, this fake cop guy and a bunch of waiters, shopkeepers and so on, I hadn't spoken to a real person for a long time. My confidence had been shattered, but it was rebuilding. There was no longer any of the 'I can't go out to the street', the crazy hallucinations or fearful predictions.

It wasn't over, but at least I was over it. I could walk around freely. It was time to start talking around. I set myself the target of talking to at least one new person. It was a start, just because the ugliness wasn't over didn't mean I had to keep the restoration on hold.

I took myself to the plaza and picked a bench in the sun and waited for the next free spirit to be gifted along. I had been to the square since I met Bill, many times, but always hesitated at anything more than the exchange of more than the briefest of words. But that had changed, I was resolute, determined to regain that part of my life. Even if this would be the only chance I would get in the coming weeks or months.

The square never changed. The people, the flora, the seasons: they all did, but their unsynchronised patterns blended into the larger pattern, creating a different kind of constant. A constant which meant, to me, that the plaza never changed.

As talking to the random isn't something you can hurry up, I quickly grew impatient. The confidence was there, but the joy in procrastination and hesitation were long gone. I had somehow been reduced to acting only open or closed. I opted for open, as it was the only thing that would actively change my situation.

People came and went, people passed and people sat. I had a few words with a few people, but being open doesn't mean the next person would be.

The square settled as *hoi poloi* went back to its grindstones. I got up and went to Raffael's for a snack and a coffee.

I thanked him for the day before and how much good it had done me. He replied almost in kind. As 'almost' as Raffael could achieve given his tendency for exaggeration. It turned out that he was suffering the same lack of neutral acquaintances. I took a panini sandwich and a very long black coffee to a street-side table in the sun. The dribs and drabs of the bustle hustled by, but the sun sat still proud, instructing them not to leave early, not to miss what would be the last rays for some time.

Some passed quickly others took heed and moved slowly. The shop was still busy and eventually somebody asked to share my table. It was a young lady, she asked if she could join me at the table with a timid forcefulness and unadulterated politeness. She looked familiar in the 'I've seen her somewhere before' sense, but the way she acted and spoke reassured me that I didn't know her from Eve. She was deeply concentrated, keying something into a cell phone.

With less important things to do, I busied myself watching her. She was young, probably the same age as I was: twenty-seven or twenty-eight perhaps. Blonde, although her skin suggested a darker colour, yet I couldn't see any signs of her having dyed it. She was very pretty, but the way she was dressed and composed gave her a hard shell, the fire seemed never to have taken hold of her belly but still raged across the surface.

She finished keying things and looked around as if to say, 'I was ages doing that, why hasn't anyone taken my order by now'.

"You're better off going up to the counter at this time of the day," I remarked.

She let out a small grunt-type sigh and stood up. She looked down to her belongings on the chair between us. I put my hand up to reassure her that they would be safe on my watch, and she smiled unexpectedly and walked off.

When she sat back down, it was to examine her direct environment carefully. She seemed so sure there was something nearby to do, something to occupy her. Uncomfortable silence? Perhaps, I wanted to say something, today was the day for saying something, but in the end this was an attractive element of the other side. It wasn't the same. There was a different motivation, which is a different starting point, and if you start from a different place it doesn't matter where you end up: it's still a different journey.

By the time my thought had processed, she had opted for something else to do on the phone. I turned my attention to judging her a little further. She was well dressed, sleek and streamlined corporate sexy. Earlier that day, she had contained it all within a very conservative suit, grey-blue and a white blouse. She had a small black leather bag with her, which sat on the empty chair on top of a leather document folder. Her hair was pulled tightly back, streamlining her further. Add to all this her plucked eyebrows, she was pulling off the 'don't fuck with me' look with the greatest of competence. I stepped off the conversation podium on this thought. Too dynamic for me.

But soon it appeared that there wasn't enough new or interesting going on within the phone and she slid it into the black bag. Then she looked up immediately seeking for the waiter. Her every move was calculated.

I went to open my mouth to say something, not really knowing what would come out, and in the end nothing did. Perhaps I didn't want to disturb the ballet. It was flustered poetry, and it was creating a conflict between my love of observation and the goal I had set myself earlier that day.

She snapped her head towards me and caught me looking directly at her. I mentally ducked behind the table, expecting the worst, but a reprisal never came. Instead, she merely took a deep breath then relaxed into her chair. It was almost an over-exaggerated movement, as if it were a difficult sequence of her routine and she was still struggling to master it. But she was genuine. She went from a bolt-upright hare's posture to being slumped into a weekend slouch.

"God, I am so sorry! Did you say something." She looked into me, her coldness had disappeared and been replaced by what seemed to be the most unpretentious manner.

"No, I didn't. But…" I hesitated.

"But what?" She tilted her head slightly.

At this point I think I blushed. I hadn't had enough experience with the other sex to be sure, but it was the only explanation I could think of.

"Nothing, I didn't say anything. I was going to, but I didn't."

"Well, what were you going to say," she said growing ever more inquisitive.

"I have no idea." I laughed, but at myself.

She smiled and told me not to worry. So I tried to stop.

"Well, I was going to tell you, firstly that if you are in a hurry you should go and talk to Raffael, then he might hurry it up. But that was just at first, then you looked at me. Then you relaxed. And I was expecting you might say something…"

"Like?"

I resisted shrinking into my chair, my heart needed all the space I could give it.

"Why are you looking at me like that?" She continued to look intently at me. So much for a slow return to talking to the world. What had happened since I had been away?

"You were looking at me?"

"Yes, I was," I said.

"Why?"

Why? She asked me! Why? It was a question for the ages.

"I don't know, I am sorry. I just look at people I guess. Kind of what I do. Besides, you attracted my attention."

"How?" She remained calm and relaxed, more intrigued than interrogative.

"You seemed agitated and hurried, I was just thinking I should try to help you out." I resisted the obvious answer; I wasn't trying to pick her up. "By saying, you know, what I didn't say."

She smiled wider. Just what I needed, sympathy.

I felt the need to escape, to get up and run home. To run anywhere to get away from her captivating captivation. Her gaze was hypnotising.

I turned to look inside the coffee shop, luckily I caught Raffael's eye. I made some facial and eyebrow rearrangements to tell him she was in a hurry. Although I think he probably understood that we were both in a hurry.

When I turned back, she was still staring at me, like some enchantress. I smiled but felt wildly uncomfortable.

"Thanks!"

"What for?" I said, assuming she meant for ensuring her lunch would arrive more rapidly.

"For thinking what you thought. Its nice to be noticed. In that sense I mean. Anyway, I'm not really in a hurry, but thank you anyway." She sat back and finally pulled apart the last stitches holding together her rigid stare. She decided to look around her. This time she did so with the air of someone taking in a green valley on a Sunday afternoon with their only plan being to enjoy a lengthy picnic.

Although, now that I had become intrigued, she had clammed up. As the seconds ticked by, however, I watched as she swallowed, took a mental deep breath and then turned back to me.

"I have a confession. I walked past you a few minutes before I sat down. I noticed you for some reason. You stood out. Anyway, before I got to the end of the block my brain had decided I had to come and sit back down. It took twice as much to do it, but… look, don't ask me why, something just told me to do it." She looked slightly embarrassed. I invented a facial expression for 'don't be, I like you too, so carry on.'

So she did, "When I sat down I really kind of panicked. So I just pretended you know, to be busy, thinking, worrying and even hoping that if nothing happened I could leave quickly. Like it was all a big coincidence."

I smiled. She was smiling too. It felt like the right thing to do.

"I see…" We both started laughing.

Raffael had approached silently with her food and caught us completely off guard, causing us to straighten up like we had been caught behind the bike shed. He winked at me as he walked away.

She started talking and eating. She told me about her and her job and how she hated it and how she had texted a colleague to cover for her in case this meeting took a long time. She talked about mundane things but with a manner that told me they weren't really that mundane.

I was caught up, transfixed by her. Was she that interesting or was it hormones or was it something else? Was it even escapism? Before I had the chance to work it out, she said something that made me nearly choke on my coffee.

Out of the blue sky and with as much reason as I could figure, out she said, "Would you like to go out some time?"

If I'd had the chance to disguise my surprise, I would have tried. She took back, to the point of dejection. I am sorry, am I being asked out?

"I'm sorry," I said apologetically, "it's just that I am not used to being asked out!"

She looked at me through slightly closed eyes before saying, "Really?"

"It's been a while," I replied truthfully. I thought about it silently, but she pressed on. I would loved to have taken her there and then. Stolen her away and gone back to the countryside. It wasn't the right time. I told her so, ending along the lines of, "Please, don't take offence or anything, I am just really tied up at the moment. And I wouldn't want that to interfere."

"None taken, but what is it that's bothering you? Is it work? You didn't tell me what you do."

"It's not that, it's other things...." My squirming was halted as I saw my ex-assailant-cum-partner waltz along the opposite side of the street. She looked across to see what had distracted me, but to her obviously no one stood out. She looked back to me.

"I'm sorry, I just saw a friend of mine. He's going to be going to my house."

I went to stand up, then sat back down. The look on the

girl's face portrayed mistaken identity mixed with deception, as if I had finished telling her I was either gay or in an unhappy marriage. "Look, absolutely nothing on this planet would please me more than going out with you."

Or someone, or being free to do so.

"It's really, just, a bad time." I looked into her eyes for some kind of response but my mind just kept on putting words in my mouth. "Wait a minute! You're single?"

"Yes, I am," she smiled timidly and flushed.

Wow, I thought, but allowed my body language to express it rather than my flailing tongue. I was still half on the edge of my seat. I had to leave, but I was torn.

"So?" I offered.

"So?" She offered in return.

I relaxed back in the chair at a loss. She had returned to upright, I sat forward and put my hand on hers.

"Look, I really do have to go. I am sorry. No, really, sorry. And, err well, what can I say? Disappointed in life. If we were six months up or down the line it would have been a different story."

We smiled again. I made to get up, but something stopped me. I wasn't going to forget again.

"Before I go. Can I know your name?"

"Penelope, my name is Penelope, but they call me Penny." She smiled and fluttered.

"Penny, words don't describe. Sammy." She smiled again.

"Next time Penny, I promise."

"OK! I am going to hold you to it."

I walked past Raffael as I sped off, telling him I had to go and to put her Bill with mine. He patted me on the shoulder and smiled. I stepped back into a different world.

I looked back twice. The first time I saw her looking at me as if she had been waiting for me to do it. The second time I saw her being told by Raffael, 'it's out of my hands.' I turned the corner and began trying to forget all about it.

* * *

By the time I reached my block, I'd remembered what it meant to be serious. I saw 'the guy' looking at my building much in the way a burglar might, but it suggested more like he was about to leave. I'd figured he would have walked back the same direction and so hadn't hurried.

I was glad he hadn't recognised me at the coffee shop. I couldn't establish if he would have done anything, approached me or waved. It didn't matter; I took it as a sign. It hadn't been the time for doing other things. For making new acquaintances. Not emotionally dependant ones at least. It was a painful sign but sensible. I had to move on.

He saw me coming. He checked his watch, as if we had made some schedule and that was how he would pass away the time it took me to arrive in the hope that I would also understand I was late. Only I wasn't, because we hadn't. In fact, I felt like slowing down, then I remembered something that made me act otherwise.

"Look, before we go anywhere, tell me what your name is. It's beginning to piss me off."

"Gil." He looked offended as if he had been expecting, 'Hi, Sweetie! and a kiss on the cheek.'

"Thanks," I said before leading him inside.

I was going to be in control again. Of the situation at least. Having monopoly over both the scene and my body had seemed previously a daunting and unachievable task. But I figured the former was the more relevant. I offered him coffee. He looked at me surprised.

"Hey, Gil." I started reinforcing the name. "I have resigned to doing this. You know I don't really want to, but I am going to. And since I haven't had a huge deal of choice in the involvement, I am going to assume it elsewhere." He looked at me somewhat confused, clearly not used to being addressed so viciously by people ten or fifteen years his junior. "So, if we are going to do this, let's do it professionally. Although I assume this is how you are used to working?"

"Uh, yes it is. And thanks."

"What for?" I said off hand.

"For taking it seriously." I didn't really register it. "It's my ass that on the line."

"You have changed your tune."

"So have you," he replied quickly.

He was right. We smiled and it didn't seem so bad after all. I made coffee and we got into planning.

"Ok, this is what you need to know, interrupt me if there is something you don't understand or don't think you can handle. To corner him, and I'll tell you more about him in a minute, we need something on him. At the moment we have loads but who's going to believe me or you? No one. So, in a nutshell we need to either catch him doing something he shouldn't be doing or at least get our hands on some solid proof of it. If you know what I mean." He winked at me. "So, the first thing we need is an angle. With you younger guys it's generally pretty easy, girls, beer, younger girls, drugs or young girls. We need to find out what he likes, what can he be tempted with. As for cops I don't know what flips their biscuits, but I think it's generally weird shit. Comes with the job."

"So what are you saying?"

"Let's deal with the basics, let's assume that he's friendly to you. Hmm, I was going to ask you, what do you think about bringing someone else in. It's ok?"

"Not unless absolutely necessary. We need to keep this on a 'need to know' basis don't we?"

"They wouldn't have to know everything that's happened, just what's going to happen."

I pondered it, be reiterated my scepticism.

"Ok, let's assume it's you in that case. Your job is to befriend our friendly neighbourhood homicide detective and convince him you are really on his side and want only the best for him. Then we need to catch him up to no good.

We can record any conversations you have with him, but it's not a huge threat. We can offer it to the media and it's likely to cause him a shit storm but it doesn't have much weight."

"So?"

"So, we need some evidence that he was up to no good."

"Wait! Evidence?"

"Yes, you know, photos, video recording, witnesses that kind of thing."

"And, no good?"

"First we need to find out what lights his buttons. All cops are up to no good, but we need something that he will not want — under any circumstances a single person, the entire world, his boss, his wife and kids, his friends, — anybody basically to know."

I wasn't sure what kind of stuff they got up to on the job, let alone off it.

"You name it. Bribes, scams, skimming money and evidence. They steal whatever they can. In neighbourhoods like our departed friend's they hold up the kids, steal their money, drugs and guns in return for not being busted. Saves them the paperwork too, I guess."

"You sound as if you approve." I looked at him in a way that would say I disagreed with his apparent approval.

"It gets the shit and guns off the street."

"But what do the cops do with it?"

He paused. "Ok, we are getting off the point. Let's leave the metaphysics debates for another day. Perhaps a lot of it ends up back on the street, it's not the best system. But it puts us on one of the right sides of it."

I felt like it was actually the right time to be starting a crusade against bent police officers, as everything that had happened was of secondary importance.

"So I lure the cop, take him somewhere, we do something bad and then what?"

"Then we tell him we caught him, threaten him up a bit and skedaddle before he gets his trousers back round his waist."

"It all sounds so easy."

Gil took me that afternoon to wait in a coffee shop across the street from a police station.

"Don't cops work in pairs?"

"You've been watching too many movies, kid."

I looked at him for a more detailed explanation.

"Look, I'm not any expert. But you have a guy who works on each case. He has a secondary or something who backs him up to go to crime scenes and all the rest of it. But it makes no difference to us. This is the guy, he's crooked and he can get us both off the hook."

We sat and watched. Gil ran over and over the kind of acting skills I would need.

"And in the end we just get him to get rid of all the things that tie me… us to the dead bodies."

I raised an eyebrow.

"Slip of the tongue." It seemed genuine. "Besides, there can't be a great deal, it's not like they have been around to arrest you yet, is it?"

He had a good point and I felt rewarded for having covered my tracks so well.

"So what do we do now?"

"Well, I am going to show you who he is. He'll be out soon. Then we'll follow him. He usually goes to the same bar and to see some young girl and then home. We'll follow him today, then from there it's up to you."

"Up to me?"

Gil looked at me. I turned back to face the street. Letting him examine the side of my face instead. He carried on looking at me. "Are you up to this?"

"Yes, I guess." I turned back briefly and hesitantly.

"Don't guess. Yes or no?" he demanded.

"Ok, yes, I am." More firmly this time. I wasn't. It sounded like the most ridiculous thing I would ever do in my life. Talk about flirting with danger. But Gil had charmed snakes that were wilier than I was. Even now as I was discovering this, I couldn't help but remember how he had hung a sword above my chest and how it was too late to back out.

"Ok, so one day you don't follow him, you wait for him. Do what you have to do and that's it. It's all over."

A few minutes later the cop came out, we watched him leave and then followed him on foot for fifteen minutes to a bar, then by taxi to a residential area. He then took a cab back to the police station and left in an unmarked car. We didn't follow him home. The bar would be the place to pick him up.

They had been two crazy days. The storm had re-entered my life. I reflected that evening. The calmness of drinking beer and chatting with Raffael. The determination of getting back the missing elements of my life, meeting the girl Penny.

The girl Penny had definitely been a highlight. I played it over in my head and wondered if we would ever have a second opportunity. Why didn't that kind of thing happen more often? Is that why it's so special, because it's rare? It shouldn't be based on resource shortage.

I thought about Gil. He fascinated me. I was drawn to find out more about him. What was he like? Where did he learn all that he knew? Why did he start what he did? What and who were his family? He was an abyss of mystery. His confidence had returned, it struck me, and he had admitted it was his ass more on the line. I don't know why he submitted that to me, but it was a clear sign that he was still confident.

I struggled against it. I didn't want to get involved with him, the less I knew the better. The sooner out relationship was severed the better. Whatever he wanted to do with whatever I would do was his business. Whoever he was,

was also his business.

Besides, I was sure no cop was going to sit back and let Gil fuck his life up. There would surely be a return of serve. I didn't want to be involved in that. Would I even be able to escape that? To get him to give up his evidence we would have to give up ours.

Some questions I dismissed, others I put to my stalking criminal encyclopaedia, and the rest I figured would be part of the learning curve.

Gil appeared again the next day around lunchtime, catching me a few minutes before I was about to leave for some food. I aired some of my concerns. He told me he had a plan to deal with the cop afterwards, and repeatedly not to worry about it. It seemed strange that he would take the rest of it on his own. I didn't know what to think. Whether he didn't trust me or whether he thought I would have done enough. I couldn't come to a conclusion and didn't want to confront him over extra responsibility. The sooner he was out of my life, the sooner it was all out of my life. I felt hurried all of a sudden.

"So, this cop we are dealing with is a dirty SOB. He's not as bad as they come, but about as amoral as they do." He told me with the vigour of someone who had just found a new book on his favourite subject. "He likes young girls. Funny that. But not young, young. Just come of age, if you know the expression. Apparently he's one, or at least was one for busting young girls for drinking or drugs then letting them off for a show or blow in return."

I had already thought of a good approach. I told Gil about it and he agreed with the new information he had that it would probably work.

"Look, we need to do this. You can get into a lot of trouble following cops around, especially when you are already a suspect. If we could find a pretty, young girl to take part all the better. But I don't know if he's still up to this or not. This girl he goes to visit some evenings is suspect, but I have no idea what their relationship is. Could be his fucking niece for all I know. And that's not going to get us anywhere."

"Hey Gil." I hadn't even thought about the question or about saying it. It just came out. "What happens if we get caught?" I wasn't even sure what you would call the crime we were about to commit. I was sure it was punishable and that whatever the punishment was, it wasn't going to be worse than that of double homicide. I hadn't thought at any point what the consequences would be, if they didn't involve me being free to do whatever I wanted I wasn't interested in knowing. Anything more than a fine would be more than I could deal with. Although such an outcome would, all things considered, be a ridiculous punishment, it still would have pissed me off.

"Well," he started with a tactician's approach, "It depends on the stage we have reached. If, for example, we get caught in the middle of it all, we're fucked. Big-time. The both of us."

It was an obvious answer, I don't know why it surprised me, the stark reality I guess.

"But, hopefully, even in that situation we bring him down with us."

I looked at Gil sceptically. Why was that even relevant? "Is that supposed to be some kind of consolation?"

"No, besides we are both going to become suspects for the murder. We become accomplices."

"And if we get to the other side without being caught."

"We'll still be up shit creak. If it all comes out, people are going to want to know the hows, wheres, whys and so on." He had definitely done his homework. But it only made me more nervous.

I thought back to the few days after the murder. I had been more worried then definitely. There couldn't have been any good evidence. And so what if they find out now. It's all going to be so crooked it might get thrown out of court before it arrived. It could still have been a set up, particularly given that Gil was becoming more confident. He had the motive. He was under suspicion. But it worked both ways, he wanted to get out. They could prove it against him in court if they really wanted to. Getting rid of the cop, of the evidence.

I was being pulled. I justified what I was getting into on the grounds that it was easier than walking away, easier than resisting. I wondered if Gil had ever contemplated handing me in after he had found me. With hindsight, I could have walked out at any point, but my mind was so occupied with calculating the future I couldn't have taken on new tasks. The only upside at any time was that I was doing another human being a favour. When he had first turned up he looked like he really needed help. Things had changed in that week and a half. Now I felt like the one needing help.

Gil's head must have been full too, but he was doing a better job of keeping all the variables in line. He seemed more logical and to have taken the thought process much further ahead. The idea of it becoming public disturbed me. They would know a certain detective had been set up, and certain evidence had gone missing. They wouldn't be that lax and let it slide.

I questioned Gil over these worries, only to become more worried that he seemed to have answers to all of them. And good answers at that.

"What if I fuck up and can't get him to confess to anything?"

"You don't have that option." Gil explained in a very matter-of-fact way. "Look, you have been on the other side of a good hustle. Do what Bill did and we'll be fine. After that, forget about it all. I can handle it."

"There's something else in it for you isn't there?"

"What makes you say that," his reply was tainted by a

hint of defensiveness.

"Something. I mean, it's not quite fifty/fifty is it?"

"You think you're doing the hard work?" Gil sounded shocked.

"No, the opposite." He didn't say anything in response, but his response said he had been caught at something. "Well? What is it?"

"The important thing is being in the bar when he arrives. You can't turn up afterwards. It's too risky, you might as well pick him up on the street."

I looked at Gil, I felt angry, I looked angry.

"Look, don't worry about it kid. What goes on between me and him goes on between me and him. That's why I am taking more than my share of it. I don't want you to be involved and you don't really want or need to be involved. Isn't that right?"

I acceded. He was right. I didn't want to thank him, I didn't know what he had. The cop was trying to frame him for his own motives after all.

I sat in the bar waiting for the cop and thinking. I thought about so many things, almost to the point I thought he wasn't going to show up.

Firstly, I thought about how I had killed someone, two people, in fact. Why had that slipped my mind? Wasn't I supposed to live with it forever, especially in situations like the one I faced? Where was the paranoia and the sweat? Where was the remorse?

It reminded me of the myth that murderers always want to be caught. They leave pieces of evidence behind, they make mistakes afterwards and they have loose lips. Would this be my time to trip? None of those amazing coincidences had happened to me. Perhaps they only arrest the wrong people, thinking it's all of them.

There is a flip side to every coin. I wondered how many undetected murdered bodies have returned to the earth without a repented soul to match. For every unlucky or fame-seeking murderer, there was an extra chance my luck wouldn't turn bad. It didn't seem obvious that they would want to be caught. Was it meant literally? Did they want the fame? Did they want to tell someone how clever they had been? How meticulously they had covered their tracks?

Once the hype dies down, you lose the feeling to scream out, 'it was me' every time you hear someone say, 'I wonder who it was'. The glory disappears with the media cameras. Once they have gone its just the fear that you are left with.

Besides I had always considered myself lucky, there had been no plan, there was luck but not intelligence or logic. For all it mattered the clothes could still be lying in my sink and the gun on my bedside table. I had nothing to brag about.

On top of that, I was rehabilitated. I didn't consider I needed to be caught. Prison wouldn't teach me anything except how to be a better criminal. If the opportunity ever presented itself a second time, I would have the presence of mind to avoid killing anyone. I was sure of that. Punishment aside, society could wash its hands of the whole affair.

But none of this accounted for the situation with which I was still dealing. Gil had pressured me into doing it straight away. Like he had more need to get on with his normal life than I did. Whether he did or, I would have rather been better prepared, and it would be difficult to disassociate his hurry and my fears.

The bar was a nice place. Quiet, lots of wood panelling, pictures of dead or dying sportsmen, green lamp shades, sports paraphernalia. You know the sort.

I had taken a booth along a wall that ran parallel to the bar. Its seediness had appealed to me; it was a good place for doing bad things.

When the cop came in, he sat at the bar with his back to me. He ordered a beer and sat drinking it slowly. Gil had said he usually stayed about forty-five minutes. I watched him drink the first beer, it was nearly ten minutes before he had reached anywhere near the bottom.

My heart was pounding at the thought of making that first move. I wiped the sweat from my palms on the tight velvet covering of the bench on which I was sat. The beer I was drinking had gone straight to my head. My stomach was drained. There was little opportunity to turn around and even less to stall. Thirty minutes should be just enough, Gil had told me. I drank down the rest of my beer and pushed it to the edge of the table.

The barman noticed the gesture and when he'd finished drying glasses he casually wandered over, picked the bottle up and wiped the table, "Another?"

"Yes, and one for the lonely guy at the bar."

He raised an eyebrow at me, as if I was trying to pick the guy up. I shook my head, but my heart was racing. 'It's just an acting lesson,' I told myself. 'Had I walked into a gay bar? Was the cop gay?' I shook it off.

The cop got up and put his hand in his pocket, about to leave. My heart pounded and my self-consciousness evaporated. Fortunately the barman had returned to the bar and was already sliding the first beer onto the bar. He put the second one on the bar and spoke to the cop.

The cop in turn looked around at me, and I raised my head. He brought both bottles over and sat at the table, sideways, keeping his legs in contact with the free world.

"And to what do I owe this?" he asked gently.

"Well, you looked like you could do with someone to talk to, and the way my day has been going so could I."

He looked blankly at me.

"You know, to take the mind off things." He relaxed a little. And put out his hand.

"Paolo," I told him.

"Yes," he replied.

"No, my name is Paolo."

He laughed, "I guessed that, so is mine."

For those first few sentences, I noticed I couldn't coordinate, neither my words with the plan I'd made, not my hand with my voice. We eventually shook hands laughing at the coincidence. But it was only me who knew it could so easily have been avoided. I would never have planned it, but it broke all the ice.

Everything left my head, I was lost but free, my confidence came back slowly and he, having avoided the awkward situation, sat himself into the chair, thanked me for the beer and we began talking.

"So why has your day been so rough?"

I wasn't supposed to give out straight away. "When we know each other a little better. Or failing that after a few more of these." I held the bottle for a toast. He looked at me a little puzzled and intrigued but lifted his bottle to mine.

We made some small talk, where we grew up, teams, neighbourhoods that kind of thing. It was all bullshit on my part, well, mainly.

He seemed like he had a lot on his mind and talking the unfamiliar familiar relaxed him more and more. I felt like an analyst. But it was going to plan.

He started talking about his job. "Lots of stress, lots of pressure. A really fucking patronising boss. But wait," he paused, "Why do we get to talk abut my job and not yours?"

"Don't know, you seem quite jovial for someone how is overworked and under paid."

"Hmph, you don't know the half of it. But, no, it's good to talk to someone neutral about it. Otherwise it's just the boys or the… hold on, now we are getting into my private life."

"Open table." I raised my glass again. He drank to it. "So what exactly is it that you do?" Like I didn't know.

"I am a detective." He announced in the way they all probably do, like you should be surprised and awe filled.

I feigned surprise. "Yes? And what do you detect?"

"Murders."

"Cool," I said with a teenage morbid fascination, not sure which approach to continue with, the fascination or the pay grade. I sipped the beer and composed myself.

I hoped Paolo would choose the route for me, but we were already heading for uncomfortable territory, and it looked like he wasn't going to pick.

"So, tell me more."

"What do you want to know?"

"I don't know, is it like the TV?" He laughed and dropped his face into his lap. "Sorry, I bet that's all you get, right?"

"More than you'd believe. But remember they edit out time doing paperwork and the head scratching when you can't figure it out. And forget about all the unsolved cases. But I guess in some respects it's the same, although sometimes its unimaginably slower than TV. Painstaking and all the rest of it."

I nodded with interest. "But, it must be fast paced sometimes?"

"Sometimes, when there is a new case it's always interesting, the crime scene, evidence, leads and that stuff. Just like you imagine it. Arrests are fun sometimes, but with murderers they are usually the most frightened by death, most of them having seen death too close to risk running. Not like the drug dealers do."

"But then there is more chance of you getting hurt too."

"Exactly."

"So why is it so stressful?"

"The frustration. When it's not open-closed, it's always frustrating. Especially when you either know who to arrest but you can't or vice versa."

Every word sent shivers running. It was all too close to the point, but the analyst inside told me not to push anything.

"Then, when the two sides come together, and the killer is lapping the sun and surf somewhere, you get your boss going, 'why didn't you pick him up while he was around, why did you let him go, why did you take so long to find this out. Those are the days I drink a beer before going home."

He came across to me as so genuine I even felt a little sorry for him. The knowledge that he was up to other things pressured me to keep on. He was the antagonist after all, he needed all of my concentration. I was sitting opposite the guy who was looking for me, but didn't know it. A guy, who could, at a moment's notice, send me to jail for a long time. That was the other motivation. It was an imminently close hurdle and I wasn't a horse that was about to bolt and be put down.

"Damned if you, damned if you don't."

"I'll drink to that," he drank the rest of the bottle and looked for the guy to come over.

"So what do you do when you aren't detecting?" I couldn't have asked a more direct question. It pounded a repetition my head like I had just sent myself to jail. But in any normal conversation it's a normal question.

"Not at work? When's that?" He let out a lazy laugh, then his expression changed to one that said he was being truthful.

"That bad, huh?"

"Not really, but the stress is what eats the time away. I seem to spend all the free time I have failing to relax enough to be able to enjoy it." A second round of beer arrived just in time. He pulled himself up, "OK, over this beer we talk about why your life is so hard."

I laughed, "It pales in comparison. It's not stress for me though, it's the frustration."

"What do you do?"

"I'm a photographer." He furrowed his forehead.

"How is that a hard job?"

"I shoot for a glamour mag. A teen glamour mag." I did my best to look embarrassed, I could feel the intention translating to my face, but I didn't know if it was actually showing.

"Still don't get it," he said lightly.

"It's like this," I shot a glance around me, "My girlfriend left me few months ago and now I'm not getting it on tap at home. And shooting these girls all day long in bikinis and tight clothing just winds me up. And they're so young some of them."

"But you can be that old?"

"I'm getting on for thirty, but that's not the point, is it?"

"Oh, you mean that young! They can't all be, so why you don't get any on the job?"

There goes the hook.

"This is respectable teen magazines. It's not pornography: they get orgies every other day. Even in the grey glamour market, there's those who'll insist on either before the shoot or after the shoot. Part of making the girls look fuckable. But what I do is sixteen years old, not a nipple in sight. It's all skimpy tops and makeup. The girls are all sluts, they offer it up all the time, but usually in front of their fucking parents. And even when they are old enough it's just too risky. They watch us all."

He shot me a sympathetic look. "Damned if you do, damned if you don't." He toasted and we drank. The plan going to plan. I left to make the call and take a piss.

When I returned the cop looked like he was in deep thought. I sat down and didn't say anything. I just waited. If Gil knew his onions, the torrent would begin as a trickle.

"I can see how that would be frustrating, you know, if you aren't getting it at home." He didn't seem sure, so I reassured him.

"Yeah, it was fine when Jade was at home, everything was taken care of. Besides, at home I can imagine it's one of those young girls." I roughed my voice a little.

"So what are you doing about it then? If you don't mind me asking."

"Nothing, I tried hookers. But it's expensive, especially when you come from teen super models at work. I mean it's not all about value for money, it's a desire thing too. It's too easy, nothing like the same process of flirting with danger. So now," I pulled the bottle close to my edge of the table, "I am trying alcoholism."

I took a swig and checked myself, both the alcohol and the character were going to my head. I didn't know if the cop was drunk yet, I couldn't exactly breathalyse him.

"I guess I should just get out more."

"I hear that."

"But even then it's so fucking difficult. My ex was an ex-model, we began back in the days when it wasn't so looked down upon. But that's gone and so has she. And what am I left with, models getting younger and me getting older."

"Standards are too high then?"

"You said it." I sipped the beer. "And you? Wife, kids, dog, pension and the rest of it?"

"You think it's that easy? That happy?"

I shrugged my shoulders in defence of my rhetorical question.

"No, now we are just two grown ups who share a house."

"So you aren't getting it at home either? Or does looking at stiffs all day kill the libido?"

For some reason he took that line on a serious note, and starting explaining that he doesn't see many dead bodies. It turned into quite a monologue, but there was just enough indifference in his voice to reassure me. He made his point that he had very little contact: just briefly at the scene and perhaps once or twice later in the morgue. With that said he came quite quickly back to the topic of more interest to him.

"But you're right, I get frustrated. But you don't have to get in to bed every night with your ex and not get any."

"That's pretty harsh. But are you still attracted to her?"

He pulled out his wallet and showed me a photo of her." She was quite attractive. "It's just a sexual thing I guess," he continued, "You know, physical hormonal thing."

"So you haven't moved onto hookers yet?"

"You kidding, right? I'm a cop. Getting picked up by a colleague, not going to look to good on a Monday morning is it?"

"You don't get some kind of special access then?"

"Haha! Right, I'd be the first to admit the kind of shit that goes on, but a cop-whore house? That would really make the front page. But it's horses for courses I guess. You have it in the day, I get it at night."

"That's the way it is."

"And you can't date models anymore?"

"Not any more, I could probably get away with it, but photographers tend to come from agencies. And so do the girls. So word spreads pretty quickly nowadays. So there's no more fucking your way to the top for the girls either."

"But did you ever?" He raised a sly eyebrow at me.

"Of course, that's how I met Jade."

"No, I mean with a model, on the set or something?"

"Hey! Aren't you a cop?"

"It's off the record I promise."

"You mean did I ever fuck one of the models? Yes, of course."

"The younger ones?"

"I told you, they're all young." I don't know why I was avoiding the question, embarrassment over lies? Didn't seem right, perhaps I thought he was recording the conversation too.

"Why?" It was a genius question when it hit me, but in hindsight it was obvious, "You like younger girls?"

"Hey, I'm a cop," he mimicked me. He looked around to clear the coast again. "Not young-young, you know, nothing illegal or perverted."

"I see, now I get it. You want me to hook you up with some models?"

"No, well, now you mention it, but no, it wasn't what I was driving at."

I avoided telling him whether I actually could or not. It felt plausible, or at least on the cusp of being plausible. I guess photographers must get asked that all the time.

"Perhaps one day you can come along and watch a shoot. Provided you keep it zipped up that is."

He laughed and said thanks, but didn't push after the offer. Thankfully.

"Anyway, I can get it away from home. I could I mean." He admitted. I raised my eyebrows to see if he would expand. "I do have a kind of mistress."

I nodded my head approvingly, but it wasn't quite what I was looking for. He explained that the after-work visits weren't to his niece. It seemed so natural that I found myself asking about it with passing interest, hurrying to look for a new angle. But his reply pricked my ears up.

"Well, and this is definitely off the record," he definitely seemed to be taking to the beer. "This, shit," he laughed introspectively, "This makes your whore-house idea seem tame. So a year or so ago, this girl turned up dead. She had died of an enormous OD, so bad in fact it looked like she had been killed by someone intentionally. So it got passed through us, not to me, I was secondary. This girl was pretty, all her photos got copied and posted around, the ones of before she was dead, that is. Turned out she had got off a plane from a well known drug country two weeks before, so we guessed she was a mule, but when they cut her open, they didn't find anything, fucking mystery, no bag nothing. And that was that. Anyway, this stiff had come over on some scholarship, three year's study plus a spot on the sports team. They'd basically brought over a whole team over to study for three years.

"Anyway, cutting to the chase, the case fell to the

wayside, but one day we were sitting around in a coffee shop and bullshitting, when someone conjured up the thought that none of the other girls died and what if they had all been carrying. What if they were as pretty as the first one, well you can follow the rest. It was a stupid joke at the beginning but it got quickly out of hand and the next thing we knew we were looking up each of these girls for interviews, official police business and the rest of it. We gave them the rough end of the stick, the affair had been covered up for PR, the stiff girl was no longer part of the team, but these girls had all probably come with something. So went bent their arms. You could tell the ones who had come with the drugs, they folded at the first question. But the others? Who knows. Anyway, one of the girls I ended up interviewing struck me quite well. And so we are still at it."

"And she had been carrying?"

"Perhaps. It's along time ago now, we've moved on. She's in the relationship willingly."

"Really?" I didn't believe him, I was shocked by what he had told me.

"Well, you know, we don't talk about it."

"And this was how long ago?"

"About eight months."

I shook my head but then nodded in manly approval. I felt quite sceptical underneath the morality of it all. "It's a fucking story man."

"Don't I know it. Perhaps when I retire I'll write about it. Provided you don't get to it first."

"Me? No chance, I am a photographer remember?" I wanted to add, if you last that long, just to shut him up. But I kept it inside. The beer was getting to me and I was playing judge over this guy: what he told me would crush him and it was a glove I could put on or take off at will. And having known someone thirty minutes before he admitted that to me made my palms very itchy.

I didn't know if it was enough, whether I should hold out

for more. I excused myself to piss once again. "But don't go anywhere, I want to hear more."

I called Gil and told him to come over. Telling him roughly what was going on, I could hear him dancing around on the other end of the line like an excited school kid.

The cop passed me as I went back to the table, he was stumbling a little, he stopped me. "Seriously, you can't tell anyone about this."

I told him not to worry and mimicked a few camera clicking movements again. He seemed happy enough with that and carried on, sending more beers to the table before disappearing down the long dark corridor to the toilets.

I sat and reflected, it was tough keeping that kind of rage inside. It was bad enough telling the lies I had told. But I stepped away. What I was there to do was going smoothly, easily in fact. I wondered if anything could actually go wrong. He was drunk enough know to never suspect anything. I was the only thing that could go wrong. And it was too late in the game for that. I was in the character and firmly there. I could probably get away with telling him I was the murderer and still have enough leverage. But it would have been pointless. As far as I was concerned, Gil wasn't even going to tell him that I was the murderer. Only in the case that I tried to fuck him over. Otherwise, I was just some extra, paid by the hour to do as I was told and not ask any questions.

The line had been crossed. It was downhill. I breathed a sigh of relief and pulled my character back over me. I saw Gil wander past the window without looking in. He must have been close by. He wouldn't do anything stupid like come in while I was still here.

The cop sat down. He had brought the beers with him. "Here's to new friends and old secrets." And we toasted.

"I am quite amazed at what you told me. Is it, you know, unusual or far out, or does is this kind of thing normal?" I said.

"This is a bit far out, it's like a scale, the less serious any punishment will be the more likely it is a cop's going to do it."

"You're going to be rich when you retire then, best start looking for someone to share the money with!" Now it was the alcohol that was talking.

"Perhaps it'll work out one day, you know with the one I've got," he said.

"For me, I knew when it was over, I guess she had done too, but we neither of us said anything. Then it all came out in the open, we both admitted we had both known. And we both agreed getting it in the open was the best thing."

He looked at me contemplating a confrontation. Like he was making the decision there and then. I didn't want him to leave anyone, I didn't really care. Surely, if we were trying to manufacture a scandal, it would be better if they were still together when it came out. I don't know why, but I wanted to cheer him up.

I still wanted him to admit the way he had set up young girls, that was something quite personal. When you know someone's dark secrets before you know them, it's impossible not to be biased. In the moment I hoped it wasn't true, that Gil had used it to influence me.

"Still, it's better than some of the things we used to do," he wanted to admit something else. His crooked life was beginning to intrigue me. I looked at him to tell me more.

"No, it's sick and depraved and I'm not particularly proud of it."

"Hey, we all have things we are not proud of. I make extra copies of photos to take home and jerk off over, it's just some people get them of their chest and others dwell on them to the point of obsession or worse."

The cop sat contemplatively swirling the beer in his bottle. Not so much making the decision but dwelling on his secret.

"It's disgusting. But every time I would pull over a pretty young girl for speeding or for whatever; I'd let them off, you know, if they did things for me."

It shocked me a bit to hear it stated in the first person, "But, I thought you were a detective?"

"Yeah, this was before, when I was a regular cop. Besides it'd always be young girls, perhaps just learnt to drive. What differences do they know?"

"You ever get caught?"

"Caught? No! Thank god. The whole fucking world knew about it at one point, though. Cops, they always stand up for each other, but the media are a different pack of animals. It started fucking with my head, knowing that someone can just flip a switch on your career like that. Made me want to clean up my act a little."

"That's pretty fucked up."

"I told you I wasn't proud of it."

I felt like walking out, I didn't care for what he had told me. I didn't because I was struck with a moment of clarity: having fallen into my path, he was clearly receiving some form of payback. Funnily enough he had already admitted to having carried on abusing his position in other scenarios without too much regret. It made me feel one-hundred per cent better for what I was doing. But I still couldn't bare looking at him any longer. I realised I would have to be patient for a while, allow the new topic to become a few minutes old. I didn't want him clubbing me on the head before I got to the door.

"But it feels better getting it off your chest?"

"Yeah, I guess. Are you going to tell me something like a problem shared is a problem halved?"

"It's the secrets that need sharing, I don't want your problems."

We laughed and chatted on some other topics and then I told him I had a tropical fish tank that needed cleaning and that it would take most of the evening. I told him to take care of himself and 'see you again sometime' and the rest of it. We shook hands and I left him at the table with a few swigs of beer left at the bottom of his bottle.

It was painful to think I was causing the guy's life to be tipped upside down. It was easier to think I wouldn't have to do anything further towards it. He hadn't been suspicious, never hesitated like he suspected me of anything, as if he really had been waiting for someone to come along and absolve him. A coincidence perhaps.

Whatever happened I felt I had left the world balanced. I may have abused his confidence and trust, but what goes around comes around. Maybe not straight away but eventually.

I zigzagged my way past the chairs and tables, paying for the beers at the very end of the bar, and then stumbled into the fresh air. The first deep breath made my head spin. I looked around for Gil, spotting him buying something from a kiosk window a few blocks down. I took the recorder from my pocket, unplugged the wire and listened to the first few seconds of the recording, at least to make sure it had come out clearly. It would have been a little late for going back to the bar and asking if he wouldn't mind confessing again, but we do these kinds of things.

"So?" Gil demanded hurriedly.

I felt very slick, just handing him the device. I was confident, not to mention a little drunk. He demanded some more information.

"Ok, it's all there. The girl he visits? Not his niece, she's a mistress who he has blackmailed into being so. She's still paying him off. He told me she was into it now, like a real relationship and so on."

Gil stood looking at me. I knew he hadn't expected anything more than me saying, 'it's all there.' I could see he want to start dancing again.

It was too easy. The planning had paid off. Perhaps, I thought, if I had even been involved it would have been even more rewarding. I am sure Gil spent a good few hours of the last few days creating the scenario. Everything he had taught me worked perfectly, and I had used everything.

"So, I guess I'll see you later." I was thinking of going straight home, via a chocolate store.

"You don't want to wait around and see what happens?"

"Not really. Why? Are you nervous? Anyway, drop by afterwards. Or give me a call. Or tomorrow even." I didn't care if I never saw or heard about it or from him ever again.

"Hmph!" He looked at me sceptically. "Ok, take care. I'll let you know."

I hurried him off telling him the cop might not be in the bar for much longer. He walked off and I went and bought some chocolate from the same kiosk window. I unwrapped it with satisfaction. I had done a good job.

Paolo and Gil were quite surprised to see each other. But only Paolo was left wondering what was going on. He had just poured out some of his lesser secrets to a random stranger, and now Gil was showing up.

Gil sat down opposite him smiling broadly. Paolo hadn't seen Gil smile before and that next experience, mixed with mild inebriation, confused him further.

"He's good isn't he?" Gil said, then paused to wait for an answer. "The kid. He's good isn't he?" Still no reply. Then, a few seconds later, Paolo burped. "Pfwah! You stink. If you're going to be sick you should go to the bathroom now."

Paolo leapt from his seat and stumbled forward towards the bathroom. He obviously had caught on. He still had no idea who the kid was, could just be Gil's new partner, being inducted into a pact. He wondered if Gil would tell him, but he had to throw up before that would happen. He tried not to look drunk; it wasn't really why he was about to throw up after all. He made it to the toilet in good time and was already washing out his mouth when Gil walked in and locked the door behind him.

Paolo looked up from the sink at Gil, still smiling, one foot propped against the wooden door that led back out to the bar. He looked next to the mirror and just caught a glimpse of Gil pulling something from his pocket.

"Do you want me to explain it or shall I just press play. I am quite eager to know what's on it. But I guess you already know."

Paolo felt sick in every direction. He had been caught with his pants down, drunk and off his guard. His head wasn't cooperating in trying to shake of the alcohol. He looked back at the blurry Gil, every time he caught sight of him smiling he felt sicker. He was expecting him to come out with some kind of statement of the charges against him but he said nothing, and just stood there seemingly enjoying him suffer. He seemed about to leave.

"You stupid fucker!" He said between spitting. He leant himself over the sink on one arm. "You stupid fucker. I got thrown off the case a week ago. Didn't you fucking wonder why you hadn't seen me? No cops, no one bothering you."

"Don't believe you."

"You don't believe me. So fucking what, it doesn't make any difference. No one is going to come around and arrest you so what do you need that for?"

"Let's call it insurance." Gil shifted back to both feet.

"Insurance against what? You didn't do the kid or the priest so what are you worried about."

"I don't know," Gil looked uncomfortable. "Well, for starters, I know you're not the only dirty cop around. Besides, you clearly have some sort of problem with me."

"Yeah, I don't like low-life criminals."

"Lowlife? You don't get out much do you?"

"To be honest with you Gil," Paolo stood up to face Gil. "I don't know what it is you have but I don't like it very much. I just don't like you very much. There is something, but I cant quite put my finger on it. Something inherent."

Gil reflected quietly positioning himself for an easier exit. "That's fair enough I suppose. Can't say that I am too fond of you either. But I am here for a reason. Whether it's to believe you or not. I want you to… are you really too drunk to figure it out? Jeez, what did the kid do to you? Let's put it like this: I want you to destroy all the files and all the evidence, everything even remotely related to this case. Then you get this little machine with all the sins you recorded on it. And no one has to listen to it. No one, no mistresses, wives, bosses, paparazzi, no one."

"You fucking stupid lowlife. It's an illegal recording. It's not worth anything."

"Lowlife." Gil switched his tone from playful to hateful. "You're the fucking lowlife who was trying to arrest me for something you knew I didn't do. And who gives two shits whether the tape is illegal, no one is going to court yet, or are they?"

"So why are you doing this? What do you get out of it?"

"I get to see you squirm and squeal like dog with his foot caught in a drain cover."

Paolo didn't see much of how the outside world saw him. He wasn't high profile, had no responsibilities. He'd have to have done something either heroic or dastardly to have even the briefest of mentions in the media. So the rest was what we're all used to. The gossip and rumours that circulated, the periodic confrontations between friends and colleagues. That was all he knew about himself.

Everything else he ignored, when he had last been reviewed at work he had told himself 'they' didn't see the world from his eyes. He'd been told he didn't have a very open view. If he could have seen himself from any other person's objective point of view, he would probably have seen something like this coming. He looked at Gil, whose actions were still light and playful despite the newfound conviction in his words. Paolo wondered briefly where this was going to go. Gil had taken in that he wasn't on the case.

He had believed it. There was no real evidence. There were the forensic samples. They could be destroyed, the files easily too. But what was the point. Did he not want the police to find out who killed Bill, sure he might not have liked him? But still?

It didn't make any difference, if Gil had penetrated him this far there was nothing to stop him going a lot further. He would get into trouble if they caught him destroying evidence. But there was a possibility they wouldn't. What he had just admitted to in front of a stranger wouldn't wash, no matter what line of defence he used. Gil looked much like he knew all about that possibility. He didn't like his job much, but this would definitely get him fired, and that was too much.

"Ok, look, what ever you want." Keeping his job was, after all, a matter of principle for Paolo. He didn't, on the other hand, care too much about the deceased father and son. "But you better be throwing straight dice, if I find you fucking around, whether I get fired or not, you'll see my nasty side."

"Unlike some people you can think of, I can be trusted."

"And that's it. This case and nothing more."

"Nothing less. But don't go lowering yourself to try and pick me up on any old charges. We can call it a gentleman's agreement."

"And that's the last we'll hear of each other?"

"That's the way I understand it," Gil's voice lightened as the words slid off his tongue.

"Anyway, I can't do anything about it locked in here." Paolo wanted nothing in the world more than to get out of the toilet. Gil started to unlock the door. "So, what makes you take your decisions?"

He stopped before leaving, "Funny you should say that, I was trying to do something for someone else for once."

Gil walked out leaving Paolo to undo his riddle. What Gil had asked him earlier had made him fell really small. And not having the ability to see himself objectively meant he'd never understand. Gil had thought his steps through, planned well ahead. Paolo's claustrophobia swelled and he ran out of the toilet. He kicked himself. Looking at the table, he remembered the stupid things he had told that photographer, things that had silently but instantly fallen into the hands of an antagonist. The word 'shit' repeated over in his head.

He regretted allowing someone to get him that drunk, telling someone the kind of information he had let slip, being so stupid and so easy to catch. But at the end of the day, he was a bad person; he still didn't regret the things he had done, just admitting them.

Paolo took a taxi, his head too full to drive. As he cruised by his car, then the police station he began to think the story over. No one was taking great interest in the case. Just take the files and lose them, then cover yourself. Do it first, think about it later.

All his alternatives maddened him. It would be having the files stolen, or having his car and the files stolen. But in every situation, he wasn't just losing the files. Reflection told him things weren't going to get better. He punched the inside of the cab softly and quietly.

The cognitive process that had locked him into his current state would carry on, unobserved by Paolo himself. He would come across new situations time again, but opportunity would slip him by with a similar frequency. He could make a new start, clean his act up, but he had neither the perspective nor the motivation to realise it let alone to do it.

Gil left smiling. What was better than going out and taking someone with you? But while he almost relished giving up the maliciousness, it pained him to admit it was the last time. The cop was just the consolation in that sense, the icing on the cake. There would not only be one less crook on the streets, but one less crooked cop too. There was social improvement to offset the inhibitions. Enough taking, time to give a little back.

The cop, to Gil, was a parasite. Sucking from the honest people under false pretences. Gil had never denied being crooked, never been proud of it either.

Gil spent the journey home fighting this battle: convincing himself he was better than the cop. He had his doubts, he had stolen, deceived, cheated and lied, and probably more than the cop. The cop stank and he was not much better. It stank, realising the hypocrisy of his statements.

If he could get the cop fired, it would make him realise his bad ways. It would be the motivation for him to change. Otherwise he would carry on in his stink, in his iniquity. So what would getting him fired do? Just increase the wrath? Make him made and want to do something more crooked?

Gil took a mental stop in his walk. He had become Paolo's deliverer, taking him from the jaws of a sinful retirement to that of a shameful discharge. Would he be able to deal with it? Would the dirty white stain come out or would the trousers have to be thrown away?

The cop uniform could be thrown away. An irreversible step in the right direction. A good place to start. The difficult steps had been taken. All that was left now was to sit back and wait for the results.

Gil itched. It was like having waited all year for vegetables to grow in the garden only to find himself now sat at the family table, where he had to wait more for them to cool to a temperature at which they were safe to eat. That was the first step. He decided he could wait, what was the point in burning his mouth. The impulse to act increases exponentially.

It was the cause of a lifetime's wait. Because he had spent a lifetime waiting for the realisation that he should be doing something with his life. Whether it was something menial and unproductive, giving and not taking, making and not breaking.

Was it something that had changed inside Gil or had it been there the entire time. Was it some external factor purely responsible? The kid was one of them. But had other things been changing anyway. Gil tried to convince himself that there were other things. But all he could see was the kid's face that Friday evening.

It freaked Gil out, having the kid so firmly in his mind. He didn't seem to care for the kid. He had done him a favour and he had repaid it. That was the kind of person Gil was aiming to be. He would tell him it was all over and say goodbye. What was all the mental fuss about? The kid didn't want anything further to do with it.

Something bugged Gil all the way home. He was approaching a bridge with the mindset of 'let's deal with the bridge when we get to it'. But it was a long, narrow and precariously high bridge. And all three of them were afraid of heights.

I heard from Gil the next day, so early I wondered if it had all gone to plan. He explained what he'd said to the cop, Paolo, and that he had agreed to get rid of the files and so on. But something stood out, not in what he said, but the tone of his voice.

"That's it kid, we're off the hook. You are at least."

"So what about you? Are you still thinking of following this through? Is there any point if he goes ahead like he said he would? It was a digital recording it's obvious I made copies."

"You did make a copy, didn't you? Because I am going to give him this one."

"Yes, I did. But if he's going to make our lives harder there's no point in doing anything else. Quit while you're ahead and all the rest of it."

He was silent before saying, "Ok, well let's just hold onto it for a while. They are going to doubly think I killed Bill now. Just keep your eyes open, check the papers and so on, if you see the cop anywhere near you let me know."

I wasn't sure about it, but I let him stay on the high ground just for the sake of peace and good relations. Gil was the last person I wanted against me.

I listened back to the recording. It made me sick to hear the stories over, and with my voice in the background. I picked out little details, give aways and slips. It wasn't so perfect after all.

Scams. They are just about taking advantages, we all do it. I for example have done it for a long time. I don't have to work, I could, but I don't. Scams are smart people taking advantage of their situation. Even if that situation is based on nothing but the scammer being an uninhibited person.

I wanted to delete the recording, but I was inhibited. Irony. I might need it one day, I told myself. Depth. Gil might come round and explode when he realised there were no copies left. Tunnel. It would prevent Gil ever being in a position to uncover this and blowing it out of proportion. It was still going to be an open case. What would Gil do? Try and implicate the cop in the murder? Uncover the dirty cop? The press find out an unofficially self-confessed dirty cop destroys or loses the evidence of a media friendly case.

It sounded like Gil. For the little I knew him. But it also sounded entirely unnecessary. So what if they think it is Gil after the evidence is gone? It was becoming to complex and convoluted. Every new idea gave way to another six branches of ramification. The kind of probabilities Gil could process easily but just confused me. I would take each crossroad as I reached it. Gil could do what he wanted.

The lawlessness of the law system wasn't something that had ever taken much of my mental occupation. It's not as well advertised as some health risks. But as time marched on never ending I became more confident in it. I should have started feeling sorry for society at some juncture. But I didn't.

Society and I had an arrangement. We didn't worry, look after or care for one another. We stayed out of each other's lives and we lived happily side-by-side. There was nothing it had for me and little I could give to it.

Paolo's boss was surprisingly clam when he found out Paolo had lost the files. What was the point in being angry? There would never be an arrest. If there were to be one, it would have been essential to have all the evidence that had mystically disappeared from the evidence department, but there was no link between any of it and the murderer.

He suspended Paolo by the book, patted him on the shoulder and didn't ask why he did it. It was the least of Paolo's worries and the third suspension of this career. The third suspension, pending review of an officer's worthiness, was indefinite and without pay. That was the most of Paolo's worries.

Even meeting Gil, and hearing that he still liked the idea of fucking him further, didn't bother him to much. Not having money and having to lean on Raffael was the thing predominantly on his mind. But still he had to deal with Gil.

"The wonders of modern technology," Paolo studied the small card and questioned how many other copies there could still be. Still, technology hadn't changed that factor so greatly.

"Ok, well you better stick to the line, I am up to my fucking neck in this." Paolo put the card in his pocket and gave Gil a cold hard and red eyed stare.

"That's the risk you run on this side of the line. Anyway, I am off to the other side, so don't worry, once I get there I wont want to be dragged back. So let's think of it as insurance."

"Ok, let's run hypothetically through this. This recording

isn't worth anything. I wanted these case files destroyed as much as you did. I'm not stupid enough to tell you why, but it's gone, and I did it because I wanted to. So what would you do with your little recording?"

"I know where the girl lives. I always knew you were hiding something on this, and I know if it comes out, the truth will too. I know the girl knows the other girls, and they will all point out the cops. She's just the first domino."

Paolo sat and contemplated. It was definitely getting to the point of everything collapsing. Best to sit tight and not break too much.

"Another thing? I didn't know you were married."

"I'm not."

Gil left him. It would only have turned to bickering and he had felt in control. Back in the driving seat, where men should be.

At any rate, he hadn't decided what to do. Making things worse on the grand scheme would only upset the balance. As rewarding as it might be.

He held execution over a man's life. Wasn't it better to keep that position rather than let him die?

Ironically Gil didn't put the two together, his happiness and his relative position.

He thought about the kid. He would call by and tell him it was all done. He felt anxious, he liked the kid and he knew that announcing closure would mean they wouldn't see each other again.

The kid would take it so easily. As he did everything. Like he did that first Friday night, backed into a corner, scared to his death, yet never anything but pure on the surface. Like a swan, Gil thought, serene, white and pure.

The kid would have made the perfect accomplice. This thought had been evading Gil, his desire to escape his underworld had been blocking him. His mind evaded all thoughts of new opportunity. He had listened to the tape:

the kid was a proper scamster. It sounded like genius and considering it was the first time. The two thoughts had been circulating in and out of Gil's conscious mind like friends looking for each other in a crowded train station, eventually bumping into each other backwards.

Indeed, when it came to it, the kid did seem relieved it was all over. He had still been hesitant on doing anything further. But there was something else too. Gil was sure of it. Disappointment perhaps. That it was all over?

He thought more about using him as a prodigy. Running the old scams with him. He would be perfect, his pretty face and his calm nature. And he enjoyed it, it was so obvious.

Would he cope over time? The others always got sick of the lies and the fear. They always moved on, they didn't build them as stubborn as Gil anymore. But perhaps this kid was different.

Gil's recent plans and his old age slowed the thoughts, but not before he had pictured working with the kid, he would have been too good for the city, they could have hit the road, any city, even the exterior. What a life it would have been.

But Gil wasn't young like the kid, he had learned to hate the reality. But he knew, at the same time, that reality obliges you to seek happiness within your limitations, not to try and escape and destroy them. Once you have accepted your reality—once it's defined and inextricably linked to the world—, it's permanent and unyielding.

If the entire scenario took the worst-case path, it'd leave a good route out. An alternative ending. The road-movie ending. It was a wistful dream, and when Gil came out of it he was a little remorseful of not having taken the grifter route when he was younger.

"Too late now, Gil, play the hand you've been dealt."

He decided to split it down the middle. Keep the kid; drop the antics. He would be the first straight friend. At least the first new friend in Gil's new life. It gave him a good goal, the next stepping stone in his new path. All he had to do was see if he could do it and if the kid wanted to be his friend. It made him feel his age once again.

Paolo spent the first few days of his suspension back in a drunken state in his escape cave. Neither feeling old nor lonely, he was merely unwashed, unshaved, naked and alone. He had broken a number of things in his apartment and was generally making the most of his ability to unwind and to embrace dereliction.

He managed to break the news to his brother, Raffael. It didn't impress Raffael much, less so given that the news came at three a.m. and in the wake of a fit of anger. The indignation wouldn't last, he told him, it was just a binge. Like thunderstorms clear the humid air, rage destroys all memories of downward-spiralling self appraisal.

Paolo's self evaluation was just that, negative and sinking. His job, his family, his life as he knew it, all spinning beyond the cusp of the uncontrolled. But he'd planned it that way. The drink gave way to inhibition. Inhibition was an outlet for anger. Anger was the expression of his depression. And once he came to possess his depression, he could start calling his family members.

After he had cried on the phone to his brother, who was not only sleepy but not in full possession of the facts, he had a moment of clarity, a vision of a perfect future. It was the highlight and it would remain a keepsake. But it was also the figurative eye of the storm. It was a moment's calm in which to stake stock of the damage done so far, accompanied by repeating pulses of mental activity which shone light on how quickly everything in his life could be returned to harmony. It was a fleeting moment's vision of how his life could become perfect, everything he'd always wanted.

The moment was closed with the thought that, eventually, the damage would be twice as great as it was for that instant. This was followed by the return of the sinking feeling. It was compounded by his thinking that even the vision might not survive the uphill struggle back to normality.

Raffael had been under the impression that things, although never smoothly, were going well in his brother's life. This new information was a sobering truth at three a.m. and only added to the confusion. Raffael told him to clean up, sober up and come and see him.

He sat for several hours after the call, awake, in contemplation and life. Family wasn't a concept in which he had experience of deconstruction and analysis. Paolo and Raffael's family functioned under the principles of 'hand it out like you receive it' and 'if you can get away with it, don't think about it too much'. But he had passed the point of being able to ignore it. He demanded an explanation as to why his family was so fucked up.

Then, he would be after a process to lift them from the mire. He thanked his lucky stars for the one good son. He made up for Frankie. All he needed to match was a brother who made up for his. He supposed that was him.

If Paolo got kicked off the force, Raffael would have to support him, for how long he didn't know, but he would have to in the short term whatever happened. He wasn't going to find another job too easily. But that's what you do in the family, you put up with them and don't think about it.

He questioned instead the appearance of a pattern in the family genes, then he thought of his mother, but decided he should think outside the family. Thinking about his mother would just make him grow more angry at his brother. If he was going to see him soon, he would have to stay clear of talking about their mother. Nothing started a fight more easily.

His thoughts spiralled, seemingly randomly, taking him

back to his youth, to early memories of his family and brother and then eventually to back sleep.

The few hours peaceful sleep were the last few such hours for Raffael. He decided against lying in any longer. It wasn't the attitude that would get him through dealing with his brother. He performed his morning rituals and drifted to work.

At work the drifting continued too. Steve told him he should go home and take a few days off without even knowing what was wrong. Raffael was in the middle of contemplating it when Sammy came in.

Sammy came in with the presence that reminds you life delivers when you really know what you want.

I ordered a cappuccino in preparation for winter. And told Raffael to start talking.

"Every god damn day they're in my life, ripping it apart to make their own personal shreds. I'm the toilet paper for their mess. It's such a banal thing to have to think about, to have to carry around on your conscience. If it's not purely human nature, it has to be cultural or social. I don't get it. It's not my fault the family structure is the way it is; I didn't design it. I didn't invent the rules, so why do I have all the consequences all the time. I'm just a step in the road, a link in the chain. And a very small one at that. Why do I have to lay my back and be the bridge all the time?

"And what do I do? I just propagate it, I don't rebel and tell them it's the wrong path they are taking, I support their behaviours. When I am I going learn, Sammy?"

Things seemed bad, but it was a sickening twist, "What's up? New at least," I joked.

"It gets worse."

"You want to talk about it?" I said, feeling the analyst personality take over.

"I don't know what to tell you, or what I should tell you. You know my brother, right? Well, anyway he's a cop, you know that much? Well, he's landed himself in a pile of shit he can't handle."

It began to creep over me. I hid behind the foamy coffee, blowing life away like the bubbles on the surface. It had to have been written somewhere, didn't I know both their surnames, the Bill must have Raffael's name on it, but I have a tab usually. Surely it must be written on the wall somewhere, some certificate of something. How had it slipped past? I swallowed a few times, then took a sip of coffee.

"Anyway, I don't know a lot, and I guess I shouldn't be telling you much either. It'll only make him madder if I go around telling people. The point is someone's got his arm twisted behind his back, and he's on the verge of losing his job."

What did I care if he lost his job? It span around and around in my head, ramping up my skull's momentum. How would it affect me anyway? How the fuck could life do this to me. The spherical mass of bone and tissue was creating centrifugal forces that I feared would soon spawn a gravitational implosion.

And where coincidences mount, probabilities follow. Everything was connected. Six degrees of being a bitch.

I had nothing to say, on another day with another brother from another mother, we would have laughed at the circumstances.

"It's going to bite you?"

"I guess so, I am going to have to back him up, financially at least, any further than that I don't know. But it's bad enough, right?" He looked around at his coffee shop.

The paranoia built. 'You can give yourself away at any minute,' she whispered in my ear, 'it's so slippery in here: you need to watch your every step.'

The conversation I had recorded with Raffael's brother was still fresh in my mind. I could have slipped up. I could have told Raffael how fucked up his brother was. I wanted to console him by telling him I knew how bad he was. But it would have been wrong. He must have known about it all. It was no consolation but you could tell in this family, family came first.

I intended to stay uninvolved. The last thing I need was Raffael saying, 'Here meet my brother, you remember, the one who just got kicked of the police force.'

My head span some more. I needed to step back, how long before he started putting two and two together. But stepping out makes me more guilty.

"Shit, look, sorry! I really don't know what to say. I wish I did."

"It's ok, just having someone else know is good enough. It's nothing to do with you, in fact, I shouldn't have told you. But, hey! You did ask!" He managed a brief smile.

"Well, if you need a shoulder, you know where to find me."

"Humph! Thanks." He sat and stared blankly out of the window. How things change. I laughed inside. He would only have noticed my head nodding gently. But he was too far absorbed in worry to take any account. When the world is sucked away, it's an amazingly numbness that prevails. For good or for bad: it's a sensation of not knowing what is going on in the current space and time.

He was there. I could see it in his eyes. Every available neurone was at work calculating the infinite arborescence of possibility. Every scenario: how would he support his brother? What had happened that was so bad? What would happen? How could he help change it to ensure the worst didn't happen? What was the worst case scenario?

I watched with avid horror. I knew the feeling too well and to have been responsible for that alone meant I was in a corner from which it wouldn't be an easy escape. For good or for bad.

I thought about what to do, to offer him a cigarette, to get up and leave him, to say something, to come clean even if just to see if he would notice. I didn't do anything. I just sat and let him have his peace, smoked a cigarette myself and watched the world drift by, contemplating the new layer of shit whose surface I had to swim to.

In my own world of artificial consequences, I ploughed on. Where did it leave me? I certainly couldn't start sharing my recent adventures with Raffael. He would have been the only, but it wasn't such a great loss. It was technically supposed to be the end of that chapter. Why need to brag about it. So I might have to find a new place to drink coffee. He wasn't one to hold a grudge, but it didn't seem comfortable.

I wondered about owning up to him. It would be a long explanation. What did Raffael really know? He had started the ball rolling after all. It shocked me how linked Raffael was to every part of this mess. It filled my head with blood and felt somewhat dizzy.

When I'd first seen him after the murders, he hadn't said a word. I'd assumed he had derived a conclusion and just not wanted the whole world to know about it. But perhaps he had always put it past me. The penny began to drop.

If Raffael had asked his brother for the information initially, he would have been covering for me afterwards. And if the cop found the same name attached to the toes of a dead kid and his father in the same period of time, he would have been covering for Raffael. Everyone was covering for everyone, and injustice spawned.

The wave regret smashed me again as it was sucked back out to sea. What if we had just asked Raffael nicely about the 'Gil' problem, he could have just asked the cop to get rid of the files. He was protecting him after all.

In all the mess, it became clear that there was no one innocent in the entire affair. If it went another day without falling into the abyss, there would be time to analyse it. But it was a looming cloud that I needed to think my way out of. I couldn't tell Raffael he could lean on me to get Gil to forget about doing anything else to hurt Paolo. That would just spur Gil on, not to mention make him as suspicious as hell. Perhaps I could confront him. I had a reason not to do anything else to Paolo. If we did anything to Paolo now it would upset the balance for good. It had been in a reasonable position a few minutes before I walked into the coffee shop.

If luck had carried me to this point, I wasn't so certain of it any longer. The fragile network of friends I had built over the last few months was about to be ripped apart. Gil didn't matter, I didn't need someone like him in my life. I had enjoyed the scam with Paolo too much to want to make it a regular part of my life.

My priorities seemed to be the only things that hadn't changed throughout the entire affair. I still just wanted to get back to my normal life. But it seemed life was yet to finish her spring-cleaning, or that there was another message embedded further along the tracks.

In any case, I had become a major part of Raffael's problems and that made it too much to think about it in front of him. Letting Gil do anything else would have been the same was handing the brothers a big fuck you and not giving them a kiss to celebrate.

I felt a trapped in the environment. Raffael was still gone, I could have left without saying a word. I snapped my fingers in front of his face and told him I was going home and that he knew where to get hold of me.

The street was unfamiliarly cold. As if life wasn't teetering on the brink of the edge I had to deal with winter too. I walked briskly, the closer I got to home the more sure I was it was the place to be.

Logic told me another decision was ahead. But it refused to help me answer it.

I called Gil and let him do the talking. He was happy, nothing had happened. No word from Paolo or anyone. He hadn't done anything else. I said that was good. "Look, Gil, the cop is about to be kicked off. It's out of his hands. He's going to fall to which ever side of the line life chooses. I don't think we need to do anything else."

"How do you know what's going on?" Gil replied.

"Don't ask, but can we reach an agreement or not?" I said.

"I don't know."

"Why are you so bent on fucking this guy over?" I tried to keep it all inside.

"Why are you so keen on protecting him all of a sudden?"

"I have my reasons."

"Look, kid, don't worry. If we release the tape we can disguise your voice or just erase it. Besides we'll dress you up like the good samaritan, you know a vigilante, tired of bad cops setting up good people. They'll lap it up. Who are they going to believe, a self-confessing child molester or you Mr. Clean."

"But I ki… look, let's just leave it. If you have to do it you have to do it. But just so you know, it's going to cause me more problems, so, I don't want anything to do with it. Take my voice off, don't play me out as a hero, don't play me out as being part of it."

I hung up. He was a stubborn character, and he definitely had a hard on for Raffael's brother.

If Raffael was to connect the dots, he still needed to process a million thought cycles. And he was actually heading in the opposite direction. He was thinking about his brother and 'the' conversation. There was nothing he could to about it. The conversation was already written.

The conversation had blown in on a wet day, amid wet customers who had been half blown in and half seeking refuge. It'd meant the floor had needed to be constantly mopped, all morning. Paolo looked particularly wet.

He was still in recovery, so Raffael gave him sympathy

and listened to his story. Unfortunately it wasn't simply an episode. Having connected so many of the dots randomly, Paolo had achieved the level of life reflection, all without creating a coherent picture. It annoyed Raffael that his brother still couldn't visualise his life clearly despite having had it all dragged up by his own will.

Why should he feel sorry for him, if he hadn't toed the line? But the past was completed. Worse still, however, was the future, a subject neither of them wanted to breach. But there was a reason they found themselves sitting opposite each other. What would happen to a lost brother in the modern world? They thought they had both learnt their lessons from Frankie, who having leeched dry life's body and fallen, cried out for a lifeline. It was the part of his family's upbringing that really made Raffael wretch. The unconditionality. The lack of choice and monotony of duty.

He would need money, what else? A spare room in the long run. Then what? Lawyers? Aren't cops supposed to stand up for one another? The questions molested Raffael but he knew they would molest Paolo even further, so he decided against pursuing them and listened further to his brother's sickening lies.

It hurt Raffael to think that his own brother had pushed someone so far into a corner that they would do what they had. He was like life's shit. When you go too near, you can smell him; but if you step in him, the consequences went beyond people assuming you weren't watching where you stepped. It said something more, something worse.

Life is the perfect subject with which to occupy the brain. It always needs a problem to solve, a schedule to plan, a corner to wriggle out of. It likes to pick and prioritise, then reshuffle the theme of our lives. What is our highest concern, dear loved one? And it likes nothing more than this kind of paradox: addicted to its life changing gravity, but repelled to the soul with its repugnance. Only when the body is unrelated to the problem does it lose is overwhelming properties, only then can it relax to enjoy other people's problems.

The thought on Raffael's brain was mainly that Paolo didn't seem too worried about the future. Or if he was, he didn't show it. It made him angry either way. Did it not bother Paolo that he would only happily let go of his job, because he had his loving brother to fall back on?

"What has gotten into you?"

"Nothing! I don't know, perhaps. I fucked up that's all. I got a bit too obsessed about this guy."

"But I don't understand, what exactly did he do to you to make you want to arrest him for something he didn't do?"

"It's not like that, Paolo got more defensive, I just… I… I guess I didn't like what he was doing, or I didn't like him. He thought he was better than me and he wasn't."

"That's it?" Raffael said disbelievingly. "It's life, not a self service buffet. You got to keep your plate clean, eat what you can. You can't go around getting into this deeper level of shit, just because you think a guy thinks he's better than you. And don't give me buts. You need to examine your outlook. You have to let people think what they want to think. You can't let their twisted views of the world ruin yours. Ninety per cent of the world might think they're better than you, but you can't arrest them all."

The conversation went back and forwards in this manner until Sammy showed up. Raffael gave advice until he was blue in the face of not having it accepted. Paolo defended his behaviours until he had forgotten himself why he had done them to start with.

Up until that point Paolo had explained in full detail what had happened. Leaving out the critical details that would have refocused Raffael's attention from his repulsion from his brother's problems to how he was part of them. He'd never mentioned which murder or which kid.

Nonetheless, the situation had heated the various elements to a satisfactory temperature for them to begin to exhibit their affinity. Their cold domains could no longer hold them, entropy had taken over and their exclusivity had adopted a much shorter time scale. Prior to Sammy's entrance, the two elements might have passed liked ships in the night, having exchanged restricted views and moved on, enjoying one like the other their relative freedom and absolute ignorance. But that was all changing, the elements of knowledge had put it upon themselves to unite. To flow freely to all spaces and to be involved in all decisions. Perhaps life no longer had any tolerance for biased decisions. Perhaps there was some imbalance she was trying to correct.

The coincidences were all in place. The ground was there, but no map had yet bee drawn, meaning the potential for a comedy-of-errors would sadly manifest as a latent tragedy-of-errors.

But as we will see, all eventuality wasn't the explosive reaction you might have been expect. In fact, the backlash shared more in common with a fusion than a fission reaction.

The next 'morning' I woke with that feeling of not being able to connect the dots, where had the previous day finished. I could remember having spoken to Gil and not being very happy. But then I had smoked before bed as well.

Had I all of a sudden been turned into the pawn of the game? Was I now the most expendable piece, ready to be ripped from the board in a flash of rashness? I experienced that 'leave the country' feeling once again.

I realised I couldn't go to see Raffael again without confessing to him. Nor could I deal with Gil's unwillingness to compromise. What else was there to do? Go to the cop? Not likely.

It was an ironic twist on normal life. No plans, no where to go to nor anyone to meet there. A day free to do whatever

I wanted, so long as I didn't do anything controversial. It was a normal day; I was the changed one. The proof of this was the storm in my head. It wasn't a familiar one; it wouldn't let me relax following my usual procedure. It did let me clear my mind, but it wouldn't let me do nothing. Things have to be moving forward, it said. Interfere, it said.

This level of motivation was new. I hadn't had it before, and I surmised that it must be a mental version of the fight-or-flight response, some form of cerebral adrenalin, if only I could bottle it and market it. My survival was on the line, however. Added to which, I'd always learned to live a life more-or-less free of predators. Call me a dodo if you will, but I had since been the predator myself, even if it was for such a short period. That must have been it: becoming fodder so soon afterwards would have been quite a demotion.

I tried to re-grow my claws. Could I drop Gil in a jail cell, where he would be safe? Going to war with Gil would be a blind alley, with a quick and precipitous ending. He was somewhat further up the ladder. It would be quick and ugly. Paolo had already tasted my claws and wouldn't fall again. That left Raffael, who was the last person I wanted to hurt.

I made my morning rituals, by which time it was already one, and lay on the sofa to smoke. Before I had even flicked on the box, the feeling had returned. Once again I had become afraid. Afraid to leave the house. I didn't want anything else to happen. As if lying still on the sofa watching shit on t.v. until the end of time would solve everything. And if I could just prevent the remote from falling on the floor, I wouldn't be stuck watching the same channel from here to infinity. The other option was letting it fall and then really moving and picking it up. But being passive wasn't going to break the chains. And to me they felt like chains.

Luckily Gil phoned, having made the decision for me.

The down side was that he phoned to tell me that, on that specific day, he hated cops more than on all other days.

"What did he do today? In particular?"

"It's not really him, it's me. I'm just feeling more resolved today."

"So you have a copy then?"

"Doesn't make any difference. I was planning to go and have a chat with this volleyball player-cum-mistress of his."

Gil was anything but a rookie. It left me not knowing which verbal steps to take. Begging or threatening? Coming clean perhaps? Time was what I needed.

"When?"

"As soon as I can find a willing reporter to come along with me. Obviously I have to find one first, then speak to the girl, then go back. So, it might take a bit of back and forth, but soon. I'm going to play the field a little, see if I can't squeeze some cash out of this cow along the ride."

"So money is really the motivation then? Anyway, if you're going to do it, leave me out of it. End of story. I don't want anything to do with it. As it turns out, I have a mutual connection with the cop."

"Really? Shit! You should have told me. Anyway! So, you don't want any of the money? That's interesting." It felt like I'd never heard him think out-loud before now.

"Look it's your call. I told you how I'd like it. If you feel like doing me another favour, then respect my request. I'm flush right now. It's more like peace and direction in my life that I need than money. But I'm human, I am not going to turn it down. Look there's someone at the door. I have to go. Just don't do anything yet."

I cut the call short and went out into the street to get some air. It was nearly three p.m. I stepped back in and grabbed a jacket. It wasn't cold, I knew that, but my sickness made me feel like it was so cold. It was uncomfortable, but I needed the air, and it was fresh enough to wake me.

I had reached a point of mental exhaustion. It had been a long period of time since I had been free of this. I couldn't remember the last time I hadn't been planning my near future without consequence to the more distant one. I wondered if it was lack of company. If I'd had more friends, I would have talked it through with them. Better still, we would have talked about other things. I had forgotten what it was like to worry about life's banalities, like in which order to perform my morning rituals. The relatively straightforward future. The next ten seconds of inconsequence. A half hour. Instead of: the rest of my life. How could I ever establish my reason for being if I was continually trying to ensure its existence?

Passivity reigned my realm of possibilities. Perhaps if I did just lie still it would all breeze over me. A homeless man asked me for the time. I told him and gave him some coins wondering where it was he needed to be.

The next mental milestone was one of action: coming clean with Raffael. He was the one I wanted to protect. He should be the one whose side I take. It would give the brothers some time to come up with something. It was below Gil's belt, but not his standards, so I could easily justify it. It would be tit-for-tat after all.

Consequences. My theory of playing everything by ear was great when it was the choice of chocolate bar, but it was different with other people's future lives. It had always seemed to have worked, but, with things progressing the way they were, I had to reconsider it. Telling Raffael would make Gil mad at me. How could I let myself wait and play that one by ear?

I needed information. I needed some counsel. I needed a fucking sign. I could have tossed a coin for all it mattered. It wasn't even funny, ironic perhaps. Of all the decisions we make, the difficult ones are the ones where we can't choose one side over the other. A perfect balance of pros and cons. I wasn't one for going against the grain, but I wasn't sure that

I wasn't already doing that. I wanted to win. Stalemate wasn't a possible outcome.

I sat down in a small enclosed square. Not far away, an old man was sat on the bench, feeding birds. He had a big bag of crumbled bread. I watched him and the birds, resenting the ease with which they carried out their respective lives. The old man asked me for the time. I felt like a public service. "They should put clocks everywhere," I told him, "that way there'd be one less entry line for hustlers. And it might make honest people come up with more original and honest introduction lines, like 'hi, my name is Sammy, what's yours?' or 'I'm bored, do you fancy a conversation?'"

The old guy leaned back and let the birds catch up with the crumbs. "It wouldn't do me any good. Unless they were also speaking clocks." He stared blindly ahead of him not really making me notice he was talking to me. "So, what is on your mind anyway, son? I could hear you grinding your teeth; there must be something bothering you."

"Decisions," I said philosophically.

"Life!" He laughed. "Life is all about decisions."

I nodded the way you do the first time you speak to a blind person.

"I know. But they tell me that some decisions are harder than others."

"That depends on what you already have invested in either side."

"And if they are equal, or there is no advantage?"

"Hah! Then you toss a coin." He laughed and threw some new crumbs to the birds.

I sat contemplating what I thought was a joke. I watched the old man. He had real vision, he knew when the birds had eaten the old crumbs. He knew when to start tossing more. He knew where the birds were and which ones were being greedy, and was throwing always to the side of the weaker, slower ones.

"Your problem is not having invested on both sides, but facing danger on both sides, am I right?" He turned to me this time. "It's never so devastating when you are only choosing two flavours of ice cream from the fifty on offer. That you can justify in advance. What did I have last time, what can I have next time and so on? When it's 'be screwed' or 'get screwed,' it's never easy to choose. And don't worry, not everyone in the world is blind, don't feel bad about nodding." He smiled and turned his attention back to the birds.

"Besides, you have to acknowledge ice cream after all!" He smiled and chuckled to himself. "But let me tell you, when you have to make a decision which holds no weight for you, it's best to think of the person involved who will benefit from your decision. And if that still doesn't work," he turned his head up to the sky, "make a decision that benefits us all."

He left me thinking about what I could do that would benefit the world. I hadn't previously reached that point. "And then? Who comes after the world."

"You mock me, young man. I told you. Toss a coin. It doesn't matter which side it comes down on. Once sides are assigned and it's in the air, you'll know. Long before it lands even!"

The next thing I knew I was digging in my pocket for a coin. "They're going to love me when I tell them this is how I decided!" The old man smiled and nodded his head. My brain was fried. I span the coin through the autumn air. It came down with a slap on the back of my hand that made the old man smile further.

It came down in favour of Raffael. But the blind man had been right, the entire time it was in the air I had dreaded it coming down in favour of Gil. Even if it had come down in favour of Gil, I would have reconsidered.

So I was wrong after all. Or rather, I had been right all along: playing it by ear did work for all hard decisions.

"Thanks, old man!" I said as I got up. He held his hand out and I placed the coin in his hand. He ran his thumb over its surface.

"You're welcome, but remember, the coin has two sides. One might tell you its value, but the other tells you where it came from."

I took it all in and contemplated it, as I walked towards Raffael's coffee shop. It would be a rough ride, but it was a future more certain and more visible than the uncertain one of before.

As I reached Raffael's place, I became increasingly apprehensive. My strides got shorter and the paranoia grew. I didn't know exactly how he would react. The street seemed normal, but I refused to treat it so. I could feel every pair of eyes breaking from their conversations to watch me as I passed. Security guards outside banks, jewellers and fashion houses, waiters outside restaurants and coffee shops, all made me feel like a marked man.

What had happened outside my head? Was the news public? Was it all really inside my head? Did I have something stuck to me? I felt naked.

I resisted the temptation to stop, to turn around and to run away. I lengthened my stride instead. A false confidence.

What would Raffael do? Punch me? Not likely. Stand up and shout? Perhaps. Sit in silence? Another possibility.

As I approached I could see Raffael sitting in the window, a solid look on his face, a man sat facing him with his back to me. I nodded to him and went to the door.

Raffael came and greeted me by the door. Under the stress of my experience—dominated by the thumping of my heart—, it escaped me to see who had been sat opposite Raffael. Now, a large pot plant blocked the view between Raffael and I and his brother who I found out was sat at the table. "My brother is here. He's just telling me about the scum who set him up."

The surge came, blocking my ability to act even further. My chest heated and contracted. My ring puckered. I swung a quick look through the leaves, and there was Paolo sitting staring out into the street. If he hasn't seen me I could still run, I thought, but I didn't.

"Raffael, I have something to tell you. I don't know if you know yet or if you've worked it out. And I am not sure how to say it." As the words were just slipping out, I just let my mouth move along with them. "I'm not looking for you to forgive me or anything. I just need to tell you and get it out. Give you a warning."

His face dropped further as the story unfolded. It was a scene of slow-moving thought processes and delayed facial expressions. The sweat started to roll off me as I watched the opera unfold on Raffael's face. I didn't know whether to run, to cry, to hug him or to prepare myself for being punched.

All the while, the clock was ticking. It wouldn't be long before Paolo started to wonder what was occupying Raffael's attention. / My legs twitched. Not only was I ready to run but it also seemed more and more like the best plan. My brain told the legs to wait, as it had no idea where to run, how fast and for how long. It wouldn't have worked anyway, as when I did actually start to move, the legs were jelly and the feet stuck to the floor.

"You better come over here then. I think my brother has something to say to you."

"Is he mad?" I asked sheepishly.

"What do you think?" It was quick and hard. "But not as mad at you as with that other prick."

In fact, Paolo had become distracted before I rounded the indoor plants. Unfortunately for me it was only by the passing by the window of an attractive red-headed lady. I tried to slow down the three steps in what had quickly transformed into the world's smallest café. I wanted to be as far away as possible at the point of recognition. I felt Raffael's hand grip my right arm to help me advance.

In the end, I was two steps from the table when he caught sight of me. Our eyes locked. In the time it took to take one more step toward the table, his eyes turned red and he leapt from his seat. He launched himself in a direct line from his chair to me, despite there having been a table in the way. A ripple passed though the room. The epicentre was the table, including the coffee, cutlery and crockery on it. It in turn knocked a series of chairs, which got people talking and mainly gasping, which brought the entire room's attention to me.

In another stroke of luck, Paolo fell, but sadly he'd already made it far enough to grab me and bring me down too. He began to swing at me wildly, in the sense of wild passion and lamentably not wild accuracy.

It shouldn't have surprised me, nor should I have considered it an overreaction. But I was the one being repeatedly punched in the face, and I felt I should object.

I tried to resist, but not fight back. He was in a red mist, and I knew he would calm down after a few minutes. I'm glad that he did, as I was verging on unconsciousness. I wriggled my way out from under his exhausted body and crawled to the first object that would help me stand up. Ironically it was the large terracotta pots that had at first hidden me.

Paolo remained on his knees, regaining his breath. He wiped spit from his lips leaving a trail of blood from his mouth to his ear. It surprised me that after murder, the fits of associated guilt, the fear of incarceration, the agony of indecision and betrayal–and with my body on the verge of both mental and physical breakdown–I could still see the humorous side to everything. I did. He looked like he had smudged his makeup.

It was a short emotion as the acute pain emanating from

my face reminded me it–the general situation–wasn't that funny.

I didn't know what to say, surprisingly. What could I have brought to the conversation? I needed to speak, firstly to see if I could and secondly to ensure my place. I needed a very high place if I was going to continue falling.

As I looked around thinking, I observed the customers rearranging their respective areas of the establishment defensively. Some were intrigued and dared to stay. Many others left, hurriedly, some drinking their drinks, others not, some insisting on paying their bills but leaving with looks of shock and offence smeared across their faces, others just took it as read that they shouldn't have to pay after such a disruption.

Was that really the actions of normal citizens? I was sure they'd be back. And when they came, they would want to know what had happened afterwards, how the narrative progressed. Why don't you stay? I felt like asking them. It was just a process, as if anyone in this city could be shocked by anything, no matter which neighbourhood you come from.

Those who stayed were mainly those whose tables hadn't been upended. They began whispering their theories, clearly not having anywhere better to go, or more politeness to do it behind our backs. They also took turns to shoot glances between pretend sips of coffee, then held each others' eye contact for long periods. I sneered at them, but that made my face hurt as well.

I looked to Raffael for something. I put my hand to my jaw, it was worse than the last time, a snap of pain pulled my hand away. I ran a cautious finger inside to make sure my teeth were still all present and correct. I found the source of my pain, a loose lower molar. I braced myself in my panic and pushed down hard on its surface. It was stubborn and I had to also push up against my jaw, but at the expense of pain I managed to get it tightly back into its hole.

"Are you ok?" A stranger asked on his way out. I groaned but was interrupted by Raffael.

"He'll be just fine, don't worry."

I wasn't sure how Raffael was using the word 'fine.' I could think of at least two bad interpretations. The stranger looked at me and I signalled the exit with my eyes. He took a deep breath but didn't say anything then walked out into the cold.

I took it as a sign to move, fortunately the rest of my body hadn't taken any blows, the main concentration had been my face. I told Raffael's waiter, who was falsely busying himself behind the counter, to give me a towel. He obliged and ran off with his tail firmly between his legs. I wiped of the blood examining my face in the mirror behind the counter. Not a pretty sight.

I turned back to find Raffael standing over his brother. They had managed to only erect one chair in the vicinity, the table and others lay either on the floor or halfway there. He was shouting under his breath at his brother, although I couldn't work out much of what they were saying. There was lots of gesticulation but mainly ringing in my ears.

The waiter tapped me on the shoulder and handed me a bag of ice. I nodded thanks, not being able to smile or speak very easily. I put the ice in the towel against my jaw, the coldness seeping through slowly followed soon by moisture. The pain of my tooth was slowly subsiding.

The conversation became more two-sided. I didn't want to stay out of it any longer. Someone had to defend me, and so I went over and put a chair into the conversation. They stopped to look at me. I had something in their favour; that was my the second half of my strategy: no time to quit now. Everything now needed to be in their favour. Time was also of essence, as I didn't know what Gil would do when he found out that I had told them. He wasn't the violent type, but then I would have said that about me too.

"Do you want to continue this here?" I looked around at the mess. "It just seems a little inappropriate."

We both looked at Raffael, he was still a little dumbfounded, still a little red, still surveying the damage and still looking a little injured. But it was more than just a few broken cups and saucers, that was easy to see.

He shook his head clear. "Let's go in the back. You two go on, I'll be there in a minute."

I wasn't entirely in favour of Raffael's plan, but the cop and I went past the counter and down the little corridor kitchenette together. The situation had the slight air of yet another set-up, but I reassured myself it wasn't the movies. I wasn't about to be whacked in Raffael's livelihood.

I hadn't been into this part of the shop before, and it didn't look like anyone came back here much. The kitchen was just the route to the office, and the office was just a store room for paper in boxes. I hadn't been in many offices in my life but this seemed the most stereotypical. I couldn't do much but examine it, timidly pressing the ice on my face while Paolo stared at me.

The emergency exit was blocked, half by a filing cabinet and half my a pile of boxes, so much for escaping. It looked like it had been a long time since any visitors had come, I took the chair that was easiest to free from its burden.

Paolo and I waited, locked in a mental mind wrestle, not uncomfortable but strenuous nonetheless. Not being trained in confrontation, I knew at least that I didn't want to appear weak.

Raffael came in. He tried to close the door, but was faced with the evidence that it rarely closed. His normal friendly countenance had transformed into school headmaster. He looked at his brother as if to say, 'don't expect me to clear a chair for you,' confirming I wasn't the only common enemy in the room. Paolo remained standing and I wished I hadn't sat down.

"You've got some explaining to do kid." Raffael stood

staring at me from behind the desk, waiting for the coin to drop.

"Ok," I started. Talking wasn't as painful as my body had been telling me. "I came here to talk to you. It's just a bad coincidence." I had developed a lisp on my soft 'c.'

"A coincidence that I found you here." I went on to explain the entire situation, from the day I met Bill and what happened subsequently to the time I told Raffael and everything since. Then the entire Gil situation, highlighting everything with accounts of my mental state and unhappiness. I went in and out of detail and Paolo confirmed that he had told Raffael the information he had passed on to me. I confessed to everything but at the same time tried to make myself the victim of circumstance and oppression. But you'll forgive me for just being a human after all.

"But how did this Gil character know it was you?" Raffael stood to mark the end of my long and impulsive monologue. He looked shocked and confused. I shrugged my shoulders. He looked to his brother. Nothing.

"Look, he turned up on my doorstep one day, what do I know?"

"You didn't ask him?" Paolo asked me in amazed disbelief. He was considerably calm, perhaps from having the answer to his murder case all wrapped up.

"I was caught off guard, and it wasn't exactly your straightforward relationship. I guess he talked to people. People saw me that day."

"Not too many white people in that neighbourhood, right?" Paolo backed up my hypothesis.

I felt invigorated by having lifted the burden off my chest. Raffael was soon to crush it.

"Look, I don't really care how who found how, what the fuck were you doing to my brother?"

"I didn't know he was your brother. If I had I would have just asked you to clip his wings a little, you know as a favour."

They looked at me without expression.

"Besides, Raffael, do you know what kind of things he is up to?" I managed to move Raffael's stare to his brother. He looked like he was about to clip something. He didn't.

"Ok, so what else have you been up to?"

"Nothing, I thought quickly to make sure. That's the reason I'm here, I told you. We never expected this tape recording to mean anything. It's what you would call flimsy, right?"

"They didn't know I had already been kicked off the case and that neither of them would have ever been arrested if they confessed to it."

"So why did you destroy the files anyway?" Raffael wasn't catching on quickly.

"That's not the point," I interrupted, "the point is, because your brother took a disliking to Gil, the feeling has reversed. I entered this with the 'liberate myself' angle. He entered it with the 'screw the dirty cop' angle. He's not happy with the files being destroyed. He wants you to fall. To be honest looking at it now I don't think he even cared about the files, I think he just dragged me in as an accomplice."

"Someone to sell out."

"Exactly."

Raffael stood still confused. "So why are you here telling us this again?"

"Because I've had enough. I don't want him spreading the bad news about your brother. It wasn't what we agreed. Besides, I don't want to be a part of that. I tried talking to him but it didn't work. The point is I came here because I wanted to give you the head start."

"Cut out the intermediary you mean."

"Exactly, I want to be involved in this as much as anyone. Besides, over everything I don't want to see Raffael suffer. He's the only innocent one, and when I realised the connection and how much of a burden you are going to be to him, I wanted to help him out."

"So what are we going to do," Raffael said with renewed team spirit.

"That's where my answers stop. Now you know everything that I know. All I want is to get on with my life."

"You should be in prison for what you did."

"So should you. Besides, I'm rehabilitated. I'm not going to go out and murder anymore priests. Provided I can get my way out of this without doing it." That last phrase had sounded a lot better in my head. I was tired, literally, and of the situation. I wasn't in the position to be the one to say it, or to feel it either, but it's how it went down.

Despite my attempts not to be, I was still the one doing all the talking. "Look, we are all in the shit here. I'm just trying to get out of this, but I have the burden of my conscience. You're going to drag your brother down if you get kicked off the police. I didn't come here to do you a favour, but I guess it's just worked out that way."

"So what are we going to do?"

I didn't care, I felt sick, all my words seemed to be lies. There didn't seem to be any solution. Paolo was devoid of the power to do anything to Gil. Gil was too smart anyway. For every angle we could cover, he would think of six more. I didn't want to be part of it any longer. Nor did I want to end up on the losing side. It wasn't merely my sports team that would be relegated, it was my entire life.

Peace eluded me still. I needed it at that point. I was feeling weak. I was further weakened by the thought of being able to attain such peace but it eluding me. The brothers looked like they were going to start family bickering again. My stomach turned, and the acid bubbled. I figured I had swallowed a lot of blood. It was trying to tell me something, 'don't let life change,' perhaps. Was it telling me life was changing or that it had. Which was worse, which was easier to deal with?

* * *

I don't know why I fear change so much. I like being able to predict my life. Not just the major decisions but the ins and outs of every single day until I die. It might be a hermit's life, but it's free from other people's interference. It carries on, always without unnecessary or unprovoked change.

I had reached the point where I couldn't stand it anymore. Raffael was back on side. At least back on his neutral objective side, which kept me safe. He was in the least trouble but had the most motivation.

Paolo had told me that nothing would probably happen to me in all of this. Logic told me I should have been relieved, but my emotions were just further riled by it.

I stood up. "Where are you going?"

"Are you feeling ok? Are you ill?"

"No, I just need some fresh air. My brain is out of service now. If you come up with anything that will help, and you can't do it alone, call me. Otherwise, I want to step well out of this situation. Anything short of violence, threats, blackmail or murder, that is. You're a bad person, Gil's a bad person and my soul's a little stained after all this. I'm not going to play any part in deflowering Raffael. That's the best I can do for the world. I'm not thinking about myself, or about Gil or either of you two. I am thinking on the bigger level."

"You've got some nerve, kid!" Paolo put an arm out to stop me as I made for the door.

"I'm not the bad guy here. Now, if you don't mind."

I stepped into the corridor-kitchenette, then into the relatively spacious coffee shop. I put the towel down on the counter. Looking around, I realised that the outside world was the only place that had enough space for me. My body lacked something. There was only place with enough oxygen to support my still beating heart.

I hadn't thought about where to go, I just needed air. The crowd swept me into motion, carrying me on the shoulders of their hurried lives. The blood drained in response to my new exercise. The need to sit down soon came, however; I went dizzy and began to panic. There was nowhere to sit down. I was lost in the crowd. Everything became instantaneously intense, and then my peripheral vision turned grey-black. I tried to stop it all but couldn't. My legs gave way. My head pounded into the concrete that I recognised only as a silent and painless flash of white light. I watched the moving forest of legs fade slowly into black and white, ever moving, then fading to black. No one stopped.

When I woke up, I realised some people had stopped. They had even moved me to the side of the street and placed me alongside a shop window.

"Are you ok?"

"Is he ok?"

"What happened to him?"

The voices buzzed around my head, as if the people were moving. I opened my eyes to try to try distinguish one voice form the next. They didn't focus very well. There were three faces very close to. I propped myself against the window.

"Are you OK?" A female voice asked me. "What happened to you?"

"I don't know. I think I passed out."

"You hit your face on something," she continued.

"He did more than hit his face," a male voice interjected. "Are you sure you're OK."

I reached for my face, and it stung. It reminded me of what had happened shortly before fainting. "No, look, I'll be alright."

I wasn't alright, but the feeling in my legs was coming back. I tested my strength by pushing my back against the shop window. The darkness began to crowd my vision again and I submitted to waiting a little longer.

"Shall we call you an ambulance?"

"No! No, don't! I'll be fine," I said, feeling my heart skip.

"What happened to your face?"

"That couldn't have happened from fainting. Are you sure you're ok?" The voices wouldn't go away, but they were starting to agree with each other.

My eyes cleared again but still wouldn't focus. My energy was concentrated on not getting an ambulance. I didn't see the point in explaining to them why my face was pushed to one side. Nor why I really didn't want to answer the questions of paramedics or policemen. But being elusive was just worse.

It cheered me, however, being cared for by total strangers. They had taken time from their lives to look after me, a stranger, nothing but a fellow member of the same species. I wondered if I would have done the same for them, or if they would have done it in another part of town, or another city or if my clothes were dirty or if I stank of alcohol. I wanted to say no, but I wasn't sure. It made me feel warm inside.

They carried on fussing even while I was inside myself. I thought of a health slogan, 'stress is a killer'. There was certain surprise and certain irony in it all.

The fear soon came back. It told me to get up and act straight before they got suspicious or really called an ambulance.

"We should call an ambulance," they continued as if on cue. "He looks beat up, maybe he was mugged or worse." They agreed. My heart and kidneys told me a new story. 'Get up', they screamed.

"Don't worry, I tried again to get up. This happens all the time. I just need to go home. I have medication there. It happens all the time honest."

Needless to say they didn't buy my bullshit. I felt sleepy. If only I could just get home. "Why don't you call me a taxi instead? I'll be fine in half an hour, honestly! I just need my sofa and some pills!" I had brief visions of being questioned by police officers and not being able to explain anything.

I pushed against the glass again. Nothing. The Samaritans were becoming firmer in the indecision. One came back with a bottle of mineral water and offered it to me. My arms were much more useful than my legs and I drank healthily. This perked the faces up.

I looked back at them. They were becoming clearer all the time. They didn't look like the kind of faces that would leave me while I was still lying on the floor, with a swollen and bleeding face and no ability to get up. It was just a matter of time before their lives would start pulling on their leashes and then they would call a figure of authority to look after me.

"He's delirious!"

"We should call for help."

My heart raced with each suggestion, only serving to drain the blood from my legs. "Look, I'll be fine. Just let me sit for a minute and I'll be in a taxi on my way."

I sat for a few more seconds and decided I would do it. I pushed my back against the glass. This time there was moderate success. I got my backside off the floor and managed half way up. I paused to gain some strength. I wanted to scream; it was so frustrating. I waited, my knees half bent, shaking slightly from supporting my half weight.

Then it struck me, one of the faces was familiar. But she hadn't recognised me. Why not? Was my face that bad? I looked into her eyes. Why don't you recognise me? Perhaps it was better that way.

I wanted nothing more but to get away. I pushed again and made it upright. I looked at them to say, 'there you go'. They looked relieved, and I felt relieved. Then their faces dropped as I fell back to the floor.

The half smiles turned back to shock, then to strange contortions as they tried to catch me. I fell like a brick. The voices faded and the darkness fell over my eyes again, and I was soon blank of mind again.

When I came around I felt comfortable. The paving stones were incredibly close to one of my eyes. I could feel the summer warmth of the paving stone still there. It radiated into my cheek. Someone had put me in this position. There was no way I could move without the window's help.

A finely modelled pair of feet danced in nervous anticipation in front of me. All I could think of was: what could be stopping her from recognising me. Was my face that bad? Paranoia? Wasn't it anything special after all? I calmed my heart with the facts. My face looked like it would have felt had all my teeth just been pulled. My own mother wouldn't have recognised me.

The voices had stopped, and only one pair of feet danced. Perhaps the rest had gone. Was she still there?

I heard the siren several blocks away. Its speed was provoking. It would advance, get stuck somewhere and stop. Its horn could be heard as it battled its way through traffic.

All my problems flooded back. I saw a shiny pair of shoes, well-creased trouser bottoms. Uniform. I couldn't see any further up; my neck wouldn't allow it.

I felt paralysed, but I knew it was just fatigue and the fact it meant I was locked into the recovery position. My body had given up its membership of the Sammy Support Club. So much for an unfailing immune system, so what if I would get better in a week, why couldn't I have made it home?

I had picked a bad space and time to pass out. It wasn't something I could do anything about, literally. I felt like I was lying perched on a thin line, but generally falling to the steep slippery side.

The shiny shoes conversed with the dancing shoes. Street noise and the ever-approaching siren drowned the conversation. I knew the first lies were being noted down in some street cop's notebook.

The ambulance pulled up to the kerb, just outside the range of my focus. Poor guys, I could see their bright trousers climb out, looking across to a swollen and bloody-faced body, lying face down, policeman taking statements and concerned looks on only a few faces.

The stuffy airless offices that I had spent my life escaping now called me like a duvet-covered hiding place. Why had I taken this path? Where had I been going? There were no answers.

But I needed answers. Soon I would be answering questions about why my face was so swollen and bloody, about why I had passed out, about why I had lied to good-hearted citizens. Hopefully some doctors would be able to explain some of the answers. So, even I couldn't make up the truth to some of the questions, I could just feed off of their worst guesses.

Nothing like this had ever happened to me before. I was supposed to be super strong, resistant to illness. That's what the doctors had been telling me all these years. That's why I had been sacrificing my time all these years. It's why I had been taking pills everyday to stop my body from overproducing some kind of cell that would coagulate. The irony of my life was that I had to stop taking pills when I felt ill.

I was awake, overtly conscious, but I could feel a large pressure from my brain, like a weight on my head telling me to sleep.

The paramedics poked and prodded me and asked me all the usual questions, well, the ones you usually hear on t.v. They rolled me onto a stretcher and placed me still fully awake but very weak into the ambulance. I was in the middle of wondering if they would charge me for the ambulance ride when the police officer climbed in. The fear of uniforms hadn't gone away. The Samaritans had all left. They had obviously seen enough squirming and lying.

Added to which, I wasn't a very convincing act. The ambulance set off and the rocking motion and safe environment lulled me to sleep.

I woke up in the hospital. In fact, it was a hospital. Although I've been in a fair few, I had no idea which one this was, or what had happened between falling unconscious in the ambulance and arriving and this new particular point in time. But there was no common factor. It didn't look like a t.v. hospital either. It was just a very quiet, very green room with beds and tables, jugs of water and a telephone chained to a trolley.

A doctor was talking to the same police officer. He was explaining that the bruises were not likely to be the result of the fall. The officer noted it. His face was free of expressions of doubt or surprise, unlike my mind which was reeling at how stage managed this all seemed. He finished writing some notes with an entirely unimpressed face and the doctor left. He came and sat in a chair that was pointed at me and my bed.

"Ok, Samuel," he began.

"Call me Sammy, please. No one's ever called me Samuel."

"Ok, Sammy. Can we start be telling me where you got the bruise on your face?"

"The bruise? There's only one?"

"It's like one big bruise," he cracked smile at me.

I laughed, but it hurt. "I was in a fight." I surprised us both with the truth.

"Really? Some fight! And who was it with?"

"With a friend's brother." Had my fall inadvertently denied me my ability to lie? The frivolousness of my answer was a million times that of anything I could have invented, I thought. He eyed me with a renewed seriousness.

"Ok, so what happened to you in the street today? According to the people who stopped to help you, you were saying it happened all time? Is that true?" He eyebrowed me as if there was a unanimous conclusion that only he knew.

I didn't think I was in a position to start backtracking. I stressed instead.

"I have no idea, I just went blank and fell over. What did the doctor say?" I looked back at the ceiling. My neck hurt too.

"I think he will be able to explain that to you more clearly than I would."

Now what could that mean? My paranoia wasn't happy with the current hospital-bed-police-officer proximity of the situation.

"But he told me it was something that might have stemmed from a large number of contributing factors." He quoted from his notebook and looked at me with a 'you should be concerned over your health look' "You haven't been using any illegal drugs?"

I shook my head, "Not today!"

"Ok, well, let's not go there. Remember you can talk to the doctor about that subject in confidence. Now, about this fight?"

"Don't worry about it. It was a family thing, I don't want to involve the police or press charges or anything."

"Well, as long as your sure. It's your call."

"Where am I? I mean which hospital?"

My eyes glazed over, as he answered. I fixated on the ceiling. I knew this hospital after all, but of course I'd never had the chance to be in the secure unit. I'd noticed the chain on the telephone, but not the restraints on the beds, not being attached myself. I was here for my own protection. My imagination took over my consciousness, calculating my next moves in the light of this absurd series of events. The police officer left, saying something about twenty-four hours of observation and him trying to come back to see me before then. "To make sure I was ok".

I didn't want to see him again. I wouldn't be able to look at him with a straight face. But in all seriousness, I was glad he had left. I didn't want to see anyone. I knew I couldn't leave early without arousing too much suspicion. But given the critical juncture, particularly that people's freedoms were hanging in the balance, I realised that not being in my life for twenty-four hours might arouse suspicion elsewhere. Perhaps that was good. Perhaps they would think I had run away from the drama. Perhaps not.

At any rate, I was a fish in a barrel at the hospital. Anyone who wanted me could come and get me. Outside, suspect or not, I at least had a chance to run.

But who suspected me? Gil? What had he been up to? Would he started putting his spanners in without consulting me? Maybe he had changed his mind. Would he ever go to the real police and tell them it was me who had killed Bill? What would he do if he couldn't find me? When had I last spoken to him?

Maybe he didn't care. Maybe he had found something to occupy his time. Someone else's life to ruin.

I was still in the open. The police had me here in the hospital. All that needed to happen was a line being drawn between the dots. What were the chances of that? What were the chances this would never stop?

The doctor came to my bed, jotted a few things on a clipboard and hung it back on the bed. "Now, Sammy, we're going to give you some painkillers, that should help in taking the swelling down. It'll probably make you quite drowsy too. If you have no objections we'll keep you here overnight. We haven't been able to determine why you passed out. I'm not to concerned. It was probably low blood pressure or sugar. When was the last time you ate?"

"I don't know. Yesterday, maybe this morning."

"Well, there you go. Try to eat regularly and go and see a GP when you get better. Especially if you are going to get into a lot of fights."

I nodded, but he carried on.

"Would you say you were stressed in your life at the moment?"

"Do you think that could be the cause."

"Not the cause, but probably a contributing factor. Something you should look after."

"Yeah? So who is it I see about that?"

He looked at me the way doctors look at you when you make a joke about health. Maybe they need to see someone too.

"A nurse will come and give you the medication." He stole away with his white coat flapping.

At least I wasn't dying. Surely, they would have told me. Not that it wasn't a way out, I thought.

My mind went in new directions. I thought about the girl I met, Penelope, Penny. Was that her today? So close to me but a perfect stranger. Really perfect. When you think of the differences in first impressions between good people and bad people, you can really see the variety in life. Bill and Gil's dark-alley fear against Penny's caramel-autumn afternoon. She was genuine, they weren't. They had both pretended. Both lied. They both changed their outside, but still there was a difference.

It was a new world opening up before me: the fairer sex. I wanted to break out and find her, to try something new. If only fate would let me get to her. But the world was still too connected to me. The tentacles I had let pervade my inner workings still gripped to me tightly. Perhaps when I had cut all the ties loose, I would find her. I would pass from the battle to the journey home. I couldn't tell her about this. This was a history to be un-discussed. I couldn't imagine telling anyone this story. I couldn't imagine a world where this kind of thing would happen. Where had my sense of reality gone? Had it hidden somewhere with normality, or did I need to leave normality to find it.

Stress was definitely behind this. Although there were

probably people tenfold more stressed than me out there, the relativity of consciousness became a stress thing in itself. I had moved from no stress ever to twenty-four hour stress ever since first meeting Bill. Everything before it was fictitious. There wasn't a single point in time that I could put my finger upon. Everyday had been free and easy and like the day before it and the one after it. Then, since Bill, life has been nothing but a cascade of negativity.

The nurse showed up with a trolley. I didn't pay any attention to what he was doing, but I soon felt the drugs as he slipped them into the drip line that was feeding into my arm. He drew the curtain fully around the bed as he left.

My eye lids felt as if they were glued open. My head wasn't moving either and my eyes were just fixated on the upper left hand corner of the green nylon curtain. It became the centre of the world. The greens and whites in front of me began to spiral, being sucked into this whirlpool at the centre of my world. It began to swallow the ceiling and the bed and eventually my consciousness in an ice-cream spiral. Even the images in my brain became caught in the pull of the whirlpool. No longer ordered by logic or filtered by consequence. They puréed into a chaotic flurry of memories. It was a little terrifying, but it didn't last. Finally everything went black.

I dreamt I was stuck in a small booth, somewhere in the barren mountains, surrounded on all sides by a windswept and infinite plain. The booth was like a border control gate, although it didn't enclose anything. It was just a space. A road ran in front of it. The bare grey gravel ran parallel to a fence, both ran into infinity.

The cold was penetrating the gaps of my hospital gown and crept into my soul. There was a stove, crammed full of pages ripped from newspapers and poor quality men's magazines. A strong young man with a dirty face looked fiercely into my exposed soul with his green eyes. He shouted at me angrily in an ancient sounding language, one that must have been forged over centuries of relatively unsuccessful attempts at civilisation. He sat back down next to the heater with a broad grin on his face. He appeared to be welcoming me, as much as his words seemed to express otherwise.

I tried to leave the booth, as I felt trapped. Like I had in Raffael's office. But his good looks and mountain charm held me heavily in my seat. He carried on in his language, loud and angrily, always stopping to smile.

When I woke up, it was to the feeling of not being safe. I hadn't felt safe in my dreams, and reality did little to restore my confidence. Silence and cleanliness greeted me.

As I came around, my head flipped from one thing to another. On the one had there was the detail: the room, the uneasiness and the probability that I couldn't just walk out if that was I wanted. On the other, there was the reflection of the detail: the people who had forced themselves into my life, they problems that had come with them, and the probability that I couldn't just walk away from them afterwards if that was what I wanted.

It was the human condition manifesting itself. I can preoccupy myself with the most pressing of issues, and even if I resolve the underlying problems, when the issues change, I resume with the next most pressing issue. Continue ad infinitum or until death strikes, but no sooner. And if by any chance I find my neighbours' issues more pressing, I am not alarmed and ensure full meddling status, it's likely they need my help.

I yearned for the cold surreal booth of my dreams. I yearned for the language I didn't understand. I yearned for the handsome smile. Nothing came of it and I started questioning whether I could escape my condition just by escaping the hospital. Perhaps it would all be over on the outside. It had to be.

I'd lost track of where my conviction had become

grounded. I didn't know and couldn't care less. There was a booth out there, somewhere lost on the barren plains. I would take on faith and religion if only I could get out and go look for it.

But the sanctuary of the hospital wooed me into waiting for at least a short while. During that time, I figured that no one actually knew I was in the hospital. I hadn't realised that inside these walls I was already in a Gil, Bill and Paolo free world. Free from relationships, association and liaisons. A world where there was no obligation to communicate.

But I had confessed to Paolo. I had told the very cop looking for me that I had done it. It stank of irony, but that wasn't the concern. The concern was that he knew. And the 'police' knew where I was. My body twitched to leave the bed. Just because one guy fucked up all the evidence didn't mean the world would forget. There would be someone new, someone smarter, someone less crooked and less prone to young girls. What if he was a friend of Paolo, what if he told him? It was like the detective show reversed. The bumbling detectives making stupid mistakes that lead to the wrong arrest for some minor offence instead of to the murderer.

Gil had a very nonchalant look on his face as he walked in. He looked around and snapped the curtain shut. He quickly displayed his mischievousness. I wondered how he did it.

He was at once the most conspicuous person on the planet and the most unnoticeable. How he had managed to remain at large all this time surprised me, let alone throughout his criminal career. His every movement disguised not only the previous misconduct but also the next. Like a rebellious teenager smoking in the park, he had a way of exaggerating a body-language confession. He had become the physical manifest of my paranoia. I wondered if there were specialists for that too.

"How do you do that?"

He looked at me with a broad grin. As if he was innocent. "Do what?"

"Appear like this."

"Ah, that. I'll teach you one day." Like it was a party trick. "Oh, you look bad, what happened?"

Was I going to lie? Was I going to ask myself that question for the rest of my life?

"I got beaten up."

"No shit! Who by? You need me to take care of them." He waved his dukes.

I wasn't sure what was going on, the painkillers were still making me drowsy and I had no idea how long I had slept.

"What time is it?"

"Ten thirty-six," he said squinting his beady eyes at a wristwatch.

"Morning or evening?"

"Morning? They've been giving you drugs then?"

"Yeah, I didn't want them, but they insisted it would help with the swelling."

"Help? Boy, I wouldn't have like to see you before."

It was all very humorous but I didn't know what exactly he wanted.

"Nothing really. I came by looking for you at home, but there was no sign last night either." He spoke like we were best friends. "Then I was a bit worried you might have done something silly. And you know, we've been hanging out a lot lately. Since, you know, Bill had stopped hanging around so much, he-he. And I know you're probably still mad over the tape-cop thing, but I... I don't want you to hold it against me. The truth is I've become a little, hmm how shall I put it, attached to you. Anyway, enough of the sentimentality, the point is I've come to the decision to let it all go. I mean I still want to see the copper squirm and all that. But, in fact I was just thinking of it. I saw a big group of them outside, chatting and laughing at all the ill people. Can't stand the bastards. They've been to see you? I guess so. What happened? You get mugged. Unusual, you know for your neighbourhood. Safe place generally."

"Have you been taking drugs, Gil?" I'd had enough of his carrying on, and it was obvious he was high.

"Sorry, the point is that I though a lot about what you said. About it was just making lots of other peoples' lives miserable. And you said you knew him, why should I make his life harder etcetera, etcetera. It's a difficult decision to come to, that's why it's taken me so long. You know how bad he was don't you. But then you probably thought the same about me. The 'old' me that is."

"The old you?"

"Yeah, that's the strange thing. I've been feeling this way for a week or two. Well, much longer really. Like I should change. You know how people always talk about changing for the better, but it's usually 'I should give more to charity' or 'I should quit smoking'. And that's why they never do it. Because it's a small thing. Well, with us it's different, it's a career change, the big going straight. But all along it's a pipe dream, something to keep us going. Something to keep the motivation above the level you'll need it to be if you're to make it to the end of the day or the week."

Gil was very edgy, but genuinely philosophical. I guess cocaine can do that to you. We caught eyes and he put his monologue on pause.

"Every one has dreams like that, Gil, not just you crooks. Even I do. But it's not about change. Just because you dream about doing something doesn't mean you really want it. If you aim to do it, then it's obvious that you want it. If you dream and don't aim then how can you say you really wanted it? That's a different dream, the 'what if', the 'wouldn't it be nice', the 'when I retire' or 'win the lottery' dream.

"I don't have those kinds of dreams, I don't have the life of Joe Schmoe. I am lucky I don't have to work to keep myself alive. I don't have to deal with society and friends, bosses and rules, Ps or Qs. All these things you have to put up with. So, I have nothing to escape from and if I wanted to, nothing to stop me. I live in my world where I am the only person whose needs need satisfying. And purely by luck my needs are few. The point is, that even if I do move back into society I would still put my needs before that of my wife, or my friends, or my boss. If I wanted something, or lacked something, I would put my own neck out and get it."

Gil looked shocked but pleased that he wasn't the only one feeling philosophical.

"What has that got to do with me and my dreams? And with me wanting to change?" He said with all the anarchism of studenthood.

"Nothing! But if you can't tell me or don't know why you are having these dreams, and still writing them off as fantasies, doing nothing about them, I guess you're struggling with basic priorities."

"You think that's the same with the tape? Is that why you don't want me to do anything with the tape?"

"It's got nothing to do with it? I don't give three shits what you do with the tape. It's not something I want to spend any more of my life worrying about. It's already taken enough time and strength out of my body, and I don't want to give it anymore. My life has been flipped upside down since I met you and Bill. And I don't want it to happen again, not even for the happy ending, the luxury yachts, girls in bikinis, palm trees and champagne ending."

"So how did you become so calm since last week? You not scared anymore?"

"Scared? No, and I'm still not going to be happy if something bad comes out of this for anyone. That's not going to change. The point is it's left my hands. I thought it was in my control but it wasn't. All I can do is deal with consequences. I don't have the control, you do. You can do whatever you want to this cop, and all I can do is deal with the results. That's why I am relaxed because I can either be stressed or relaxed. It's a choice."

I felt stressed from explaining it.

"Besides, I don't think you're going to do it."

"No, why not?"

"Well, because you've been talking about the 'old' you. Tell me where does one end and the other start? Do you want to go out with a bang or to start with the right frame of mind? And you wouldn't have come here looking for me either. I am the last person you would come to for advice on that if you though I was still scared. So what was it? Missing me? Well, I'm touched, but come one, we're from different worlds. I'm not trying to give you a hard time or tell you to fuck off or even tell you off for that matter. I mean I miss you too, but for different reasons and not to the extent of putting on a city wide search. Honestly, how the fuck did you find me here?"

He pulled up a chair and sat down. The smile on his face gave away that he was enjoying every last word of mine. It set me thinking about it too. During my yapping, I had realised things: some hypocrisies, mainly some loose ends in my personality that I should have tied up. My outlook had changed in those few flitting minutes, speaking from my heart and not weighing, twisting or inventing the words. To use the words I always think of but never use, without socially evaluating them.

Those seconds would become minutes and go on to become the rest of my life time. I told myself to take heed of them, embrace them even, just in case these were to be my the last seconds of consciousness.

"You're smarter than I thought, but you shouldn't be so arrogant, especially in your position."

He wouldn't give up his fight. Every word had been forged and sharpened through years of habit. It was his instinctual defensiveness. What was worrying me was that he defended like this but never carried through with things?

He fought the consequences before they happened, only to be too tired and let them was him away when they manifested at his door.

What worried my somewhat more was that he was the type of person who did follow through when it came to promised actions. We all strive for this, but the bitter irony is that only a few succeed: reaching great heights and depths. Was it the effect of lifestyle? It was possible, but it's one thing knowing when to bark and when to bite and another to live in a dog eat dog world. I knew myself too well, I wasn't going to waste any more time barking.

I saw several possible paths along which to extend my life: First, somebody killed Gil. The first wasn't the most serious contemplation, besides I couldn't really summon the moral justification for his death. It was just the most easily explained. The one that granted the most peace of mind. But I wasn't up for anymore dead bodies either, that's why it had to be someone else who did the deed. Death had entered my life seemingly from nowhere. The first time I'd ever seen a dead body was after I had just put them in that state on the ground. I didn't want to be involved with the shady player any longer. All the reasons were there: the sudden entry, never having lost anyone close or even been to a funeral. It all made me want to steal back so many moments from my life. I've witnessed a few car accidents, heard pleas for witness, but then it repeated in the form of help in murder cases, could I return to the crime scene. Each unassisted victim that had slipped away was now stealing back their time, while I lay in bed. But although death had a strangle hold, my lungs were still working. Every time I auditioned my mind for the role of murderer or murderer's accomplice, I found fortified my link to the living. 'Being in the audience was as close as you will get,' went the whisper. And with me that was fine, somewhere near the back, under the circle where there is less light.

Second, Gil steps out of his rotten life. We get him to

surgery, stet. We debride the half eaten, brown soft tissue and reveal what's left of the living inside. The remains can be left for the scavengers that would otherwise have kept him in business. Imagine a world where you rely on parasites to survive. Imagine a world where if lying isn't high on your personal-skills list, you will go down sooner, not later. Imagine a world where lying is so high on your skills list, you forgot what was second. Gil's world was shitty, his happiness was delivered momentarily on cheap paper destined to flow quickly back to the earth, not even rewarding him with loyalty. I didn't know anything about his family or his life, I didn't care to know. The more I though about him the more likely he would try and populate my life with the many versions of his self. It would have helped my appraisal of the situation but I couldn't really face asking him. I couldn't imagine it held anything that would make him any happier.

The third option was the Sammy option, the one I preferred. I had to eject him myself: push him, kick him, haul him crying, until he was out of my life for good. Running away was not even an option. I could walk without compass for six months nomadically across Mongolia and any given day could expect the tent flaps to be thrown open by him punctually expecting elevenses. He wasn't a threat, just a looming shadow that would probably prohibit me from executing the rest of my life in a free fashion. I was more worried about him showing up than about what he might do when he did. He'd quickly become an enigmatic nemesis.

"So what's it going to take?"

He looked at me as if puzzled by my question, not having been party to my high-speed thoughts.

"When are you going to stop?"

He opened his mouth only to knit his eyebrows and let out a little gasp. We both had thought he would say something. We both realised the ambiguity of the question.

At least it brought Gil's wandering mind into the sterile reality.

The walls emitted silence. Here in the hospital you could hear everything: any corridor in any department in any wing. What wasn't heard was amplified by the walls: the squeak of shoes, the patient noises, intermittent and mutually exclusive, and the pumping of machines giving life. Then there was phones ringing and buzzing, other items beeping and chirping each to their rhythms and arrhythmias. The tannoy's faceless voice moaned its content-free messages. Nothing was constant and nothing happened together, as if one person was staffing the foley for the whole hospital. He cycled though his sound effects with only one rule in mind: never repeat the same two sounds too close together. In a way, it added to the unsupporting continuity, never letting the restless rest.

My thought and mood followed similar patterns: never deviating, living their short lives in shorter times. My thoughts were quick expirers. They abandoned the path to fall by the way side where they would remain until a passerby offered them a ride to where ever he or she was going. But hospital roads are quiet, passing traffic did come from all sides and was heading in all directions but just with low frequency and high irregularity.

A pair of white shoes squeaked by the curtain. Gil tensed up slightly forgetting the moment we'd been sharing. I recollected some nearby thoughts and ordered them as best I could.

"What are you going to do?"

"Now?"

"In general, this episode has blown out of proportion. Not that that is difficult in my world. Anything that gets me out of bed before eleven a.m. is an event in my life. But even in the life of an adventurous person, we are looking here at something quite out of the ordinary. It's prompted me to do things differently, to take the next decisions of my life with a different approach and different variables. But what about you? You need to do something, to make a change or to do things differently too. I don't know you, but I know that about you. And what do you do? You come here looking for me! Whether or not it's a big thing to you, you have the opportunity to reassess. To take a new angle on your life. Why don't you do it?"

Gil still looked puzzled, but I could tell he was actually weighing the words. If not for an answer he already had, then to establish how I knew. Nevertheless you could tell he was resisting inside all the way, like the old dog he was.

"You don't have to do it because I told you to. Or because I was around when it happened. You have to do it for you and because of you."

I felt like I was selling him something, perhaps even something he didn't really want. The life of a convinced salesman must be a life. Option number four was just tell Gil to fuck off. Not the most diplomatic answer. Besides I felt for him, for what he represented at least. He wasn't the orthodox example of a criminal mind, nor was he the type to find happiness in any corner of positive thought. Some people are put here to struggle, designed with internal conflicts, designed for the creation of fresh gossip.

I had it too. I was wrestling with it in that same moment, hating myself for even caring about him or being concerned with his well-being and his future, hating myself more for letting our lives become so interlinked. I couldn't imagine my future with the preoccupation 'is Gil alright', with him calling every six months to tell me he's staying straight. Or worse still, he calls at midnight for spiritual advice. I could become his analyst and probation officer rolled into one. I resisted his sad cheeks as they told me to care for him. He was the cartoon puppy.

I made my resolution resolute, solid. Help him now and if he doesn't go away fuck him later.

"It's just seems such a big step," he said with his

resurgent weak side.

"I am sure it does, Gil. But all that tells you is that it's a step worth taking. That it has value, that not everyone can do it. Besides you need to get far enough away from it all so that it can't drag you back in. You need to distance yourself."

As a bigger metaphor began to emerge, I realised I could sit back while he unravelled it all. It was a quiet few moments. My soul felt weak for having let, even if momentarily, Gil's life supersede mine in terms of importance. His future had become my life, his worries my problems. For those few moments his life was more important than mine. But that just made me want the best for him, to send him off into the world happy and without the need to come back.

The tannoy announced the approaching end to visiting hours. Reality returned. I shook the sentiments and sentimental feelings out of my wet hair. I immediately accepted the challenge and went straight into the first task: eliminate this man from my life in the next fifteen minutes. It was nothing short of monumental. But anything is possible. And that was what I wanted. I didn't want him to come back the following day to drink from my fountain of information and good company.

The tannoy had made him look sad.

The thought of him being a future friend made me sad, not directly but in a way that made me think I'd never want another friend.

I've been though many lonely periods when I wouldn't have turned down a leper. But at this point I was strong. He could have promised me he would clean up his life and I still wouldn't have flinched. I made a note never to think of it as a possibility again.

But what lay under this thought was my curse. My former life of solitude and independence dancing further and further away form the fire. It was now out of my grasp.

With every second of visiting hours that I wasted, my life danced further from my grasp, tantalising me with her golden fingers and magical meringue.

Gil got up. Attempted several times to say something but in the end didn't. He did get out a barely recognisable farewell but that only stirred my imagination as far as wanting to see him culled by a truck or bus as he wandered —dispossessed—from the front doors of the hospital. Well, if he was lucky it would be an ambulance that hit him.

Voices approached. They were discussing visiting hours and how they must be strictly adhered to for the sake of the patients health. They were familiar voices and had approached the curtain. They stopped short, and a disgruntled foot stamped itself and went off in search of a senior authority. Only then did the curtain rustle, and Raffael and his brother walked in with the sort of inseparability usually reserved for twins.

Raffael looked first like he wanted to mother me, or at least father me. But he checked himself in front of his brother, making sure he hadn't seen him. The big brother role had switched.

I smiled. It hurt. Just as I had earlier, I opened my mouth and couldn't say anything, struck by last minute doubts. All I could think was that we all needed to get really drunk and let the truth flow like wine. There was no way they had seen Gil. If they had, it would have been evident. Besides, I knew Gil now, he knew how to slip by unnoticed and could summon that knowledge at the drop of a hat.

In fact, they looked happier than they were when I had left them earlier. There was a hint of bitterness, but it didn't spoil the flavour. Raffael was the first to break the increasingly uncomfortable silence.

"So what happened to you?"

"Yeah! We thought you had done a runner," Paolo joined quickly enough.

"But then we couldn't think of what you were running from."

"It was like you just disappeared."

"What have you done to yourself?" Raffael moved cautiously to his fathering self. "Is this because of what he did to you? Look what you have done to him!" He turned to scold his brother but received a colder look and forgot quickly.

"This wasn't from me, was it?" Paolo asked, concerned about a law suit probably.

I couldn't help but see them as a nightmare double act in a comedy of errors. I resisted laughing, although my fragile face would have probably stopped me. I managed instead to nod a little. "Thanks for coming to visit me!" I layered it with as much sarcasm as possible.

Paolo recognised it and smirked. "He's fine. Well, at least he's got his nerve back. You got a nerve kid. I feel like telling you."

I felt like telling him he was a cliché, but resisted.

"So who sent you guys? Patch Adams?"

"What happened to you? Tell us come on, we came so far to visit you."

I decided to cut Paolo's growing sarcasm with an answer to his question that he hadn't expected. "And in the end, you didn't bring flowers or grapes. You didn't come to visit me right? You can't tell me there is some ulterior motive. If you really came to visit me, I would tell you the visiting things. But I know you are here for something else. Same as that nurse knew."

I was stressing again, with Gil, now these two clowns. My life was being arrested from its solitude. It was like I would never escape. Well, in truth I didn't want to escape. Running was not the answer. If I couldn't create my own life with all the time and leisure I'd had all these years, there was no way I could cope with anything else, especially if it involved anything even slightly less familiar. What I had in front of me was already more than I could handle. As much as I had learnt about life and decisions, as a result of this episode, I still didn't like it or treat it as a positive experience. I liked it better in my shell. The bubble island life for me works just fine. If only I could seal the hole once more. Close it off and make these others leave.

It had all been an act, everything I had done was either clichéd or copied straight from the t.v. or the movies. There was no reality or originality on my part. Fake—one-hundred per cent—and I was tired of it. I couldn't live like it anymore. I had to learn to make my own decisions. It was not the way to start a life, whether it was achievable or not. Nobody had invited them into my life, but still I couldn't get them to leave. They were unwelcome guests in an unwanted way of life.

I know that my actions are my responsibilities, I have no arguments, I think that if anything it was my lack of patience that had begun to cause my downfall.

"So?"

They looked a little offended at my order. It didn't bother me; they were both grown men. They didn't mince their words, so why should I? Just because I was lain up in a hospital wasn't a reason to act soft.

"Err, well, we were worried. You said something about there being a risk involved with telling you what this peckerneck was up to. So, when we didn't hear anything from you, we thought maybe he'd done something to you." Paolo appeared surprised at having managed to fish a logical statement from somewhere.

"I'm fine. I just passed out and some good citizens dragged me here. Nothing more, nothing less. I don't even need to be here, they're just keeping me for observation. And they did it by filling me full of drugs, so the streets really weren't that safe."

"What kind of drugs?"

"To take down the swelling!"

They looked at me and I pre-empted what they would say.

"Well, put it this way, I've been drifting between sleep and hallucinations for the last eighteen hours."

"What's that supposed to mean?" Paolo snapped. "You some kind of druggy?"

"Calm down, leave the kid alone. How is he supposed to leave pumped full of that shit?"

"What are you talking about calm? I am calm. The kid's clearly a stoner."

They carried on like brothers for a while and eventually I took it upon myself to remind them that people were busy trying to recover from illness. They both calmed down.

"So, did you come here to tell me something specific, or were you just looking for a new place to carry on your domestic dispute?"

"Yes," Raffael sucked his stomach into his chest, "We have come up with a plan."

The words span in my head like the devil's real name. Was it childishness or snobbery, were we children on summer adventures or lifeless morons trying to make our lives more exciting with words stolen from the Hollywood dream factories? Making pretend good crooks and bad cops. I couldn't help but believe it was the truth, nor could I help feeling sick at this ultimate truth. I bit my tongue: another plan!

"We spoke to a guy who works for the press. Made some stuff up and asked him whether a story like your friend has would interest the media."

Paolo took over and gave the idea a more professional aspect.

"He told us, if it came to him, he would run it. They don't go around digging up dirt on cops, as it makes everybody look bad."

The very tip of my tongue fell off, freeing the stump to

speak. "Wait, you already did this? I thought you said it was a 'plan'. Why did you do this? You know they're going to look for it now. You didn't give them a copy of the tape at the same time did you?"

They looked at me a little scared by my outburst. Raffael jumped in as if to excuse them. "That's just the first part! Don't worry! Paolo has got someone to follow the same hack until he finds Gil."

"Your buddy's smart enough to clock him, and he'll be real obvious, and hopefully he'll walk away from the entire thing."

Raffael smiled at the eloquence of his brother's interruption. I pictured him panting yeah-yeah-yeah, tongue lolling to one side and teeth glinting.

Well, I had to give them some credit; it was pretty foolproof. But then it would've had to have been. That way I wouldn't actually have to reward them for it. Besides it wasn't a plan. They had done it.

"We couldn't find you. Your cell phone was switched off. You weren't at home."

"Don't worry! What's done is done. I can't change that now. I can only face the consequences. But tell me what exactly did you tell the press?"

"Nothing, we just made up some details, changed the story a little. You know, to see if they would bite. If they hadn't been interested then it didn't matter what our friend got up to. And if they were, then we had a back up plan."

"And?"

"And what? Oh I see, yeah. They were interested. Very interested. Did a real bad job of disguising it too."

"And you really planned it this way? Or are you just covering your tracks and sending your mutts out to do the dirty work? You fucked up, am I right? Sent someone else to sort it out for your and now you're coming here with smiling faces, hiding your sticky fingers behind your backs. You are more stupid than I thought," I told Paolo, "You should know fucking better than to send a cop to follow a snoop."

"It doesn't fucking matter. It's completely fool proof. Gil is going to bin the tape and forget about it."

"Great, works just fine for you guys, but look where it puts me. Gil is only going to think of one person responsible, because only three people know about the tape. He's going to think I sent both the press and the police after him. If you have so many unpaid favours, why don't you just have him arrested and make the tape disappear."

"Are you angry at us?" Raffael tried to change the subject.

"Yes, I'm fucking angry, if my face wasn't in so much pain, I would show you how angry I am. That's not the point, whether we are all friends after this is least of my priorities right now. But since we aren't going to be: let me provide you with some friendly advice immediately. Think stupid things through before doing them or you'll never know by whom you're going to get fucked."

"Well, he might take it as a prank call," Raffael offered sheepishly. "We tried to make it as vague as possible."

I looked at Paolo. This was clearly his entire work of genius. He was looking blankly into space with a stone look of disappointment and realisation of failure. It was the face of someone who had failed previously and who was just beginning to accept it as an integral part of life. Once it is done, there is little going back. There's just the future and the attempts to sweep it under the carpet. He shook his head, as if he were weighing it with his neck.

Raffael was unaware, thinking things through at his usual pace. If you live a slow life, you live it slowly. Other people, however, are more accustomed to change and can summon a plausible range of consequences to mind in the style of a chess player. The magnitude hadn't reached Raffael yet. Or, at least, he hadn't reached it. A dumb look was frozen onto his face: half in realisation, half in tenaciousness.

I was different. I had passed the consequences to the history file. I was lying in a bed of rage. I wanted nothing but to get out. Storm through hospital doors and corridors. Even just out of the room. To demonstrate to them how foolish their imprudence was and how it affected me. I felt a sharp pain as the new, unknown and unpredictable variables squeezed through the gap and into the situation. I was struggling keeping track of the four main sets of variables. Adding two more would probably eliminate me from the game. Then there was the army of journalists who sit up and beg at the word 'exclusive'. What had appeared at first just to be a simple scenario was merely the reflection of a lack of imagination. Only as the game had proceeded had the complexity been revealed.

What could I do? Praying had been banned by the semantic, rational regions of my brain. For them, there was already a hoard of journalists barricading the doors to my hope, praying themselves for the story. The story of a double murder, based on revenge, ended in chaos. The story of surprise deception and blackmail, the mixings of a corrupt cop and his innocent brother who was probably the instigator of everything. The story of Gil. Gil who was the key to the story but who didn't even want to do anything with the tape. It was nothing, if it wasn't ironic.

What broke the camel's back for me, however, was the falling value of instructing them: giving them the information that would prevent any further complications. If they had found me first, I would have said: 'He's not going to do anything except go straight, and it would have all been avoided.' What good would it have done to tell them that, here in the hospital?

My muscles had been contracting throughout the two encounters and eventually gave up on me. My body sank back into the bed and the blood flowed to all the parts again, making everything below my brain stem tingle and everything above hallucinate. I clutched strongly to the sheets and at the possibility of a miracle as I fell into a semi-unconsciousness, but firmly believing that all I had left in my power was wait patiently for the next thing to go wrong.

Shortly after Sammy had left and passed out in the street, Raffael and Paolo had sat down to put their heads together and a strange thing happened. It wasn't what they did, it wasn't the stupid plan they came up with nor was it any of the obvious things that changed. It was something unspoken. If only one good thing came out of everything, it was this silent reunion of love between two brothers.

The unfortunate and less romantic non-event was that Paolo would neither see it nor change his attitude to life in any way. He would still see his brother as he always had, perhaps he would actually regress and see him as clearly as he had during childhood. Raffael had been his hero and protector. For the rest of his life nothing would change that, even Paolo's attempts to become the bigger and stronger of the two.

Stinking, polluted and unworthy of even him, his inertia went against the romantic progression of that scene of fraternal love, working with his brother but against Gill, exploiting the media's pursuit of public upset for his own self-purpose. It was as if he only vaguely understood the idea of cleansing.

What Paolo did understand was his brother's affection for the kid. The kid had entered the equation under Raffael's belt and so Paolo had to consider him a family member. Paolo disregarded the fact that the kid was the murderer he was too lazy to look for a week earlier. He couldn't blame him for the murder, but he would protect his brother's son as he would his own brother.

From any direction, it is easy to see how narrow his perception of society is, for that we can easily point the finger. But yet we can sympathise with his actions only because we know them so well ourselves. We know his feelings and his motivation. Given some objectivity you cannot let a murderer go no matter how closely he may be attached to your family. This case is just a reflection of the power we give to people: Paolo's folly and lack of social responsibility mocked his lack of suitability for the role he had been pretending so long to fill.

But who are we to judge who should be president, police officer or coffee shop owner? Who is good, bad or murderer? The answer is no-one. We can't, we can't make this judgement. We pick our own roles in society. Sometimes of our own will, and if not, then through the support and advice of significant others. Then we do it and stick to it with all the determination we can muster. And provided no one bothers us or tries to upset the balance, we are free to execute our own will. We can stay happy and un-judged, provided we don't step over the lines and bother the next man.

That is when the problems occur. Then we are thrown kicking and screaming from our lives. Caught for something we did or didn't do. How many people live their entire lives in pure iniquity without disturbing anyone's peace? I would really like to know a figure. It's only those who step outside and get caught that are punished.

The advantage we give them? We give them the opportunity to go back to their lives or to start fresh. So why do they go back to…?

The old life? Because we tell them to. The only way to change is to do it ourselves. To pick a new role in society, through individual will.

Some people can have their entire lives tipped into the street in front of the cameras. They can have the public dissect their every move and have neither the shame nor the humility to change. It further confirms the mould they have made themselves. And like fish out of water, they flap and struggle to futility. The unlucky ones make it back into the green murky darkness that teems with their kind.

Others don't flap so much. They focus on growing their fins into feet, and the gills into lungs. They learn to learn to cope and avoid.

And what became of me? I got out of the hospital, from one green cell to another. I went to my apartment and migrated to the living room. There, twenty hours a day, I watch twenty-four-hour news channels, switching only to view local broadcasts. I get out of bed at the crack of dawn and I buy a copy of every newspaper then come back to examine them.

And? Nothing. Exactly. My breathing would shallow out as I scanned the papers. Every headline soothed me, every non-event relaxed my mood, every hour of time horizontal on my couch, not being dragged in handcuffs had similar effect. Every morning would reset my anxiety a little, but as those days passed it all changed.

Angry became positive. Fear became hope. Avid reading became accessible knowledge. After a few days, I cut out the stitches myself. My face was still purple, yellow and black, but it had begun to resemble me again. I began to move around my flat. I even ate food.

In between times, I would watch the telephone and the intercom, struggling with the temptation to destroy them or at least disconnect them. My reason prevailed every time realising they were chiefly lifelines. Early warning signs at best. I resented them all the same, not knowing if they would ever bring good news again. But for every time they didn't ring, I felt rewarded for not having destroyed them.

My predictions of the outside world were just that, predictions. My four walls couldn't contain my mind, just my body. I hadn't the courage to go out and verify anything. Ignorance wasn't bliss. Silence only represented the clock ticking downward.

It didn't matter. I could convince myself nothing would happen. Gil had bigger fish to gut than me. He had realised that the chase never ends unless you say 'stop'. He was out there somewhere being a citizen. The press? The rage I had suffered as a result of coming down off the drugs had led me further from the real facts. And I came to accept that facts didn't even matter. They don't. There are only two things that matter. One is individual perceptions. The other is individual interests. Takes Gil and his tape for example: the facts were there. The tape could be found by any reporter, but whilst no reporter is looking for it… So, I kept on working on my perceptions. Sometimes hope helped to sooth me, other times it agitated the fire.

Hope was a double-edged sword for most of the week that followed. The more you have on your hands, the more time you have to lose. It felt like getting your head back above water just long enough to take a good lung-full of air before being dragged back below. I suffered this constant fluctuation into and out of the depths of furious despair, where jail was a place I could imagine being before the sun went down. Every day, every week were periods where freedom was not guaranteed. The one thing I had always owned had become something slipping from my grasp. I wanted to pray.

Hope against the truth is not a game of equal opponents. Truth was an unfamiliar opponent. It had no counterpart. I wasn't ready to consider reality and its strategy. The extremes of my situation where casting dark enough shadows as it was. Life was the only dimension I had been aware of, and it was no longer being portrayed in the same colours. I was cast into a no-mans-land of obscurity and torment. Fear was no longer in charge, reality had become the chief gaoler.

I wanted nothing less in the world than to know the truth. Stepping out of my front door could reveal my worst expectations, my worst hopes. A pack of blood hounds with cameras and notebooks. A flurry of black ants with infra-red scopes pointed at my throat. The neighbours with their careful eye watching over their daily broadsheet. The entire cast of my life screaming bloody-double-murder.

The more I thought about going to the outside world, the more intense the extremes became. Freedom became delirium. I lost the ability to imagine the outside world as a real place; it no longer existed in terms of houses, trees and cars. When I opened the door in my mind, I was confronted by light, bright white light, too strong for the iris of my mind. The blinding white light was as bright as godliness and suggested a paradise conditional on my ability to open my mind to its reality, a scene of unrevealed utopia. It was a paradise I never knew existed. It had colours never painted, birds never flown trees never climbed and fruit never tasted. Beyond my fear was a peace never enlightened.

It was more than a few worlds away from my old one, but not so many from the end. My feelings fluctuated, sensations chilled my spine, and from time to time I would return to the semi-reality I had: the t.v., the characters in this play, my fear. I would mimic their actions and feelings, their situations and sensations, simulating time's continuation in the framework of my imagination.

I imagined Gil—with his coldness, habitual decisiveness and sparse regard for the consequences suffered by others— was shifting his balance, becoming considerate and responsible to multiple others. He created a new beginning, a new first day in the rest of his life. He created new criteria. He understood how he owed it to himself to make a change, probably to any family he might have too. I had a lot of hope for Gil and my only concern—that he might consider me the key to his new life—started to dwindle from my mind. I may have been his first straight friend for a while, but there was no way I would or could be his oracle in a queer and new-fangled world.

Raffael couldn't change, not even in my mind. Maybe I

couldn't bring myself to change him, maybe he was my constant. He had been there since I was dragged kicking and resisting into this institution for the sane. He had been the father I needed, the friend I could talk to. He was my mentor. His life had been flipped by three members of his family in less than a year. First his son, then his brother and then finally me. But he stood strong. He was the only one I felt sorry for and the only one whose respect remained intact. His world was infected, for no reason and by his loved ones, not by strangers as had been my case. But he had survived, remained strong and intact. Perhaps he was the sole survivor, never flinching, never frowning.

Paolo was the most difficult to predict. His life was almost as hard to calculate as mine. He was a random entity, a free radical. His anger and conceit, mixed with a rowdy disregard for the rules, made him both avoidable and not. Maybe society was better off without him trying to uphold its laws. He was a loose cannon. There was no predicting what he might damage next.